Confessions of an Ex-Girlfriend

Lynda Curnyn

D0097114

RED DRESS INK
™

First edition April 2002

CONFESSIONS OF AN EX-GIRLFRIEND

A Worldwide Library/Red Dress Ink novel

ISBN 0-373-25015-0

Visit Red Dress Ink at www.reddressink.com

Printed in U.S.A.

"Sometimes an Ex-Boyfriend is just an Ex-Boyfriend."
—Sigmund Freud's Ex-Girlfriend

Brittany

This book is dedicated to:

My mother, Marianne Nappo.
You gave me not only love, but courage. Congratulations
on finding your soul mate.

My father, James Curnyn, for always believing.

Rose Nappo and Lillian Curnyn, the original city girls.

Linda Guidi, my redheaded sister,
and most inspired and inspiring friend.

Tony Chiaravelotti, my love, my friend,
my "Dear," and my Ex-Boyfriend Extraordinaire.

Special thanks to the following people
for advice and endless support:

Joe and Joanne Scotto di Carlo, for believing in the
magic of the Skinny Scoop man. My lovable brothers,
Jim and Brian Curnyn. Kim Castellano-Curnyn
and Trina Palumberi, who not only had cool
NYC apartments, but snagged great guys.
Dave Webber, the great guy who snagged my mom
mere moments after I penned the proposal.
Linda Jean Curnyn, whose struggle to maintain sanity
on the home front did not go unnoticed.

All the city girls, ex-girlfriends all at one time
or another, who lent their womanly wisdom:
Anne Canadeo, Lisa Sklar, Jennifer Bernstein,
Alison Stateman and Karen Kosztolnyik.
My editors, Joan Marlow Golan,
whose encouragement and creative spirit
guided me through this first writing adventure,
and Margaret Marbury, whose hipness I trust
emphatically and whose solid advice I came to count
on. Margie Miller, for creating the coolest cover!

My wise, dear friend, Roberto Lugo, for keeping me not
only blond but sane.

Laura Wilkes and Todd Smith, the most lovable lawyers
I know, for helping me keep the details straight, and for
cheering me on. And let's not forget Bismarck (the
rabbit), of course, who, like Lulu, may just have
matchmaking qualities. You never know....

One

Confession: I should have seen it coming.

My friend Jade claims that if you're dating a serial killer, he will, however subtly, let you know his intentions from date one. And if you are especially attracted to said serial killer, you will merely nod and smile at this admission, then promptly forget it.

It's true that on our first date Derrick told me he'd be moving to the West Coast just as soon as he sold his first screenplay. But since this comment came just moments after our first kiss—complete with a sunset view of the Hudson, along which we were romantically strolling—I did not register that he would one day be leaving me but only that a) he was an amazing kisser, and b) he was a writer, which essentially translated into soulmate for me. I was a writer...of sorts.

Now it's a horrible fact of New York City life that every man you pine for is either too ambitious, too creative or too desired by the rest of the world to even have the time of day for you. Yet somehow, after spending the past two years of weekend nights curled up with Derrick on the futon in my rent-stabilized studio, I had mistaken us for a couple Meant-To-Be. Especially considering how we got together against all odds.

We met on the West 4th Street Subway platform, the uptown side. The main reason I noticed Derrick was that we were dressed similarly, in black T-shirts and jeans. And there was something so stumbling and shy about the way he was trying to catch my eye, I could hardly resist. "Hi," he said, meandering closer.

For a neurotic instant, I thought of those nutballs who had lately been pushing unsuspecting women onto the tracks, but when I saw his neatly trimmed goatee, I felt an odd sense of security. There was something soothing, yet edgy, about a man with a goatee. I also remember being startled by the clear blue color of his eyes behind his wire-rimmed glasses. Oh, and the glasses got me, too. I love a man in glasses.

It was summer, and the air hung thickly around us. "Hot down here," Derrick remarked.

"Like an armpit," I replied, not thinking.

This was exactly the kind of blunt little vulgarity Jade had warned me against time and again. "There are some things you just can't *say* to a guy if you ever hope to have sex with him."

Derrick did look at me rather oddly, then gave a half laugh and proceeded to move on to introduce himself, "I'm Derrick, by the way."

"Emma," I blurted, as the subway car pulled up, rescuing us from our awkward dialogue.

In fact, the thing I loved about Derrick immediately was that he was so "unsmooth"—so unprepared to seduce me that I was immediately seduced. "Heading out of town for the weekend?" he asked, eyeing my oversize pocketbook.

"No," was my less-than-scintillating rejoinder.

"Oh." He studied my bag with a frown. "I am. Jersey shore." And he held up a bag which, to *me,* looked like it would barely hold a bottle of suntan lotion and a change of underwear. But then, I was talking to an attractive man—this was *not* the time to mince words.

When the train pulled into Penn Station—his stop—just moments after I had explained that I was headed up to 85th Street to check out the Guggenheim exhibit on "Phallic Inevitability and the Surrealist School"—a conversational gambit that earned me an eyebrow raised in admiration—I made my first tactical error. Although Jade had advised me endlessly never to make the first move, I jumped off the train right after Derrick. What could I do? Seeing him on the platform fumbling for a pen to take my number as the doors stood temptingly open but in serious danger of swinging shut at any moment—destroying my every hope for happiness—I panicked.

"Oh, I thought you were going...'.' he began, puzzled.

"It's better if I transfer here," I replied quickly, hoping he wouldn't realize this didn't exactly make sense.

With a look that resembled relief, he produced a pen and a small scrap of paper and handed it to me. When I was done, he wrote his number down on the same paper before nervously tearing it in two and handing me half. Glancing at his watch, he mumbled a brief but endearingly warm goodbye. Then he was gone, leaving me dreamy-eyed on the platform.

Dreamy-eyed for all of three minutes.

Because as I stood there contemplating the two of us entwined in intimate conversation over drinks at some hip little boîte downtown—maybe Bar Six or Lansky's Lounge—I felt a flicker of doubt. To verify that I did, in fact, score an incredibly cute guy's phone number, I glanced at the folded scrap of paper still clutched in my hand. With sudden horror, I realized the number I held was my own.

"Made for each other," Jade said when I told her the story. "Neither one of you is ever going to get laid, judging by the number of attempts you probably have between you."

I turned to my friend Alyssa for comfort, instead. Unlike Jade, Lys always managed to see a brighter side to things. When I explained how I hadn't even given him a last name so he could look me up, she said hopefully, "Maybe he'll take out an ad in the personals, looking for you. You know, some people do that. They even have a page devoted to things like this in the *Voice*. You've seen the ads: 'Saw you on the A train. You, brunette, soft green eyes—'"

"My eyes are hazel."

"'Shy and sweet.'"

"Me?"

"Well, on first impression you can be!" Once again adopting the voice of the man she had never met but believed capable of such grand romantic gestures, she continued, "'Me, writer looking for a beauty like you. Thought I found you but you got away. Please call....'"

"Not a chance. Guys don't do that sort of thing."

"Then *you* do it, Em. Take an ad! C'mon, what have you got to lose?"

"My sense of self-worth?"

"What are you talking about?"

"I used to read those ads, Lys," I explained. "All the time. I used to think they were romantic, too. But the more you read the personals, the more you realize there are a lot of pretty desperate people out there. I mean, c'mon. To think that somebody might mistake a random encounter—the equivalent of stepping on someone's foot in a crowd—for Kismet. Gimme a break."

"Oh, here she comes. The cynic."

It's true I was a cynic in the pre-Derrick period. But who could blame me? At the time, I was twenty-nine years old, and had dated enough men to know that my soulmate would likely turn out to be nothing more than a good-fitting pair of shoes.

But then, destiny intervened. Two weeks after the hapless subway encounter, as I shared coffee and the Sunday night blues with Alyssa at the Peacock Café, I spotted Derrick, sitting two tables away and wearing the most perfectly faded pair of Levi's I had yet to find in my own endless thrift-store searches.

"Hey," he said, jumping up and almost knocking over the tiny table in front of him. "It's you." And suddenly he was standing over the table looking down at me in amazement.

I stood, too, staring at his adorable face in disbelief and leaving Alyssa to gawk up at us, a smile spreading across her features.

"I can't believe what an idiot I was that day," he said.

"Me too." I replied, Jade's warning voice a mere whisper as I stammered through a ridiculously elated dialogue about how absolutely retarded I'd felt when I discovered the mix-up.

"I told you it was fate," Alyssa said dreamily when he left our table fifteen minutes later, my number safely tucked in the pocket of his denim jacket.

Fate. This had come from the very same Alyssa who days ago had officially declared Derrick the man I needed to put out of mind. Forever.

Confession: Contrary to popular belief, I am not better off without him.

Even Derrick had the gall to attempt to come up with reasons why I should be happy, even though he was leaving me. According to him, I had a dream life. How many people, he argued, could claim that they had spent the better part of their twenties in the best city in the world?

"If it's such a great city," I argued back, "why are you leaving it?"

Then he explained once again, in the calm, rational voice I had begun to abhor in him during those last, angst-ridden days, that all his career opportunities were in L.A. That now that he had sold his screenplay, the studio wanted to hire him on as a script doctor. That he was better off on the West Coast.

Without me, I thought in silence that followed his speech. And as I considered throwing myself at his feet and begging him to take me away from this glorious city, he changed tactics.

"You have so much here," he argued. "Your own apartment. A *career.*"

Now this statement requires some clarification.

First, my apartment. If the words "walk-in closet" send a tremor of longing through you, think again. My walk-in closet contains a bed, a dresser, a desk and a bookshelf that has seen better days. Oh, and did I mention the Barbie kitchen along one wall? Yes, that's right. My apartment *is* a walk-in closet. Of course, there is something to be said for the fact that it's not only rent-stabilized but below 14th Street—the only neighborhood really worth living in, in my opinion.

Now as for my career...when asked the inevitable "what do you do?" question at parties, the answer I give is that I am a writer for a national women's magazine. This is not a lie, though my job is hardly as cool as this sounds. In truth, I am a contributing editor at *Bridal Best,* where I compose captions, headlines and—with ever-increasing frequency—articles on such subjects as "Hot Honeymoon Escapes" and "Wedding Dresses You Can Breathe In."

At best, my illustrious career at *Bridal Best* could be called a happy accident, for it started as a two-week stint as an office temp which turned into a permanent position when Carolyn Jamison, the senior features editor I work for, took a personal interest in keeping me on. How could I resist all her encouragement when, up till then, the master's degree in Creative Writing I had gotten at NYU had resulted only in a handful of unpublished stories and a full-time waitressing position?

Now, as I sat filled with self-loathing in an editorial meeting on the Wednesday morning of Derrick's departure, counting the minutes until his plane left the ground and carried him away from me, I began to wish I hadn't resisted the impulse to call him at 3:00 a.m. to let him know what a heartless bastard he was.

Looking up from my cloud of despair, I saw Patricia Landers, *Bridal Best*'s editor-in-chief, stand up to give us her weekly address. "At *Bridal Best* our editorial mission is to speak to the bride in *every* woman," Patricia began, "whether she is simply dreaming of that special day, or taking the first steps toward making that day happen."

Step 1: Don't let your boyfriend leave the state.

I sighed, suddenly weary of the wedding planning mantra that was sure to issue forth from Patricia's thin lips. As I studied her wispy blond hair, pale face and crisp blue eyes, I wondered if this would be my fate. To be the ultrathin, somewhat prim yet rather well-kept editor-in-chief of a national magazine. A career woman who needed no man, only a fat paycheck and enough take-home assignments to make her forget that there was so much more to life than work.

Then I remembered something else.

Unlike me, Patricia was married. And as dubious as that marriage was rumored to be, it set her miles apart from a manless and struggling contributing editor like myself.

My eyes moved frantically about the table, where the illustrious editorial team of *Bridal Best* sat, seemingly transfixed by Patricia's words. There was Rebecca, the only office colleague I deigned to call a friend and who shared my enthusiasm for taking pott shots at the powers-that-be. But Rebecca had a boyfriend—worse, an incredibly perfect boyfriend, who not only had a high-paying accountant job but came from money. Big money. Then there was my boss, Caroline, of course, who was round with her fourth child, compliments of the hardworking husband she kept back at her sprawling Connecticut home. The other three senior features editors were married, too. Sandra, whose wedding to Roger two years earlier had been almost as splashy as Patricia's; Debbie, pushing fifty and married for so many years no one even remembered what her husband looked like; Carmen, who not only had a husband but— according to our production assistant and resident office gossip Marcy Keller—a boyfriend on the side. Janice in production was married two times over, despite the hairy mole on the side of her face. Who was left among us single folk but the editorial assistants, who were too young to care?

I glanced down at the end of the table and swallowed hard as I caught sight of the strange trio who sat clustered there: Lucretia Wenner, the angry copy chief who neither woman nor man could truly love; Nancy Hamlin, the bodily pierced and butch admin everyone suspected was a dyke; and Marcy Keller, who spent so much time studying everyone else's personal life she barely had one of her own. I quickly closed my eyes, shutting out the hopeless look in their eyes that not even their bitter smiles could mask.

Oh God, was *this* what I had to look forward to?

Confession: I am not ready to be an ex-girlfriend.

This fact became glaringly apparent on my first real weekend of singledom. Derrick had flown out only three days prior with a promise to call once he was settled, though we had agreed that from now on, we were strictly friends. I will confess right now that he is the only "friend" I have ever had whom I secretly wished would fail miserably. In fact, I was practically preparing for the day when he would return to NYC, tail between his legs, begging me to take him back.

Though Jade had invited me out for a girls' night out with a couple of her friends from *Threads,* the fashion magazine where she worked as a clothes stylist, I opted to avoid an evening of gyrating on a dance floor looking fat and unfashionable next to Jade and her pseudosupermodel friends, in favor of a quiet evening at Alyssa's.

"You've been denied your right to be angry, Em," Alyssa explained after she'd set me up with a martini. Two sips of it made me fall into a state of self-pity that I was attempting to wallow in until Lys cut me off with her "I'm Okay, You're Okay" brand of advice.

Sighing long and deep, I watched as she slid mushrooms expertly into a pan for the gourmet dinner she was cooking for her live-in boyfriend, Richard, who had yet to arrive home from his high-powered—and, need I say, high-paying—job as a corporate lawyer. Alyssa was a lawyer, too, but one of those earthy-crunchy ones who fight to save trees and make tap water fit for human consumption. In addition to being a top environmental lawyer and all-around hell of a gal, she liked to whip up heart-healthy, mind-expanding meals with names like wheat gluten casserole with roasted baby corn. Somehow these qualities, which I'd always admired in Alyssa before, began to depress me as I watched her cook. Is this what it took to maintain Girlfriend status? Maybe I should have made more of an effort with Derrick, whipped up something heartier than coffee with Cremora on all those Sunday mornings we spent together.

"Just because he had a perfectly good reason to leave doesn't mean you don't have a perfectly good reason to be angry," Alyssa continued, sautéing in earnest now, her curly brown shoulder-length hair swept up into a ponytail, her brow furrowed over her bright blue eyes.

Though Alyssa knows me better than most, when it comes to this ex-girlfriend business she cannot relate. After all, Lys has been successfully dating since puberty. Once I asked her how she always managed to have a boyfriend on hand, and she laughed, saying she usually hung on to the guy long enough for them to grow completely sick of each other, then broke up with him just as New Boyfriend stood waiting in the wings.

Now if this were any other girl, I might have said Alyssa suffered from Chronic Boyfriend Syndrome—a condition that leads many women not only to date, but also to plan their lives around men who are for the most part reprehensible but seem preferable to the other option...which is no boyfriend at all. But I can honestly say that despite her claims, I am sure Alyssa never dated a guy out of this kind of neediness. It is just that she is utterly lovable—so lovable, in fact, that most men upon meeting her wish they had an Alyssa of their very own.

Her current beau, Richard, the first man Alyssa has ever dared live with and, I must admit, the best guy she's ever been with, is a perfect example of this. Richard was the roommate of Alyssa's last boyfriend, Dan. They were all in law school together, and since Alyssa pretty much lived at Dan's place in order to avoid her own awful roommate, Richard took every opportunity to bond with her whenever he was in her warm and fun-loving presence. I can just imagine his joy when Dan up and moved back home to Ohio to practice law with his father's firm, leaving Alyssa free and clear for Richard, who had already fallen hopelessly in love with her from the sidelines.

Now, as Alyssa looked up from her mushrooms, silently demanding my assent to her psychobabble, I struggled for words to explain how I felt.

"I don't think I'm angry, Lys. I think I just miss him, is all."

"Well, get angry, Em," Alyssa said, turning from her sauté to look at me. "You're not going to get over this unless you do."

The thought of getting over Derrick horrified me. Derrick was the man I loved. My soulmate. Getting over him was *not* an option.

"Mmm-hmm," I muttered vaguely in response, and while I sat pondering the audacity of her suggestion, I found myself agreeing to stay to dinner with her and Richard, which, I realized later, was a mistake. As I watched them exchange tidbits of their day along with meaningful glances, one thing became very clear: I needed to get a life. A life that didn't involve...couples.

Confession: I have been operating under the mistaken belief that I would never, ever, have to enter the dating world again.

I called Jade first thing Saturday morning and practically begged her to have brunch with me. And despite a slight hangover, best bud that she is, she agreed to drag herself out of the house before dusk.

We met at French Roast, mostly because they had outdoor seating and Jade would be able to smoke. As I sat waiting for her at five to one—I am chronically early, a habit I developed probably to have something to hold over the chronically-late-but-otherwise-perfect Derrick's head—I looked forward to some solid single-girl bolstering. After all, Jade was one of the few friends I had who seemed fearless in the face of the battleground that was the NYC dating scene. She never seemed to suffer the same kind of losses other women did. When she gave out her number, the man always called. Sometimes she didn't even pick up the phone—that's how sure of herself she was.

At one-fifteen, she breezed up to the sidewalk table I had secured, looking effortlessly gorgeous in capri pants and a tank that showed off her toned shoulders. Jade is one of those women who was born to wear clothes—a perfect size 6 with just enough bust to matter and no hips. Her hair, a deep, rich shade of red, fell in soft waves down her back, seemingly without effort or design. Her eyes are green, her skin smooth and flawless over high cheekbones. She is the kind of woman other women would hate if they could, simply by virtue of the fact that no man can ignore her when she is in a room. But there is something about her that is irresistible to both men and women. It amazes me sometimes that we are even friends, she graceful and self-assured, me always fumbling and often angry. Yet we've known each other since grade school and are bonded together by shared memories of first bras, first boyfriends and first successful undereye coverage finds. When she was edging toward twenty, a photographer encouraged Jade to put together a portfolio and she did, but when the time came to submit it to modeling agencies, she shrugged off the opportunity, as if it were something anyone could do. As it turned out, after various attempts at other careers, she landed a job on the other side of the camera, working as a clothes stylist for *Threads* Magazine.

"Sorry I'm late," she said, giving me a solid one-arm hug, then pulling back to look into my eyes—gauging my mood, I suppose— before she slid into the chair across from me. First we ordered, she the niçoise salad—not because she needed to eat light, but because she *liked* to, believe it or not—me, the smoked salmon hash with eggs—a fancier version of the kind of greasy, carbohydrate-laden meal I chose whenever I was throwing myself a pity party. Then she said, "Okay, spill. What's going on with you? Are you moping? I can see you're moping. He's not worth it. No guy is, really."

And so I began my discourse on how my life had suddenly lost all meaning now that I had gone from Happily Coupled-Off to Horribly, Achingly Single...and all before Memorial Day weekend, no less.

"Alyssa says I'm unable to get angry because he left me for a good reason. It's true I can't really get angry at Derrick for going after his dream. I mean, all he's ever wanted to do was make a living at writing, and when he sold that screenplay, he got the chance to do it—in L.A."

Jade lit a cigarette, making me painfully aware that I no longer smoked, despite the occasional desperate urge I suffered. "So let me ask you something. If you are so heartbroken without him, why don't you go after him? Move to L.A."

Leave it to Jade to go straight for the jugular, asking the question I didn't even want to ask myself. "And give up my career?" I said, practically parroting Derrick's rationale for not inviting me with him, a point that still jabbed at my ego.

"At *Bridal Best?*" she asked, her eyes bulging in disbelief.

"I *am* next in line for a promotion, you know," I said defensively, realizing how ridiculous I suddenly sounded, glorifying my day job. The very job I took great delight in mocking whenever Jade and I got into a gripefest about work, usually over drinks during a Friday night happy hour. But how could I explain to Jade, who knew that all I'd ever wanted to be was a writer, that for the past two years of my life—The Derrick Years as I imagined I would one day call them—my creativity had been confined to my role as editor at a magazine? A magazine, as I often joked, that thrived on the fact that happily-ever-after was not only every woman's ambition, but a prosperous industry. There had been room for only one writer in our relationship, and Derrick, with a screenplay under his belt as well as a string of short stories published in literary journals, had won the role hands down. As for myself, I hadn't written a word for the last year and a half. Not that Jade knew that. No one knew, really. Except Derrick. There was no hiding your failures from someone who spent seventy-five percent of his life in your one-room studio.

"Besides, how could I give up my rent-stabilized apartment?" I added weakly as the waitress came by with our meals.

While Jade blew out a last puff of smoke, staring at me as she stubbed out her cigarette in the ashtray, I tried to bury myself in my meal, avoiding her gaze. Jade knows me better than anyone, sometimes even better than I know myself, and I was not yet ready to face whatever ugly truths I was hiding from myself.

"Emma—"

"The truth is, Jade, he didn't *want* me with him while he went off to become rich and famous. He doesn't want—me."

Her eyes were soft when I looked up again, and somehow her pity stung more than her anger might have.

"What you need is a nice rebound relationship. And I know just the guy," she said, resolve firming in her eyes as she dug into her salad. "I just styled him the other day for an outerwear shoot."

"I don't date models." Translation: they don't date me. "*You* don't even date models anymore." After months of trying to keep one around long enough for at least one evening of unparalleled ecstasy, even Jade finally realized they were too self-absorbed to truly seduce. At least I *hoped* she realized that.

"C'mon, Emma. You know the best thing you can do for yourself is get right back out there. Besides, this guy might even be nice."

"Then why don't *you* go for him?" I asked, studying her expression. I always distrusted the idea of dating the men Jade passed over herself. She was such a solid judge of masculine virtues, I knew that if she didn't want the guy, she must have found some serious flaw she would never fess up to while she was trying to sell me on him.

"He's not my type."

Now I knew he was flawed. "Forget it."

"I might even be able to line him up for next weekend."

"Next weekend?" I said, shocked she might even suggest that I—with that extra five or so pounds of relationship flab firmly intact on my thighs and my emotions still tattered and flapping in the wind—might be ready to sit across a smoke-filled table from a startlingly handsome man and utter meaningless words designed to make myself seem just as accomplished and attractive as he was. "Thanks, but no thanks."

"Well, what *are* you going to do?"

"I don't know. I'm just trying to get through *this* weekend, never mind next. Speaking of which, what are you doing later? Want to see a movie?" I asked, hoping to avoid an evening alone.

"Can't. I have a date."

"Really? With Steroid King?"

"You mean Carl? No, he's history," she said. "I told you—he couldn't, you know, perform. I don't think you should have to deal with penal dysfunction in a man unless you're in love with him. You remember what I went through with Michael?"

Michael was the man I would say came the closest to being the love of Jade's life, except that he brutally dumped her for some dippy little blonde from his office after she struggled for over a year to put up with his vanity, his immaturity and, worst of all, his impotence—not that *he* ever called it that. He just claimed not to be interested in having sex with Jade, which did wonders for her ego. Ever since their breakup two years ago, Jade has done everything in her power to keep her heart out of it and go strictly for kicks—all those kicks she never really got from Michael, sexually speaking. But the great irony of her life has been that despite the fact that she is beautiful, intelligent and financially self-sufficient, she can't seem to find a man in all of NYC capable of delivering a satisfying sexual experience. Having gone through some dry spells myself since moving to NYC, I could sympathize. In fact, we often joked that we could start our own sitcom, called *No Sex in the City*. Carl had merely been Jade's latest dating experiment— a musclehead so pumped up on steroids, he couldn't seem to get a rise out of any other part of his anatomy.

"No, this is a guy from the gym, too, but he's the real thing. Gorgeous, in that lean, surfer's body kind of way."

"Let me guess…he's a model."

"Yeah, but he's very down-to-earth," she argued, leaning back from the salad she'd barely touched to sip her water.

Though Jade didn't like to hear it, I firmly believed her trouble with men began with her selection. She had always been a connoisseur of the beautiful people, which was probably why she was such a high-in-demand stylist in the fashion industry. But what she apparently hadn't figured out yet was that that beautiful men all had one thing in common and that was an inability to love—or even desire—anyone more than they loved themselves.

"I know what you're thinking, Em," she said, "but this time I have the best of both worlds. Ted is beautiful, but I get the feeling he doesn't even realize just *how* beautiful."

"Hence, his career choice."

"Please. The guy was living out in the middle of a cornfield in the Midwest when a scout spotted him at a club."

"This story sounds familiar." Why was it that no models ever seemed to actually apply for the glamorous, high-paid jobs they wound up in?

"He almost seems...innocent," Jade continued. "I mean, he practically blushed when I gave him my phone number."

"You're kidding?"

She started to laugh, then lit a cigarette. "So what are you going to do tonight? Go out with Alyssa?" Jade and Alyssa had become fast friends from the moment I introduced them in college, despite their very different personalities.

"No, no. She'll probably be doing something with Richard. And there is *no way* I can deal with a night of hanging with the Happily-Almost-Married."

"Well, I don't think you should stay home," Jade advised. "Want to meet up with me and Ted for drinks?"

"His name is Ted?"

"I know. Doesn't it sound almost...harmless?"

"Very boy next door."

"Well? What do you say? Drinks with me and Ted Terrific?"

"Naw. No, really. I want to stay home. You know. Get into myself again. Maybe I'll do a little renovating. I've been meaning to move my bookshelves. Maybe hang a few pictures."

"Are you sure?" Jade demanded.

"Of course I'm sure. It's not like I've never spent Saturday night alone before."

Confession: I have not spent Saturday night alone for two years.

This wasn't *exactly* true, as there had been times when Derrick spent Saturday night home writing, and I spent Saturday night home alone, also writing. Or at least that's what I told Derrick whenever he suggested we take Saturday off to catch up. "Oh, sure. I've been meaning to get started on a short story I've been thinking about," I would always say. After we hung up, I would turn my computer on, and as it booted up, I would start hand-washing all my lingerie or organizing my sock drawer. If things got really desperate, I would take an old toothbrush and some cleanser to the grout in the bathroom. If Derrick happened to call during these binges of avoidance to ask what I was up to, I always replied, "working." It wasn't exactly a lie.

Now I didn't dare turn on the computer. Couldn't even bring myself to gather up the hand-wash, for fear of the memories it might conjure up. Instead I curled up on the bed, fetus-style, contemplating the night ahead of me.

I had already called Alyssa and learned that she and Richard were going to Richard's sister's house for dinner, confirming that I was, indeed, alone for the evening, without even friends to call. There was always my office pal, Rebecca, but she and I have never ventured into weekend territory together. Then there was Sebastian, my hairdresser and sometimes friend—that is, when Fire Island or some handsome new man didn't beckon him away. But I hadn't spoken to Sebastian in a while and felt like a fraud calling him up now, expecting him to be there for me when I hadn't been much of a friend to *him* lately.

"Do something for yourself," Alyssa had said when we spoke on the phone, "take a hot bath, do one of those home facials, curl up with a good book." I knew she was right. That *was* what I should have done. It was, in fact, what was advised by every woman's magazine and every relationship self-help book—not that I'd read any, but my mother always reads enough for both of us.

Instead I gorged myself on a pint of Ben & Jerry's Chocolate Chip Cookie Dough, overplucked my eyebrows and proceeded to pore over old photos of Derrick and me on vacation last summer in East Hampton, where we had rented a house with some of his friends. I studied that face I loved so much, saw the happiness in his eyes as we stood, arms entwined, tanned, rested and utterly in love. Or so I thought.

What had gone so *wrong?* I wondered now.

The phone rang, shattering the gloomy silence of my apartment. I picked it up, then remembered—too late—that I *should* be screening on this first Saturday night alone.

"Emma! You're home! I didn't think I'd catch you—"

"Hi, Mom." There I was, caught by my mother, home on a Saturday night. "Yeah, well, figured I'd stay in tonight, catch up on a few things. How are you?"

"Fine, fine. Clark just went out to get some milk and eggs for the morning and I just thought I'd try you, see if you were around."

Clark was my mother's current boyfriend, and despite the fact that they had been together close to three years, I didn't trust things to last. It wasn't that Clark wasn't the greatest guy in the world for my mother, it was that my mother didn't have the best luck with men. I was starting to wonder if it was hereditary.

"So how's everything with Derrick?" my mother asked. This question was a fairly routine one, occurring as it does at least once during our weekly phone calls. There was a subtext to it, which my mother will firmly deny if challenged: *Is everything progressing normally? Will there be an engagement announcement soon? Am I ever going to see a grandchild?*

I tended to ignore the subtext and answer with a cheerful "Everything's fine." And somehow, despite the fact that my mother would more than likely never see that grandchild now that her thirty-one-year-old daughter's last chance had just up and left for L.A., putting that daughter—who had an average rate of two years between boyfriends, with one in three of those boyfriends actually being tolerable enough to consider propagating with— pretty much out of the running for motherhood. Despite all of that, I stuck to my faithful reply: "Everything's fine. Derrick is fine. We're fine."

I don't know why I lied. Maybe I didn't want to get into it. I knew I would tell her. Eventually. I just didn't want to hear how I had failed while my insides were still aching with the loss of him.

As it turned out, my mother had other things she wanted to talk about anyway.

After babbling on for a few minutes about her job as office manager at Bilbo, a pharmeceuticals company where she'd worked since I was a kid, she got to the real reason for her call. "I didn't want to tell you this on the phone, but I don't know when I'm going to *see* you again—" This was another point of contention with my mother, who apparently didn't believe my monthly treks to Long Island to pay homage to her in her cozy Garden City home were quite cutting it.

"What's going on?" I asked.

"Well, Clark and I have decided…that is, we're going to get married."

Now I must admit that upon first hearing, I was ready to completely disregard this statement. After all, this would be husband 3 (almost 4) and another in a long line of men my mother fell hopelessly in love with and considered marrying. Admittedly one could make the argument that my mother always went into marriage with the best intentions. It was the men she chose who always threw a kink into things.

There was my father, first of all, whom my mother discovered— after twenty years of marriage—to be a raging alcoholic. "He was always such *fun* at parties," she once declared, remembering happier times. Then there was Donald—almost husband 2. After a whirlwind courtship that ended in a trip to Las Vegas to tie to knot, Donald was nailed by airport authorities with a warrant for his arrest…on three counts of embezzlement. Then came Warren, whom I would venture to call my mother's true love…had their marriage lasted long enough to stand the test of time. After an eight-year courtship—my mother wasn't taking any chances that time—they were wed in a small ceremony in our backyard, with me standing in as maid of honor. Unfortunately, Warren died of a heart attack within weeks of the honeymoon.

Now there was Clark. Sweet, lovable Clark, an English professor with a lopsided smile and a fondness for quoting from seventeenth-century metaphysical poetry, a trait my mother found absolutely charming.

But there was no shrugging off this announcement, I realized, when she began rattling off the details of the ceremony. "...I'm thinking mid-September...a small cruise ship, just the family. Clark and I, of course. Grandma Zizi. You and Derrick. Shaun and Tiffany..." Shaun is my married brother. Married *younger* brother, I might add. "Clark's son and daughter and their kids," she continued. "We'll take a short sail through the Caribbean to St. Thomas, where Clark and I will be married with the waves crashing in the background and the family standing by. Kind of like a family vacation and a wedding all tied up into one. Won't that be fun?"

Loads.

Two

Confession: My breakup has turned me into a pathological liar.

The following Monday at work, I slid into the guest chair of Rebecca's cubicle. Though Rebecca is mainly an office buddy, we have been known to make excursions out to local bars for happy hours together, to commemorate a good review or gripe over a particularly menacing co-worker. However, these outings have become few and far between, mostly due to the fact that I have been doing the relationship thing, avoiding all friends other than Jade and Alyssa, in favor of takeout and a video rental with Derrick. Though Rebecca had been with her boyfriend, Nash, for about as long as I was with Derrick, she always seemed to make time for friends, and never seemed to mind the occasional late-night crunch to make a special assignment deadline, even if good old Nash had made them dinner reservations. In fact, I think she prides herself on her ability to be both good friend to all and steady girlfriend to one, which makes me suspicious of her, and somewhat jealous, I'll admit.

"My mother is getting married again," I announced, with some exasperation.

"What fun," Rebecca replied, peering up at me from a layout she had been reviewing, her eyebrows raised and a bright smile on her face.

Something about her cheerful reaction to my news made me immediately put up my antennae. One of the things Rebecca and I had always shared, especially during our after-work-cocktail outings, was a healthy disdain for the perky little world of wedding planning that is *Bridal Best.* How else could we separate ourselves from an office of people who waxed poetic over everything from choosing the right place settings to the proper thickness of paper for invitations, except by mocking them? If I didn't know Rebecca better, I might have thought she'd been bitten by the *Bridal Best* marriage zest after all. Because at *Bridal Best,* every marriage, even your mother's third, is an event worth getting hysterical over.

"Yeah, well, it's hard for me to summon up any sort of enthusiasm for this wedding. I mean, my mother's track record is a lesson in how *not* to find everlasting love."

Rebecca studied me for a moment, as if I were speaking in a foreign language. "You should be happy for your mother. It's not every woman who can fall in love again after so many missteps. She has a lot of courage."

"Either that or she's taking enough Prozac for it to not matter." Ever since she lost Warren, my mother was a firm believer in the kind of happiness that was available in easy-to-swallow caplets.

"What's gotten into you? You seem more cynical than usual. Did you fight with Derrick this weekend?"

Her question caused a minor panic inside me, as if my sudden state of stressful singledom had somehow become glaringly apparent. I stumbled around for a moment or two as I studied her careful blond bob and perfectly plucked brows, the neat way she had lined up her pencils on her desktop. Suddenly I was filled with distrust. Even the shiny eight-by-ten framed photo of Nash she kept in her cubicle seemed to glint evilly at me. There was no way I could tell her the truth.

"No, no. Nothing happened with Derrick. Everything is fine. Great, in fact."

"Terrific," Rebecca said, turning back to the layout before her. "Then that will give you a clear head to help your mom out with this wedding. Gosh, you could practically plan this thing yourself, if you had to."

"Sure, if I had to." If I didn't die of heartbreak first.

Confession: Marriage suddenly seems like a social disease.

Back at my desk, I was faced with my greatest challenge since The Breakup: attempting to muster enough perkiness to write a short to-do list for the bride-to-be that I had secretly titled, "How to Make Your Wedding Day Happen Without All Hell Breaking Loose." As I struggled to come up with an opening paragraph, I started to feel some of that anger Alyssa had encouraged in me. What about us non-bride-to-be's? I wondered. Even my own mother had put me to work in the service of her wedding day by asking me to start looking up cruise ships and "getaway" weddings on my handy little database. Worse, she had gleefully offered to take one of the many vacation days she'd accumulated during her twenty-year career at Bilbo to meet me for lunch the following week to see what I had come up with.

Why was my job so convenient for everyone else? Why was it that everyone else had a burning need to pick my brain for suggestions on everything from romantic-honeymoons-that-don't-require-a-tan to effortless-and-elegant hor d'oeuvres? Working in the warped little world of wedding planning had led me to one conclusion: If you don't get married in this world, you get nothing. Once, in an editorial meeting, I jokingly suggested that a woman should get a bridal shower when she turns thirty, wedding or not. Everyone looked at me as if I were some kind of nut. I am thirty-one years old, am I not entitled to free Calphalon yet?

The phone rang, saving me from starting the dreaded article.

"Hey, Em," came Jade's voice over the line.

"Jade. Thank God."

"Were you expecting someone else?"

"I was hoping for anyone who is *not* getting married."

"No fear here. What's going on?"

"Nothing, nothing. You know, the usual. Deadline pressure high, motivation factor low. How did the date with Ted Terrific go?"

"Terrific, of course. We did drinks, went to shoot some pool. Did I mention that he has the most beautiful forearms I've ever seen? Nice and thick and just the way I like 'em. He's even got a couple of tattoos. And you know how I feel about a man with tattoos.''

''Uh-oh. You're finished.''

''If I don't sleep with him, I don't know what I'll do.''

''Marry him?''

''What's gotten into you this morning?''

''It's my mother. She's getting married again.''

I held the phone away from my ear as Jade shrieked with joy. ''That is *so* wonderful! She and Clark are too cute together. Oh, I have to call and congratulate her. I should probably pick up a card at lunch....''

I should have figured Jade would be my mother's biggest champion. After all, she'd known my mom since husband 1. ''Jade, am I the only person in the world who's not excited about this?''

''Well, you should be,'' she said, censure in her tone. ''She's your mother! Don't you want her to be happy?''

''Happy, yes. I'm just not too clear on the fact that marriage is the way to get happy. You *do* realize that this would be Husband 3, almost 4?''

''Em, I think you need to get over that. Not everybody lives a cookie-cutter life. So what if your mother has spent a lot of her life searching? As long as she finds what she wants in the end.''

''I suppose you're right.'' I let out a sigh. ''Maybe I'm not looking forward to the Big Day, especially since she's got the whole family cruising to the Caribbean together for the ceremony. And guess who will be the only guest in the single cabin? Of course, my mother doesn't know that yet.''

''What do you mean?''

''I couldn't bring myself to tell her about Derrick. I don't know why...I just...couldn't.''

''You're going to have to tell her eventually. When's the wedding?''

''She's hoping to get something together by the end of September.''

There was a silence, as if Jade was pondering. "That's not much time, but who knows what could happen before then. You might be in love with someone else. Or you might find yourself a cute waiter on the cruise ship to share that single room with."

"Somehow I doubt it. But maybe I can dig up someone to take with me."

"Ah, yes. The old Boy Under the Bed." This was our term for the ever-present male friend who was suitable to take to such events as weddings or office picnics, though for one reason or another not someone you had any sort of desire to *truly* date. Mine used to be Cal, who'd been a fellow waiter at Good Grub, the restaurant I waitressed at during grad school. Cal was a perfect Boy Under the Bed—a great dancer, tall enough so you didn't tower over him in heels, and just unattractive enough not to cause any instances of drunken groping on the dance floor that might later prove embarrassing. The problem was, Cal had up and gotten married during the Derrick Years. Men were such bastards.

"I just realized my Boy Under the Bed went AWOL. Cal got married last year, remember?"

"Oh, yeah." She paused, and I heard her inhaling on a cigarette. "What about Sebastian?"

Sebastian was always a possibility, of course. But he was more a Boy Out of the Closet than a Boy Under the Bed, which made choosing him as a wedding date a bit of a problem. "I don't want to be the fat older sister turned fag hag at this affair."

"You're not fat."

"Well, you never know what could happen by September. I ate an entire pint of Ben & Jerry's Chocolate Chip Cookie Dough over the weekend. And not even the frozen yogurt version. I went for the gusto—twenty-four grams of fat per serving, four servings per pint."

"Big deal. Don't worry, Em, we'll find you someone. There's always that model I told you about."

"You know how I feel about models."

"Well, you don't have to *marry* him. And consider how good you'll look together in the wedding pictures."

"I'll think about it," I said, reluctantly.

"Now there's the Emma I know and love. Don't worry. Everything will be just fine."

Confession: I would marry for a below-market one bedroom.

I somehow managed to muddle through the rest of the week without any major emotional disasters. And after making it through a second weekend alone without completely falling apart, I felt almost proud of myself. In fact, as I walked down my tree-lined street on my way home from work on the verge of week three of the Post-Derrick Period, it suddenly occurred to me that being single in the greatest city in the world wouldn't be all that bad. I even lived on the nicest street, I thought, as I passed the pretty brownstones on West Thirteenth Street.

Then I reached my building, with its faded facade of peeling paint and row of dented garbage cans and I couldn't help but sigh with dismay. Why, oh, *why,* couldn't Derrick and I have made it as far as shared real estate? He would never have left me if we had landed a below-market one bedroom downtown. No man in his right mind would walk away from that kind of find.

And no woman, I realized now, hating Derrick more for denying me my real estate dreams. With another sigh, I started up the steps.

Derrick was fond of calling my twenty-four unit apartment house The Building of the Incurables, because it was filled with tiny studios that housed—other than students struggling through until graduation—old people with ailments either mental or physical, which kept them from moving on to apartments with a living space large enough for an area rug that didn't say Welcome on it. There was Beatrice on the first floor, for example, who had been hit by a piece of scaffolding on West Thirty-ninth Street sixteen years ago and whose injury required a metal plate in the head that had put her on the permanently disabled list. Now in her fifties, she was collecting social security and painting watercolors, which decorated the walls of her tiny cube on the first floor. Then there was Abe, who could have been anywhere from sixty-five to eighty-five and who, every morning, emptied the entire contents of his apartment (except for the furniture, which wasn't much) into two trash bags, loaded them into a shopping cart, and went off to God knows where for the day.

Then there was me. Neither student nor psychotic, yet stubbornly holding on to my rent-stabilized studio as if my very life depended on it. Now don't get me wrong, it's a great address—just a few short blocks from the subway, the Film Forum, the downtown bar scene, the Peacock, NYU and just about anyplace anyone wanted to be in the downtown area. And it was easy enough for me to bear up to my lack of closet and living space for the kind of location that drew looks of envy whenever I spouted my address at parties. Besides, with Derrick in my life, there was always that lingering hope of the one bedroom we would one day share, once Derrick realized the two-bedroom dive on the Lower East Side he shared with a foul-mouthed bartender just wasn't cutting it. I used to fantasize about our dream apartment, complete with wall shelves displaying our combined, heady collection of film and literature titles. It was that hope that kept me sane, and safely apart from my incurably psychotic and old, or annoyingly young and transient, neighbors.

But once Derrick was gone from my life, I fell out of my Safely Coupled category and into…Something Else. And that something else was yet to be determined, I realized, as I entered the building.

"Emma!" came Beatrice's shrill cry as I stepped into the foyer and found her at the mailboxes, arms laden with every mail-order catalog you could imagine, and an assortment of envelopes.

"Hi, Beatrice, how are you?" I said in the usual singsong voice I reserved for small children and adults like Beatrice, who weren't, as they say, all there.

"Oh, I'm all right—"

"Good," I replied quickly, starting for the stairs.

"—except for this crazy sinus condition. Every morning I wake up, stuffed nose, clogged ears. And my molars. Oh—'' Her gray eyes opened wide behind her thick glasses. "It's unbearable."

"I hear what you're saying, Bea," I replied, bracing one foot on the steps, preparing for flight at the first opportunity. Beatrice did like to get into a thorough discussion of her ailments, and I still hadn't managed to figure out how to effectively avoid listening to her litanies. She's lonely and it means a lot to her that I listen, I often rationalized after a good ten minutes hearing about everything from nasal congestion to hot flashes.

But instead of carrying on with the details of sinus drainage, which I thought was sure to come next, she abruptly stopped talking, her eyes roaming over me from head to foot in a way that made me feel faintly ill. Beatrice, with her thick, squat body shoved, more often than not, into flannel shirts and stretchy pants, always looked to me like the butch half of a lesbian couple—except she was permanently sans her other half—and so her inspection, especially during this vague Post-Derrick Period of my life, was anxiety-producing. "You *do* understand, don't you?" she said, her mouth dropping open as it did whenever she was captured by some thought.

As I started to proceed up the stairs with a hurried wish that she feel better soon, she called out, "Wait!" and turned her attention to the mail in her hands. Shuffling through the catalogs, she pulled out a thick, glossy volume and held it out to me. "I thought you might be able to use this," she said as I reluctantly took the catalog from her.

I stared dully at the cover, which featured a tall, large-framed woman dressed in a flannel shirt similar to the ones Beatrice favored, and dark jeans.

"It's got great deals on styles for women like us," she continued, staring up at me, a pleased expression on her face.

Women like us? I started to get defensive, but thought better of it and made my escape. "Thanks, Beatrice. I'll return it when I'm done."

"Oh, no need," she replied, beaming a mouthful of brown teeth at me as I fled up the stairs.

Confession: I'm not convinced a fish wouldn't be happier with a bicycle.

"Why aren't we married yet?" I asked Jade later that night on the phone.

"Because we're strong women," she replied.

This answer was beginning to bother me. "What does that mean, exactly? That I've got metal in my head and can withstand numerous blows?"

"What are you talking about?"

"Maybe we aren't looking hard enough."

"Oh, I've been looking all right."

"Oh, yeah. So how are things going with Ted Terrific?"

Big sigh. "Turns out he's more likely to be Ted Bundy."

"What?"

She sighed. "He didn't call."

Needless to say, I was shocked...and slightly horrified. Of every woman I knew, Jade was the only one who never got snubbed by a guy. Men *always* called Jade. She was my one last hope that women didn't have to forevermore be left waiting by the phone. Good grief. What did this mean for the rest of us if Jade, the Über-Single Girl, was having trouble getting to date number two?

Understanding all too well the frustration that followed such blow-offs, I offered the one thing every woman who has been left hanging by a man always needs: anger. "Clearly he's an asshole."

"Hmm."

"Or gay. Or mentally deficient. I mean, what kind of moron goes out with a beautiful, intelligent girl like you and then neglects to pick up the phone, even just to tell her he's happy she's alive and he had the opportunity to spend a few hours in her presence?"

"He probably couldn't handle the fact that I beat him in two out of three games of pool."

"Wimp."

There were a few moments of silence, while we ruminated over the question of how Ted Terrific had taken a turn for the worse.

"Maybe I was too aggressive," Jade offered.

"You're kidding, right? Jade, I'm sure you did nothing—"

"I did invite him up. I mean, not to sleep with him or anything. But I'd just gotten the new Jamiroquai CD, and I knew he was into the same kind of music, so…"

"Did he come up?"

"No. He said he had to get up early. Gave me this killer kiss in front of my building, then took off. It just doesn't make sense. The whole night, right down to that kiss, was amazing. We had drinks, shot pool and talked like we'd known each other all our lives. We liked the same music, hated the same clubs. I couldn't believe how well we clicked. How much we had in common. And the chemistry…forget about it! I wish he *had* come up, so at least we could have had sex before he disappeared. I'm sure it would have been nothing less than incredible."

In truth, I was stumped, but concluded that maybe we had just assumed things all wrong. "Maybe he'll still call. What night did you guys go out?"

"Last Saturday. As in the weekend before last. Granted, I did leave town on Thursday to go on a shoot for the weekend, but he didn't know that. I came home on Sunday morning to no message."

It didn't look good. One week, okay. But to go to week two without even a quick hello-had-a-great-time-wish-I-could-see-you-again-when-I'm-less-busy call, was not a good sign. He was history. "Maybe he got hit by the Second Avenue bus. Doesn't it run right past your gym? He could have been coming out late, after a workout, and wham-o."

"Yeah. If he's lucky."

I knew we would never truly find an answer. Why He Didn't Call was one of the great mysteries of single life. A life, I realized, I was now reluctantly a part of.

Confession: Marriage—any marriage—is beginning to look good.

As if the idea of newly tackling single life wasn't exhausting enough, the next day at work I was forced to take on the facade of one of the Happily Coupled-Off when Rebecca dropped by my cubicle to regale me with tales of her romance-filled evening with her boyfriend, Nash. "He just seems different lately," she said with a glimmer of excitement in her eyes. "More *committed.*" Then she went on to tell me about the great little French restaurant on the Upper East Side where they'd had dinner the night before. "Maybe if you and Derrick ever venture uptown," she added, "we could all go to dinner there together sometime." To which I responded, with what I hoped was a convincing smile, that maybe we would, all the while knowing that it would be a miracle if Derrick ever ventured to the East Coast again, never mind the Upper East Side.

By the time I dragged myself home that evening, I was convinced that the key to life was finding someone—anyone—who would stick around long enough for you to lure him to the altar. Someone stable and reliable like Nash. Or better still, Richard.

As if to punctuate this realization, my father called. Though he had managed to drown a good portion of his life in Johnnie Walker Black, there was no denying that my father had been a good catch in his day. By age thirty, he had worked his way to the top of a financial investment firm. Even when he'd asked my mother to marry him at the tender age of twenty-five, he was making a respectable salary and had "upwardly mobile" stamped all over him. Life had been pretty cozy growing up in our sprawling Garden City home. It was no wonder it took my mother twenty years to realize her husband loved no one and nothing more than the bottom of a bottle.

"Hi, Dad," I said, "how are you?" This question was still asked with some trepidation, despite the fact that it had been over a year ago that my father's second wife, Deirdre, had dragged him off to the rehab center for the third time in their twelve-year marriage. It amazed me that Deirdre, who hadn't realized what she was getting into when she'd married him, didn't leave him at that point, despite his big house and fancy landscaping. But maybe she had made the right choice. After all, he had managed to stay sober since that last incident, and passing the one-year mark constituted a new record for him. Still, none of us quite trusted that he wouldn't fall off the wagon again.

"I'm fine, fine. Finally got that settlement on that toaster oven that exploded on us," he said, satisfaction in his voice.

The end of my father's drinking career did have one side effect: He had become extremely litigious. Ever since he'd made his first attempt to go off the bottle a few years back, he'd begun suing anyone he believed had slighted him—whether it was his firm, which forced him into early retirement three years ago without (according to my father) sufficient compensation, or this most recent episode, in which his toaster oven allegedly burst into flames unbidden. It only took a little research for my father to find out the model had been recalled six months earlier.

"How's my little girl?" he asked now. "Make your first million yet?"

"You'll have to count on Shaun for that, Dad." At twenty-nine, my baby brother was making more money annually at the dot.com he'd gone to work for three years earlier than I'd ever hoped to make in my four years combined at *Bridal Best*.

He laughed. "I don't know, Em. You might still be in the running, with that good noggin of yours. How's what's-his-name?"

Despite the fact that I had been with Derrick for two years, my father always made a point of not remembering his name. And though I knew it would give my father great delight to know I was no longer dating a dog-walking, bartending "bum" (my father never did buy into Derrick's claim that he was in the service of a higher cause and thus couldn't chain himself to a real profession), I could not seem to tear myself from the path of lies I had only begun to traverse. "He's okay," I replied. "Did I tell you he sold his screenplay?"

No matter what had happened between Derrick and me, somehow I still felt the need to defend him to my father as a perfectly suitable and upwardly mobile sort of boyfriend. It all seemed silly now, but here I was babbling on about how many opportunities would open up for Derrick now that he had his foot in the door. I neglected to mention that the rest of his body had followed that foot to L.A.

"Hmm," my father responded, distracted. This was the part of the conversation where he usually tuned out, probably to contemplate how his daughter would survive if she married a man who had no hope of a pension plan. "How's that Alyssa doing?" he said now. "Still dating that lawyer?"

As my father had been handing most of his own pension over to the attorneys he hired for his various lawsuits, he had developed a new respect for this particular breed of boyfriend material. "Yes, they are still together. I imagine they'll eventually get married, though Richard is so focused on trying to make partner, he probably won't pop the question until after that happens."

"That's what I like to hear," my father replied.

"Jade's doing great, too," I continued. "One of the layouts she worked on last year just won an award."

"Oh, yeah?" he replied. Then he laughed. "That Jade. She always was an artsy one. I guess she's still not dating anyone, huh?"

"You know Jade. She's always dating someone," I replied, trying not to remember that her latest someone had suddenly turned into a no one.

"Hmm…" Again my father had tuned out, probably worrying that Jade's success at singledom might spur me into some kind of complementary spinsterdom.

"So how's Deirdre?" I asked.

"Oh, she's having a ball now that I've given her my blessing to purchase a new living-room sofa. I've never seen so many swatches of material pass before my eyes in my life. She was just asking about you. Wants to know if you're planning on coming in for Memorial Day weekend."

Uh-oh. How was I going to come up with a Derrick-double by then? "Umm… I haven't really decided. Uh, Derrick and I might be doing something in the city."

"You're going to spend Memorial Day weekend in the *city?*" he asked. My father, who had spent the last thirty years as a commuter into this "dirty rathole," as he referred to Manhattan, still couldn't believe I willingly chose to live here, and in a postage-stamp-size apartment no less. He was one of those homeowners who always went bigger with each new house he bought, despite the fact that his family had gotten smaller after the divorce. His current house, a sprawling Victorian in Huntington, was a monument to this philosophy.

"I don't know what I'm doing over Memorial Day. I haven't decided yet," I said, anxiety creeping into my voice.

"All right, all right. No pressure. Deirdre was just asking because we were thinking of going away that weekend."

"Oh." And here I was worried my father and Deirdre would suffer from my absence at the annual family barbecue. "Okay, well, don't let me stop you from making plans," I said, hoping he and Deirdre would go out of town and leave me and my phantom boyfriend to ourselves.

We talked for a little while longer before hanging up. Then, with a sigh that descended into a groan, I gave in to temptation and grabbed a photo album off my bookshelf. Flipping to the first photo of Derrick and me that I came across, I stared deeply into his enigmatic eyes looking for answers as to what went wrong. And as I studied his smiling face, I realized that despite all the good times we'd had, our relationship had amounted to a whole heap of nothing. Then I remembered the admiration in my father's voice when he'd asked about Richard.

Maybe my father had something there. Maybe I should be going for a man with more prospects and a solid career. A man who had made a name for himself in the world and was now looking for a wife to come home to. That's the kind of man I should be dating. Someone like Richard, where there wasn't a question of Will He Ask, only How and When.

I called Alyssa, hoping to hit her up for a hot lawyerly prospect.

At the very least, I would get a date for Memorial Day weekend. Maybe even for my mother's wedding as well.

"Why a lawyer?" Alyssa asked when I made my request.

"You say that with such disgust in your voice, Lys. And last time I checked, you were not only living the life of a lawyer, but living *with* one."

"I'm talking about you, Em. You never wanted one of my fix-ups before."

"That's because I hadn't realized the value of dating a lawyer until now."

"Uh-oh. Here it comes."

"Well, all my observations of the male species over the years have led me to one conclusion: Men will only consider marriage when they reach a certain income level. And assuming most lawyers our age would be just about hitting that comfort mark—or are even likely beyond it—I figure my odds of marriage are better with a lawyer. At the very least, I could argue my way to the altar."

"Wait a sec here. Back up. Since when are you so gung-ho about getting married?"

"I'm thirty-one years old. I ought to start thinking about it, don't you think?"

"I'm thirty-one, too, and you don't see me rushing out to buy a dress."

"Lys, not to be mean or anything, but it's a lot easier to be brave about your unmarried status when you have Husband 1 living under your roof."

"Nothing's definite between Richard and me."

"Yeah, but you guys are clearly in—" A twinge of panic shot through me as realization dawned. Something was up. "Wait a sec. What's going on with you?"

"Oh…nothing."

"Please don't tell me you and Richard are on the rocks. You would be destroying my last lingering belief that soulmates do exist. That people can actually follow falling-in-love with happily-ever-after."

"Everything's *fine,* I guess."

"Lys—"

"Okay. I met someone else."

"What?"

"It's not like I planned it or anything." She never did. Men just fell in love with Alyssa without warning.

"Who is it?"

"Don't laugh."

"I promise."

"Dr. Jason Carruthers."

Leave it to Alyssa to go from a lawyer to a doctor. "Let me guess...your ob-gyn?"

"Don't be ridic—"

"Your optometrist? Your dentist?"

"My vet."

"Your *what?"* Suddenly my head was filled with images of a scrawny, softspoken man with patchy facial hair. After all, I had never seen a vet who hadn't eventually turned out to look somewhat like the patients he treated.

"I told you Lulu has been having trouble with her bowel movements? Well, I went to her old vet, except he had retired. And in his place was Jason."

"Jason? You guys are on a first-name basis already?"

"I know what you're thinking. It's just that I never met anyone like him before. And it's not only that he's gorgeous. There's a certain...tenderness about him."

"Oh God. Don't tell me. Have you guys—"

"No—no! Nothing like that. I mean in the way he handles Lulu."

I began to become suspicious. Lulu was Alyssa's Lhasa apso, the dog she grew up with on the Upper East Side and the last vestige of her mother, who had died two years ago. Alyssa's father had a fatal heart attack when she was a teenager, and her mom had gotten her a puppy during that difficult year. Alyssa loved that dog as if it were the last family member she had. And Lulu was, really. If you didn't count me and Jade, of course.

"How is Lulu?"

"Not good. Jason thinks it may be her kidneys."

Aha. "Well, don't do anything rash, Lys. Just see this thing through with Lulu, and then look at where things stand. You and Richard have a long history together. That's not something you should regard lightly."

"I know. I know. It's just that…things have changed between us. I…I sometimes feel like I don't even know Richard anymore. Maybe *he's* changed. Hell, maybe *I've* changed."

"Lys, all I'm saying is don't do anything—"

"Oh, shit. Got to go. Richard just got home. Listen, Em, let's keep this between us. I haven't even told Jade. You know how she can be—and I don't feel like being ridiculed right now. I'll look into the lawyer date thing. Maybe Richard knows someone. I'll call you…."

"Alyssa—"

"Hey, maybe we should all get together for dinner Saturday night? Richard's going out of town on business, and it's been a long time since we've had a real girl's night out. Is Jade around? Let's plan something."

"That's fine, Lys, but don't think I'm letting you get off easy with this one."

"Okay, okay. I promise I'll be good. At least until Saturday."

Three

"Getting married is the easy part."
—Virginia McGovern, mother of Emma Carter

Confession: My mother's wisdom is starting to make sense to me (God help me).

The next day was my planned lunch date with my mother, who was still under the lovely-though-absolutely-untrue assumption that her only daughter was on the sure path to happily-ever-after with her own dream man. Though I hadn't yet decided how I was going to handle the Derrick subject, I headed off to the restaurant she'd chosen near my office, armed with catalogs and travel brochures filled with all sorts of ideas for how to pull off this wedding she was dreaming of.

She was already there and seated at a table in the back when I arrived, and suddenly I realized where I might have gotten that five-minute-early arrival technique. Was I more like my mother than I realized? I wondered with sudden horror.

"Emma!" she exclaimed as I approached the table. She got up and gathered me into a warm, apricot-scented embrace. When we pulled back from each other, I realized that taking after my mother wouldn't be so bad after all, at least in the looks department. Though she was fifty-nine years old, she was still a beautiful woman, with wavy chestnut-brown hair framing her high-cheekboned face. Other than the fact that she had the same hazel eyes as mine—though hers seemed more definitely green—no one would have guessed we were mother and daughter. How had I wound up with straight mousy-brown hair and no cheekbones to speak of? Maybe these things skipped a generation.

"How are you, sweetie?" she said, studying my face once we sat down across from each other.

"Good, good," I said, immediately hiding my face in the menu to disguise any glimmer of unhappiness that might betray me. "Tired. Work is nuts, as usual."

"Sometimes it's nice to take a break in the middle of the day. I was just reading this new book, *A Mental Space of One's Own,* and it talks about how we can renew our creative energies just by taking as little as fifteen minutes each day to meditate."

"They won't allow us to burn incense in the office, unfortunately."

"Oh, Emma, you don't have to—" She stopped, probably realizing she was going to get nowhere with me, as usual. "Why do you always have to be so difficult?"

"I'm sorry, I—" Then I caught sight of the ring, a large deep blue stone that sparkled magnificently on her left hand. "Oh, is that it? I mean, is that the ring Clark gave you?"

She beamed and held out her hand. "Isn't it absolutely perfect? We decided to stay away from diamonds after— Well, you know, I'm starting to think they're bad luck after the first two… Anyway, when Clark gave me this sapphire, he told me that the ancients believed it to be the truest blue in the world, a reflection of the heavens above. He wanted me to have it as a symbol of his faith, his sincerity." Then she blushed. "You know Clark. Always thinking like a poet."

The look on my mother's face was positively beatific. I began to suspect that maybe this *was* the real thing. Until her next words.

"Clark and I have decided to take a vow of celibacy."

"What?" Now my mother's sex life, or lack thereof, was a subject I strictly avoided. But I couldn't help asking, "Forever?"

"Oh, no. Of course not!" Then she glanced around and leaned close, confiding, "It's only been a week, and Clark's having a hard enough time as it is. Just the other night—"

"Okay, okay," I said, interrupting her, not wanting her to get into any details I couldn't bear hearing. Over the years, my mother's intermittent single status often put me in the position of confidante, given that I was the only other close female in her life for long periods. But despite that, there were some lines mother and daughter could never cross. "Let me guess. Until the wedding night?"

"Yes! So you've heard of couples doing this?"

"Yeah. I think we did a story on it once in *Bridal Best.* Something about recapturing the romance of an old-fashioned wedding night."

"Exactly. I knew you would have heard of it. Clark thought I was crazy at first, but you know how agreeable he is."

"Can I bring you ladies something to drink as a starter?" the waiter said, when he finally showed up at our table.

My mother looked up and beamed him such a smile he almost blushed. "We're ready to order our meals, I think," she told him. Then looking over at me, she asked, "Have you decided, Emma?"

No, but that wasn't about to stop my mother, who's had this thing for time-efficient behavior ever since she read *Twelve Time-Saving Strategies That Might Just Lengthen Your Life.* "You order first. I'll be ready in a minute," I said, my eyes roaming frantically over the menu.

"I'll have the grilled chicken salad, dressing on the side and a sparkling water," she said. Then, looking up at me, she continued, "The salads here are really good, Emma."

Now this is the kind of statement my mother makes that immediately sends me into paranoid speculation. Clearly I had gained weight, and my mother was subtly guiding me back from the brink of bulging midsections and mornings spent obsessing in front of my closet in search of an outfit to disguise my sudden change of dress size. If there was one thing I could count on my mother for, it was a careful monitoring of weight fluctuation. If I relied on my own eyes, which tended to deceive me during periods of my life when I felt a pressing need to gorge myself at any opportunity, I

worried I would wake up one day requiring a crane to get me out
of bed. "I'll have the Cobb salad and an iced tea," I said, handing
my menu to the waiter, who gave a quick nod and scurried off.

"So have you told Derrick about the wedding yet?"

"Oh, yeah, sure," I said, then quickly moving on, "Told Jade,
too. She's thrilled to pieces for you."

My mother stopped, staring at me hard for a moment. "And you
aren't so thrilled, I take it?"

Here it comes. Confession time. "It's not that I'm not *happy*..."
I began.

"You don't trust it," my mother said. "I was worried about this
happening."

Whew. I was actually going to be saved by psychobabble. I felt
my mother about to take over from here, explaining away her reasons for running to the altar for the third time.

"I know for much of my life I've looked like I've had my head
in the sand, and in truth I probably have," she acknowledged.

She was looking at me in earnest now, and I saw a burning need
in her eyes to make things make sense to me. "It hasn't been so
bad for you..." I said, attempting to erase whatever anxieties she
might still be having about the zigzagging course her life had taken
thus far.

"It has been bad at times. And I think it was because I simply
refused to see what was in front in me. But I look at Clark and I
see everything. His warmth. His compassion. His kind, kind heart."
Her eyes misted. "But I also see his flaws. For example, I know
he sometimes gets so wrapped up with his work or with his students
that he tunes out my needs. And he sometimes has a hard time
adjusting to change—and you know my life is nothing but change,
it seems." Then she smiled. "And he snores. Loud."

"You snore, too, Mom."

"Oh, Em, I'm quiet compared to him." She laughed before
growing serious again. "But the one thing I know for sure is that
I love him in a way I've never loved anyone else. I would do
anything for him. Go anywhere to be by his side. Tend to him if

he were ill, God forbid. And I know—this time I know for sure—that he would do the same for me."

Her words rang through me, clanging in ways I wasn't ready to hear. The question rose, unbidden, of whether Derrick and I were really the soulmates I dreamed we were if we were so unwilling to give even a little of our lives to each other. But I quickly swallowed this doubt down around the lump in my throat. And, fortunately, the waiter took that moment to come by with our salads.

Once he was gone, Mom said, "Does any of this make sense to you?"

I saw in her face how much she needed my acceptance of this latest turn of events in her life, and though for various reasons I wasn't ready to swallow it whole, I was ready to start seeing her hopes and dreams in a more sympathetic light. "I understand. And I'm happy for you, Mom. In fact, I've got a stack of ideas with me on just how we can make wedding number three the charm." Then I laughed, not able to end things without some kind of ironic touch. "Because you know as well as I do, Mom, it isn't really about *who* you marry. It's *how* you marry."

And with that, we dug into lunch, as well as the stack of wedding-day dreams I had packed into my tote bag. Things were pretty much on an even keel after that, which is why I didn't understand the lump of emotion that emerged once our salad plates had been cleared away and we sat poring over the last few pictures of brides gazing thoughtfully into the camera as they stepped beneath various archways and gazebos that could be rented and transported to the location of your choice.

Suddenly, out of nowhere, I felt something inside of me go slack. And before I knew what I was saying, I had told my mother everything. About Derrick's disastrous departure and my newfound misery. And after we shed some tears and angsted together over the "whys" behind the breakup—my mother is especially good at this type of relationship analysis, having submerged herself in self-help books as each relationship ended in her own life—we indulged in giant slices of Mad Mocha Mud Cake for dessert. Even ate it with heaping clumps of vanilla ice cream on the side.

"You know what you really need," Mom said, when we'd finally emerged from our dessert dishes. I stared at her, sensing some significant bit of wisdom would be forthcoming.

"Highlights."

Confession: There are some ailments only good hair can cure.

Though agreeing with my mother is not my strong suit, I had to admit, she was right—I had relationship hair. Long brown locks that spoke of Saturday nights at home, wrapped in Derrick's sweatshirt and boxers while we watched videos and stuffed ourselves full of whatever goodies we had managed to find at the bodega on the corner. In order to remedy the situation, I did what I had done in the Pre-Derrick Period when dye jobs were a regular part of my regiment. That night I called Sebastian, my erstwhile hairdresser.

"Emma, what a surprise!" he said, a hint of censure in his tone, when I got him on the phone. This is the problem when you first befriend the person who ultimately becomes responsible for your hair. They expect you to adhere to the boundaries of friendship, even when all you need is a few blond streaks. And since I hadn't spoken to Sebastian in more than six months, I had to smooth things over by inviting him out for drinks.

"Oh, I don't drink anymore, Emma. Tea, perhaps?" he said, naming some veggie joint on West 3rd Street and suggesting we meet there the following evening.

The nondrinking stance should have forewarned me, but I was so focused on my forthcoming transformation, I missed the signs. So as I headed down to West 3rd Street after work the next day, I looked forward to catching up with Sebastian and swapping zany stories of New York men and other strange creatures. When Sebastian and I first met, he was dating a college friend of mine, Keith. And though Keith and Sebastian lasted no longer than a semester, it was enough to seal the bond between Sebastian and me. I held his hand through the breakup, downed some serious drinks with him and bitched about the sad state of the male species, excluding Sebastian, of course. And when all was said and done, Sebastian started dyeing my hair.

It was a difficult relationship from the start, though my hair never suffered. Sebastian took me through every shade of blond, a few hues of red, and even a rich chocolate-brown—which, coming from his magic hands, even seemed a bit dangerous and exciting. He was an artist, but like all artists, he was temperamental. He insisted his friends didn't have to pay, then complained he was being taken advantage of. It got to the point where I was forced to surreptitiously leave money on his countertop as I left his apartment after a color session, like a lover leaving secret gifts for his inamorata. And he was alternatively open, then secretive, about his love life, so I never knew when it was a good time to ask how things were going between him and whatever luscious boy—and they were *always* gorgeous—he had in his life.

"Emma," he called, waving lazily at me as I detangled myself from the velvet drape hanging between the juice bar and the dining area where Sebastian sat, presiding over his surroundings like the queen that he was. Somehow Sebastian had managed to find a place that matched his unique look—a mixture of wholesomeness and exoticism. Amid gilt-framed pictures of various plants and herbs and swaths of rich fabric hanging from the windows and walls, Sebastian, with his lush golden curls and Asian eyes set in a cherub's face, looked at home.

Once I reached his table, he enfolded me in a hug—a departure from the practice of kissing both cheeks he had instituted the last few times I saw him.

"Sit, sit! Isn't this place fabulous?" Sebastian insisted, studying my face with a mixture of reverence and concern. Whenever I was with Sebastian, the same insecurities came over me that I felt whenever I was in the presence of a beautiful woman—that my eyebrows needed shaping, my lipstick updating. In short, I felt woefully subpar in the femininity department.

"How *are* you?" he asked once we were sitting across from

each other, giant scarlet menus—in some textured fabric that was clearly impractical for a food environment—before us.

"Good, good. How are *you?*" I said, peering at him over the top of the menu. "You look...relaxed."

"Do I? Oh! I have so much to tell you."

"Can I take your order?"

Turning away from my menu, I was confronted with a pierced belly button and low-slung jeans. The waitress, a lanky girl whose bored expression spoke of her utter indifference to our needs, stood beside our table poised and waiting. She looked exhausted and I noticed a faded ink stamp on the back of her hand, probably from some East Village club. Had it not been for her softly spoken question, I might have thought she was going to lie down on the bench beside us.

"Darjeeling for me," Sebastian said, naming some substance I assume was tea.

Noticing a woeful lack of caffeinated beverages on the menu, I ordered chamomile, deciding that if I wasn't going to get a jolt, I might as well go to the other extreme.

"So, tell me, tell me, tell me. How're things? Derrick?" Sebastian asked, settling into the cushions surrounding his seat.

"Things are fine. Derrick's...gone."

"Gone? As in...?"

"Got a job offer, moved to the West Coast."

"Oh, dear." Sebastian's pretty little nose scrunched up in sympathy.

"Yeah, well, I guess you can't say he didn't warn me."

"That's the trouble with ambitious, creative, gorgeous men. They've always got something better to do than you."

Picking up my glass of water, I clinked it into Sebastian's. "Here's to slackers."

"Slackers with trust funds," Sebastian replied, picking up his glass to drink. "Men without money are no fun."

"It's true," I agreed. "I've been thinking of going upscale in the man department. I've got the boobs, all I need is the dye job.

What do you say, Sebastian? Are you up for it?'' I laughed, trying not to sound too desperate. I needed to be blonder, and Sebastian was the only one I trusted to take me to that next level.

''Oh, Emma. I've discovered that hair color—even *good* color—can't solve all your problems.''

Now this is where I began to realize that Sebastian had changed in some elemental way. Fear began to invade me. ''Do tell,'' I replied, trying for a light tone.

''Remember John? Impossible John?''

''Are you guys back together?'' I asked with disbelief. John was the man who had tormented Sebastian for the better part of three years. A struggling actor, John was notorious for pledging his undying love to Sebastian just moments before he ran off with some buff production assistant or wardrobe boy from whatever set he was currently working on.

''No, no. Never, in fact,'' he said, puckering his lips as the waitress placed our tea before us and slithered away once more. ''John has been permanently replaced.'' He began fishing around in the shiny tote he had with him. Pulling out his wallet, he flipped to the photo section and handed it to me.

I was shocked to find myself looking at a photo of an Indian woman dressed in traditional robes, a bindi firmly in place on her forehead, a gentle smile on her lips. Not only was she female—an unimaginable possibility as a new partner for Sebastian—but she was alarmingly unfettered by the kind of female things that normally gave Sebastian pleasure—like lipstick, cleavage and a well-groomed brow.

''Meet the woman who saved my life,'' he said, smiling.

I stared at him, perplexed. ''I don't get it.''

''Emma, I have undergone the most *amazing* transformation.''

''You haven't gone straight, have you?''

''God forbid!'' he cried, shaking his head. ''No, it's nothing like that. This is my guru!''

''Guru?''

He smiled pleasantly, as one might at a small child in serious need of enlightenment. "Let me start at the beginning. I ran into John a couple of months ago, and you would not *believe* what he looked like. Completely bald, for one thing."

"*John?*" I said, remembering how much he had always treasured his long dark locks.

"I know, I *know,*" Sebastian said, looking sad for a moment, as if the loss of that beautiful head of hair might still hurt, despite whatever revelations about life he had recently been given. Getting hold of himself once more, he continued, "He had this look of serenity about him. It had almost changed his face—he was even more gorgeous, if you can imagine that!" His eyes widened at the thought. "I asked him how he'd been, and he began telling me that he was following a new path in his life. When I questioned him further, he told me he was practicing a form of Hinduism—and was training to be a healer."

"Wow. Who would have thought," I said, gulping chamomile and suddenly wishing it were something else…like a martini. I had a sinking feeling about my hair prospects, especially when I suddenly noticed that Sebastian had let his eyebrows grow in. Not a good sign in a man I once worshiped for his beauty regime.

"Next thing you know, he was inviting me to a meeting," Sebastian said, lifting his teacup and holding it between his hands in front of him. "I will confess that when I first agreed to attend, I had sex on the brain. You know that no matter what happened between John and me, we never had trouble in that department. But from the moment I stepped through the doors of the Holistic Center for Life Healing, I was a new man. Within weeks, I was on the path, and now I'm close to being certified as a healer myself. I've even planned a trip to India in the fall, to meet the guru. I can't wait to go."

I felt contrite. He did look happy. Who was I to mar his happiness with my own selfish desires? "That's wonderful, Sebastian."

"I knew you'd understand, Emma. In fact, I've been meaning to call you and invite you to a meeting. I think you, especially, could really benefit from it.'' He put down his tea, then reached across and grabbed both my hands in his.

I will admit, I felt something like a soothing strength in those fingers. Of course, unable to acknowledge such things, I made one last halfhearted, half-humorous, plea.

"So I guess this means a few ash-blond highlights are out of the question, huh?"

"Oh, Emma," he smiled beatifically at me, releasing my hands. "That world seems so removed from me now." Then he winked. "Besides, you know I always saw you as a *golden* blonde."

Confession: I get in touch with my inner career woman—and discover she is out to lunch.

The next day as I was poring over some old notes in an attempt to put together a piece on current trends in floral arrangements, Marcy Keller, the production assistant and resident office gossip, slipped into my cubicle.

"What's up, Emma?" she said, sitting down in my guest chair.

I immediately went on red alert. The only reason Marcy Keller would ever sit down in my guest chair to chat would be a) because she had some juicy bit of gossip she had already shared with everyone in the office and I was her last resort or, b) she had some juicy bit of gossip about *me* that she was coyly trying to verify.

A shiver went through me. They knew. They knew about my recent, brutal breakup. But how?

"So what brings you to this corner of the world, Marcy?" I asked with trepidation.

She looked up and leaned close, her eyes narrowing to slits behind the big square black frames she wore on her sharp little hook of a nose. "Sandra quit," she hissed at me. Then, smoothing her short, dark brown hair behind her ears, she leaned back, folded her arms over her painfully thin frame and watched her words take their effect.

Relief swept through me, followed by a realization. Sandra was one of the three reigning senior features editors at *Bridal Best* and had just given up one of the few management positions a contributing editor like myself could aspire to. Now I understood why I had been chosen to receive this particular bit of gossip. Since I was the contributing editor with four years' experience under my belt and the most seniority, I was the most likely candidate to apply. So Marcy *had* come on a verification mission. I decided not to give her the satisfaction.

"Sandra quit?" I began, leaning back in my chair. "That's wild." I paused, pondering this for a moment to increase the dramatic tension. "Huh. And I thought she'd be a lifer. What has she been here, five, six years?"

"Seven and a *half*," Marcy said, glee in her voice at the scandal created by such a long-term employee's leaving. "I heard that she and Patricia had it out."

Now I knew she was embellishing. Our editor-in-chief was soft-spoken, poised, and probably the least likely person to start a brawl at *Bridal Best,* the magazine that was her life's blood. Which made me wonder about this battle she'd allegedly had with Sandra, who wasn't exactly a brute, though she had been rumored to have a temper. "Huh. That's hard to imagine."

"Yeah, well, you know *Sandra.* She can be a bitch when things aren't going her way. And they haven't been, ever since her husband left her."

"Her husband *left* her?" I asked, suddenly sucked in, in spite of myself.

Marcy rolled her eyes behind her square frames. "That was six months ago. God, Emma, where have you *been?*"

I snapped my gaping mouth shut. "Well, usually I'm too *busy* with work to pay attention to the gossip," I replied, deciding now was probably the perfect time to put Marcy in her place.

Marcy swallowed hard and began backpedaling. "Yes, you do work a lot. I've even seen you here late a few times," she said, changing tactics when she realized ridicule wasn't going to get her anywhere with me.

"Yeah, well. Once in a while. When I'm on a deadline," I replied, embarrassed that someone might think me one of The Devoted, some of whom had given up their lives, their dreams and, apparently, in the case of Sandra, their husbands, for the sake of getting out a monthly magazine on how to make happily-ever-after a reality.

"No, you work hard," she protested, gazing at me steadily and making me notice for the first time that her eyes were actually gray behind those thick black cakes of liner. "I read your piece 'The Cinderella Syndrome: Finding the Perfect Wedding Day Shoe.' It was amazing."

Now she had me. "Ah, well, thanks. I kinda liked working on that piece."

"I just *loved* the way you captured the anxiety of finding a shoe that's both comfortable and captivating. And the fairy-tale angle was *very* clever. What was that line you opened with?"

Leaning back in my chair with something close to an embarrassing pride curling my lip, I quoted, " 'Now that you've found a Prince Charming who's your perfect fit, it's time to get serious about the shoe you step into to take that long—and potentially painful—walk down the aisle.' "

"Yes, yes!" Marcy said, sitting up higher in her chair. "That was *awesome.*"

"Thanks, Marcy. Gosh, I hadn't even realized you *read* the magazine."

"Are you kidding?" Marcy leaned back in her chair once more. "You're good, Emma. Really good. How long have you been here now? Three and a half years?"

"Four years and two months next week."

"Wow." She beamed at me, then her eyes narrowed speculatively. "You know, you'd be a shoo-in for the senior features position."

"That's nice of you to say, but—"

"I mean, you've got the most seniority of all the contributing editors."

"I know, but that doesn't mean—"

"And *everybody* knows you're the best writer we have on the staff," she finished, throwing in the pièce de résistance with a gleam of satisfaction in her eyes.

"They do?"

"Oh, Emma. You don't have to be so modest with *me*. I mean, I just assumed you'd be going for that promotion. You *are* the strongest candidate, after all."

I leaned forward in my chair. "Well, now that you mention it, I had thought of talking to Caroline about opportunities within the company." It was true that I had recently had vague thoughts about talking with my boss regarding my future. But in my fantasies I always imagined entering her office with a prepared speech, then arbitrarily breaking into a rant about how no one recognized what a huge talent I was. It was this that always kept me from initiating any sort of dialogue with Caroline on the subject. But now it seemed—according to Marcy anyway—that everyone was quite impressed with me.

"You should talk to her."

"Hmm. Maybe I'll talk to her some time next week. I mean, I've got this piece to finish and another one to proof—"

"I wouldn't put it off *too* long," Marcy cautioned. Then she stood, leaning in close for the final kill. "I mean, you don't want someone *else* to move in first."

She had a point. "Yeah, that's true." I looked up at her, trying to find some glimmer of camaraderie on her face, and discovered *something* there that resembled sympathy and goodwill, but I was too far gone to discriminate at the moment. "I'll do it. First thing Monday morning. Then maybe she can advise me on how to approach Patricia." Though the thought of approaching the editor-in-chief regarding the position put a pit in my stomach. I doubted Patricia even knew I existed. But it was necessary if I was really going to go through with this.

And it looked like I was, judging from the triumphant smile on Marcy's face as she made some hasty excuse and rushed out of my cubicle, more than likely to find someone worthy of her latest bit of news—that Emma Carter, disenchanted editor on the verge of career despair, had just put herself on the block for the highest promotion a girl with no giddiness over marriage and all its mayhem could ever hope to aspire to at *Bridal Best.*

Oh God. What had I done?

I immediately sought out Rebecca, hoping that she at least might be able to offer some insight on this latest development.

"Hey," I said, sliding into her guest chair.

"Hi," she said, slowly pulling herself away from her computer screen, where she'd been typing furiously.

"I'm not interrupting, am I?" I asked, suddenly aware that she seemed so focused on what she was doing, I was more of an obstruction than an office buddy at the moment.

"No, no. Just wanted to tie this article up before lunch," she said, saving her file and turning to me.

Finish an article before lunch? When had Rebecca become so efficient? Not having the time to ponder such matters, I started in, "Did you hear about Sandra?"

"Oh, yeah. Marcy already made the rounds," Rebecca said, rolling her eyes.

"I'm thinking of going for it."

She hesitated for the briefest moment, but long enough for me to see the surprise on her face.

"You don't think I should?" I said, suddenly becoming defensive. Just what was it about me that Rebecca thought wasn't senior features editor material yet? And who was *she* to judge, having signed on only a year and a half ago?

"No, no. That's not it." Then she smiled. "You should go for it. If that's what you really want."

"Of course it's what I want! I mean, what am I going to do? Sit around here for another four years, making the same schlocky salary? After all, it's not like these opportunities happen every day. It took Sandra seven and a half years to up and leave that position open."

"That's true." Then she sighed. "Things haven't been the same for her since her husband left."

"Gosh, I just heard about *that* office shocker. They only got married two years ago. Didn't that throw you for a loop?"

"Yeah," Rebecca replied, "I always thought she and Roger had the perfect marriage."

"You've *met* him?"

"Uh-huh. Sandra had Nash and me over to dinner about a year ago. She went to Sarah Lawrence, too, graduated a few years ahead of me. I guess she figured we had a lot in common. It was a fun evening. Sandra's really down to earth, once you get to know her."

"Yeah…" Now this bit of news *really* threw me. I never would have envisioned Sandra and Rebecca as pals. Again my suspicions about Rebecca were aroused. Just how entrenched in this loony little world was she, anyway?

I found out, moments later, when I heard her next words.

"I think you should go for the senior features editor position, Emma," she began, "if you feel that's the direction you want to take." Then she looked down briefly at her hands clasped in her lap, before meeting my eyes again. "But to be fair, I think you should know that I've already applied for the position myself."

Confession: My inner career woman has left the building.

"Who does she think she is?" Alyssa asked, her brow furrowed in indignation as she stared at me across the table in the dimly lit restaurant. We had met for dinner at Bar Six, one of our favorite haunts in the West Village. Jade was joining us, too, though she had yet to arrive. We sat in the bar section, so that Jade could smoke once she got here, and drank cosmopolitans while I filled Alyssa in on the gory details of my newfound competition with, of all people, Rebecca.

"She hasn't even put in the *time*," I complained. "Of course, she *has* put in the time with good old Sandra. Sandra probably primed her on how to get the position without even trying." I took another slug of my drink, hoping to dull my senses and ease the irritating ache between my eyeballs. "Why does this kind of thing always happen to me?"

"What kind of thing is happening to you now?" Jade asked, arriving just in time to hear me gripe. She quickly swooped down to embrace each of us in greeting, before sliding into the third chair.

"Rebecca is competing with Emma for a senior features editor position at *Bridal Best*," Alyssa informed her.

Jade's gaze swung to me, assessing. "*You're* going for a senior features editor position?"

"*Yes*," I hissed at her. On the defensive, I argued, "Why is that so hard to believe? I've been writing and editing for the magazine for the past four years—and quite brilliantly, I might add. Just the other day my boss commended me on a piece I wrote about under-garments to wear with your gown. It was positively brilliant—I mean, for a piece on underwear. I even had this great inspiration for the title—'The Bride Beneath.'"

I sat back, breathing hard, as I contemplated Jade's carefully blank expression.

"Sounds…clever," she said, lighting a cigarette as the waiter approached to take our order. He was young and gorgeous, as the waiters at Bar Six tend to be, with a vaguely Mediterranean look about him. I watched Jade give him the complete once-over as I retreated into myself to sulk.

I knew what was going through Jade's mind. She was thinking about the fact that I had suddenly pledged my heart and soul, staked my entire self-worth, on a career that up until a few weeks ago, I couldn't care less about. But she was wrong. She didn't know that during the Derrick Years, my role at *Bridal Best* had taken on epic proportions. It had become my whole raison d'être. No one knew—besides Derrick, of course. Derrick, who had always admired the fact that I was one of the lucky few who had actually gotten a day job writing, while he had done everything from waiting tables to walking dogs in order to make a few bucks while practicing his "art." Derrick, who admired me so much, he hadn't even called yet to let me know he'd settled into his life without me.

When I tuned in again, I heard Alyssa calmly laying out the reasons why I was eminently more qualified for the senior features editor position than Rebecca was. Good ol' Alyssa. I could always count on her to stand by me while I harbored my illusions. Jade, on the other hand, was a bit trickier.

"Okay, okay," Jade was saying now. "I see your point." The waiter came back, carefully placing a cosmopolitan before her while she took in his forearm, his hands. Then she glanced up at us with a look that said, "Look who's coming for dinner." Once the waiter had safely escaped her perusal for the moment, she lifted her glass. "So if we're going to get behind this promotion thing, let's do it right." When we had lifted our glasses, too, she said, "To Emma's next incarnation—as Leader of the Stepford Editors."

We froze, glasses in midair. Alyssa cracked an exasperated smile. "Jade!"

"Okay, okay. Forget it. Let's move on to a toast I can really get behind," she said, sending a last cutting glance in my direction. "To our waiter. For being just luscious enough to keep alive that lingering hope that I will have sex again."

We clinked, Alyssa laughing and me relieved that we had moved on to topics that didn't have anything to do with my sudden touchiness over my next career move. Though Jade wouldn't allow me to delude myself, she knew when to back off.

"So what's going on with you?" Alyssa said to Jade. "Emma told me you met a great guy. Ted, was it?"

"Ted." Jade sighed. Then, sipping her drink, she shrugged. "I guess Emma didn't get to the part where Ted disappeared off the face of the earth."

"What happened?" Alyssa asked.

"What else? He didn't call." She stamped out her cigarette, then gave another shrug.

Though she carefully tried to mask it, I saw something in Jade's eyes which made me think this particular failure somehow got her where she lived. I wondered why. Then figured it was probably because Ted had been the first guy she'd ever dated who *had* disappeared into that giant vacuum of Men Who Never Call. It was the kind of void that left a woman aching not with heartbreak, but a resounding *why?* which tended to turn against *her* rather than *him,* with responses like "Maybe I'm too fat too boring too broke too confident too insecure too aggressive too passive too happy too depressed...." But this thought was followed by the realization that this was not Jade's normal line of thinking but mine. Still, even the strongest could waver in the face of the silent-but-deadly blow-off. Perhaps she needed another reminder that Ted Terrific was not so terrific anyway.

"I read somewhere once that muscle size is directly dispropor-tionate to brain size," I began. "Didn't you mention that Ted was pretty thick in the muscle department?"

Jade gave a half smile. "All right, all right. I know what you're trying to do. And no, I said that Ted was lean. Like a surfer. But that's not the point."

"What is the point?" Alyssa asked, and I could see she, too, was aware of some simmering unease in Jade.

"The point is, I thought we really had some kind of connection. I mean, we liked the same music. He was into the same clubs. And he even liked Simply Red. And you know how I feel about Simply Red."

"Well, it was only one date," said Alyssa, ever the logical one.

"One amazing date," Jade argued. "And that doesn't happen too often."

Jade had a point. If there was one thing I knew, it was that in a city this large, where any sort of interaction with the opposite sex is swallowed up by the rush of time or traffic or whatever it is that keeps people from their mating rituals, one meaningful evening with a man constituted a serious beginning to something. Which was why losing Derrick, after two years of sharing everything from soulful conversation to toothbrushes, was something just short of disaster.

"They're all heartless bastards," I chimed in.

"Yeah, well, if I ever hope to have sex again, I have to figure out how to keep one of those heartless bastards around long enough.''

"Maybe you're focusing too hard on the end result, Jade," Alyssa said. "Maybe you should take a more Zen-like approach to this whole dating thing.''

"Easy for you to say when you have a live-in boy toy," Jade said, though it was hard to envision Richard as a boy toy in his dark suits and tasseled loafers. Don't get me wrong—with his chiseled good looks and tall, athletic build he was quite delectable. But Richard was the kind of man women fantasized about marching down the aisle with, not swinging from a rope in the Tarzan room of the Fantasy Land Motel. Then again, Jade did like to say I lacked vision when it came to men.

"The grass is always greener," Alyssa said, dropping her gaze.

"Oh?" Jade countered, warming to the subject. "Let's see about that. It's been six weeks and four days since I last had sex—and I'm not counting Carl, because I'm talking penetration here. When was the last time you and Richard did it? And if you say last night, I will be forced to be envious.''

Still regarding her glass, Alyssa replied, "Three months ago.''

"What?" Jade and I said in unison.

Alyssa looked up at us and sighed. "Well, that's not exactly true. We did have sex about three weeks ago, but it was the kind of effort that's better left unmentioned. All mechanics, no emotions. As if we're just blowing off some steam after a hard day at work.''

"What's going on with you guys?" Jade asked.

"I don't know. Everything has just been…different between us the past few months. As if we're only going through the motions of a relationship.''

"Maybe you're just in a rut," I said, desperate to find any reason why things had suddenly gone astray for the last two people in the world I was sure were Meant-to-Be. "I mean, isn't Richard trying to make partner? He's got to be under enormous pressure at work. And you've been working on that class action suit for quite some time….''

"Maybe." Alyssa sighed. "But it's like we don't really even *see* each other anymore. I feel more like a roommate. The girl he shares the laundry hamper with."

"You just gotta shake things up," Jade said. "Do something to remind him that he's living with a beautiful, intelligent woman who any guy would snatch up." Then she arched her brows as sudden inspiration hit. "What you need is some serious competition to suddenly show up, give old Richard a run for his money."

Alyssa immediately glanced at me with a guilty smile, and I couldn't help but smile back, thinking of her vet and imagining how a man who probably spent a good deal of his day dodging dog feces was going to give Richard, a successful corporate lawyer who could probably eat him for lunch, a run for his money.

"What's going on?" Jade asked, suspicious.

I looked at Alyssa, leaving the confession to her.

"Well...the truth is...I *have* met someone else."

"You're kidding," Jade said, and I had a feeling she was wondering, as I had, how Alyssa always managed to keep the men coming, no matter what her circumstances. "Who? And most importantly, *how?*"

"You have to promise not to laugh." Alyssa looked hard into Jade's eyes.

"Laugh, nothing. If you've got some method I should know about, who am I to judge?"

"Okay. Well, I don't know if this method would work for you, because it requires you to get a pet." Alyssa paused, glancing at me for reassurance. "You see, Lulu hasn't been feeling well lately, so I took her to the vet. And, well, the old vet retired, leaving his practice to a new, young...gorgeous...vet."

"You're sleeping with Lulu's vet?"

"No!" Alyssa and I shouted in unison, the sound of my own anxious denial making me realize just how important it was for me that Alyssa didn't do anything to jeopardize what she had with Richard.

"Then what? You're sharing housebreaking tips? Flea baths? What?"

"Nothing is going on *really*," Alyssa said. "It's just…"

"She has a crush on him," I said, butting in. "You know, puppy love." Then I glanced at Alyssa. "Uh, no pun intended."

"I don't know if it's just a crush," Alyssa protested. "I mean, it's just like you said you felt with Ted, Jade. I feel a real *connection* with him."

"Yeah, well," Jade said, "you can take that for what it's worth, Alyssa."

"I'm sorry, I didn't mean—" Alyssa began.

"Look, no apologies needed, Lys," Jade countered. "There's just one thing you need to think about, and think hard. Just how important is this cute little pooper scooper to you? Enough to risk losing Richard for?"

When Alyssa didn't respond, I turned to gape at her. "Alyssa!"

"Hey," Jade said, lighting a cigarette and leaning back in a sort of blasé-about-relationships pose she'd adopted ever since Michael had torn whatever romantic streak she'd formerly had out of her. "If it means that much to you, I say go for it."

"Jade, don't encourage—" I began, but Jade leaned forward then, confidingly.

"But whatever you do, please do it outside of his office. I can't imagine all those wee wee pads and antiseptics making for much atmosphere."

"Ha, ha," Alyssa said, lifting her drink to her mouth to try to hide her smile.

A smile, I might add, which said she was planning on doing just what Jade suggested, and with a man whose only distinction so far was in making Lulu's most recent bellyache go away.

I had to face facts. Alyssa and Richard were truly on the rocks. And Jade, who I saw light up as our handsome waiter returned, had gone from Girl Who Couldn't Get Enough to Girl Who Couldn't Get It At All.

Then there was me, of course, who didn't have a hope in the

world of convincing the man I loved that he'd just made the greatest mistake in the world by moving across the country away from me, especially considering the fact that the creep hadn't even taken a moment to call yet, even to say hi.

The question that was stuck in the recesses of my mind, wedged in tight by anxiety, suddenly wafted up, unbidden.

What would become of us?

Confession: Things could definitely get worse.

After an evening that ended with Jade—egged on by Alyssa— successfully securing our waiter's phone number, I woke up the next morning resolved to make myself a smash success at *Bridal Best*. Maybe it was Alyssa's encouragement, or maybe it was a rebellion against Jade's utter disbelief in my decision, but I wound up spending part of Sunday preparing a presentation to make to Caroline on Monday, and giving myself a French manicure that I hoped would somehow raise me to some new professional level. On Monday I donned the only thing in my closet resembling a suit—a pair of black trousers that didn't look too faded against the one black blazer I owned, and a white shirt that looked less than my others like your standard T—and headed for the illustrious midtown office where my new destiny awaited me. My intention was to discuss my decision with Caroline and get her approval to move on to the next step: persuading the Powers-That-Be at *Bridal Best* that not only was I the best candidate for senior features editor they could hope to have, but that I was, in fact, of one mind with the editorial mantra "Give me marriage or give me death."

Once I arrived, I walked with purpose to my cubicle. I kept my gaze focused forward to avoid seeing any raised eyebrows over my sudden upgrade in office attire. "Confidence," Alyssa had said as she hugged me goodbye after dinner. "All you need to do is show them how sure you are of your ability to do the job." But all I could do once I sat at my desk in order to practice my seemingly unrehearsed speech was think about Sandra and Rebecca, sitting over lunch while Sandra dictated the surefire route to senior features editor to her protégée. How could I compete against that kind of inside track? Everyone knew what an incestuous business this was. It was as if the most coveted positions were carefully kept open for those chosen few who managed to emulate their superiors so per- fectly that the Powers-That-Be couldn't help but strive to make the little mini versions of themselves grow up to be the new Powers- That-Be.

Now one could argue that Rebecca, with her perfect boyfriend and her perfect bob and her stylish little silk blouses and knee- length skirts, did not even remotely resemble Sandra, who tended more toward a disheveled, layered look. But I was certain now that a bond had formed between them from the moment Rebecca had joined the staff. At the time, Sandra had recently joined the Happily Married, and I imagined her taking one look at Rebecca, with her pedigree schooling and her upwardly mobile boyfriend, and seeing enough of herself and her happy little life to reach out. After all, it had been only mere months since Sandra had landed her own financially stable husband and Upper East Side Duplex, and I'm certain she couldn't help but see a dinner party with Rebecca and her beau as nothing less than a prime opportunity to bring out the Lenox china she had obsessed over and ultimately registered for in the months before she marched off to her ill-fated marriage. And despite the fact that Sandra had now, for whatever reason, just joined the Disastrously Divorced category, I knew that ultimately she had shared something with Rebecca that night—something that would only grow now that Sandra had given up her role as Suc- cessful and Married and needed to hand the mantle on to someone else. Someone as polished, as poised, as perfect as Rebecca.

How was I going to compete with that? Me, with my scuffed pumps pulled from the bottom of the closet and phantom boy- friend?

"Looking sharp," came Marcy Keller's voice as she popped her head around the wall of my cubicle and gave me a conspiratorial wink.

Feeling horribly grateful for the compliment, even coming from a woman more known for her calculation than her camaraderie, I actually smiled at her, which gave her just enough invitation to slide her spindly form into my guest chair.

"So you're finally going to do it, huh?" she asked, in a kind of harsh whisper that suggested I was going to take a machine gun to my colleagues rather than go in to my superior to ask for a promotion.

"No better time than the present," I replied with false bravado.

"I agree," she said, nodding vigorously, eyebrows arched above her big black frames. "Especially since Rebecca has already put together her clips and her résumé and handed them in."

"She *has?*"

"Of course."

I glanced over the gaping "to be filed" box where I had stuffed everything of personal relevance, from bedraggled clips and old vacation memos to takeout menus for local eateries. "Do you think I should put together something before I go in to Caroline?"

Her gaze followed mine to the pile of papers, and I saw her eyes widen briefly. "Nah," she replied, swatting her hand through the air in a gesture that suggested I was worrying for nothing. "That would take too long. You're best off going in there and at least letting her know you are interested. Then, *afterward,* you could pull together something for when you go in to see Patricia."

Suddenly I saw the benefits of befriending Marcy. She was a wealth of information on how to negotiate the politics of getting promoted. I hadn't even *thought* of putting together my clips. I just assumed Patricia would have seen my work at one point or another. I mean, she *is* the editor-in-chief of this fine periodical.

"And I would probably try to include some clips outside of what you've done for *Bridal Best,*" Marcy continued, as if reading the unasked question that lingered in the back of my mind. "I think Rebecca included a bunch of stuff from that trade newspaper she used to work for."

Panic began to invade me. Rebecca had other clips. What did I have, other than a few half-finished short stories and some self-deprecating poetry I had written during a previous post-breakup pity party? "Other clips?"

"You know, stuff you might have written freelance, or in a previous job," Marcy continued, then sucked her cheeks in when realization struck. "Oh, that's right. You've never *had* a previous job."

She was right, other than my stint at waitressing and a run of office temp jobs that had resulted in nothing but callused feet and bad fiction. Even my illustrious career at *Bridal Best* was really a result of random luck and Caroline's somewhat misguided belief in me.

"Have you ever done any freelance?" Marcy was asking now. She actually seemed really concerned for me, which I found oddly heartening. Maybe I'd had Marcy pegged all wrong.

"Not really," I replied, my confidence slumping to an all-time low.

She studied me for a moment, as if trying to assign a promotability value to me and coming up short. Then she shrugged. "I wouldn't worry about it," she said, standing up. "I mean, after all, Rebecca was working on a *trade* publication anyway." Her nose wrinkled, as if the idea that anyone would work for an industry newspaper that languished on the desks of some back office somewhere, rather than a magazine being prominently displayed on the racks at your local newsstand, was somehow distasteful.

"I guess," I replied, unconvinced.

Glancing at her watch, she said, "Well, duty calls. Knock 'em dead, Emma." Then after skipping somewhat merrily out of my cube, she popped her head back in, "Oh, and *good luck.*"

You'll need it. The implication she had not voiced sped through my mind nonetheless as I stared at her retreating back.

Confession: My life has become some sort of inside joke—and I'm the only one who doesn't get it.

"Come in, come in," Caroline invited, once I finally gathered up the courage to actually go in and make my now somewhat pathetic-seeming bid for the senior features editor position. Thank God, I had Caroline to practice on first, before having to make my case to Patricia. Ever since I had come to *Bridal Best,* Caroline had been my champion, lavishing praise on my early writing efforts and encouraging me to go for the contributing-editor position when it opened up. Now, as I headed into her sunlit, plant-filled office, the shelves overflowing with everything from the international dolls she collected to photos of her and Miles, her husband, and their three picture-perfect children, I was glad she was my manager. But as I seated myself before her, it suddenly occurred to me that the theory I had recently constructed of the solid bond formation between Sandra and Rebecca didn't hold water when it came to Caroline and me. There was no way I was the miniversion of Caroline, with her warm, loving home in Connecticut strewn, I was sure, with the hand-made crafts she excelled at and smelling of the fresh-baked cookies she tucked into her children's lunch bags before sending them off to posh private schools carefully chosen according to each gifted child's unique talents. Even her husband, a general contractor who was ever ready to build a new wing onto their already sprawling home to accommodate the next adorable addition to the Jamison family, seemed from some male mold I had yet to encounter in my own life. Not that I had ever been invited to said happy home or met the husband and kids, but I had gathered much from Caroline's softly spoken stories at the communal lunch room table of the joys of family life. Even now, she was radiantly pregnant with Perfect Baby Number Four beneath her floral and feminine maternity dress. Everyone was always faintly amazed at how she returned to the office baby after baby, ever ready to do her part for the greater good of *Bridal Best.*

"I'm glad you stopped by," Caroline said now, once I had made myself comfortable in the chair parked next to her wide desk, which was a maze of carefully stacked papers. Somehow, no matter how busy Caroline was, she was always prepared to offer you a chair and an ear to discuss just about anything that was on your mind, whether righteous indignation at your piece getting bumped from an issue, or dismay of a more personal nature, should you dare to share it with it a superior. Not that I ever did. And I wouldn't dare share my recent Derrick Disaster with anyone in the office now that I was allegedly making so much progress in my life that a promotion seemed like the next, natural thing. After all, whoever heard of a disgruntled editor and new member of the Recently Dumped making senior features editor at the nation's most comprehensive guide to happily-ever-after?

"Did you want to talk to me about something?" I asked now, worried suddenly that Caroline, in her gentle way, was about to inform me that she had realized how seriously lacking I was in most areas of my life and work.

"No, no. Nothing specific. It's just we haven't really spoken in a while, and I was wondering how things were going. You know, sometimes with all the flurry of deadline pressures and, well, life, we forget to take stock of things. How *are* you?"

"Good, good. Great, in fact," I replied, striving for the tone of a woman in charge of her life and ready to tackle any professional challenge that came her way.

"Wonderful." She smiled, her hand going to her softly rounded abdomen and caressing it gently.

"How's everything with you? Feeling okay, with the baby and all?"

"Oh, yes." She laughed. "I'm an expert at this baby thing by now. Miles always jokes that I'm going to be given my own monogrammed paper gown by the maternity ward."

My glance fell on the photo of Miles smiling out at me with the strong white teeth and tanned skin of a man designed to make a woman happy. "I bet you and Miles are just as excited about this baby as you were with your first," I said, suddenly realizing I had forgotten the name of her first baby and hoping I would be saved from an awkward moment in this all-important friendly banter. After all, I didn't want my seeming indifference to the children she loved more than life itself to become glaringly apparent. It wasn't that I didn't care—her kids were actually quite adorable, at least in their photos. It was just that I couldn't keep up with her output.

Fortunately Caroline saved me from disgrace. "Oh, we are excited. But my Sarah never lets us forget who is the oldest in the house. I swear the way she bosses her brother and sister around, I wouldn't doubt she has a management position in her future."

"Funny you should mention that," I said, finding my segue and readying myself to take the plunge and launch into how I was verifiably the smartest, sanest and strongest candidate for a senior position with the magazine. Oh God.

"As you know—" I began, gripping the armrests in an attempt to take the tremble out of my fingers "—I was promoted to contributing editor two years ago."

"Yes, and you've been doing a fine job," Caroline said with a smile.

"Thank you," I said, feeling a measure more confident and relaxing my grip. "During that time, I've been a solid contributor, often initiating ideas for articles and getting more involved in layout. I even wrote a lot of the promotional copy on our most recent subscription contest."

"Your copy was lovely, Emma, as always."

"Thank you," I replied once more and rather calmly, I thought, considering that my insides were shrieking *I'm in, I'm in!* "I think my writing skill, as well my strong knowledge of the magazine gained over the past four years," I continued, "make me an excellent candidate for the open position of senior features editor."

Caroline's expression fell, eyebrows dropping down as surprise spread over her features. "Oh."

Oh? My stomach plunged.

"Interesting," she murmured, her brow becoming furrowed as she studied me.

Interesting? What did *that* mean, I wondered, my newly fostered hopes crumbling. "Um. I'm wondering. That is, I want—uh, what do I need to do to…uh, apply for the position?"

Finally she smiled, her trademark warmth returning and giving me a small shred of courage once more. "Well, the first thing you would need to do is talk to Pat, of course," she said, her use of the editor-in-chief's nickname a privilege allotted to management, apparently, as I had never heard anyone else refer to Patricia in this manner.

"And would you recommend pulling together clips for Patricia?" I said, hoping my question would show her how aware I was of the next steps in the promotion process.

"Good idea," she replied. "You also might want to update your résumé, to give Pat some sense of your whole career."

Gulp. I wondered how my stint at Good Grub and string of temp jobs was going to hold up against Rebecca's experience as a trade editor and God-only-knew what other accomplishments. "Hmm. Yes. That is a good idea," I agreed.

Caroline's brow furrowed once more as she studied me. After a few painful moments she said finally, "As you go through your clips and update your résumé, Emma, take the time to take stock. It's a good opportunity for you to see the work you've done, analyze your strengths and think about future directions." Leaning back in her chair, she continued, "After all, it's not every day we think about what we want to be doing over the next few years."

Wasn't that the truth? In fact, if I *had* thought about my future, I might have realized a few things: like the fact that there was no way in *hell* I would ever be able to compete against Rebecca, who seemed to be growing in accomplishments by the minute. I might have even figured out, for that matter, that I would be manless at thirty-one years old rather than married to Derrick, seeing as he had scheduled his departure from our relationship from day one. But I said none of this to Caroline as I stood up, murmured a few words of thanks and headed off, I was sure, to my next and imminent disaster.

Four

"To binge, or not to binge, that is the question."
—Weight Watchers escapee

Confession: I am not as thin as I think I am.

On my way home from work, after managing to convince myself that I had an absolute right to an all-out binge, I stopped at the bodega on my corner.

"Hello!" called out Smiling Man behind the counter, so christened by Alyssa and me, due to the fact that despite his likely status as a minimum-wage worker being exploited by his own bodega-franchise-owning family, he was relentlessly cheerful, no matter what hour of the night you came in—and he worked all night.

"Hello!" I called back cheerily, masking my feelings of despair and heading straight for the Hostess rack in the back. As I contemplated the Ho-Hos and Suzy Q's—even turned over the Twinkies package to shamelessly check the fat content with some vague hope that a nonchocolate selection might save me from utter overindulgence—I realized that for the first time in two years, I was about to head to that counter up front (with an armload of snack cakes) alone. No Derrick by my side to pawn off three-quarters of the booty by making some offhand joke about how *he* should have limited himself to one or two selections. Picking up a Suzy Q—the largest little cake on the rack by far, and containing the most chocolate per square inch—I actually considered buying one cake here and then hitting another bodega or two until I had enough fat-filled treats to obliterate any glimmer of unhappiness I might be feeling about my prospects at *Bridal Best* and in life in general.

But then an old, familiar anger gripped me. What the hell did I care what Smiling Man thought about my fat intake? I told myself, furiously grabbing a coffee cake to add to my Suzy Q before moving on to the next rack for a bag of sour cream and onion potato chips. I realized now that was exactly my problem: I cared a little too much about what others thought. Forget Caroline and her enigmatic expressions. (What the hell did *interesting* mean anyway?) And who did she think she was, with her Earth Mother approach to life and that perfectly constructed bubble she lived in out in the burbs, to judge me just because I wanted something better for myself, I thought, grabbing up a Yoo-hoo from the dairy section before I headed for the front and, with a look of false bravado, plunked everything on the counter.

"Is that it?" Smiling Man asked, his grin seeming somehow wider as he gazed on my selections.

"Yes, that's it," I said, standing strong as I counted out the obscene amount of money the register showed after he had rung up my purchases.

"Goodbye! Have a good night!" he called out in a singsong response to my muttered thanks.

Marching down the street to my building, I tried desperately not to let any thoughts creep in about how Derrick and I used to wander this way, arms linked, gazing at all the beautiful brownstones and dreamily picking out ones we'd like to live in. Of course, he was only caught up in the moment, while I—

"Hello, neighbor," Beatrice said, holding open the door to the only dilapidated building on this magnificent block—ours.

"Hi, Beatrice, how are you?" I said by rote, then cringed for the response.

"Well, I'd be a lot better if I hadn't let myself eat pastrami for lunch. I've been tasting it ever since! Oh, the indigestion that stuff gives me, and I don't know why. In truth, I—"

"Mail come today?" I asked, not wanting any more information on the particularities of pastrami the second time around as I made my way into the foyer.

"Of course it came," she said, following me to my box and

standing a little too close for comfort as I pulled out a wad of junk mail and bills.

Eyeing a clothing catalog in my hand, she asked, "Did you ever find anything you liked in that catalog I gave you?"

In truth, I had glanced through the catalog before dumping it in the trash, probably out of some vague curiosity about the shopping worlds of lonely old women. Not that I planned on being one or anything, God help me. "No, no, I couldn't find anything." Closing my mailbox, I poised to say my hasty goodbyes and make a quick exit, when Beatrice's next words stopped me.

"I'm surprised. I mean, it's perfect for women like us. I usually—"

"What does that mean exactly—women like us?" I demanded, cutting her off. I knew I should just leave it alone, but I couldn't help myself. I had to know.

Her eyes widened behind her thick glasses. Probably because I was glaring at her. "Well, I just meant size 14 and up. You know. *Large* women. Don't you find it's hard to find clothes that fit right and are comfortable? I know I..."

The sack of snacks sagged in my hand. Beatrice's voice faded away as a larger version of myself swam before my mind's eye. Much larger. One I somehow managed to miss every morning as I stood before the mirror.

Then my defenses got the better of me. "Well, that's very *sweet* of you, Bea, to think of me, but I'll have you know that I am a size *10.*" And with that I marched up the stairs, leaving Beatrice staring up, I was sure, at my suddenly oversize rear end.

Once safe inside my apartment, though, my mind exploded with thoughts of all the skirts I had slid to the back of the closet in recent months because the zipper closed up a little too snugly for my liking. And all the waistless cardigans and tunics that had taken the forefront in my attempt to disguise my somewhat bulging mid-section. Then I remembered the new trousers I had bought two months ago, and I dropped my bag of illicit treats on the counter and rushed for the closet, searching frantically. Pulling out the hanger where the pants hung, I quickly glanced at the tag in the waistband. Size 12.

I was finished.

Hanging the pants back, I took off my blazer and went to stand in profile before the mirror, noticing—for the first time, apparently—how my stomach billowed out just enough to make my pants look sloppy, my physique unappealing.

I slumped in a chair, eyeballing the Hostess cakes that peeked out of the bag on the counter as if they were the demon seed. How had I let this happen to me?

To make matters worse, I began cataloging every time that I had made a comment to the effect that I had gained weight, and realized, with sudden horror, that no one had denied my declaration once in the past few months. Not my mother. Not Alyssa nor Jade. Not even Rebecca, who despite all her newfound faults, always came through with a "you look great," no matter what state I was in. And, worst of all, not even Derrick.

In the early months of the relationship, while we were still basking in the glow of our first lovemaking and first shared words of deeper affection, I had made some joke about how I had acquired an extra roll of flab due to all the comforts of loving him. Of course, our food and sex fests never had any effect on Derrick, who somehow managed to retain his lanky frame through it all. Seeing my sudden insecurity, Derrick pulled me into his arms and told me he would love me no matter how I looked.

Now my mind skittered forward to six weeks ago, when I was trying to cram myself into a miniskirt to attend a film festival in which Derrick's friend had a short film. I had asked the fatal question: "Does this make me look fat?" only to have Derrick look up from the magazine he'd been reading and say, "Well, do you have anything else to wear?"

I should have seen the signs back then. Now I wondered if this was one of the things that had doomed my relationship with Derrick in the end. Maybe he *had* planned on taking me to L.A., only to discover the woman he once loved had turned into a candidate for the Big Beauties catalog. Maybe I had become…completely undesirable.

My gaze fell on the phone. I wanted so desperately to talk to him all of sudden. I needed confirmation—but of what? That he had left me because he didn't want me anymore? That the reason he hadn't called yet, despite the fact that he was probably more than "settled in" by now, was that he was already dating some wand-slim blonde who didn't even need to rely on the whimsy of her hairdresser to maintain her golden status? I could see them now, marching off to the premiere of Derrick's movie, she leaning on his arm in some strappy little number that only the malnourished could pull off with any sort of aplomb. I hated her. I hated him even more.

I called Alyssa. "Why didn't you tell me I got fat?"

"What?"

"The woman downstairs—you know, Beatrice?—just accused me of being a member of the size 14 and over set."

"Oh, and now you're suddenly taking to heart the opinions of a woman who has a metal plate where part of her brain once was?"

"Do you think Derrick left me because he suddenly realized if he stuck with me, he'd wind up married to one of those double-chinned, muumuu-wearing housewives who have a penchant for finding any excuse to keep the old cake-hole full?"

"Em, Derrick left you because he got a job on the West Coast."

"He could have taken me with him."

"You didn't want to move to L.A."

"That is *so* not the point, Lys. He didn't even ask!"

I heard Alyssa sigh. "Look, if you want, you can come to my gym with me. I have loads of guest passes I've never even used."

"Oh my God. You just admitted it. You think I'm fat, too, don't you?"

"Emma—"

"You can tell me. I can take it—"

"Emma! Will you listen to me for a minute? I think you look fine the way you are. The problem is, *you* don't think you look fine the way you are, and that's no good. I only suggested the gym because a good workout always makes *me* feel better about myself. Plus, it's good for stress. And clearly you've got a lot of that going on."

"Can you blame me? I went in to Caroline today to tell her that I wanted to apply for the senior features editor position, and you know what she mumbles while I'm sitting there all suited up and ready to receive her blessing?''

"What?"

"*Interesting.* Two years ago she is practically pushing me into the contributing ed position. Now I want to move up again, and she calls this *interesting.* What the fuck does *that* mean?''

"That *is* weird."

"See what I mean?"

"Well are you still going to go to the editor-in-chief?''

"I guess I have to, now that I've set the ball in motion. Caroline told me I should update my résumé, so Patricia could see all my previous publishing experience—you know, the experience I *don't* have?''

"I'll help you with the résumé, Emma. There are ways of making yourself look like a strong candidate even if you don't have lots of experience. But let's take one thing at a time. Come to the gym with me tomorrow. You'll feel better after a good workout.''

"All right, all right," I said, calming down finally. Alyssa had that kind of soothing effect on me. We hung up a short while later, after I learned that Lulu was having trouble with her new medication and that Alyssa might have to take her in to the irresistible Dr. Jason Carruthers again. At least I had tomorrow at the gym to try to talk her out of any designs she still had on the doc himself. Feeling safe and satisfied for the moment, I allowed myself half a Suzy Q—I mean, I *was* going to work out tomorrow, surely I was allowed *something* to take the edge off a particularly taxing day? Then I went to bed, keeping the phone close in case Derrick came home from an off night with his new blonde beauty and wanted to talk to the one woman he had just discovered he truly loved.

Confession: I have a deep-seated fear of fitness clubs.

The next evening, I practically had to drag myself, kicking and screaming, to the gym. My day had gone no better than the previous one. While I was struggling to create some compelling argument why I should be promoted by going through my collection of clips to find my most distinguished selection of blurbs befitting a so-called wedding expert, Marcy Keller dropped by my cubicle to gleefully inform me that Rebecca had somehow landed next month's cover story on "World's Best Wedding Venues." To top it off, Derrick still hadn't called, despite the fact that I had gotten myself to sleep the night before by convincing myself that he would most definitely call while I was at the office, rather than risk getting my machine at home, where I might be screening. But no amount of mental telepathy had managed to make my phone ring all day long—except when my mother called to remind me that the weekend after next was Memorial Day, and I, being the dateless single daughter with nothing better to do, was naturally expected to attend the barbecue she had planned for Sunday. "Maybe we could even shop for my dress on Monday," she enthused, with barely contained excitement. With so much to look forward to, how could a girl *not* get depressed?

Now, as I stood outside the gym waiting for Alyssa, constructing elaborate excuses why I needed to head home immediately to my darkened apartment and half-eaten Suzy Q, I began to crumble under the weight of everything.

"Hey," Alyssa said as she approached, dressed in a dark gray suit, a bright blue gym bag slung over one shoulder.

"Hey, spiffy girl," I said, trying for lightness. "What—did you go to court today?" Office attire at Alyssa's earthy-crunchy law firm was usually more casual, unless they had to argue a case in court.

"I did." She leaned in for a hug, then looked in my eyes. "How are you?"

"Miserable. And I don't even think the Stairmaster can save me now."

"What's going on?"

"Do you realize Derrick has been gone almost three weeks and has yet to call?"

She studied me for a moment. "Was he supposed to call?"

"Wouldn't *you* call the woman you once pledged your undying love to if you had just moved across the country from her?"

"It was a big move, Em. Maybe he's still settling in," Alyssa replied, though her expression said she was not convinced by her own words.

"Settled in? He could be *married* by now."

"Somehow I doubt it."

"Well, I wouldn't put it past him. He's not that far from Vegas. And you know how men are after they get out of a long relationship. Sometimes they're feeling so bereft, they're suddenly willing to shackle themselves to any willing female just to get through it." As the horror of this fact sank in, I suddenly envisioned Derrick lying on some cot in a dingy apartment, desperately dialing my phone number out of sheer loneliness, prepared to demand that I move to L.A. and marry him. At the sound of my answering machine clicking, he becomes frustrated, disillusioned. He heads to his local watering hole to drown his sorrows, and within hours he's off to Vegas for a quickie wedding with some leggy stranger who smiled at him too long.

"I've got to go home."

"What?" Alyssa said, holding the gym door open for me with a look of disbelief on her face.

"I just have this strange feeling he's going to call tonight and that my not being there could have huge ramifications. Maybe he's decided to come home for Memorial Day. I mean, there's still time for me to get out of my mother's Memorial Day shindig, which, by the way, will not only be featuring my married younger brother, Shaun, but the latest blushing bride in the family—my mother. Besides, I don't really need this gym thing anyway. Derrick always liked me with a little meat on my bones."

"Forget it, Emma. You're not getting out of this one," Alyssa said, grabbing my arm and pulling me after her into the gym's entrance. "C'mon."

Beaten, I followed her reluctantly, though the thought of Derrick standing before an Elvis Impersonator and gazing into the eyes of some equally besotted stranger still ate at me.

Down in the locker room, I found myself surrounded by women in various modes of undress that seemed directly proportional to how toned and slender their bodies were.

Now, I had been to the gym before precisely twice in my life:

once when I had been persuaded by a zealot from my college days—one of those girls who were born with enough elasticity to do a split with little effort and lots of smugness. And once with Derrick, when a friend of his got us free passes to the Y, and we spent the whole time in the shallow end of the facility's pool, seeing who could squirt water better from between their teeth. On both occasions I was slightly aghast at how the locker room, with its bevy of scantily clad women doing everything from blow-drying to hamstring stretches, seemed designed to make you feel self-conscious if you happened to have, God forbid, a little cellulite here or there. Where were my fellow flabby girls hiding? I wondered, turning toward the wall and reluctantly beginning to unbutton my blouse. More than likely they were home with their Hostess cakes, and feeling quite happy with themselves.

While managing to reveal little more than a roll or two, I quickly slid my oldest—and only—pair of gym shorts on, along with one of the few T-shirts I owned that I didn't consider office attire. At first I had packed an old concert jersey with the sleeves cut off in my bag, but as the soft fabric slid through my fingers I suddenly remembered that it was Derrick's jersey—and one of the few remaining articles of his clothing I had left. So I had carefully tucked the T-shirt in a bottom drawer, along with a printout of every e-mail he'd ever sent me, a dried-up rose—a momento from one of our early dates, a cartoon he drew of us watching a movie—written and directed, as the screen happened to reveal, by Derrick Holt, and various other tokens of our ill-fated two years together.

Once dressed, I turned to find Alyssa, who had donned a well-shaped sports bra and a pair of color-coordinated running shorts, waiting for me. "Ready?" she asked, a determined smile on her face.

"Be gentle," I said, following her meekly to the stairs after my request to take the elevator was firmly denied.

When we got to the third floor, ominously labeled Cardiovascular Training, I was greeted with rows and rows of gleaming machines manned by rows and rows of sweating-and-motivated-by-God-knows-what men and women.

"We should stretch first, then do a little cardio warm-up before we hit the weight room,'' Alyssa said, heading for some mats in the far corner of the room.

"Isn't that a lot for my first workout? I don't want to overdo it. I mean if I ache *too* badly, I won't be able to come back to the gym for a while, and that will sort of defeat the purpose, won't it?''

She just rolled her eyes at me and sat down on the mat. "Come on, Emma. You'll like this part.''

And I did, I realized, as I sat beside her, legs outstretched as I pulled my upper body from side to side. I almost fell asleep during the lower back stretch, until Alyssa prodded me into action. I got up and followed her to those dreadful-looking machines. "Jade told me she's going out with that waiter guy,'' I began, hoping to distract her.

"She *is?*'' Alyssa asked. Even though I encouraged her to get his number, I thought it was all a joke. "I mean, he seemed a bit young, didn't he?''

"I guess. But he works in a bar. Don't you have to be at least eighteen to serve alcohol? Jade doesn't mind them young, as long as they're legal. I mean, she doesn't want to get arrested or anything.''

Alyssa laughed. "When Jade first started hitting on him, I didn't think he even knew English, the way he was stammering.''

"Just barely,'' I said. "His name is Enrico, and I don't think he's been in this country too long.''

Despite my efforts to detain or distract her, Alyssa stopped right in front of the most torturous-looking machine in the room. The StairMaster. Not that I'd ever tried it, but I'd heard scary stories from the few people in my office who had attempted it in the past.

"You know, I think this one might be redundant for me,'' I said, "seeing as I live in a fourth floor walk-up. Maybe I should try something I don't normally do.'' I glanced around frantically and, spying a girl on a stationary bike with a book propped in front of her on a reading stand and not a bead of perspiration on her brow, I said, "Like that one.''

"Just try this, Em,'' Alyssa said. "It gets you the most results. My butt lifted at least an inch when I first started doing it.''

Eyeing Alyssa's butt, which I'd always thought was rather perfect and probably a key factor in her year-round girlfriend status, I stepped on the machine and waited while Alyssa punched in a few keys to start up my workout. Once she was done, I started moving, legs going up and down in the kind of rhythm I normally dreaded whenever I came home and faced the four flights up to my apartment. I smiled meekly at Alyssa, who had stepped onto the machine next to me.

Before five minutes was up, I was so winded that any hope for an irresistible rear end was replaced by the fear that I would surely die of a heart attack at the tender age of thirty-one. I let my stairs sink to the floor and stepped off. "I can't...go—" I puffed out to Alyssa, who was still stepping away, not even a tiny bit breathless.

She looked down at my reddened face with concern. "The pace of this one is hard to get at first. Why don't you try something else for now?"

Something else? Like the shower maybe?

"The treadmill is also good," she said, gesturing behind her to a row of people running on what looked like some sort of conveyer belt. I suddenly thought of the hamster I had growing up. "Do they have a pool?" I asked, thinking I might be able to brush up on my water-squirting skills. Because if Derrick ever did return, I was going to douse him good for putting me through this particular hell.

"No. Not at this location," Alyssa replied. "Try the treadmill. You'll *like* it."

Yeah, right, I thought, walking past the treadmills and discovering, much to my delight, that they were all occupied. For Lys's benefit, I gave an ostentatious sigh. Then I headed for my novel-reading, sweatless role model who was still pedaling away effortlessly next to a fortuitously empty bike. I grabbed a women's magazine from the magazine rack conveniently located on the wall next to the bike machines. Once seated comfortably, I opened to the article that had beckoned to me from the cover as I made my selection, "Ten Sure Signs that He Is In Love With You." Choosing a preset workout course of rolling hills that seemed leisurely enough, I began to pedal and read.

Hoping his heart is in the right place? the article began perkily.

Read on to discover if your man is exhibiting signs that he is hope-lessly devoted to one special woman—you! Pedaling ruthlessly, I scanned the list, which was bullet-pointed with little red hearts.

♥ *He buys you flowers, for no particular reason.*

I smiled as the memory of that dried-up rose in the Derrick Drawer came back to me.

♥ *His friends like you—more than likely because he's always telling them how wonderful you are!*

A vision of Ed Riley, Derrick's best friend, popped into my head, filling me with disgust. Ed had a way of always inviting Derrick out for events that suspiciously never included me. Hmm…

♥ *You are the first person he calls when he gets the big pro-motion.*

Well, I *was* at Derrick's apartment the night his agent called with the news that he'd sold the screenplay. The moment Derrick hung up the phone, he pulled me into his arms and kissed me soundly. Hugged me like he'd never let me go.

♥ *He thinks you look beautiful, morning, noon, or night—and even without a hint of makeup!*

My mind rolled over a memory of Derrick and me, lying in bed on a Sunday morning, *The New York Times* laid out before us on the rumpled bedding. I remember feeling suddenly aware of my tangled mop of uncombed hair and my makeup-free face when Derrick reached over to graze my bare leg with his long fingers. I also remember the wolfish smile he gave me before he proceeded to pull off my ratty T-shirt as if it were some gossamer gown, stroking my face, and then my body, as I were the most desirable woman in the world.

A lump thickened in my throat. I pedaled harder.

♥ *He goes away on a business trip and calls you every night just to tell you how much he misses you.*

The page blurred before me, and I was suddenly breathless. Slamming the magazine shut, I discovered that the preset course I'd chosen indicated I was about to traverse a hill I was not phys-ically—or emotionally—ready for. I stopped pedaling, grabbed my towel from where I'd draped it on the back of the seat and headed straight for the StairMasters and Alyssa.

"Hey," she said, her cheeks pink, making her eyes look bluer than ever, as she continued stepping relentlessly.

"I'm gonna hit the showers," I said, dabbing my face with my towel and hoping to hide any inner turmoil written there. "I didn't realize this would take so long, and I have things to do at home." Like bawl my eyes out.

She let her steps sink to the floor and got off. "The weights will only take about a half an hour." As she studied my expression, I knew she was somehow seeing into my emotional distress. "You'll feel better for it," she continued. "I promise."

After I stammered through a few more lame excuses, I found myself reluctantly following Alyssa to the weight room, where at her instruction, I pitted every bit of misery, anger, anxiety and utter despair I felt against great concrete blocks of weight designed to make me, somehow, a better, stronger and ultimately trimmer person. I pushed. I pulled. I sweated and I cursed. And once we were back on the mats doing our final stretches, I discovered Lys was right. I felt better. Much better.

"I'm going to be working out Saturday morning if you want to come," she said, as we glided into a final stretch. "But earlyish. I have to take Lulu to the vet afterward. I told you her medication wasn't working?"

Uh-oh. "I'm coming with you."

"To the vet?" Alyssa said.

"Yes. I think Lulu needs the support. And *you* need a chaperone."

Alyssa rolled her eyes, but she smiled and I thought I saw something like relief in her eyes. Maybe she was just as scared as I was that she'd do something that might just destroy whatever happiness destiny had in store for her and Richard. "Okay. It'll give you a chance to check out Jason anyway. And then maybe you'll understand how I got myself in this dilemma."

"Yeah, yeah. You and your dilemmas. A great guy at home. Another one in the wings. I'm having a real pity party for you."

"Oh, that reminds me. I have a man in the wings for you," she said, standing up and wiping her face with her towel.

"What?"

"Remember that lawyer you imagined might be your next Mr. Right? Well, I have someone for you. Or Richard does. A guy from his firm—Henry Burke."

"Henry?" I asked, realizing the only "Henry" I knew was my mother's neighbor on Long Island—a short, balding man with a rounded belly who leered at me whenever I happened to see him standing in his yard, bare-chested and feverishly watering his lawn.

"He's a very nice guy. I met him at Richard's Christmas party last year."

"Does he ever go by Hank?" I said, standing up and trying to wrap my mind around the idea of dating a man named Henry. *What did you do last night? Well, Henry and I went bowling.* I didn't even think I could cry that name out in the height of passion.

"What difference does it make?" Alyssa asked, heading for the steps down to the locker room. "He's very sweet. And—" she turned to look at me "—he seems like he's looking to settle down."

"I'm not ready," I said, glancing down at my sweat-damp body and realizing one workout did not a beauty queen make.

"What are you talking about? You *asked* me for this."

"That was before I realized I was a strong candidate for the 'before' photo in a Jenny Craig advertisement."

"You are *not* fat," Alyssa protested as we made our way into the locker room, and I was surrounded, once again, by the next generation of lean and limber supermodels.

Tell that to Henry Burke when he finds himself feeling like a sucker for agreeing to give a fat girl a night on the town, I thought, wondering just how many of these adventures in self-torture it would take until I was truly ready to join the single world.

Confession: Selling out is easier than I thought.

The next morning I awoke with a vague sense of purpose, though it wasn't until I had perked myself a cup of coffee that I remembered today was the day I faced Patricia. With the help of Alyssa the night before, I had reconstructed my résumé to show that I was not only ready and willing to be the senior features editor, but that, with the long list of carefully delineated skills I had acquired during my four years as contributing editor, I was more than qualified. It amazed me how, with Alyssa's guidance, I had managed to turn four years of regurgitating the same wedding planning wit and wisdom, of oohing and aahing over layouts I couldn't care less about and of writing headlines designed to capture the attention of the anxiously altar-bound, into the kind of diverse and exciting experience great editors are made of.

This morning I had even discovered a long-forgotten gray skirt to pair with my trusty black blazer. Though I was horrified to discover that it fit, since it had been purchased during a previous bout of flabbiness, I realized that it had stayed in its time capsule in the back of my closet long enough to meet the new knee-length, A-line style requirement for the current season. At least according to Jade, whom I called for a wardrobe consultation.

Now all that was left was to meet with Patricia. And since ours was a fairly informal workplace, all that required was a short walk down the hall to her corner office to see if she was available. I already knew she was in today, having memorized her schedule and obsessed over when the best moment to pounce on her might be. I had decided that a prelunch visit was in order. After all, I didn't want her too carbohydrate-laden and sleepy to see how perfectly suited I was to the position.

"Is she in?" I asked Nancy, her admin, who, aside from an eyebrow piercing that lent her the air of the illicit, seemed like just the kind of capable, no-nonsense type to keep Patricia's otherwise hectic life in order.

I tried to ignore the fact that both brow and earring raised at the sight of me in a blazer and skirt before her. "Sure," she said with something that resembled a smirk on her lips.

She always looks like she's smirking, I told myself as I stepped daintily past her—with my new jacket-and-skirt combo and sore-yet-seemingly-firmer frame, I felt almost dainty—into Patricia's doorway.

I knocked softly, and Patricia looked up from a document she had been poring over at her desk. Seeing me, her eyebrows raised in question.

"I wondered if you, um, had a few minutes," I said so softly I could barely hear myself.

"Of course. Come in. Sit down. Give me a minute, though, while I finish this up."

I slithered in and carefully sat before her desk, staring at the side part in her honey-blond hair, which was pulled back into the usual soft French twist, as she bent her head over the paperwork before her. My gaze shifted to the photo she kept on the shelf behind her, of her and her husband on their wedding day. Patricia's wedding was legendary in the office, taking place at it did in a romantic villa in the South of France and featuring Patricia in a $17,000 Vera Wang dress, holding a flowing bouquet of lush and exotic orchids she'd had imported from South America. The only bizarre thing about Patricia's marriage was that once she'd wed her husband, a successful trader on the stock exchange, he'd virtually disappeared. Not one appearance at an office Christmas party or even the fund-raisers Patricia—who came from old money and had a standing invitation to such events—attended frequently. Once I had even seen a picture of her in the society section of *The New York Times,* looking stunning in some designer concoction but essentially alone. It was as if she'd hired groom-to-be Lawrence Landers along with the five-star French chefs she'd had cater the event, and then promptly dismissed him along with the rest of the hired help once the last crème brulée had been cleared away. The only thing that assured her loyal staff that she was, in fact, still married, was the 2.5-carat emerald-cut diamond that sparkled from her left hand. Some of the staff speculated—Marcy Keller chief among them—that Patricia was a lesbian who had only married to save face. After all, how could the editor-in-chief of *Bridal Best* not spend two years' salary and eighteen grueling months planning her own wedding day? Hell, we devoted a whole *issue* to her big day.

Now, as she looked up from the document she'd been reviewing, a serene smile spread over her smooth, almost plastic features, and her navy-blue eyes looked expectant. "What can I do for you, Emma?"

Amazed that she even remembered my name, I took the plunge. "Well, I don't know whether Caroline mentioned it to you or not,"

I hedged, starting off in an unplanned direction and mentally cringing. *Don't mention Caroline,* an inner voice chided. God knows what kind of *interesting* preview she might have given Patricia. "That is, I would like to apply for the senior features editor position that will become available shortly." I swallowed, then went on, shifting into autopilot as I began my rehearsed speech. "Over the past four years, I've been a solid contributor of articles for both the Style and Beauty sections of the magazine. I even contributed to the Travel and Honeymoon section, when that section was short-staffed six months ago," I continued, showing, as Alyssa had instructed me, how I had come through for *Bridal Best* when the magazine was in a pinch. "In addition, I worked with Production on layouts for the anniversary edition last year, and I am often instrumental in the development of headline text, as well as copy for special promotions." Having really warmed to my subject, I began to wax poetic on my knowledge of the market, my ability to lead and inspire others, and my indispensable talent for spotting trends. By the time I was done, not only had I convinced myself of my promotability but, judging from the look on Patricia's face, I had convinced her as well.

"Well, Emma, you've presented a strong case for yourself," Patricia said with a smile. "Truth be told, I *have* noticed your work. Your piece on undergarments was wonderful, and Caroline has often mentioned how instrumental you are in the development of headline copy."

Encouraged, I handed over my folder, bulging with the clips I'd obsessed over all week, as well as my carefully tailored résumé. "I hope these will help you to review my qualifications for the position."

"Wonderful." She took the folder, then stood, signaling the end of our meeting. "I will certainly take these things into consideration. Thanks for coming in, Emma. I appreciate your enthusiasm, and I'm delighted you're interested in pursuing a career with us."

I stood and walked on air out of her office, smirking at Nancy as I passed her desk and even cruising by Rebecca's cube in my smart outfit, just to show her the competition had suddenly gotten fierce. All at once, everything seemed possible. I could get promoted. I might even fall in love someday, not that that mattered, at least as far as Patricia was concerned. Clearly she didn't need anyone, judging by the way she kept that pseudohusband of hers at arm's length. Maybe we were kindred spirits, Patricia and I. Maybe that gleam I saw come into her eyes as I announced my interest in the position was the hope of the already-accomplished for the destined-to-succeed. Maybe there was more to me, Emma Carter, than Caroline, or Rebecca—or, hell, even Derrick—could see.

Hah. I was going to be a smash success. And make him rue the day he ever left my illustrious side.

Confession: I am ready for my miniature schnauzer.

As promised, I met Alyssa at the gym on Saturday morning. And after an hour and a half that I spent pumping my legs, lifting my arms and sweating more than I ever imagined possible, we went to Alyssa's apartment to pick up Lulu for our appointment with the allegedly irresistible Dr. Jason Carruthers. I tried not to get on Alyssa's case too much in the locker room as she showered and carefully reapplied all her makeup for the occasion, but I was clearly ill at ease with the whole thing. My feelings worsened when we entered Alyssa's apartment and I discovered Richard lounging on the sofa, looking oddly vulnerable in a pair of boxers and an old NYU Law T-shirt. "Hi," he greeted me cheerfully, oblivious to the deceit that I had now tangled myself up in.

"Hello, Rich, how've you been?" I said, almost too brightly, as out of the corner of my eye I watched Alyssa round up Lulu.

"Great. How are *you* doing?" he said, studying me, probably wondering if I was still as much of a basket case as I had been the last time I saw him, just days after Derrick had left. If he only knew what *he* was in for, I thought now.

I swallowed. "I'm okay. Keeping busy with work and all."

"Alyssa tells me you're up for a big promotion."

"Oh, that. Yeah, well, I did just speak to the editor-in-chief about it and she was very encouraging, so…"

"Great." He smiled so sweetly and innocently I wanted to gather him close and warn him of the dangers of letting Alyssa go out in the world unattended. But then Alyssa was suddenly by my side, Lulu smiling up happily at us now that her leash had been snapped on. Even Lulu was oblivious to the fact that this was no joyful little walk she was going on, but a dreaded trip to Dr. Jason Carruthers— a man who would only probe her with cold metal tools while he gazed with longing at Alyssa.

"You guys all ready to go?" Richard said, hopping up from the couch and going over to scratch Lulu playfully behind the ears, all the while muttering endearments that caused Lulu's tail to wag furiously. My heart sank.

Richard walked us to the door and kissed Alyssa on the forehead, much in the way my father used to kiss me when I was six.

"Take care of yourself, Em," he said, turning to me. "And don't be a stranger. In fact, if you and Henry hit it off, maybe we can double date. You did tell her about Henry, right, Lys?"

Gulp. Now we were double dating. I wondered if Henry would even talk to me, much less date me, if he ever found out I had stood by while some womanizing veterinarian made off with his best buddy's girl.

"Yeah, I told her," Alyssa said as she led Lulu to the door. "Remind me, Em, to give you Henry's number."

"He's a great guy," Rich said, encouragingly.

So are you, I thought sadly, following Alyssa and Lulu out the door to meet their fate.

Once we hit the pavement, I found myself racing to keep up with Alyssa, who seemed to be in too much of a hurry for my taste. "I don't know if this is such a good idea," I said when I had finally matched my pace to hers.

"I need to know if this is an irritable bowel or something more serious," Alyssa replied, glancing down at Lulu with concern.

"No, no," I said, annoyed at her denseness. "I mean this Dr. Carruthers character. You and Richard have been together a long time. You have a *dog* together, for chrissakes."

"Lulu is *my* dog, Em. I've had her since I was sixteen."

"Yeah, and why did your mother give her to you, huh?"

Alyssa marched on, her face a mask. "I was a good kid?"

"No, because your father had died a month earlier. She was trying to get you to move on, enjoy life again. You told me that yourself."

She stopped now, stood looking at me while Lulu sat expectantly at her feet. Then she gazed down at the dog, who cocked her head questioningly before cracking a doggy smile. "What does that have to do with anything?"

She started walking again, and I followed suit. "Maybe you're afraid of losing Lulu. Or even Richard, on some level. I mean, you only lost your mother a couple of years ago. Maybe this thing with Dr. Carruthers is just your way of controlling the marbles. You know, if you keep moving on yourself, you can't get hurt."

"That's ridiculous," she said, then stopped again, this time before the large wooden doorway of a brownstone. A shiny brass plaque affixed just above the intercom read, "Dr. Jason Carruthers, D.V.M." She pressed the button on the intercom, and at the sound of an answering buzz, she pushed the heavy door open with renewed determination, barely glancing back at me as she held the door open for me to follow. After we passed through a small foyer, we found ourselves in a cozy waiting area that was decorated with paintings of dogs and cats in various poses, as well as pillows embroidered with sayings like *Bark If You're A Dog Lover*. Behind the reception desk, a woman with a cloud of gray hair and the softest voice I have ever heard greeted Lulu, then raised her eyes to Alyssa as we approached.

While Alyssa checked in, I made myself comfortable on a cushion that proclaimed *Cat Love Is Purr-fect Love*, and contemplated an empty pet carrier that stood waiting in the middle of the room to be filled with some ideal companion. As I sat there imagining the kind of muumuu-wearing cat-lover who might be the owner of such a garishly colored carrier, the door to the inner office opened, and out stepped a tall blonde in a skirt the size of a postage stamp, carrying the tiniest dog I had ever seen. I immediately eyed the blonde's long legs with suspicion. What kind of woman wears panty hose on a Saturday—and to the vet, no less? As the woman stooped to put the dog in the ostentatious carrier, all the while murmuring words of comfort through brightly painted lips, I began to wonder what kind of operation this Dr. Jason Carruthers was running.

"He's ready for us," Alyssa said, having finished whatever paper-work she had to fill out and gesturing for me to get up.

"I'll just bet he is," I muttered, following her and Lulu through the office door.

As I stepped inside a gleaming white room that smelled like a mixture of antiseptic and kitty litter, I fell into a stunned silence.

There, dressed in a white lab coat and a blue button-down shirt that brought out the stunning color of his eyes, stood Dr. Jason Carruthers: six-foot-two, broad-shouldered, lean-hipped and one hundred and seventy-five pounds worth of the most incredible male I had ever seen.

I swallowed hard, studying his beautiful features as he stood behind the examining table, his hands folded comfortably behind his back, a brilliant smile on his—dare I say sensual?—mouth.

"Jason," Alyssa breathed next to me, and I suddenly remembered why I was here.

"Alyssa, how are you?" he said, then kneeled down to Lulu. Weirdly enough even Alyssa's dog seemed deliriously happy to see the man who would soon be the instrument of her torture. He scratched her behind her ears with his big tan hands, before scooping her effortlessly into his arms and rising to his full height once more. "I see you brought a friend this time," he said, nodding to me in greeting.

"Oh, yes," Alyssa said, as if suddenly remembering I was in the room. "Jason, meet my good friend, Emma Carter."

As his hands were full of Lulu, I merely smiled my greeting at him. I don't think I could have spoken anyway, judging by the way I was salivating.

"Emma was concerned," Alyssa continued, glancing at me. "About Lulu, that is."

He nodded, as if this answer made perfect sense to him. "You mentioned on the phone that she wasn't responding to the medication," he said, placing Lulu gently on the examining table, all the while caressing her with those broad, tanned fingers.

I was mesmerized. And quite frankly, I was shocked, because

suddenly it was very clear to me that this man could be Alyssa's next Mr. Right. He was kind to animals, gorgeous beyond compare—and those hands, I thought, watching as he pulled a stethoscope from around his neck and placed it carefully on Lulu's chest. The dog's tongue lolled out of her mouth as if she were receiving a full body massage.

He didn't even look like a vet, I realized suddenly. Well, maybe a vet on TV.

"We're going to need to run some tests," he was saying now, his beautiful gaze fixed on Alyssa's face. "Some of them will be pretty extensive and may require an overnight stay." He paused, as if he were about to suggest an overnight stay for Alyssa as well. Then, as if remembering something, he pulled himself from Alyssa's gaze and began moving about the office, collecting instruments, then pausing to flip through a chart on the counter. Facing Alyssa once more, he continued, "Today I'll just take some blood, but make an appointment to bring her back in the next two weeks so we can run the next battery of tests. By then I'll have her blood work done, so that if we need to take, um," he paused, as if caught again by Alyssa's gaze, "if we need to take any further steps, we'll be ready to go."

"Further steps?" Alyssa replied.

He studied her for a moment, looking as if he were about to pull her into his arms at any moment to comfort her with caresses. "Well, surgery for one thing. But I want to eliminate a few other options first. Lulu's a bit older, and surgery would be the final option, if it is, in fact, a viable or necessary one." Then he smiled gently. "In the meantime, you keep up the TLC with her, and everything will be just fine. Trust me."

Looking into those baby blues, I knew I would have trusted him with *my* life.

When Alyssa snapped Lulu's leash on once more and gently took her off the examining table, I realized that we were leaving and hated myself for the ping of disappointment I felt.

Jason shook my hand. "It was nice meeting you," he said.

The strength in that hand moved through me, and suddenly I was contemplating stopping off at the pet store on my way home to pick up the miniature schnauzer I had been eyeballing ever since Derrick made his departure. Hell, I'd take on a pet python if I thought it might bring me back into this man's life.

Then I remembered myself, and more important, Alyssa.

"I'll probably see you after Memorial Day," Alyssa said. "I'm, um, going out of town."

"Big plans for the holiday weekend?" he asked with what seemed like sincere interest.

"Oh, nothing special," Alyssa replied, "just some family stuff."

Yeah, *Richard's* family, I thought to myself, remembering where my loyalties lay.

Still, as we said our final goodbyes and headed for the door, I couldn't help but turn expectantly along with Alyssa when Dr. Dreamboat called us back. "Oh, I almost forgot."

"Yes?" Alyssa said, her eyes wide with anticipation.

He smiled. "Next time you come, don't forget to bring a stool sample."

Ah, the romance of it all, I thought, giddiness bubbling up inside me as Dr. Carruthers showed us out.

Though I had almost lost my head at the sight of the good doctor, now that we were safely outside his office, I was relieved we had made it through with no major flirtation. No matter how gorgeous Dr. Jason Carruthers was, I couldn't—wouldn't—allow myself to see him as a part of Alyssa's life.

We walked in silence on the way back to Alyssa's apartment, each lost in our own thoughts. And when Lys stopped suddenly, two doors away from the brownstone where she lived, I was surprised to discover her eyes were glassy with unshed tears. "What am I going to do?"

I blinked. "Lys, don't get upset. Whatever happens, you'll make the right choice. You always do." I sighed. "If it makes you feel any better, I thought he was gorgeous. I can see why you would consider—"

"No, I'm talking about Lulu. Oh, Em, if she needs surgery, she'll never make it at her age." The tears sprang forth now as she looked down at Lulu, who pressed herself against Alyssa's leg and whined at the sight of her beloved owner's distress.

"Oh, Lys," I said, hugging her close. It was all I could do, really, because I had nothing to say. No answers at all. And no way to stop whatever sadness was bound to come her way.

Five

"All anyone really needs in life is a good lawyer."
—Burt Carter, Emma's father

Confession: I could more easily submit to bodily torture than wear a seafoam silk dress.

Maybe I was hiding from my emotional distress, or maybe I had been spurred on by Patricia's encouragement, but the following week at work, I made a bonafide attempt to become the one thing I never dreamed I'd be: a career woman. I organized my files, answered all the e-mails I hadn't got around to responding to and even handed in my copy ahead of schedule. I began to feel like management material, capable of sending some editorial assistant scurrying over to a photocopier or fax machine to do my bidding.

That is, until Rebecca showed at my cubicle on Wednesday afternoon in the kind of navy suit that commanded others to cower before her and a thousand-watt smile on her face.

"I think it's finally going to happen," she said, her pretty blue eyes alight with excitement as she sat, uninvited, in my guest chair.

Alarm shot through me as I attempted to hide my pièce de résistance from her prying eyes—a memo to Patricia, with ideas for our next subscription contest. "What's going to happen?" I asked, panicked.

"Nash is going to propose. Memorial Day weekend. I'm *sure* of it," she said, studying my reaction.

Of course, I thought to myself. Not only was Rebecca probably the best woman for the senior features editor position in the eyes of my superiors, she was apparently the prime candidate for Wife

Number One—and maybe even Wife Number One and Only—in the eyes of her boyfriend. Bitch.

"That's wonderful," I said, hoping my smile didn't look too pasted on. "How...um, how do you know?"

"Well, we've been planning to go away for Memorial Day for some time now. As far as I understood it, we were going to his family's cabin in the Berkshires. Then, last night, he tells me he has a surprise—he got us a reservation for a bed-and-breakfast out in East Hampton!"

I nodded, not getting how East Hampton equaled Big Proposal Scene. According to Jade, it was more of a Big Blow-Job Scene for the rich and disillusioned.

As if reading the confusion in my face, she continued, "It's not just any B-and-B—it's the exact same bed-and-breakfast we went to on our very first weekend away."

Ah. Nash was going for real romance. I could just picture him with his chiseled features and wire-rim glasses—though a bit too strait-laced, Nash was just the type of Bespectacled Babe I lusted after—gazing up at Rebecca on a moonlit beach, a monstrously large diamond in hand. "Wow," I replied. I thought of my own holiday weekend plans, which would more than likely entail basking in the glow of my mother and Clark's love while listening raptly to my brother, Shaun, and his wife, Tiffany, detail their plans to make their new house bigger and their lives richer.

"I could hardly keep the smile off my face last night as I packed my lingerie," Rebecca was saying now. "I even brought along the underwear I wore the first night we made love," she continued with a blush.

"You remember what underwear you wore?"

"Of course I do!" she said.

Now *that* was special. "Wow," I replied again, seeming to have lost the capacity for any type of prolonged speech.

"I know." Then she gazed down at her hands folded in her lap before she lifted her eyes to meet mine once more. "I wanted to tell you first, because you're one of my closest friends."

I am? "That's, um, sweet of you, Bec," I somehow managed to mumble.

"And I want you to know that when Nash and I do get married, I'm going to ask you to be part of my wedding party."

What? "Uh, that's really, um— Don't you think it's a little premature to be planning the, uh, wedding?" Then I laughed uneasily, hoping to lighten the mood. "You don't want to jinx yourself by jumping the gun."

She smiled. "Are you kidding? I've already decided on my colors! How do you feel about seafoam for your dress?"

Oh, God.

She sighed, and went on as if my feelings about seafoam were irrelevant. "I can't believe it's finally going to happen. I've been thinking about this wedding ever since I was a kid!" Then she laughed.

Huh? "I thought you met Nash in college?"

"I did." She looked puzzled. "What does that have to do with anything?"

"Well, you just said you've been thinking of this wedding since you were a kid—"

"Oh, you know what I mean. Every girl dreams of getting married someday. When I met Nash, I just knew he was the one who'd be part of that dream."

I better start dreaming, I thought now, realizing that maybe I hadn't put any real strategy in place for the sort of thing every girl wants. It seemed so simple the way Rebecca put things. Maybe I made everything too damned complicated.

"Don't say anything to anyone," she said then, getting up to leave. "Not even Derrick. I mean, you're right. I shouldn't tell *everyone* until I have the ring. Though I don't know how I'm going to get through the next couple of days without bursting."

No problem-o, I thought as she skipped away, realizing that if I ever did talk to Derrick again, I had a few things I wanted to say to him, none of which had to do with Rebecca's sudden windfall of happiness.

One thing was sure: I knew there was *no way* I could ever tell Rebecca now that Derrick was irretrievably out of my life. But how to hide this fact while I was busy showering her with gifts and lavishing her with all sorts of bridesmaidlike camaraderie? I would

have to do something to get out of this wedding when it happened.
Like fake my own death.

Confession: Dating might just be my only resort.

By the time I stomped up the stairs to my apartment that night,
I found myself with a head full of steam over Rebecca's presump-
tion that I wanted to participate in her personal bridal hell. I even
considered defrosting the Hostess cakes I'd stashed in the freezer
for safekeeping, until the soreness of my abdominal muscles reminded me of my last blistering workout and kept me from in-
dulging in the sort of angry binge I was by now certainly entitled
to.

How dare Rebecca ask me to be in her wedding party? Me—a
mere co-worker and now all-out *competitor!* Leave it to Rebecca
to be the bigger person and keep office grudges out of the way of
the grand friendship she saw between us.

Needing some perspective, I called Jade. "Rebecca asked me to
be in her wedding party."

"You're kidding. I didn't even know she was engaged."

"She's not—yet. According to her, Nash is going to pop the old
question this weekend."

"Oh? And how did she figure that out?"

"Who knows? Everyone at *Bridal Best* seems to have some kind
of radar when it comes to imminent proposals."

She was silent for a moment, and I heard her inhale on a cigarette. "I didn't even know you guys were that close."

"We aren't. At least not in my mind. I've been picking apart
this situation all afternoon, and I think I have it figured out. Rebecca
is an only child. Nash has two brothers, plus he's still pretty close
with many of the guys from his old fraternity. As far as I know,
Rebecca has only a few close friends outside the office and very
little close family. It basically boils down to a numbers game. She's
got a load of groomsmen and no bridesmaids for them to escort.
And you know how unbalanced that makes the photos look."

Jade laughed. "That's pretty shallow, if that's her reason."

"I wouldn't put this kind of bridesmaid-recruitment maneuver past anyone at *Bridal Best*. I sometimes think Patricia—our editor-in-chief—picked her groom out of a catalog and just had him show up once she put together her lavish little affair.''

Jade chuckled gleefully.

''Now all I want to do is cram down a coffee cake or five and feel sorry for myself, except I'm in deadly fear of getting any fatter than I currently am.'' I sighed. ''It would serve Rebecca right if I started stuffing my face every night so I'll be good and round by the time I have to squeeze into whatever taffeta nightmare she selects for me to trail down the aisle in.''

''You mean you're actually going to go through with this bridesmaid thing?''

''How can I get out of it? Then Rebecca will know how much I've grown to despise her. I mean, I don't want to hurt her feelings.''

''That is the most *ridiculous* thing I have ever heard.''

''You're right,'' I admitted. ''I can't exactly pack on the pounds when I'm about to embark on the cruelest journey known to woman-kind—dating in NYC.''

''So you've decided to join the living once again?''

''Alyssa's already got some lawyer guy from Richard's office lined up for me.''

''You're kidding?''

''No, I'm not. She gave me his number after our little trip to the vet over the weekend. I haven't called yet, but there's no turning back now. He's waiting to hear from me, though I'm not quite sure he knows what he's in for. You know how kind Alyssa can be when giving descriptions of people. Although I have to say, she didn't quite prepare me for that hunk of a veterinarian she and Lulu have been spending time with.''

''Oh, yeah?''

''He's the George Clooney of the four-legged set. Except he's got blue eyes. Sparkling blue eyes, I might add, with thick, dark lashes.''

''Hmm. Maybe I should get that pet chinchilla I've been thinking about. Where did you say this vet was located?''

''Jade!'' I said, about to reprimand her for moving in on Alyssa's turf. What was I thinking? Alyssa's turf was Richard. *Richard, Richard, Richard,* I repeated silently, though my inner voice sounded like a mere whisper at this point.

"Don't tell me that since having made his acquaintance, you haven't contemplated picking up, say, a guinea pig, at Petland?

Thank God Jade couldn't see my face. I think I blushed as I remembered the minischnauzer that had beckoned from the moment I laid eyes on Dr. Jason Carruthers. I decided to change the subject. "So whatever happened to your little Italian import? Enrico, wasn't it?"

"Oh, man."

"This sounds promising already."

"Emma, he's amazing."

"You slept with him already? Where have I been? Details, please."

"No, no. We just went out dancing last night. He is the hottest thing. We could not keep our hands off of each other on the dance floor."

"And then?"

"Then nothing. I wasn't going to take him home and waste all this presex sizzle. Besides, there's something I'm worried about."

"Just use a condom."

"No, it's not that. It's just that he's very young."

Uh-oh. "How young?" I asked, worried Jade was about to incriminate herself in some sort of sex scandal.

"Twenty-two."

Whew. No jail bait there. "So what's the problem? You've never taken issue with the young ones. What about that acting student you took on for a while? Mark? Wasn't he just over the legal limit, too?"

"Yeah, but Mark was different. He had that tough veneer that NYC ingrains in the young, struggling types. I mean, he was only twenty-four, but he'd been around the block a few times. Enrico seems…almost innocent."

"Jade, I saw him myself. There was nothing innocent about the way he was eyeballing you while he took our drink orders."

"I don't mean sexually. It was clear to me from the way he was moving on the dance floor last night that he would know his way around a woman's body.''

"So what's the problem?"

"He just seems so vulnerable somehow. Especially at the end of the night, when he walked me home. He started talking about how much he missed his family back in Italy. Then he gave me this gooey look and made some joke about bringing me back to Italy with him.''

"Uh-oh. Preejaculatory emotion," I said, using the phrase Jade and I had developed for the wealth of emotion some men seemed to have just before you slept with them.

"He just seems like he's looking for a girlfriend or something. And you know how I feel about the whole relationship thing.''

Yeah, I knew. And I still wondered if Jade's attitude was good for her, or whether she was still fending off all those feelings she'd wasted on Michael. "Why don't you just take one step at a time, and see what happens.''

"I guess I'll have to. Because there's no way I'm letting this one get away without getting him in my bed. Did I mention how *promising* he felt when he pressed up against me on the dance floor?''

"So you're going to have him even at great risk of breaking his boyish heart?''

"Yeah, well. That's life in the big city." Then she sighed. "Maybe I shouldn't worry so much about his heart anyway. It's not as if I have any hard-and-fast evidence that he even *has* one. And you know as well as I do, Emma, though you're loath to admit it: Most men don't have any deep feelings for anyone but themselves.''

I was powerless to argue with her, I realized. And when I found myself staring at my silent telephone after we hung up, I even started to believe her. Apparently Derrick was so wrapped up in his new life as Big Screenwriter, he couldn't be bothered calling me. I didn't even exist in his mind anymore. With a sigh, I dug through my pocketbook and pulled out Henry Burke's phone number, then carefully tucked it into my wallet. I would call him tomorrow. To hell with waiting for the love of my life to realize I was still alive and aching for him. I was moving on.

Confession: I discover you can't go home again (at least, not without marriage prospects).

The following afternoon, I called Henry Burke. His secretary answered, advised me that he was in a meeting and took down my phone number so that he could call me back. I hung up, feeling vaguely titillated. A secretary. I was going on a date with a man who had a secretary. How very adult. I answered the phone all afternoon in my best sexy-yet-unconcerned voice, until he called back just under two hours later. Perfect timing, in my opinion— not long enough to torture me with waiting, but not quickly enough to make me think he was some hard-up geek. The first few awkward minutes of conversation were filled with his bemused commentary on how all his Happily-Coupled-and-Practically-Married friends were always trying to fix him up. Of course, I made some sympathetic response. What else could I do? Admit that I had shamelessly prodded Alyssa to find me some suitable replacement for the man who had torn my heart to pieces?

After navigating a few more clever quips about single life, I learned that Henry was going to the Hamptons for the holiday weekend. Since I was going to my family's torture chamber— which I cheerfully described as a barbecue on Long Island—we made plans for the following Thursday. I hung up ecstatic. It was official. I had a date. With a successful lawyer, no less. Gone was the Ex-Girlfriend, replaced by the Woman-in-Demand.

As I packed a bag for the weekend, carefully folding the kind of flirty combinations that said I was carefree, fun-loving and free as a bird, I banished all thoughts of minischnauzers and lonely late-night TV. Yes, I was still that career woman whom Patricia would one day make her protégée, but I was also a single girl with a Big Date on the agenda. It amazed me how one little promise of drinks had changed my perspective, but I wasn't about to question my newfound cheerfulness. Even spending Saturday night at home with a video felt like a personal choice, rather than a concession to the fact that I was dateless and all my friends had gone away for the weekend. Jade had invited me out to Fire Island with her, but I'd begged off. After all, now that I'd committed myself, I had to be at the family barbecue on Sunday, and there would be no getting out of the big Memorial Day Bridal Dress Run with my mother on Monday.

Still, I was in good spirits as I stepped off the train at Garden City on Sunday afternoon and found Clark waiting for me.

"Ah, the fair Emma has arrived on her trusty steed," he said as he stood beside his sporty compact car, waiting for me. Leaning over, he planted a kiss on my forehead and declared, "You've never looked lovelier, my dear." Then he took my overnight bag, tossed it in the back seat and held the passenger door open for me. Usually Clark's habitual chivalry embarrassed me, though today I was somehow able to accept it as my due. Must have been the soft pink sundress I had donned for the big family shindig—the only garment in my closet that could disguise the recent rolls and bulges I'd acquired.

"So how's everything, Clark?" I asked, once he had successfully negotiated the vehicle into the traffic.

"Fine, fine. Your mother is putting the finishing touches on some gelatinous dessert, so I thought I'd make the rounds and gather up her chicks for her." He smiled at his own joke, dimples forming in his cheeks and bringing a sparkle to his dark eyes. He really was a handsome man, I thought now, eyeing his thick salt-and-pepper hair and wondering if he had managed to avoid baldness at age sixty-three through some sort of technology. He wasn't really the type to resort to such vanities, but one could never tell with these things.

"Have Shaun and Tiffany arrived yet?"

"Oh, yes, yes. Tiffany has already filled us in on her five-year plan, and Shaun has the cocktails flowing. I think he's whipping up piña coladas as we speak." Then he winked at me, as if we were sharing some secret about my baby brother and his uptight wife.

Maybe today wouldn't be so bad after all, I thought, feeling as if I had Clark in my corner. Suddenly remembering his upcoming nuptials to my mother—as if I could have forgotten them—I congratulated him.

He positively beamed in response and quoted John Donne: "'Love these mix'd souls doth mix again and make both one each this and that.'"

Feeling too much a mixed soul to even *begin* to ponder that one, I simply nodded, and we fell into a companionable silence for the short trip home. Once we pulled into the driveway and disentangled ourselves from the seat belts, my mother appeared at the front door, waving ecstatically at us.

"Ah, there she is now, my queen," Clark said as he ambled toward the door, a broad smile on his face, as if he hadn't seen her in months, when it couldn't have been longer than the twenty minutes it took him to get to and from the train station.

I followed, watching as my mother kissed him sweetly on the lips, then swatted his behind as he walked past. Then she opened her arms to me, her eyes taking me in.

As her gaze roamed over me, I immediately jumped on the defensive. "I know I'm fat. Don't you dare say anything."

"Oh, Emma!" she cried out as she folded her arms around me and clutched me to her. Releasing me with a playful pinch to my waistline, she said. "More of you to love." Then she smiled, relenting. "You look beautiful."

As I studied her shining eyes, I almost believed her. Then, embarrassed, I excused myself and bounded up the steps to toss my overnight bag in the guest room, knowing that if Shaun and Tiffany decided to stay, I would be banished to the couch, where all the Single and the Sorrowful were doomed to sleep alone.

By the time I made my way back to the kitchen, my mother was at the stove, putting a cover on whatever she had cooking there. She turned to look at me, beaming as if this were our first get-together in months, when it had only been mere weeks.

"Where is everyone?" I asked, suddenly afraid to be alone with her. My mother was known to habitually delve into deep emotional territory at the most inopportune times—like right before I was going to face my successful brother and his perfect wife. And as I had just put my Happy-Career-Girl-With-Prospects facade carefully in place, I didn't want to do anything to jeopardize it.

"In the yard. Shaun made piña coladas." Lifting a glass filled with a frothy concoction to her lips, she winked mischievously. Ever since her marriage to my father, my mother could no longer allow herself that daily drink after work others felt entitled to without thinking she was still somehow part and parcel of my father's particular brand of madness. Now, on those rare occasions when she did indulge in a cocktail, it was always with a sense of a forbidden pleasure. "Let's join them," she said, ushering me out the sliding glass door that led to the back patio.

Seated at a round redwood table laden with a large sampling of every chip and dip known to humankind were my brother, Shaun, looking tanned and relaxed in khaki shorts and a terra-cotta polo shirt probably picked out by Tiffany, and Tiffany herself, looking a bit like a cheese danish—an expensive one, of course—in a cream and yellow short set and matching sandals. Grandma Zizi, so dubbed because as a baby Shaun hadn't been able to pronounce Zelda, sat off to the side, under a small clump of trees.

"Hey, Em, what's up?" Shaun said, lifting his face for a perfunctory kiss as I approached.

"Hi, Shaun. Hi, Tiffany," I said, gliding by both their cheeks as we kissed the air. Straightening, I stared at Grandma Zizi off in the near distance. "Why is Grandma sitting all the way over there?"

"She doesn't like the sun," my mother said, seating herself next to Clark with her cocktail in hand.

"It's probably all that polyester," my brother said, his laughter trailing after me as I walked over to Grandma Zizi to say hello.

"Hey, Grammy!" I said, loud enough for her to hear—she usually kept her hearing aid turned down for some reason.

She looked up, startled, and stared at me momentarily as if she didn't recognize me. Then her soft, wrinkled face broke into a wide smile. "Emma!"

I hugged her, kissing both cheeks and then her lips, which was our tradition ever since I was a little girl. When I leaned back, I saw a look of accusation in her soft brown eyes. "You lost weight."

I smiled, wanting desperately to take her comment to heart but knowing that this was an assertion Grandma Zizi made fairly regularly to all the females in the family who suffered from fluctuating waistlines. I think it was her way of being encouraging—the senior equivalent of "You go, girl."

"Thanks, Grandma. I'm trying. How are you?"

"Oh, you know. Old. How are *you,* dear?" Then, suddenly, as if struck by a memory, she stared over my shoulder, her eyes searching. I knew exactly who she was looking for, though I didn't offer any assistance as she struggled to come up with the name of my missing better half. Finally she asked, "Where's Derrick? You're still seeing him, right?"

I mentally cringed. Either no one had told her, or she had forgotten. More likely it was the latter, as Grandma Zizi's memory was not what it used to be. "No, Grandma. Derrick and I broke up." As her mouth descended into a puzzled frown, I hurried to explain. "He got a job in California. He moved there."

"Oh, dear." Still that perplexed look. Then she looked up at me, her eyes filled with sympathy. A sympathy I could not handle at the moment.

"Let me get you some more ginger ale," I said, carefully pulling her half-full glass from her fingers as she gazed sadly at me.

I made my escape to the cooler, slowly filling her glass with ice and pouring in some soda, in an attempt to give her enough time to lose her train of thought.

By the time I returned to Grandma Zizi, it was clear all memory of my previous visit moments earlier was erased. "Emma!" she said, leaning in close for our ritual series of kisses.

"You lost weight," she insisted once more, and just as her gaze began to wander over my left shoulder in search of Derrick, I gave her a quick kiss to the forehead, muttered something about needing a drink myself and headed off to the relative safety of the picnic table.

As I sat down and pulled the pitcher of piña coladas toward me to fill a glass, Tiffany was talking about the new job she had just landed.

"They practically doubled my salary," she was saying now, "how could I *not* take it?"

Tiffany was a financial analyst who received bimonthly phone calls from competing firms, attempting to woo her over to the other side with promises of huge cash bonuses and extra vacation time. I suddenly felt ridiculous, pining away for a raise of a few thousand dollars and a semi-major title adjustment at *Bridal Best.* But I swallowed the thought, along with a mouthful of piña colada, which, I noted with satisfaction, had enough rum to keep me warm and friendly.

"Well, it sounds wonderful," my mother replied, smiling at my brother as if *he* had just doubled his salary.

"I know I've been switching around a lot, but this seems like a company I might be able to stick with for a while," Tiffany continued. "At least while Shaun and I work on getting our family started." With this announcement, a flush covered her normally composed features, and she turned to smile at Shaun.

Looking at them together, I couldn't help but picture how outrageously adorable their children would be, dressed in designer duds and sporting her honey-brown hair and creamy coloring, with his green eyes.

Clearly this was also the direction my mother's thoughts had taken, as her eyes had misted over with a mixture of joy and, I suspected, grandmotherly greed. "Oh, you don't know how those words make me feel. Grandkids!" She turned to Clark, as if she were unable to contain her happiness and needed him to shoulder some of it. He, of course, leaned forward and plopped a kiss on her mouth as we all stared into our piña coladas with new interest.

"Not for at least a year," Tiffany warned, but she was smiling off into the distance, probably mentally highlighting a block of space in her day planner for childbearing. It seemed to me that everything Tiffany had was the result of careful planning—the kind of purposeful strategizing I had yet to contemplate until Derrick up and left me with no game pieces.

As if sensing my unrest, Tiffany turned to me. "So how's everything going with you?"

"Fine. Great, in fact," I replied, plastering what I hoped was a convincing smile on my face.

Tiffany's neat little eyebrows raised over her wide blue eyes and pert nose.

"We heard about Derrick. That must kinda suck," Shaun said, with his usual aplomb.

"Yeah, well, you win some you lose some," I said, ignoring the sight of my mother's concerned frown. "Besides, it's not like I could have *gone* with him to L.A. Especially now that I'm up for a promotion to senior features editor."

"Oh, Emma, why didn't you *tell* me?" my mother chimed in.

"Well, nothing's been decid—"

"Big salary jump?" Tiffany asked, leaning in close.

"Not bad, not bad." *Not great.* But I wasn't about to tell that to Ms. Meet Me for Lunch at the Plaza.

"Cool," Shaun said now, picking up the pitcher of piña coladas and topping us all off.

Taking a sip from her glass, my mother licked her lips with a satisfied grin. "I think this is just what you need, Emma. There's nothing like a salary increase to make you feel human again. Maybe now you can start paying down some of those student loans, think about saving some money. I was just reading a book, *The Ten Steps to True Wealth*—"

As my mother rambled on about my apparently horrific financial outlook and how this meager yet somehow miraculous salary increase was going to change all that, I wanted to burrow into the patio floor. From the way Tiffany and Shaun kept throwing glances at me while she spoke, I got the feeling they had suddenly discovered my future prospects were even less cheery than they had realized. I mean, there was no room for a house, much less a BMW, in my future, while theirs was unthinkable without both these items. And though I never really craved material things, other than the season's offerings at Banana Republic, I suddenly felt the hole in my single life grow wider and wider.

Oddly enough, it was Clark who seemed to notice my sudden

state of despair. Cutting my mother off just as she leaped into the seventh step to true wealth—which was something about recognizing your own true worth—he said, "You know what, my love? I think we should toast all that Emma is now. Because oftentimes we forget to acknowledge all our existing triumphs in our race to new accomplishments."

"Oh, Clark!" my mother said, her eyes glowing with pride and happiness as she leaned in close to give him the kind of kiss that probably curled the toes of everyone at the table. When she sat back in her chair once more, she asked, with apparent amazement, "What have I done to deserve such a man?" Then, remembering herself, she lifted her glass. "To Emma. For all you are, my darling daughter."

Everyone clinked glasses and drank, some of us—like me—more than others. And maybe it was the alcohol coursing through my system, but suddenly I did feel a sense of well-being breaking through my despair. Overwhelmed by the sudden rush of emotion, I quickly got up. "I'm gonna see if Grandma Zizi needs anything."

"Give her this," my mother said, handing me a plate with an assortment of pretzels and chips.

Grandma Zizi looked up as I approached, a smile of surprise spreading over her features. "Emma!" she said, pursing her lips to kiss me, as if I had just arrived.

Out of the frying pan, into the fire, I thought, going through the motions of the kiss.

Then she stared at me, hard, as if something ate at her feeble memory. "Still seeing Derrick?" she asked hopefully.

I sighed, realizing that I would be in for it today. Whenever Grandma Zizi sensed something was not quite right, she fell into the unfortunate habit of asking a question repeatedly, as if she feared the answer she might receive would be disturbing. And I was quite sure it was greatly disturbing to Grandma Zizi that her thirty-one-year-old granddaughter had just lost the man she had hoped to see her marching down the aisle with.

"Of course, Grandma," I lied, giving her what we both needed to keep our sanity. "Derrick couldn't make it today, but he sends his love." Then, distracting her with the plate of goodies, which she eyed greedily once I placed it on the folding table beside her, I kissed her forehead and hurried away once more.

Sitting down with the others again, I topped off my glass with piña colada just as my mother joyfully announced that she and Clark had finally settled on a cruise line for their wedding.

"Which one?" Tiffany asked.

"Carried Away Cruise Lines. It came highly recommended by one of the source books Emma gave me." She beamed at me.

"Oh, I've heard of that line," Tiffany said, nodding her head approvingly. "It's supposed to be excellent."

And she would know, I thought.

"So where will we be cruising to?" Shaun asked.

"Well, it looks like St. Thomas. What do you guys think?"

"Wonderful," Tiffany and Shaun answered in unison as I nodded my head meekly.

Clark smiled, and we all knew that just about anything my mother decided would be fine with him.

"Emma, we just need to figure out a venue on the island—I was thinking a gazebo on the beach, but I don't know if that's possible. Fortunately, I can draw on your expertise in these matters."

"Gosh, Emma," Tiffany said now, "I wish I'd had you around when *I* got married."

Well, maybe she would have, I thought uncharitably, if she hadn't married my brother when she was like, twelve. Tiffany hadn't even hit the big 3-0 yet, and she'd been married for five whole years.

What had I done so wrong to wind up thirtysomething and single?

"I was about to book rooms for all of us this week," my mother continued, "when I had the most fabulous idea."

Uh-oh.

"Emma, since you won't be sharing a room with anyone, I thought maybe you and Grandma Z could bunk together! Wouldn't that be fun?"

I looked over at Grandma Zizi, who had fallen asleep sitting up, her glass of ginger ale still firmly in her grip as her head lolled over to the side and her mouth fell open on a soft snort.

Barrels.

Confession: All I have to look forward to now is support hose and short-term memory loss.

Later that night, after a barbecued feast that left me fuller, fatter and even more unsatisfied, I was nominated to drive Grandma Zizi back to the nursing home, just a few short miles from my mother's house, mostly because no one else was available to do it. Shaun had fallen asleep on the sofa after an afternoon of slaving over a hot barbecue pit, and poor Tiffany had a headache—probably from hunger, as she'd barely even touched the rack of ribs my mother had put on her plate despite her protests. Mom was in the midst of kitchen cleanup duty, and Clark—well, *someone* had to gaze upon my mother with rapture while she scrubbed pots.

"Just make sure they don't leave her in the hall too long before they put her to bed," my mother said, stopping scrub duty momentarily to press her car keys in my hand and hug and kiss Grandma Zizi, who was starting to kick up a protest about the fact that my mother was letting Clark stay over. Apparently Grandma Zizi hadn't grasped the fact that Clark had moved in six months earlier. "They'll never buy the cow when they can get the milk for free," she muttered as I led her down the driveway to the car and folded her into the passenger seat. It didn't seem to matter to Grandma Zizi that my mother was married two times over and a grown woman. She still saw Mom as a young girl in serious danger of losing her unalienable right to new cookware by letting "that man," as she referred to Clark, "keep company" with her while their wedding vows were still unspoken.

As I started the car and backed down the driveway, I was secretly relieved Grandma Zizi had turned her thoughts to my mother's alleged disgraceful lifestyle. Over the course of the afternoon, Grandma Zizi had inquired about the status of Derrick and my relationship no less than six times, and I was finally forced to hit her with the truth: that her last remaining single granddaughter would probably remain so for quite some time.

By the time we arrived at the Happy Hills Nursing Home and I had maneuvered Grandma Zizi out of the car and into the wheelchair that waited just inside the doors to escort her, she had dropped into what I might term a pensive silence if I thought Grandma Zizi still capable of holding a thought in her head long enough to reflect on it. After rolling her down to the lonely little room she shared with a cranky old woman with a penchant for shrieking in the middle of the night, I alerted a nurse that she was back and needed to be put to bed. Then I leaned in to touch my lips to first one cheek, then the other, all the while staring beyond her shoulders into the dark and lonely room that awaited her, wondering if, after all the struggle to marry, have children and get those children married, this was all there was. But before I could finish with a parting pat on her lips, she grabbed my face between her two bony hands and stared at me as if truly seeing me for the first time all day.

"You're too good, Emmy," she said fiercely, her grip tightening. "Too good for any of 'em. That's the problem." Kissing my lips, she released her grip with a wise smile. "Besides, that fella was no good for you anyway."

"Derrick?" I said in disbelief.

"That's right, Derrick. No good *at all.*"

"What was wrong with—"

"Well, for one thing," she said, "he was too short for you. You need someone tall." Then she dropped her hands in her lap, winking slyly at me. "And rich."

With that the nurse arrived to wheel a smiling Grandma Zizi into her darkened room, as an image of some tall, rich man lingered in my mind's eye for just a moment, filling me with vague hope before doubt drove the vision away.

Six

"A woman's got to use it or she will surely lose it."
—Betty, salesclerk, Dream Bride Boutique

Confession: I convince myself that marriage is nothing more than the opportunity to wear a great dress.

Bright and early the next morning, I found myself embarking with my mother on the shopping trip from hell. For Mom was determined to find a dress that would not make her look fat, old or virginal, or too much like she was trying not to look fat, old or virginal. Though I had tried to convince her that she might have more success with some of the New York bridal salons, like Kleinfeld's—I half hoped to put off this quest for as long as possible—she wouldn't hear it. She *would* have her dress that day and she *would* get it at a deep discount. According to her logic, she had spent enough money on designer dresses. This time, she was going for off the rack. "No one will even be the wiser," she said, revving the engine on her sporty compact and taking off down the driveway with me hostage in the passenger seat.

My mother had invited Tiffany, but she'd graciously begged off, explaining that she and Shaun had to get home early to clear the kitchen for the cabinet men who were coming on Tuesday. Not a bad ploy, since we all knew that my mother would never stand between Tiffany and a renovation project. I think Mom secretly admired her daughter-in-law's ability to find new reasons to tear out cabinets and pull up floors at the drop of a hat. Now I wished Tiffany were with us, as her cheerful chatter might have eased some of the tension I felt over this particular shopping spree. A tension that only worsened when we entered the first shop and an overzealous salesclerk tried to entwine me in measuring tape the moment my mother announced we were shopping for a wedding gown. Imagine her surprise—and my humiliation—when she discovered the bride was my mother, not me.

Things only got worse from there. After eight unsuccessful stops at various warehouse-style bridal bonanzas, my patience was wearing thin. I was just mentally putting together a convincing argument as to why it would be okay for my mother to recycle the dress from her last wedding when we pulled up in front of a tiny shop strategically sandwiched between an accessory boutique and a shoe store on a small strip mall. Dream Bride the sign declared in flowing script against a neon pink background. *Dream on,* I thought. Reluctantly sliding out of the car, I studied the window, where a mannequin with a pinched expression stood dressed in a frothy taffeta concoction that seemed to overwhelm the small storefront and was beginning to look slightly yellow with sun damage. Still, my mother couldn't be stopped. Grasping my hand, she made the same declaration she had made before the eight previous shops: "I have a good feeling about this one."

I felt a shiver roll through me as we entered a door beneath a sign which read, Where Wedded Bliss Begins! and found ourselves standing in a long narrow room lined with rows and rows of dresses in every shape and size. For my mother's sake, I tried to stifle the sigh that escaped. After a day of battling bulging garment racks and curt salesclerks, I realized there were other reasons to drop a load of cash on a designer gown; reasons that had nothing at all to do with the wedding day and everything to do with personal sanity.

At the back of the small shop, half-hidden by a long, beaded number that I could imagine Ivana Trump wearing if she decided to go bargain basement on her next wedding, a tiny woman was seated behind a counter, a bored expression on her tired features. As we approached, she slowly dragged her eyes up from the crossword puzzle she was working on, and seemed to be sizing us up, probably trying to determine if we were worth any sales effort she might expend on us.

"Good afternoon!" my mother greeted her.

The woman looked at her watch, as if surprised to discover it was close to three o'clock. "Afternoon," she said, with a crack of her gum. Her face was fleshy and her lips had bled whatever color she had dabbed on them hours earlier into the tiny wrinkles around her mouth. Beneath her oversprayed, overblond hair, which looked long overdue for a touch-up, her eyes were a faded blue.

"I'm looking for a dress for myself," my mother began. Then, hesitating, she finished, "for a third marriage."

The saleswoman seemed to perk up at this, her eyebrows raising in what looked like interest. "Well, that narrows things down considerably," she said, waving a hand dismissively toward the miles of gleaming white on the left side of the room. Hopping off the stool where she sat, she began walking toward the back of the shop with an air of confidence that could almost be called graceful, despite the garish, oversize top and stretchy black pants she wore.

I could tell my mother had regained her spirit when she started babbling to the woman about how we'd been searching all day, how many dresses she'd tried on, how helpful I had been.

"My daughter is an editor at one of the biggest bridal magazines—*Bridal Best?* I'm sure you've heard of it."

The woman stopped and turned to look at me. Then, glancing at my mother with an expression that said she wasn't the least bit impressed by this information, she asked, "When you getting married?"

"Uh, the third weekend in September," Mom replied, off balance. "In St. Thomas," she finished with a brave smile. The woman digested this information and continued toward a rack of dresses in various shades of off-white.

I liked her already. Maybe it was the lack of response my illustrious career invoked, or maybe it was the no-nonsense way she shoved through the rack as if she knew exactly what she was looking for, but something about her said she was the kind of woman who wouldn't get caught up in the madness that getting married entailed, yet would somehow get the details just right. After fishing decisively through the rack, she yanked out a dress that looked closer to white than to ivory, and had a long, flowing skirt topped by what looked like an ultrapadded sweetheart neckline and illusion sleeves.

Mom stared alternately at the dress and then at the clerk, as if trying to decide if she should let this little scrap of woman in a beaded top and Day-Glo lipstick make one of her most important wedding-day decisions. "I, uh, I was thinking maybe something…less white. And less…flowing. Maybe a suit?"

The woman slapped the hanger onto a rod above her head and turned to face my mother. "First, let me tell you something, sweetheart," she began, leaning in close, confiding. "I don't care what they say about what you should or shouldn't wear for a second or third marriage—no woman over the age of fifty looks good in ivory. Unless she's a blonde, and, clearly, you are not."

My mother glanced at me, but I was staring steadfastly at this little dynamo turned prophet.

"Second," she continued, with a crack of her gum, "you been down this road before. The first time you did it for your parents. The second time, maybe love. Maybe loneliness. Who knows?"

My mother's eyes widened.

"But if you're lucky enough to get to number three," the woman said, her mouth moving into a wise smile, "I'll put money on it that you're doing it for *you*."

Finally my mother smiled, as if the woman was speaking her language.

Tugging on the skirt of the dress, the saleswoman said, "See this fabric, this cut?" At my mother's nod, she continued, "You have a little pre-wedding stress, decide to eat that extra piece of coffee cake in the morning, you got some give here. And no one will even see what you've been up to."

I smiled. It was as if she'd seen into our feminine souls.

"The sleeves are sheer enough to keep you cool, yet don't require four nights a week at Jack La Lanne for the next six months to look good. And the cut of the neck—no woman, even one your size," she said, with a nod to my mother's all-but-nonexistent chest, "will look bad in this."

As she glanced down at herself, Mom looked uncertain.

"Trust me," the woman said, picking the dress up and pressing it into my mother's hands, "try it on."

A few minutes later, my mother stood on a pedestal before a three-way mirror, a vision in off-white.

She smiled tremulously, and I knew she knew she looked good. The salesclerk, who had introduced herself as Betty as she helped my mother into the dress, stood looking on, a satisfied expression on her face.

"You look beautiful, Mom," I said.

She beamed at me. Then, with a nervous glance at her generously padded bustline, said, "But I think I must have gone from a B to a C cup."

Betty smiled wryly. "Listen, sweetheart. Even a woman going for number three needs *some* illusions."

With that, my mother's decision was made. And once Betty had taken a few measurements, she turned her focus on me, having learned that I was to be the maid of honor, and—as my mother had told her in a moment of camaraderie—that I had just been brutally dumped by my longtime boyfriend.

"Cruise ships are the best places to meet men," Betty said. And since she'd just finished showing us the beautiful necklace and earring set she'd made from the diamonds received from her first three husbands, I submitted meekly to her choice of a slinky little number in a soft lavender, with just enough shirring around the waist to disguise any last-minute anxiety binges.

Everything was going to be all right, I thought, as we paid for our dresses and waved goodbye to a satisfied Betty.

And even if everything wasn't all right, at least I would be wearing a great dress.

Confession: I am ready to chuck any future prospects for misguided hopes.

Though I usually find a return to the city after a weekend at home redeeming, on this particular Monday night after a long holiday weekend on parade as the last unmarried member of my family, I did not find the same solace I normally did at the sight of the cafés and shops twinkling in the growing dusk. Instead all I saw was couples walking arm in arm, or bent toward one another in

conversation over tiny candlelit tables. As I trudged up the stairs
to my lonely apartment, I even found myself wishing a good ran-
sacking had occurred while I was away. Nothing too serious—just
a couple of thugs who slipped in through the window by the fire
escape and stole a few essential items: like my laptop full of half-
baked dreams and my collection of Derrick memorabilia. After all,
anything was possible in New York City, right? Even sentimental
thieves. But as I slipped into the dark, quiet apartment and flipped
on the light, everything was just as I had left it. And so was my
life.

With a sigh, I began to unpack my tote, when I noticed the light
was blinking on my answering machine. I slapped the Play button
with something resembling indifference, though what girl living
alone in NYC is ever truly unfazed by the sight of a blinking red
light on her answering machine?

After the sound of fumbling, as if the caller couldn't get a grip
on either the receiver or his thoughts, a voice filled the air that
stopped my heart: "Hey, Em, it's Derrick."

My tote bag hit the floor with a solid thud.

"Just calling to check in. See how you're doing. Um. Was going
to call sooner, but it took me a little while to find a place. Believe
it or not, rents in L.A. are almost as bad as NYC." Then he
laughed, that soft chuckle he always gave when something defied
his inner sense of logic. Warmth curled through me. "Anyway, I
didn't think you'd be home this weekend—you're probably out on
the Island, beaching it or whatever. But I was just sitting around
thinking about you, so I figured I'd give you a call...." Pause.
"Give me a ring when you get in. The number here is 213-555-
5684. Anyway, hope to talk to you soon. Miss you."

Stunned, I lurched for the machine and hit Rewind. I needed to
hear it again, every breathtaking word—but especially the last two.
He *missed me.* Missed *me.* I played it back, my heart gliding over
the sound of his voice, which to my undernourished ears sounded
filled with longing...for me. I scribbled down the number, once on
a scrap of paper I found by the bed, and again in the more secure
place of my address book. As I stared at the unfamiliar phone

number I'd jotted down right beneath his old Rivington Street address—which I still couldn't bear to cross out—I contemplated whether or not I should call him back right away. A glance at my watch told me it was nine-thirty, which meant six-thirty his time. Would it seem too desperate of me? Maybe I should torture him for a few weeks, make him think I'd forgotten about him the way he'd seemingly forgotten about me. Then, realizing that *I* would never survive those few weeks, I picked up the phone and dialed.

He answered immediately. "Hello?"

"Derrick?" I inquired, though I knew that voice better than I knew my own.

"Emma." The relief in his husky voice set my heart hammering triple time. "I was hoping you would call tonight. How are you?"

"Great, great," I replied, and suddenly I was. "How's L.A.? The new apartment? What am I saying? How is the new *job?*"

He laughed. "Everything is good, good. The job is fine. A lot of big egos, but I'm managing okay for the moment, as long as I tiptoe through."

"You hate it?" I asked hopefully.

"No, no, not at all." Then he laughed again. "God, do I miss you, Em—sarcasm and all."

I ignored the fact that I wasn't being sarcastic and latched instead onto the fact that he missed me. He missed me! "So tell me everything. The apartment is okay? Not too lonely?"

"Naw, in fact, rents were so crazy, I had to do the roommate thing again."

"Anything like your old roommate, Craig the Crud Monger?"

"No, thank God. The apartment is actually terrific. It's a short ride from the beach, and it's got a great view of the water from my bedroom window."

"Wow," I said, turning my head to gaze through my own window at the brick wall of the building next to mine. "That sounds incredible." And incredibly romantic. A heaviness developed in my chest.

"You really have to come for a visit, Em. I think you might like it out here."

The heaviness dissipated. "Yeah? Well, as it turns out, I still have a week's vacation left to me, and I could probably even take it before the end of June."

He paused, and in the brief silence I cringed at the sound of my own desperation. "Well, it's something to think about," he said, then graciously changed the subject before I uprooted my entire life and put it on a plane headed for the West Coast. "So how's *your* job going?"

"Great," I said, still mentally chastising myself for seeming too needy. Hoping to recoup some of my self-esteem, I elaborated. "In fact, one of the senior features editors just left, and I'm up for the promotion." Hah. That ought to salvage me. Let him see just how grand I was doing despite his abrupt exit from my life.

"That's wonderful, Em. I always knew you were destined for greatness."

He did? I filed that one away—I didn't have time to contemplate all the reasons a man would leave a woman he deemed destined for greatness. I was too busy basking in the warmth, the pure, unadulterated love, I heard in his voice. "God, Derrick, it is really good to hear from you."

"Yeah, and it's good to hear your voice. I was so caught up in the craziness of the new job, settling in, that I didn't have a chance to miss you. Then came this long weekend, and all I could think about was how the hell we managed to share that house in East Hampton with sixteen people last Memorial Day weekend." He laughed. "Remember that? I never thought I'd find myself sharing a bedroom with you and *Sid,*" he said, referring to a guy he used to work with during his waitering days at Reservoir, "and Sid's nutty pseudostripper girlfriend. What was her name?"

"Barbie, I think. Or was it Bambi?"

"Something like that." He chuckled, then in a lower voice, he said, "But somehow we managed to escape them all for a little strip show of our own...."

A silence ensued as we both remembered the night we snuck off and made love on a deserted section of beach, the moon high above us, its light filling us with both the thrill of desire and the anxiety of being exposed completely to anyone who happened to stroll by. It was one of the most exhilarating lovemaking sessions we'd ever had, and the sizzling memory of that heady night fairly crackled over the line between us now. As heat flooded through my veins and set my skin pulsing, I suddenly understood why people resorted to phone sex.

"You looked so beautiful that night," Derrick was saying. "Your hair was long, and it almost covered your breasts."

My hair was never *that* long, but I wasn't about to destroy his fantasy, especially since I had a starring role in it. "You weren't so bad yourself. All tan, with that little shadow of beard on your face."

"Ah, Em, those were good times."

"They were." I let the truth of that zoom home, hoping against hope it would spur him into some sort of action, like packing a bag and catching the next flight out for a week of debauchery at Chez Moi.

Instead he said, "I ought to let you go."

No! "We can talk some more, if you'd like...." I offered, as if *he* were the one in desperate need of keeping the connection going.

"Yeah, well, I have to be in early tomorrow for a meeting with one of the producers, and I have all this stuff to prepare tonight. You know, duty calls."

Since when had he become so responsible? I thought, then realized he'd never had a job he cared enough about to be well-prepared and well-rested for. "I understand," I said.

"Talk to you soon, okay?" he asked hopefully. "You have to keep me posted on the big promotion."

"Of course," I said, wanting to leave the lines of communication wide open enough for him to call every time the mood struck him, and hoping that would be often. "And you need to keep me posted on how the big screenwriter is doing."

He laughed. "Good night, Em,"

"Good night, Derrick." *Love you,* my brain echoed, partly out of habit but mostly out of pure longing, as the sound of the dial tone filled my ear.

Confession: I am ready, willing and able to harbor a few illusions about my love life.

For the first time in a long time, I hesitated before calling Jade or Alyssa. I knew both were more than likely home from the long weekend, Jade full of ribald tales of Fire Island finds and Alyssa full of future-in-law angst. Yet I could not bring myself to dial a single number in the warm, cozy afterglow of Derrick's phone call. I didn't want Jade to tell me, in that bland voice she gets whenever she's referring to the ills of mankind, that Derrick only called because he was lonely. That his warm and fuzzy words meant little in actuality. And Alyssa...Alyssa would see right through my sudden happiness. She'd recognize it for what it was: false hope.

But false hope was better than no hope, right? Besides, I was still addicted to the idea that Derrick and I were Meant-To-Be. I was only waiting for *him* to figure it out. And judging from the lonely ache behind his voice, I thought he was on the path to the higher truth. My truth.

I opted to call no one, nestling in for the night and shamelessly listening to my Sade CD, reveling in her lush, sexy lyrics about true love as if they applied to me.

I even made it safely to the office the next day with my illusions intact, resisted answering the juicy e-mail from Jade I received once I opened my computer, despite the fact that she alluded to what sounded like a meaningful sexual encounter. In fact, I was just heading safely off to lunch with my illusions, when Rebecca showed up at my cubicle. The first thing I noticed was that she looked terrible. And Rebecca *never* looks terrible. Her face was solemn and her eyes red-rimmed as she asked in the kind of small, pathetic voice I would never have expected to come from her lips, "Have lunch with me? I really need to talk to someone."

With a glance at her ringless left hand, I remembered. The proposal scene. Apparently it hadn't happened according to plan. Nodding helplessly, I grabbed my purse and followed her to the elevators.

As we headed over to Tivoli, a small Italian restaurant only a few blocks from the office with prices even the lower echelon publishing set of midtown could afford, we said very little. It wasn't until we were seated across from one another, menus in hand, that Rebecca finally spoke about the subject that clearly weighed cruelly on her mind.

"It didn't happen. No ring, no proposal, no…nothing."

I saw tears threaten, and a stab of sympathy shot through me. I grabbed her hand across the table and gave it a squeeze. "What happened?"

"Well, we drove out to East Hampton, like we planned," she began, blinking back her tears as if she were taking strength from the memory. "All the way out, we're having a grand old time, talking about the last time we were there, how much fun it was."

I nodded encouragingly.

"We get to the B-and-B—the one I told you about, with all the antique moldings and authentic landmark window casings? Well, the first thing I notice is that the whole place has been renovated. That should have been my first clue."

I smiled weakly, not getting what a little fresh paint and spackle had to do with anything.

"Naturally Nash sees how surprised I am, and he explains that they renovated the whole place. He actually *liked* it." She rolled her eyes. "I mean, it wasn't *bad,* though I would have left more of the original effects. Thank God they had the sense to leave the staircase, which is a real nineteenth-century beauty."

Another nod, my plastered on smile diverting into a faux frown. As if I knew anything about what constituted a landmark staircase.

The waiter came by, took our orders, then politely disappeared, allowing Rebecca to go on with her seemingly senseless tale.

"The whole weekend, he just seemed…off, or something. I mean, every time we were in the room alone, he started waxing poetic about the new shower massage they'd put in, or how he preferred the new carpeting to the hardwood floor they had previously. Well, I figured out where all that was coming from."

Oh? I leaned close, hoping it would all come together for me, too.

"I was down at the front desk, asking about renting sailboats in the area, because Nash likes to sail and I thought that might not be a bad place for him to pop the question. Out on the open sea. Just the two of us. Well, I get to talking with the front desk clerk about all these seemingly marvelous renovations and she lets slip how they had sent twenty percent discount vouchers to all their previous guests to welcome them for their first season under the new renovation.''

Ah. "Well, he *is* an accountant. And isn't that one of the things you told me you loved about Nash—his good head for money?''

"Yeah, I'll give him a good head," she muttered. "I thought we were there for *romance,* not discounts."

Though I was shocked at the level of bitterness Rebecca was showing, I said nothing.

"Anyway, the whole weekend, all I kept wondering was when he was going to do it, when, when, when. At one point we were eating at this restaurant overlooking the water, and I thought for sure the moment had arrived. The sun was setting. We'd just been served a beautiful little bottle of Bordeaux. Nash was looking at me. I was looking at him. And then he launches into some stupid story about how his boss hadn't called him yet about some meeting he was planning for next week. I don't even remember what it was about, exactly. All I know is that this was definitely *not* the moment to be thinking about work!''

"Maybe he's having a little anxiety about work and needs to come to terms with it before he can make his next move," I counseled, as if some age-old wisdom about why men do the things they do was suddenly welling up inside of me. "You know, some men don't even think about the marriage question until they've got a solid six figures and a fat 401K."

"Oh, he's got all that," Rebecca said dismissively, then sipped her water daintily, as if dating a penniless man was never an issue with her. She sighed. "It was as if he wasn't even thinking about our future. About *us.* By the time Sunday rolled around and I knew there was gonna be no ring coming this weekend, I was furious!'' Her lower lip trembled and curled.

I have to admit, I felt a bit of alarm at the sight of her rage. Was this what happened to women when they didn't get what they wanted? Did veins bulge in my neck every time I brought up Derrick nowadays? I felt a sudden urge to soothe Rebecca. To tell her anything to stop the fury from engulfing us both. And now that I had mastered the art of snowing myself, I was sure I could initiate Rebecca in the ways of self-delusion.

"Bec, you *know* it's going to happen. You're just upset because it didn't happen when you wanted it to." I smiled now. "Look, you're better off anyway. I mean, you didn't *really* want to get engaged in a house that didn't even have the original window casings, did you?" I stifled a chuckle as I watched her actually consider my words with a great deal of seriousness.

"That's true," she said, her expression cautiously hopeful.

"Besides, I bet Nash has got an even more exciting proposal dreamed up than you could possibly think of."

She smiled now. "You're probably right."

That was way *too* easy, I thought. "All I'm saying is, keep an open mind. You don't know what Nash is thinking," I hedged, feeling guilty for throwing her a bone now that she had latched on to it so quickly. I didn't worry too much, though. I knew in my heart that Nash was going to ask Rebecca to marry him one day. He had marriage material stamped all over him, and Rebecca... well, who wouldn't want to marry a woman with a filing system that rivaled the Library of Congress's and the kind of creamy complexion that probably looked fresh and lovely from the moment she lifted her head from her Laura Ashley pillow sham?

Our lunches arrived, mine the grilled chicken over field greens, lemon vinaigrette on the side, and Rebecca's thick burger oozing with melted cheese and surrounded by a hoard of crisp shoestring fries. And though I had been trying to maintain my holier-than-thou position as newly reformed heath nut, I wished I had joined Rebecca in her pity binge as I watched her take her first mouthwatering bite.

With a sigh, I drowned my greens in dressing, then dug in. And as Rebecca went on to talk about how good Nash was to her most of the time, how much fun they had together, I felt myself dreaming of how it all used to be with Derrick and me, as if it all were *still* that way with Derrick and me. After all, in Rebecca's eyes, I continued to be Derrick's warm and loving girlfriend.

And I wasn't ready to prick that happy little bubble just yet.

Confession: I am hopelessly unprepared to meet Mr. Right.

"Where have you been?" Jade demanded when she caught me
at home the following night.

"Been?" I replied innocently.

"I left you an e-mail, tried you last night—oh, never mind. How
are you? How was your weekend?"

"You tell me," I said, carefully deflecting the subject away from
me. "Sounds like someone finally had sex?"

"Who?"

"You! Didn't you mention something in your e-mail about some
hot guy you hooked up with?"

"Oh, no, no. That was Ricky Phillips I was talking about. I told
you about him before. Has his own line of motorcycle jackets? Big
garmento. But totally hot."

"And the problem with sleeping with him is…?"

"He's the biggest slut on Fire Island."

"Can you call a guy a slut?"

"You can call Ricky Phillips a slut. That guy has slept with
everyone in the industry."

"Except you, of course."

"Of course not me. I may be hard up at the moment, but I'm
not stupid. Sleeping with that guy—on a holiday weekend in Fire
Island when everyone I know is there to witness—is like the kiss
of death. You sleep with Ricky, you become known as one of
Ricky's girls—and no one wants to sleep with you."

"Why not?"

"Because then you are easy game. And that's no fun for anyone.
Most guys like a challenge. And if you give it up for Ricky, you'll
give it up for just about anyone."

Apparently I had forgotten everything I needed to know to effectively manage my sexual encounters. "So whatever happened
with Enrico?"

"He's still around, but he's starting to annoy me. I swear, if it
weren't for the fact that I felt this great little package waiting for
me beneath those jeans of his, I'd lose him."

"What?" I was beginning to suspect Jade's lack of a sex life had more to do with her pickiness than anything else.

"I come home from Fire Island Monday night, and there's two messages from him. So I'm tired and stuff, and I don't call him back. The next day I'm at work and he calls me up and blasts me about how I didn't call him back. Then he goes into this jealous rage over these other guys he imagined I was with all weekend on Fire Island."

"Poor Enrico."

"Poor nothing. We had like one date, and he's pulling the possessive boyfriend act."

"Isn't that terrible? He actually likes you enough to want you for his very own."

"What's that supposed to mean?"

"It means cut him some slack, Jade. He *likes* you. Of course he doesn't want you going off to Fire Island without him."

"Yeah, yeah. Well, I'm giving him another chance, aren't I? We're hanging out this weekend. And I'm getting that boy naked before he completely cracks on me and I have to dump him and do without for three more months. Though I'm a little worried about what will happen when I do sleep with him. He'll probably drag me off to Italy by my hair to meet his mom."

"A trip to Italy wouldn't be so bad."

"It would under those circumstances." I heard her light a cigarette. Then she asked, somewhat suspiciously, "So when did you become the spokesperson for the testosterone set? I never knew you to be such a great champion of the meaner sex."

Uh-oh. She knew. "Uh, well, I've just been thinking that maybe women are too hard on men. I mean, here I was all bitter about Derrick, when all he's doing is living his dreams...I mean who am I—"

"He called, didn't he?"

"Yeah, but that has nothing—"

"Let me guess...it was Memorial Day weekend, and Derrick Holt, new boy in town, had no one to play with for the holiday, so he figured he'd call the ex and pour his heart out."

An ache filled me, but I immediately squashed the feeling by rushing to Derrick's defense. "He just called to say hi. I mean, he *said* he was going to call once he was settled—"

"Don't tell me you let him have the friendship clause in this breakup?"

"Of course we're going to remain friends. Why wouldn't we?"

"Listen, Em," she said, inhaling hard on her cigarette, "take it from an ex-girlfriend who knows. The *only* reason guys ever want to remain friends with their exes is so they can get 'friendship sex' during the dry spells."

Ah. I had her now. Laughing confidently, I said, "Yeah, like Derrick and I will be having lots of sex while living on opposite coasts."

"His family's still here. He *has* to come home some time. Wouldn't it be convenient for him to have a nice piece of ass to keep him happy during his stay?"

"His family's in Jersey," I replied, trying not to feel hopeful about the prospect of Derrick coming home and ravishing me. Was it too much to wish for this Christmas?

"Yeah, well. They'll take anything. I mean, when things are dry, even phone sex starts to look appealing."

Gulp. "Look, Jade, it's not like I could tell him I was never going to talk to him again." Even the thought of it sent icy fear through me.

She sighed. "Okay, okay. Talk to him. I'm just saying to be careful. You talk to him enough, you'll start thinking you have a boyfriend when you don't. Then you'll be turning down *real* boyfriends left and right out of some warped sense of loyalty."

Suddenly a memory stabbed at me. Of a man, potentially rich, potentially tall, and potentially marriage material. She was right. I had already forgotten about my next potential boyfriend. Henry Burke. "Oh my God. I have a date."

"See what I mean? Already you're feeling guilty."

"No, it's not that. It's tomorrow night." Looking ruefully down at my bulging midsection, I whined plaintively, "And I have nothing to wear!"

Confession: I have discovered temporary relief without paying department store prices.

Jade came to my rescue, meeting me for lunch the next day and dragging me off to a sample sale for a designer she swore by. When it came to fashion, I trusted Jade emphatically. Not just because I was desperate, but because I truly believed she understood what looked good on me better than I did. It always amazed me how she could give a man or a woman the once-over and rattle off their dimensions, everything from waistline to shoe size. This probably accounted for her unerring ability to size up a man's equipment while he was still fully clothed, thus saving herself any disappointments once she got the guy home.

By the time my lunch hour was up, Jade was hugging me goodbye and sending me back to the office with a swingy little black skirt, a clingy knit tank in a shade of deep blue she swore made my eyes positively glow with color, and a one-button black shimmery cardigan to guard against the evening chill. Not that it was very chilly in the evenings anymore, but I couldn't bear to leave the sale without it once I discovered the fabulous price.

I came back to the office to find a message blinking on my voice mail from Henry, who had done the gentlemanly thing and called to confirm that we were, in fact, having drinks that evening. I called him back, brimming with confidence and offering to meet him at Karma, a little bar conveniently located on W. 4th Street, mere blocks from my apartment. Not that I planned on bringing Henry back to my place. Quite the contrary. I just wanted to be able to hurry home in the event that the date was a complete disaster, and wait for Derrick to call again.

Later that night, as I was getting ready for my first foray into the singles world, I began to have misgivings. I wasn't ready, I thought, as I took a quick shower, hoping to wash away whatever residual anxieties I was feeling. Then I spent an incredible amount of time blowing out my hair, trying to convince myself that no matter what happened with Henry Burke, at least I had Derrick…on some level. I mean, I had a phone number, didn't I? An invitation to visit? That was *something*.

Once my makeup had been carefully applied, I got dressed in

my new duds. From the moment I felt the silky fabric of my new skirt slide against my freshly shaved legs, my confidence was bolstered. After pulling the top carefully over my head and slipping my feet into my always-reliable-yet-subtly-sexy slides, I stood before the full-length mirror and gawked.

I was gorgeous. I felt it, from the tips of my freshly painted pink toenails to the top of my shiny tresses. Not a bulge threatened to disrupt the smooth fall of my skirt, and the knit top managed to make the most of my bust and even showed off what looked like the first results of my gym workouts: subtly toned arms and shoulders.

Checking my watch, I saw that I had a little time. I called Alyssa.

"Hey," I said when she answered on the second ring. "I'm going out with good old Hank tonight."

"You are? Why didn't you *tell* me?"

"I *am* telling you. Besides, I figured you had other things more important on your mind," I continued, neglecting to mention that I myself had almost forgotten about good ol' Hank after Derrick's phone call. "How's Lulu doing?"

"She's still pretty much the same. I'm taking her in to see—" she stopped herself short of saying the *J* word, and I knew Richard must have been in the room. "I'm taking her for those tests on Saturday."

"You need company? I could meet you there and we could go to the gym after—"

"You know, I think it might be best if I go myself, Em," Alyssa said, her voice full of meanings I couldn't decipher at the moment.

"Well, I'm here if you need me," I said, hoping she understood that meant no matter what happened with Lulu, Jason—whatever.

"I know, I know. Don't worry about me. Just go and have a good time. I only met Henry once, but he really seemed like a genuinely nice guy. And Richard likes him."

I smiled now. "Well, if he has Richard's and your blessing, how bad could he be?"

Confession: Yes, looks matter to me. More than I ever realized.

The first thing I realized as I walk into the dimly lit bar is that I have gone on this blind date under the illusion that my friend

Alyssa understands me well enough to know what kind of man I find attractive. But as my eyes scan the room, looking for a dark-haired, bespectacled type gazing thoughtfully over a freshly poured martini, I realize that man isn't here.

The second thing I realize, as I see a stranger in a dark gray suit stand and wave a thin white hand hesitantly in my direction, is that Henry Burke is not that man. It wasn't the fact that he wasn't wearing glasses, or even drinking a martini. It was that he was incredibly short. And completely bald.

Well, not completely, I discovered as I walked toward him, a smile plastered on my carefully made-up features. He still had a widow's peak in the front, which sported just enough light brown hair to comb over that vast bald patch between his hairline and the crown of his head. Still, I mustered up at least the appearance of enthusiasm as I stopped beside the small table for two he had chosen for our tête-à-tête.

"You must be Emma," he said, grasping my hand in his thin, somewhat damp one.

"Henry, right?" I said, summoning the courage to make it through the date.

"Oh, you can call me Hank," he replied.

Not even that could save him now, I thought as I smiled at him anew. Then he smiled back at me, and his whole face changed. As he flashed me a row of even white teeth, I realized he could pass for one of those cool CEO types that I imagined spent Saturdays on the golf course with the boys, looked tanned and confident in khaki shorts and a polo shirt. I felt a small flicker of hope, wondering when would be too soon in our budding relationship to recommend Rogaine.

"Have you been waiting long?" I asked, as he pulled my chair out for me, surprising me so much with the chivalrous gesture that I almost tripped over the chair leg when I attempted to sit down. I prayed he didn't notice, composing my features quickly as he sat down across from me.

"No, no, I just got here." He smiled again, then signaled the waiter. "What would you like to drink?" he asked, as a buff, well-clad young man approached our tiny table with a cheerfulness that did not match his position—or my mental state, for that matter.

"A white wine spritzer," I replied, even while I felt some surprise at my own choice. I never really drank white wine, let alone *diluted* white wine. I must have been suffering from some strange belief culled from years of reading women's magazines that a spritzer would make me seem feminine, health conscious and, ultimately, more appealing. Henry—Hank, I should say—ordered a Dewar's on the rocks, impressing me further with his manly choice. *Maybe this will work after all,* I thought, glancing away from his thin white fingers to focus somewhere safely below that bald patch and those incongruously beautiful white teeth. Those teeth said money, I realized now, wondering if he'd had them whitened.

"So Richard tells me you're a writer," Hank said, diving right into things.

He did? I thought, but managed a politely modest, "Oh, well..." as I wondered how Richard knew anything about my previous incarnation. Then I remembered that I had still been busy at work on that ill-fated novel when Alyssa had introduced me to Richard as her "writer friend" years ago.

"So what type of things do you write?" Hank asked.

I decided not to shatter any illusions Richard might have encouraged in Hank about my artistic abilities and reverted for the moment to my former writer self. "Oh, mostly short stories. Though I have thought about a novel."

"That's impressive. And quite a commitment."

Uh-oh. I began to fear the one redeeming quality Hank might have was slowly slipping away. Was he a commitment-phobe? I thought that only poor, struggling artist types were afflicted with that condition.

Still, I sallied forth. "Yeah, well, I haven't exactly, uh, started the book yet."

"I admire anyone who can write." Then he laughed ruefully. "You know, I once thought I could be a writer. Back in college."

Big uh-oh. Suddenly that confidently tanned and smiling man on the golf course was transformed into a pale, disgruntled paper pusher who vaguely yearned for a more bohemian life. Luckily the waiter came with our drinks at this point, rescuing us from this dangerous turn in the conversation.

"So have you been at Holworth, Barnes, and Steingold a long time?" I asked, proud of myself for remembering the name of Richard's firm and safely steering the conversation to topics that might somehow revive the idea of Hank as Perfect Husband Material.

"Ten years. And partner for two of those," he said, his eyes crinkling appealingly as he flashed me those expensive teeth.

Hank was back on the putting green again. "Must be pretty interesting work. What kind of cases do you generally handle?" I asked, then realized too late my fatal mistake. For Hank began to tell me, over the course of the next hour, every excruciating detail of the cases he handled. And I will say, right now, that corporate law is not cocktail chat for the uninitiated. As Hank chattered on, obviously unaware of his utter charmlessness, I found my eyes straying to his widow's peak, which upon study was starting to look like an island of hair unto itself. I began to wonder if he'd ever considered shaving his whole head bald, instead of trying to maintain two different looks, one for the front of his head and one for the back.

Fortunately Hank eventually realized he was rambling on and on, for he suddenly wrapped up his obscure explanation of some minute point with a trite, "Well, enough about me. Now tell me, what do you think about me?"

I laughed graciously and realized that maybe my date with Henry Burke wouldn't be a total loss. At least I'd learned how to feign interest, which was a key single-girl survival tool. It was a tool I would be wise to learn how to wield, and wield well.

After all, I had only just begun to date.

Confession: I have forgotten the art of the casual blow-off.

By the time Hank dropped me off in front of my door a couple of hours later—yes, I had gone so far as to allow him a glimpse of my hovel—I was slightly tipsy. This was probably due to the fact that I had ploughed down three spritzers on an empty stomach, in some vague attempt to keep things interesting. Why was it that you never got dinner on a blind date anyway? I wondered now. As I glanced up at Hank when we came to a stop in front of my building, I realized that it was probably because no one wanted to risk spending more than a couple of hours with a person you were utterly unattracted to.

"I had a nice time," I said, smiling what I thought was probably a sincere smile. After all, I had had a pleasant enough time, I realized now that alcohol warmed my blood and fuzzed my brain. And it must have been that alcohol-induced blur that caused me to blurt out, "We should have dinner some time."

Why? My brain screamed back at me silently. Why had I said those fatal words? Was it the wine? Or was it the vague fear that had filled me when I realized that within moments I would be watching Hank walk away and then would have to head up the stairs past Beatrice and on to my own lonely little existence?

As I saw Hank's smile deepen into a confident grin, I realized the damage had been done. That grin smacked of satisfaction. He had me, or so he thought. And now I had gone and left it up to him what to do with me. "Sure," he said now, then leaned in for, God help me, a kiss.

It was mercifully brief, a mere sliding of lips—his surprisingly soft. Then, with a wink and the famous "I'll call you," he was gone.

And I was worse than alone now. I was, at least in Henry Burke's mind, waiting for him to call. Oh yuck.

Confession: I don't need a man, just a lobotomy.

"What were you thinking?" I asked Alyssa the next morning. I had phoned her as soon as I got into the office, partly because I was curious to learn just what she thought I might find appealing about Hank, and partly because I hoped to procrastinate starting my next article, which was tentatively titled, "Managing Your Future In-laws Before You Marry Them."

"You asked for a lawyer," Alyssa said.

"Did I specify short and bald?"

"I thought he was a nice guy. Warm. Sweet."

"I guess you're right. He *was* nice. Maybe I'm just hooked on handsome and evil."

"Or maybe you're just hooked on Derrick."

I sighed. "Well, even if he hadn't called—"

"He called?"

Oops. Now I had to 'fess up. "Yeah, well. He did. Monday night. I think he...I think he misses me."

"Of course he misses you."

I felt a warm glow inside at her insistence.

"But that and a dollar fifty will get you uptown."

I slumped inside. "I know."

"Men are essentially selfish creatures, Emma. They only care about what *they* want, what *they* need. And it doesn't matter whose feelings they hurt in the process."

Suddenly I was suspicious. This wasn't the lover of all humankind I knew Alyssa to be. "What's going on with you?"

"Me?"

"Don't get me wrong, but I've never known you to notice the evil that is man."

She sighed. "Richard and I had a fight last night."

Uh-oh. "About?"

"Well...in a word, sex."

I took this as a good sign. Chances were someone wanted sex and the other didn't. And as long as someone's desire was at stake, there was still hope. "What happened?"

"Well, in some pathetic attempt to salvage our sex life, I planned this whole romantic evening. Candlelight dinner—the works. Afterward, we're on the couch fooling around and we decide to move it into the bedroom. Well, I go into the bathroom to put in my diaphragm—which took exactly three minutes—and he's out cold by the time I come out."

"Maybe you served too many carbohydrates at dinner. You know that rice pilaf dish you once made me knocked me right—"

"Don't you dare find excuses for him, Em. Believe me, I was trying to sympathize. I even crawled into bed and attempted to kiss

him awake, only to have him roll away from me and mutter that
he was too tired and couldn't I wait?''

"Well, maybe he was tired. I mean, isn't he trying to make
partner? That's got to be a lot of work. And the stress—"

"Emma!''

"Okay, okay. I won't make excuses for him. All I'm saying is
that there may be a reason why he's tired."

"Yeah, well, that reason, whatever it may be, is about to lose
him his girlfriend," Alyssa said darkly. "If Jason so much as
makes a suggestion of a get-together now, I'm not going to stop
myself—"

"Now wait a second here. Don't go using this fight to justify
your desire to do the very hot Dr. Carruthers. I mean, I'm pretty
good at deluding myself, Alyssa, and I have to say, that's pretty
lame."

"Well, lame or not, it's how I feel. I'm tired, too, you know.
Tired of being the one who has to keep things together all the time.
I mean, why is it always the woman who's responsible for rekin-
dling the magic in a relationship? Someone has to do it, I suppose,
if people are going to stay together, make a life together. Marriage
would be a dead institution if it weren't for our efforts. And you
know what, Em? I'm starting to think we should just let it die!"

Suddenly all the fight drained out of me. I mean, if Alyssa
couldn't find it in her heart to commit to Richard, the last perfect
man in all of New York City, who was *I* to argue? Maybe marriage
was overrated. Maybe it was even…unnecessary.

Seven

"Love really *doesn't* have anything to do with it."
—Alyssa Reynolds, Girlfriend-on-the-Make

Confession: I realize marriage might best be left for the truly committed—or the mentally insane.

Alyssa definitely had a point, I realized later as I sat in an editorial meeting, listening to Patricia, who had just stood to address us, her face solemn.

"Circulation of the magazine is down," she began. "Even with our Spring and Summer issues, when our circulation is usually at its highest, the numbers are just not there. And though we can attribute a lot of this to changes in the marketplace and tougher competition at the racks, we need to work harder to put out a product that stands above and beyond our competition...."

Maybe it was a sign, I thought now, glancing around the room at the "Marrieds" and realizing most of them—witness Patricia with her pseudohusband, for example—were not living the dream lives their illustrious wedding days promised. And marriage among the junior staff was spotty, I thought. Sure there were Grace and Penelope from the Honeymoon and Travel section, but with their sweater sets and good hair, they were practically poster children for the kind of solid WASP marriages most of us thought only existed on the society page of *The New York Times.* The editorial assistants were too young to worry about, and the admin...well everyone knew she was a dyke. True, most of the older staff were married, but they were almost a whole generation away agewise and really didn't count in my informal survey of the state of the institution. Then there were the contributing editors, with two gone to the altar and holding steady and Rebecca well on her way to engaged, at least in her mind. Once through with my count, I realized that despite the fact that we were a magazine that based its whole existence on the institution of marriage, more than half of us were single, divorced or just plain indifferent.

What was going on? If the illustrious staff of the nation's most popular bridal magazine weren't all happily married, who was?

Suddenly my new single status made me feel…trendy.

"…Since I'd love to hear your ideas on how we might take the magazine to the next level and make it a cut above the competition," Patricia was saying now, "I'd like to turn the rest of this meeting into a brainstorming session. So let's open the floor to your ideas."

Maybe it was the adrenaline racing through me as I reached my antimarriage conclusion. Or maybe I was just yielding to some strange tendency I had to sabotage myself and my career for the sake of a good one-liner, but suddenly I found myself speaking up, skating dangerously over the silence that had descended upon the room once Patricia had finished her speech.

"Maybe circulation is down because marriage is out," I said, then made a meager attempt at laughter as everyone simply turned to stare at me. "What I mean to say is that maybe there just aren't as many new brides as there were before," I continued, backpedaling in the hope of saving myself from further disgrace. "After all," I rambled, "women are getting married later and later. Maybe the market has…aged."

Though Patricia seemed to be gazing thoughtfully at me, absorbing my comment, I could swear that beneath her furrowed brow she was questioning the sanity of even keeping me on the staff, much less promoting me.

Suddenly another voice piped up, and I realized I was about to be rescued. And by Rebecca, of all people.

"Maybe Emma has a point," she was saying.

If I did, I couldn't wait to hear it.

"Perhaps we have put too much focus on the *younger* bride. The twenty-something woman who is going to the altar for the first time."

I leaned forward, waiting for my idle, idiotic comments to make sense. I saw that Patricia waited, too, her gaze trained hopefully on Rebecca.

"Maybe we need an issue devoted to the older bride and her concerns. The woman who may have waited until later to marry. Or—" and she glanced warmly at me, as if there were inspiration inscribed on my blank expression "—the bride who's getting married for the second or even third time."

My mother's upcoming nuptials loomed suddenly in my mind. Now at least I knew where Rebecca had gotten her inspiration. Dumbstruck, I watched as the others reacted.

"But there already is a magazine devoted to second-time marriages," someone was arguing.

"I'm not advocating that we change the editorial direction of the whole magazine," Rebecca replied. "Maybe just make it a feature in one issue. Or even a regular feature, so you get both market segments—the first-time bride *and* the older bride."

Patricia was beaming, I realized to my dismay. Then she dropped the bomb. "I love it, Rebecca. Why don't you develop the second-time bride idea some more—perhaps give me some ideas for approaches and potential articles. We might even be able to pull something together for our next issue." Then her gaze fell on me, and the gleam in her eye suddenly seemed a tad malicious. "Emma, why don't you work on some thoughts for an issue devoted to older brides—women who marry for the first time in their late thirties and forties. Let's see what the two of you can come up with. Maybe we can do two separate issues, depending on how much material there is."

I glanced at Rebecca, a tremulous smile on my lips as I met her triumphant gaze. Oh God, what had I gotten myself into?

Confession: I am not above the desire to bitch, bitch, bitch.

"What really pisses me off," I said to Jade, whom I had dragged out to the Whiskey for drinks after work that night before her big date with Enrico, hoping to wash away my ills with alcohol and a solid bitchfest, "is that she couldn't have planned it better if she'd scripted the whole thing."

"So what are you going to do?" Jade said, reaching for her cosmopolitan and sipping gracefully.

"I have to at least try to compete with her. What else can I do? My older bride issue versus her second-time bride issue. And I'll put money on it that she's going to gleefully probe me for stuff about my mother's third marriage, then get all the credit for this thing. I mean, already Patricia thinks that it was *her* idea."

"Wasn't it?"

"Well, it was probably *my* mother who inspired it!"

Jade put down her drink, studying my expression.

"What?" I demanded, desperate to break the uncomfortable silence.

"Nothing," she said, then picked up her drink again, eyes scanning the room. "Why do we always come here after work?"

"It's conveniently located near both our offices?" I asked, still wondering what conclusions Jade had drawn about my work situation that she refused to share.

"Hmm. Lots of Eurotrash. I never realized it before," she said, then turned back to face me again.

"I know what you're thinking," I blurted out, "you're thinking Rebecca is more qualified for this job."

"I did not say—"

"You didn't have to. I can tell. You think she deserves to be promoted and I deserve to roll around in the mud for a few more years, waiting for someone to notice I'm the best damn writer they have on the staff!" I downed my drink in one swoop, setting my glass on the bar with a plunk.

"You *are* the best damn writer on that staff," Jade said. "But that doesn't always mean you get to be queen. You know as well as I do that any manager starts out as a kiss-ass. And you're not a kiss-ass."

"Neither is Rebecca."

"Yeah, well, she's a bitch. That's the other person who gets to be a manager."

"You're not kidding. I can just see her kicking and screaming if she doesn't get this promotion. She looked ready to poleax Nash when he didn't embellish her with a big rock last weekend.''

"Oh?'' Jade said, a gleeful little smile on her face.

"Yeah, apparently Rebecca misforecast her engagement. I'm starting to wonder if Nash even realizes how very serious their relationship is.''

"Yeah, men can be a little lame at figuring out whether they're just fucking you or marrying you.''

"Hmm...'' I mumbled, wondering how I felt about being tossed into the "fuck'' category on Derrick's relationship barometer. Clearly I didn't fall into the marriage category. And judging from his phone call the other night, I could be anything from soulmate to potential East Coast screw.

"Take Enrico, for instance,'' Jade continued, warming to her subject. "He thinks we're practically engaged when I go to Fire Island for the weekend without him. Yet when it's just me and him on the dance floor, I'm clearly the girl he's fucking. Or I will be, if things work out that way.''

"So you're saying it's the old double standard.''

"No, I'm saying guys are just assholes.''

I looked at Jade as she lit her cigarette, then dragged deep. Every time she made one of those male-blasting statements—not that they weren't true most of the time—I worried that the residue of cynicism Michael had left on her life was going to keep Jade from ever having a satisfying relationship with the opposite sex. "Why don't you want to date Enrico seriously?'' I asked.

"He's too young. Besides, except for the killer body, he's not really my type.''

"What is your type, exactly?''

"You know—tattoos. A bit of an edge. Kind of like...Ted.'' She sighed. "But you know how that is—the ones you want are the ones who never call again.''

I suddenly wished I could find something encouraging to say on this front, but really there was nothing I could do but commiserate with her. "Yeah, well, I can almost guarantee I'll hear from Henry Burke, considering the fact that he was short, bald and utterly unappealing.''

"Oh, man. I meant to ask you how that went. No good, huh?"

"I couldn't even muster up enough interest to remold him. I mean there's always Rogaine...."

Jade stubbed out her cigarette. "The last thing you need right now is a man-improvement project. Believe me, I've been there," she said, and I knew she was thinking of Michael and her attempts to persuade, cajole and just plain seduce him out of his impotence, but to no avail.

"The thing that really blows me away," I continued, "is that Alyssa picked him. She knew what he looked like and still thought I might find him remotely attractive. I'm a little...insulted."

"Yeah, well, that's the way those fix-ups are. I mean, would anyone really set you up with someone they might consider fucking themselves?"

"Alyssa has Richard. She's not in the market for—" I stopped dead in my tracks, thinking of Dr. Jason Carruthers, doggie doctor and ladykiller extraordinaire.

Raising her eyebrows at me, Jade polished off her drink.

I signaled the waiter with a sigh. "I think another round is in order."

"Count me in," Jade said. "Listen, if you want to go pick up your own man, I have a couple passes for a magazine launch party for that new men's monthly, *Bone.*"

I rolled my eyes. "You don't really expect me to hook up with any man associated with a magazine devoted to the adoration of his...his..."

"Look, you don't have to like a man to sleep with him. And I know some of the models they're using for their first issue. To die for."

"You know how I feel about models."

"Emma, there will be all kinds of men there. Editors. *Writers.*" She raised her eyebrows at me, knowing she had me. And she did. Already visions of Derrick lookalikes danced in my head.

"Okay, okay. What time do I have to be there? And where?"

"Envy, around ten o'clock tomorrow night."

"Well, at least I have something to wear," I thought, thinking I could recycle the Henry Burke date outfit.

All was not lost yet, I thought. New York City was full of interesting men. Surely I could find one to distract me from my post-Derrick depression?

Confession: I discover hope—and a new exfoliating cream.

After coming home from drinks with Jade and finding a message on my answering machine from Hank, telling me what a nice time he had last night and how much he hoped we might get together soon, I had a definite attitude adjustment. Suddenly I was a Woman In Demand. I didn't dare call him back. Not only because it was Friday night and that would be the desperate thing to do, but because I didn't want to risk spoiling my newfound fantasy of being the much-desired woman with any sort of blah conversation or bad attempts to give him the brush-off. In fact, I was in such a good mood after his call, I even found myself standing in the lobby of my building on Friday night for a full ten minutes before I headed out to Ricky's Beauty Supplies for a hair-product binge, charitably listening to Beatrice as she described her current dyspeptic state. I discovered I could be generous. I could be kind. After all, I had a message blinking away on my machine from an actual man. And even though I wasn't the least bit interested in Henry Burke, I hadn't been able to bring myself to erase it.

Add to that the fact that I had a free pass to the hottest party in town this weekend. I didn't even mind that the bulk of my Friday night would be spent alone in my apartment. In fact, I rushed back from Ricky's planning on pampering myself with a full-body scrub using the new peach exfoliating creme I had purchased along with a fresh tube of Bedhead styling gel. I even gave myself a pedicure in Just Do Me Red, a new shade I had bought at the encouragement of the salesclerk, who seemed to sense my newfound sexiness. The four walls of my apartment couldn't intimidate me tonight, housing as they did an address book with the carefully inscribed phone number of a certain budding screenwriter whom I hoped couldn't get me out of his mind. He might even call again if he happened to be in on a Friday night, all alone and remembering just how desirable I am.

Once my skin was scraped baby smooth and my toes shined alluringly, I nestled down in my freshly laundered bedsheets with a good book. I was feeling so content, so utterly worthy of male attention, that I briefly considered calling Derrick. I did have his number, after all. But then I realized I had talked to him less than a week ago, and that in order to dial him up—on a Friday night, no less—I would need some pretext.

My mind roamed over the possibilities. I could call him to rant about the Rebecca situation, but all that work-related angst seemed so removed from me now. Besides, I didn't want to spoil his image of me as the highly promotable editor capable of "greatness." Then I remembered that I hadn't told him yet about my mother's upcoming nuptials. That was certainly phone-call-worthy. But as I reached for the phone, I hesitated. It would be so much more satisfying if he called me....

Suddenly the phone rang, causing my heart to nearly burst out of my chest. Was it possible Derrick and I were connected by some spiritual bond that allowed him to feel my need for him even from three thousand miles away?

"Hello," I answered on the third ring, hoping my voice sounded sufficiently subdued and raspy.

"You're *home?*" my mother's voice barked back at me in disbelief.

All hope drained out of me in one swoosh. "Yes, I'm *home,*" I said with exasperation.

"Oh," she replied, backing off.

"What's up?" I asked.

"Is everything all right?"

"Everything is *fine,* Mom, just fine. How are you? Did you go for your first fitting yet?"

"Oh, no, no. It's too soon," she protested. "Besides, I have a few pounds to lose, though Clark, bless his heart, thinks I'm just perfect the way I am."

Oh, brother. "You look fine, but if you want to wait, I'm sure it's not a big deal."

"Yes, I think I'm going to wait a bit. Besides, there are so many other details to attend to. Like the cruise ship. I booked us some rooms, like I said I was going to.''

"So I guess I'm sleeping with Grandma Zizi, huh?'' All hope of scoring a date to drag on this wedding cruise from hell fell away. Even a cruise ship romance seemed like an impossible dream now.

"Well, actually, I got you and Grandma Zizi connecting rooms— that way you could be close by if she needed help, but you could also have a little privacy, if you, uh, need it. You know—after all Betty's talk about available men on cruises.'' She giggled girlishly.

Now I felt even worse. It seemed my mother's hopes for me had dwindled to the level of cruise-ship romance. "Or I might have a boyfriend by then, who knows?''

"Oh, Emma, wouldn't that be wonderful?''

Maybe it was the wistfulness in my mother's voice. Maybe it was the hopeful little message light blinking beside me, reminding me that I wasn't without prospects, but something made me blurt out, "I had a date just last night. With a lawyer. A partner, actually, in Richard's firm.''

"A partner! In Richard's firm? Alyssa's Richard?'' I heard a deep intake of breath. "Oh, Emma, that's *wonderful.* I mean, that Richard—he's quite a catch himself.''

Tell that to Alyssa. "Yeah, well, he was a nice guy and all.''

"What's his name?''

"Uh, Henry. Hank, actually. Hank Burke.''

"Nice-looking?''

"Well...''

"What am I saying? That stuff doesn't matter to you anyway. I mean, look at Derrick.''

"What about Derrick?''

"Oh, I'm sorry, dear. I just didn't think he was attractive enough for you. I mean, you're beautiful—''

"Derrick was good-looking!'' I protested, full of disbelief that anyone would question the beauty in those eyes I'd stared into for two dreamy years, those heavenly lips...

"I don't know, Emma, he seemed a bit of a...nerd. But what do I know? I'm fifty-nine years old!''

"Well, Jade thought he was good-looking. And so did Alyssa,''

I argued childishly, desperately trying to remember if they'd ever commented on Derrick's looks.

"Oh, Emma, what's the difference now?"

"What's the difference?" I said, my temper having spiked in Derrick's defense. "The difference is that I love Derrick!"

A concerned silence greeted my declaration. And suddenly I realized I had revealed way too much.

"Now, Emma, I don't think it's healthy—"

"Please," I begged, "don't give me that self-righteous self-help drivel now."

Again silence, but this one seemed filled with hurt.

"I'm sorry," I backpedaled. "I didn't mean that. I just—can we talk about something else?"

"That's fine with me. I mean, somehow we went from your great date with a successful lawyer to, to…Derrick!" she said, not bothering to disguise her distaste for the very sound of his name. "Why don't you tell me about this Hank Burke? When are you going out again?"

I glanced at the blinking light on my message machine, resolving to erase Hank Burke from my life as soon as I got off the phone with my mother. "We're not."

"What are you talking about?"

"I can't, Mom. I'm just…not interested."

"Oh, Emma." Then there was another silence, and I felt her struggling not to go places I didn't want to go. Finally she said, "I swear this is the last thing I will say on the subject of Derrick, but it needs to be said."

I sighed. "Go ahead."

"You need to forget about him, Emma. You need to move on with your life."

As if I didn't know that, somewhere deep down inside. But I couldn't tell Mom that. After all, no girl should ever admit to her mother, of all people, that she's hanging on against all hope to a man who's living another life, three thousand miles away. Without her.

Confession: A woman doesn't need a man, just a loftlike space and lots of disposable income.

The next day I woke up with the sound of my mother's warnings still ringing in my ears. As if on autopilot, I clicked off the ringer on my phone and scrubbed down my kitchen until it shined. By the time I was done, I'd resolved to banish all thoughts of Derrick and have a good time with Jade tonight. I even imagined that I might meet my next Mr. Right Now, which was good enough for me, as I also realized that I had banished, along with Derrick, all dreams of Mr. Right.

But once I had donned my swingy new skirt, paired with the reliable all-purpose black tank top that I kept at the ready in my top right-hand drawer, I had an attack of nerves. I realized I was about to plunge myself into one of the hippest scenes going on in NYC tonight, and I hadn't even taken the time to update my lipstick. Thank God for my sexy little slides and newly painted toes, I thought, eyeing my feet in an attempt to summon some courage. As I studied my freshly made-up face and carefully blown-out hair, I cursed Sebastian and his newfound inner peace. What I would do for a few highlights right now. Maybe I should just say the hell with it and seek out a new salon. What did I stand to lose, except a month's worth of groceries?

Popping my most fashionable shade of red lipstick into my most minuscule bag and grabbing my keys, I headed out, determined to blast through my last-minute crisis of faith. I was meeting Jade at her apartment, as her Soho loft was on the way to Envy. As usual, I was running a little early, and when I buzzed her apartment, she begged me to come up, which usually meant I would spend the better part of an hour watching Jade put the finishing touches on her makeup and hair.

But when the elevator opened up on her apartment—yes, Jade could afford one of *those* lofts—she was lounging on the sofa, crystal flute in hand. "You ready?" I asked, as the elevator door slid closed behind me.

"Yeah, yeah. But we're early. Come in, sit down. Have a glass of champagne."

"Champagne?" I said, plopping my bag on the kitchen counter and spying an opened split of champagne by the sink. "What's the occasion?"

She hopped off the couch, cruising toward me in a little black dress and bare feet and looking almost tiny against the background of her soaring ceilings, "Jade got laid," she said, stopping before me.

"You're kidding," I replied, but I knew she wasn't by the satisfied grin on her face as she opened a cabinet, pulled me down a champagne flute and filled it.

"Nope. And Enrico was everything I dreamed he would be. *More,* in fact."

"Oh?"

"Not only does the boy have a nice package, but he knows how to use it."

"I never doubted it. I still don't know how you're able to size up a guy's equipment from five hundred feet."

"Yeah, well. You can tell by the forearms. And the attitude. A guy with a big dick always has that extra edge. Plus, it didn't hurt that he's only twenty-two, in terms of sheer stamina at least. In the past twenty-four hours, I've had sex no less than five times. Three last night. Two this morning."

"Here's to youth," I said, clinking glasses with her.

"To youth," Jade said, a dreamy expression on her face as she sipped.

"So where is our fine young stud tonight? Is he coming with us?"

She slurped down the rest of her champagne. "Please. It took me all afternoon to get rid of him."

"Get rid of him?"

"Yeah, I told him I had plans tonight, and he was getting all possessive again. Even more so now that we've had sex. I actually had to resort to lying to him. Told him you and I were doing dinner and a movie. No boys allowed."

Leave it to Jade to be irritated by a guy who actually wanted to be with her all the time. "I suppose it's better than the usual scenario. Guy sleeps with girl. Girl waits by the phone. Guy vanishes into thin air.''

"Oh, he's not going anywhere after last night, that's clear.''

"So enjoy it, Jade.''

She looked at me funny. "Oh, I plan to. Don't get me wrong. I'm not about to walk away from a guy who is ready, willing and able.'' She rolled her eyes. "Especially now that I know what a rare commodity they are.''

"Good.''

"Don't get all gooey-eyed on me, Em. I'm not after what you're after. I don't want a relationship. If I did, why would I be dating a twenty-two-year-old?'' She placed her empty glass in the sink, and with a glance at the art deco clock on the wall next to her fridge, she said, "I'm gonna just get my shoes, my bag. Then we're out of here.''

I studied Jade now as she headed for her bedroom in her Calvin Klein dress, probably in search of an equally expensive pair of shoes, and wondered how she managed to maintain such an aloof distance from the diseases of the mind caused by men. And as I glanced around her spacious apartment—the walls lined with stunning black-and-white photography by a colleague she admired, paintings she picked out over years of gallery hopping and tasteful retro furniture, I realized it was probably because Jade didn't *need* a relationship. Why would she, with her closet full of killer clothes and enough disposable income to satisfy her taste for vintage furnishings and expensive, exquisite meals at all the hottest new restaurants?

And as she came back down the hall again in a pair of Dolce and Gabbana slides, her red tresses spiraling perfectly around her clean yet exotic features, I realized that maybe it was my own personal impoverishment that might be motivating me to immediately seek out soulmate 2. Maybe if I had a Soho loft, a closet full of fashionable threads and a personal budget that allowed for major furniture purchases on a biyearly basis, I wouldn't give most men a second glance.

"Ready?'' Jade asked, rubbing her lips together to even out her lipstick.

As ready as I'll ever be, I thought, as I headed for the elevator down to a world I had neither the apartment nor the income to truly belong to. But what the hell? I was living Jade's life tonight. I was a woman in charge.

Confession: My previous incarnation as a Girlfriend has made me unfit for the club scene.

After a short cab ride Jade insisted we take, despite my protest that we were within walking distance, we arrived at Envy. From the moment we stepped past the bulked-up bouncer with the ingratiating smile and into a low-lit room pulsing with music and barely heard conversations between scantily clad women and hulking men, I realized there was only one way I would be able to survive this kind of scene.

"Let's get a drink," I said to Jade, who had already spotted a tall, incredibly striking man she apparently knew and was about to walk over to before I was sufficiently lubed to be her charming companion.

"Sure," she said, forgetting the hottie for the moment and following me to the long bar lined with a new crowd of women thin enough to bare it all and the men who loved them.

When we finally managed to slither our way through the hordes to a spot at the bar just wide enough to accommodate both of us, I pulled out a twenty and began waving it, knowing it was the only way I'd be able to tear the little blond bartender in the tight tank top away from the pack of fawning men at the far end of the bar.

"What can I get you?" she said, once she finally caught sight of me out of the corner of her eye and came over.

"Tequila Linda?" I said to Jade, naming the Cuervo, ginger ale and Rose's Lime juice concoction that Jade herself had invented during her short stint as a bartender during college.

She nodded, her eyes scanning the crowd for familiar faces or hot new prospects, I couldn't tell which.

I ordered us drinks, and once they were promptly poured and paid for, I took a long, soothing sip.

"You forgot to toast," Jade said, just touching her glass to her lips as she eyed my drink, which was already a third of the way gone.

"Oh," I said, momentarily embarrassed. But I saw Jade had already forgotten my transgression and was sizing up a spectacular specimen clad in the tightest pair of leather pants I'd ever seen.

Turning her attention to me, she held up her glass. "To well-blessed men," she said, using a term we had both learned from Grandma Zizi, who had felt a pressing need to inform us of the finer points of selecting a mate when we both turned sixteen.

"Amen," I said and drank again, alcohol coursing through me like newfound courage.

And thank God for that courage, because before I knew it, the most incredibly beautiful man had planted himself in front of us. I was momentarily speechless until he opened his arms around Jade and enveloped her in a hug, complete with two-cheek kiss. "How *are* you sweetheart?" I heard him shout above the music that throbbed around us.

With something like relief that I was momentarily saved from being sized up by a prospective date, I realized he was gay. I couldn't think of a heterosexual in my dating history who would call a girl sweetheart with that kind of lilting cadence.

"This is my best friend, Emma," Jade said, once her acquaintance had finished gushing over how great she looked. "Emma, this is Davis. He and I used to work together when I was styling for *Vogue*. Davis was the man behind the makeup palette on that first layout I did for them. But now he's moved on to bigger and better things."

"Oh, stop. You're making me blush," Davis said, and I found myself amazed, as I always was, at how this kind of comment coming out of an otherwise striking man could make him suddenly seem so unattractive, on a sexual level at least. I mean you really couldn't call a man who was tall, broad-shouldered and as pretty as Cindy Crawford exactly *unattractive.*

"I'm not saying anything that isn't true," Jade said. Then, turning to me again, she continued, "Davis does makeup for network TV nowadays. You are looking at the man responsible for making Heather Locklear look so utterly fuckable on *Melrose Place.*"

"Please," Davis protested with a roll of his eyes, "Heather doesn't need *me* to look fuckable. She's *gorgeous.*"

"So what *is* the secret to making a woman look fuckable?" I asked, deciding to take my beauty tips straight from the master.

"It's all in the lips, sweetheart," Davis said. "All in the lips." Then he barked out a deep laugh, his teeth gleaming in the lights flashing our way from the dance floor. When he recovered from this burst of hilarity, he looked at me with new interest. "So what is it that *you* do, Emma?"

Ah, the moment of truth. That predictable question one could always count on when surrounded by people richer and more successful than you were. As I began to sputter my usual I-am-an-editor-for-*Bridal-Best*-yes-that-*Bridal Best*-isn't-that-a-riot? speech, Jade cut me off with, "Emma's a writer. And a damn good one." Then she clinked her glass into mine with a wink. "Let's drink to that."

I gulped down the rest of my drink as Davis fluttered on about how he absolutely adored writers, how he once dated one and how to this day he still lived in fear that his ex was going to write an exposé about his sex life once he got famous. Then Davis spotted someone else he knew, and with another kiss to Jade and even a hug for me, he bounced away, already shouting lavish compliments at a handsome black man who waited with arms open for the expected embrace.

"Looks like you're ready for another," Jade said, spying my drink and dragging me off to the bar for a refill.

Several hours and a few drinks later, I didn't even need Jade to introduce me as her writer friend to the numerous new people I met as we mingled, danced and lounged on the long sofas that lined a room bathed in scarlet light in the back. I had already adopted the persona myself—except with three drinks in me, it felt more like a real vocation than just party chat. I even found myself boldly flirting with a twentysomething model named Cliff with the most amazing blue eyes I had ever seen. And I might have even convinced him to come home with me, which in my state of spinning drunkenness seemed like a pleasing prospect, if I hadn't—during a sudden spate of nervousness when I feared his attention was beginning to wane—dropped my drink on the floor, causing the contents to splash all over his Armani loafers.

After Cliff had excused himself to the bathroom with a look that spoke of his complete disgust at my utter disregard for his footwear, I came to the somewhat sobering conclusion that there was no way in hell I'd ever hook up with anyone at a scene such as this one. I sought out Jade, who was gyrating wildly on the dance floor with an even more exuberant Davis. "I'm outta here," I shouted, touching her arm to get her attention. She looked surprised at first, then resigned. "Okay, okay. I'm leaving soon, too. Just one more dance?" she pleaded. I was powerless to resist the request I saw in her eyes not to leave her alone at the club with Davis, who, she had mentioned earlier, was notorious for seducing his companion of the moment into pulling an all-night dance party. "I'll be in the lounge," I said, pointing toward the back of the bar. At her nod, I headed off, sinking gratefully into the first available sofa I came across.

And just as I had reduced the couple necking on the sofa across the room from me to the kind of desperate, clinging types who sought out whatever affection they could find, I became achingly aware of a tall, dark-haired man standing in the entrance to the lounge, looking deliciously handsome in the kind of offbeat way I adored.

I fought not to stare. In fact, I struggled so hard to seem like I was completely unaware of his lean, lanky presence that I feared I might be sending out negative vibes. *Sit down, sit down,* I willed him silently, desperately afraid to glance up at him for fear he might see the positively needy look in my eyes.

Either he heard my unspoken plea, or my couch was conveniently located—in any event, miraculously, something made my new dream man sit down.

I leaned back farther into my seat, striving for the kind of indifferent, languorous beauty that drove men wild with desire. And as I struggled to come up with some sufficiently nonchalant conversation opener, he suddenly spoke.

"Are you as bored with this scene as I am?"

Something resembling relief was released inside of me. But it only lasted for a moment. For when I turned to look at him I realized he was even more incredible-looking than I first realized. And he was wearing glasses! How had I not noticed the glasses? "Totally," I finally managed to say.

"Just not my scene. The club thing."

We were even on the same wavelength. After two years of weekend after weekend of me, Derrick and some carefully selected movie title from the neighborhood indie video store, I had developed a decided distaste for the kind of romance that required an evening spent with a pack of perspiring strangers in a dimly lit room. "Yeah, well, this is my first time here. And probably my last," I said, rolling my eyes and hoping to show how ready, willing and able I was to forego this glamorous life for something more sedate and meaningful. He looked like the philosophical type. I could tell by the collarless shirt he wore, which gave him a somewhat scholarly look.

"Max Van Gelder," he said, holding out a hand which I only touched briefly, hoping he wouldn't notice the layer of sweat on my own.

"Emma Carter," I replied with a smile.

"Emma. Emma. What a good solid name. Like you stepped right out of a British novel."

So he was a literary type, I thought, my heart beating faster. "Yeah, sort of like Clarissa after Lovelace got through with her," I bantered back before I realized I sounded awfully like the bitter, recently dumped ex-girlfriend I was. After all, Clarissa pretty much died after Lovelace left her, if I remembered the novel correctly.

But he only laughed, and I liked the rich sound of it. Strong. Confident. "Whoa," he said, "let me guess. You're a writer, too."

Too? "Yes," I sputtered helplessly, "how did you know?"

"Because only a person devoted to the word would bother reading the rest of *Clarissa* after Lovelace 'got through with her,' as you put it."

Devoted to the word. I liked that. I believed it. Heck, I would believe anything while sitting so close to the most heavenly man I'd encountered in a long time. "So, do you write for, uh, *Bone?*" I asked.

"God, no. I just came to this party because a friend of mine dragged me. I mostly freelance. In fact, I'm currently working on an article on transcendentalism and the remaking of Times Square for *The New Yorker*."

Oh, God. I was way out of my league. "That's sounds incredible. Wow, *The New Yorker*."

"Yeah, well—" then he smiled the most endearingly modest smile "—got to do something to pay the bills while I work on my novel. So what do you write?" he asked.

Novel. He was writing a novel. My own unfulfilled dream swam before me, blurring my eyes and clogging my throat. "A novel?" I asked, ignoring his question about what I was writing. Better to leave *Bridal Best* out of this relationship until he was hopelessly hooked on my wit and charm.

"It's my second actually," he said, with another one of those smiles I was becoming addicted to. "The first is tucked away under my bed."

"Better than still being tucked away in the brain cells," I said, gaining another one of those great chuckles of his.

"Well, my agent thinks this one has potential," Max continued.

He even had an *agent*. Suddenly I felt my heart skittering between hope and utter despair, as my mind leaped past this chance meeting to the day when he sold that second novel and left for a book tour and a better life without me as a *New York Times* best-selling author. And just as I was about to make some self-deprecating joke about how my latest writing achievement was purchasing a new computer to surf the Web with, Jade suddenly appeared, her face flushed and, surprisingly, anxious. "Let's go," she said, then realizing that she had just waltzed in on what probably looked like a very cozy moment between me and my next heartbreak, she backpedaled. "I mean, if you're ready, that is."

"Uh, I can go if…" I began, suddenly unsure how to maneuver this next crucial moment in my budding relationship with Max Van Gelder.

"You know what," Jade said, as if realizing I was about to blow it, "I'm going to the bathroom. Meet me out front whenever you're ready."

"Okay," I said, relieved. And just as I turned to Max to introduce him to Jade, she disappeared.

"Gosh, sorry about that," I began.

"Hey, not a problem. I was thinking of heading out of this gin joint anyway."

I smiled, then just when I was trying to figure out some non-desperate-seeming way to get his phone number, he asked, "Maybe we can finish this conversation over a cup of coffee some time?"

"Sure," I said, wondering at my good fortune.

"Do you have a card?" he asked.

"Uh." I started fishing around in my bag, then realized that even if I did have a card, I wouldn't want to scare him away with it, featuring as it did a wedding cake and the *Bridal Best* motto, *Making wedding dreams come true for over a decade.* "I don't think I have one with me."

"Hang on just a sec," he said. Getting up, he headed for the bar, allowing me a nice view of his perfect little ass. After a brief conversation with the bartender, who looked over Max's shoulder at me and winked, Max came back and handed me a pen and a cocktail napkin.

I quickly jotted down my home phone number and handed both items back to Max, hoping my hands weren't shaking because I was absolutely strumming with joy inside. "Well, it was great meeting you, Max."

"Great meeting you, too," he said, then took my hand in his and held it long enough to fill me with a tingly kind of hope. "I'll call you, Emma." And with that, he smiled and released my hand.

I stood there stupidly smiling at him for a few moments before I realized this was the part where I was supposed to smoothly make my exit. Finally, with a nod of the head and a small wave, I headed out of the lounge, feeling his eyes burning into my back and praying that my skirt hadn't somehow gotten tucked into the underwear or that my ass didn't look too fat.

I couldn't believe my luck. By the time I got out front where Jade stood, puffing, somewhat angrily it seemed, on a cigarette, I felt as if I were in some sort of strange dream.

"I hope you didn't leave without his number," Jade said.

"I gave him mine."

"Oh, well. I guess that will have to do. But in the future, don't be giving away your phone number. Always get his."

Fearing I had messed up already, I asked, "Why?"

"Because then it's up to you whether or not you want to see him again. Puts all the power in your hands."

Damn, I thought, realizing that if Max Van Gelder didn't decide to call, I would never forgive myself this fatal error.

"Don't worry about it. Let's just get the hell out of here," she said, and started walking, her hand in the air to hail whatever cab might come rolling by at 2:00 a.m.

I noticed a stiffness in her movements, and as I hurried to catch up to her, I asked, "Is everything all right?"

"Everything's fine," she replied without looking at me.

But everything wasn't fine. I could tell by the tightness in her expression, and the way she wouldn't look at me once I was walking side by side with her. "Jade—"

"Okay, okay. Michael showed up."

"At Envy?"

"Yeah. And he had this adorable little brunette on his arm." She swung around to face the traffic and began to walk backward, her eyes scanning the empty avenue. "Where the fuck are all the cabs?"

I was in shock. Not just because Michael had shown up at a club—Jade always said he hated them—but because Jade was clearly shaken by the sight of him. After two years.

"Are you okay?" I asked.

"I'll be fine. Don't worry about me. I'm immune to that asshole."

"Jade—"

"He looked pretty cozy with that brunette. Maybe she managed to figure out what it takes to make that prick hard."

"Jade, if you couldn't do that, I seriously doubt—"

"I don't care. What do I care? I've got someone who knows how to treat a woman in bed. I really don't—"

"Hey, Jade, why don't we go to the diner," I said, cutting her off. "Get some breakfast like we used to do when we went clubbing.'' My plan was to get her seated and calm somewhere so she could talk this through.

But Jade was on to me. "No way," she said, as a cab finally pulled over to the curb. "I know what you're trying to do, Em, and you can just forget it." As she held the door of the cab open and gestured for me to get in, she continued, "I've done enough crying over asshole men in my lifetime, thank you. I'm going home to bed."

And as we rolled down the dark and empty streets, I didn't push her. Apparently she had been managing her angst over Michael just fine up till now. Who was I to force her to open those wounds again, when I couldn't even find a way to close up my own? But it bothered me that even after two years, her breakup with Michael still caused her pain.

I began to worry that maybe there were some men you just never got over.

Eight

"There are very good reasons to medicate oneself."
—Dr. Steven Coburn, author of *The American Family:
A Survival Guide*

"Read this book!"
—Virginia McGovern, Emma Carter's mother

Confession: I discover dysfunction is only a phone call away.

The next morning I woke up to the sound of a ringing phone, which reverberated maddeningly in my alcohol-soaked brain. I picked it up, if only to stop the sound.

"You're still sleeping? It's ten-thirty already. Whatsamatter?"

It was my father, full of the usual moral indignation he suffered whenever he was forced to recognize that neither of his children had inherited his solid discipline of early to bed, early to rise. My father was a firm believer in the early bird catching the worm. Even during his darkest drinking days, he always managed to pull himself out of bed, as if getting up before dawn might somehow save him from whatever damage his night-before debauchery had done.

"It's Sunday," I said, knowing my protests were falling on deaf ears. I settled the phone comfortably against my ear, nestled farther into my pillow and prepared for the long haul. My father didn't call me on Sunday mornings without a very good reason.

"I've been up since five-thirty," he said. "Not that it did me any good."

"What happened?" I asked, bracing myself for whatever disaster he had heaped on himself.

"I had a little accident while I was replacing some roof tiles on the house."

"Are you all right?"

"I'm fine, fine. Nothing that a couple of months in a sling won't cure."

"What?"

"Well, I broke my right shoulder," he finally admitted, sounding almost embarrassed.

"What?" I repeated, alarmed.

"And my right arm. But it's no big deal," he said, brushing off the concern he must have heard in my voice.

"What happened?" I asked again, waiting for an opportunity to give him my biannual speech about how he had reached a time in his life when home repairs, especially ones that required him to scale the house, might best be left to professionals. Somehow my father could not bring himself to pay for the kind of repairs he still felt young and able enough to do himself, despite all the mishaps he brought on himself.

"I was up on the roof, working, you know," he began. "Everything was going fine. I even had on that harness Shaun bought for when he used to go rock climbing. I found it lying around in the garage and figured it might keep me from falling off of the goddamn roof. And then what do you know? One minute I'm working, the next I'm on the ground."

"Did the harness break?"

"God only knows. It was all in one piece, according to Deirdre. But there must be something wrong with the clasp. In fact, I called Bernie—" my father was on a first-name basis with his lawyer these days "—to talk to him about it, and the bastard would barely listen to what I had to say. All he kept telling me was that I didn't have a case!"

I was immediately suspicious. "Were you drinking while you were working?"

"No, no," he muttered, though the quickness of his denial made me even more suspicious. "Can you believe that bastard won't take my case, after all the business I've given him?"

"Hmm…" I replied, suspecting I was about to be brought into

my father's latest plight. When I heard his next words, I knew I was right.

"Anyway, I was wondering how that friend of yours, Alyssa, is doing. She still wasting time trying to save rain forests with that law degree of hers?"

"Alyssa can't take on your case, Dad, and I don't—"

"What about that lawyer she's dating? Where does he practice?"

"Dad, Richard practices corporate law. He's not an…an…ambulance chaser!"

"Ambulance chaser? What kind of thing is that to say? Your old dad wants someone good. Respectable. Not some ambulance chaser. I mean, I'm hurt here. I got pain shooting up my arm."

A stab of sympathy went through me. "Are they giving you anything?" Then I realized what I was asking. Would they give painkillers to a man who had struggled with substance abuse most of his life? To me, it seemed like giving a loaded gun to a suicidal maniac.

"Of course they're giving me *something,*" he replied. "But it's not enough. This arm is killing me. And to top it off, I've got to look for a new lawyer now. Because I can't let these bastards get away with this. You use a product, you expect it's not gonna fail on you. What kind of world are we living in, here? Those bastards are gonna pay through the nose this time. I'm not kidding…."

After listening to his diatribe on the injustices of the world, I finally managed to calm him down by promising to ask Alyssa and Richard if they knew any good lawyers for his type of case. Satisfied, he made the usual inquiries about my life—had I made my first million and/or found a decent husband yet? Feeling a sudden urge to shake him out of his delusional state, I blurted, "Derrick and I broke up."

"Is that right?" Dad replied, a mixture of surprise and sympathy in his tone. "Did the bum finally figure out he wasn't good enough for you?"

No, I thought dejectedly. He became *too* good for me. "He moved to L.A. Got a job as a script doctor for a studio out there."

"Huh," he replied, and I could tell he was surprised Derrick had managed to do so well for himself. Then, "I'm sorry, sweetheart."

"Yeah, well," I replied, not knowing what else to say.

"You know, you could sue," he said finally.

"What?"

"I'm not kidding," he said, warming to his subject. "I was reading just the other day how this woman sued her fiancé for emotional distress when he broke it off right before the wedding."

"We weren't engaged, Dad."

"That's true," he said, and I could hear the wheels turning. "Did he ever give you any gifts? Love letters that might be construed as promises of commitment?"

"Forget it, Dad," I said, not wanting to 'fess up to the fact that I had allowed myself to fall in love with a man who said from day one that he wasn't going to commit.

"Well, if you ask me, Emma, I think it's for the best," my dad said soothingly. "Who knows, maybe you'll meet a nice lawyer. Then we could kill two birds with one stone!" And he laughed in some misguided attempt to cheer me up, but all I could think of was Henry Burke's shiny bald head and how utterly unable I was to love such a man, despite my father's wishes. I mustered up some halfhearted reply, then moved on to safer ground, like my job and how I was angling for a promotion. By the time I hung up, I had managed to convince my father that my life was a lot cheerier than it seemed. But as I stared at the receiver, I felt emptier than I had ever felt.

When I thought about it, I realized a lot of my dismay had to do with being almost certain that my father was drinking again. And there was nothing I could do about it. I understood perfectly why Bernie wouldn't take on my father's latest case. How could he argue the harness was defective when, in fact, it was my father with the defect? And the worst of it was, in my current hungover condition I was really in no position to judge. People did what they needed to do to get by, right?

But I could just hear my mother outlining a few psychological paradigms that might give shape to this particular dysfunction. And at the moment, most of them also applied to me.

Shrugging off the thought as the truly dysfunctional are wont to do, I called Jade, my comrade in debauchery, to see if she was okay. I still thought she might need to meet over coffee and talk about this whole thing with Michael. But as I dialed, I knew I would have to tread lightly, because when it came to Michael, Jade tended either to clam up or get defensive.

I got her machine and wondered if she was screening. "Jade, are you there?" I paused to give her a chance to pick up. "Okay. Well, can't say that I am envious of your ability to get yourself out of bed so early after our raucous evening last night. My head is killing me." I paused again, wondering once more if she was there and just didn't want to talk. "Anyway, I just called to see if maybe you wanted to go get breakfast, talk about last night. Not that I think you *need* to talk about last night," I added quickly. "All right. Well, call me when you get a chance."

I hung up and sat wondering where she might be. Then I dialed Alyssa, figuring I could both see how she was doing and get my father's request out of the way.

Richard answered the phone. "Hey, Em, how are you?"

"Good, good, how are you doing?" I replied. The image of Henry Burke rose before me, and I suddenly felt embarrassed. As if Richard had offered me a Mercedes-Benz that simply needed a wax job and I had politely declined.

"Great, great. So I heard my pal Hank and you had a good time the other night."

"Oh, yeah. Well, we, uh—"

"Said he just picked up tickets to the Sting concert at the Garden this weekend. You going with him?"

"He did?" Maybe there was reason for me to return good ol' Hank's phone call, I thought, then was immediately horrified at the discovery that I was in danger of becoming one of those girls who would do anything for a free meal, a free concert, free anything.

"Yeah. I think he said he got floor seats."

"You're kidding," I replied, wondering why I *wasn't* one of those girls who would do anything for a free ride.

"Hank's the man. He's got connections everywhere. You'll never have to worry about a thing when you're with him."

Except footwear. Could a woman really commit to low heels for the rest of her life? "He seemed like a nice enough guy. I mean, he was very *sweet*."

Richard was silent for a moment. "Oh, I get it. You weren't into him."

Relieved that I wasn't going to have to live another lie, even for the sake of floor seats to Sting, I replied, "No, I guess I wasn't. He called...but I never got back to him," I confessed guiltily.

"Hey, that's not a big deal. It was worth a shot, right? These blind-date things are tough, you know?"

He was so sensible, so good natured, I thought. Alyssa better not break his heart. "Yeah, I guess you're right. I feel bad, though, because he *was* a nice guy, and I don't want to hurt his feelings. Maybe I *should* call him back...or something."

Richard laughed. "Are you kidding? Don't worry about Hank. He's probably lined up someone new already. In fact, I was out with him for happy hour last night, and I saw him talking to some pretty blonde. I think he may even have gotten her phone number."

The creep. "Oh, well. That's...good, I guess."

"Oh, yeah. Don't you worry about Hank. If you want, next time I see him, I'll cover for you. Say you left the country or something." Then he laughed. "Hank will get over it. I mean, the guy *never* lacks for women."

Suddenly Hank, with his gleaming bald spot and blah conversational skills, grew incredibly appealing in my mind. I quickly shook the feeling off. What was I, crazy? What kind of world are we living in here when short, balding men had dates lined up back-to-back and beautiful single women like Jade—and, yes, I would even venture to include myself in this category—could barely find someone to stick around long enough for meaningless sex? Oh, right. New York City. Where the women are plentiful and the men...pitiful.

"Well, I'm glad poor Henry won't suffer on my account," I said.

He chuckled. "I miss that sarcasm of yours, Emma. When are you going to come over for dinner again?"

Just as soon as you and Alyssa are safely married and I don't have to feel guilty looking at you, I thought. "Soon. Soon. Hey, listen, I'm wondering if you can recommend a lawyer for my litigious dad."

"Uh-oh. What did he do now?" Richard was well versed in my father's lawsuits, as we had spent many an evening analyzing the sheer audacity of many of them.

"Fell off a roof." Then I added, "He was wearing one of those mountain-climbing harness things, and apparently the clasp wasn't working properly." I didn't mention my suspicion that he might have been drinking. I always hesitated when it came to revealing my dysfunctional upbringing, especially to men like Richard, who grew up in Westchester in a perfect house with perfectly nice parents, one a doctor and the other a lawyer. His parents even had a golden retriever named Skip, for crying out loud.

"Is your dad okay?" Richard was asking now.

Depends on what you mean by okay, I thought, but aloud I said, "Well, he did break his right shoulder and right arm."

"Ouch," Richard replied.

"Yeah, you're not kidding."

"Well, let me think about it. See if I can come up with a good lawyer for him. Sounds like he might have a case, who knows?"

So sweet, Richard was. So very, very sweet. Damn Alyssa and her raging hormones. "Thanks, Richard. So, is Alyssa there?"

"Naw. She's at the vet."

Oh *God.* "On a *Sunday?*"

"Yeah, well, you know Lulu went for those tests yesterday, and Alyssa was really worried. She didn't want to have to wait the whole weekend for the results. So the doctor offered to meet her today and talk to her about the results. Nice guy, huh?"

Helluva guy. "Uh, yeah."

"I offered to go with her, but Alyssa wouldn't have it. She seems to think she's gotta manage this whole thing with Lulu on her own." He sighed. "I guess it must be hard for her. She's had that dog since she was a kid."

"Yeah." My heart was doing a sad little plunge to my ankles as I listened to the concern in Richard's voice.

"I'm just hoping for the best," he said. Then he chuckled ruefully. "You know, I used to tease Alyssa about her attachment to that scruffy little ball of fur. I have to admit, though, I've grown quite attached to the old girl.''

"You are *not* going to lose Alyssa," I said, my voice full of determination.

"Alyssa?" He chuckled. "I was talking about Lulu."

Idiot! "Right. That's what I meant. Lulu." I bit my bottom lip. Hard. "Anyway, don't you worry about anything, Richard. You and Alyssa are going to get through this thing. With Lulu. Everything is going to be just fine.''

And when I hung up the phone a few minutes later, I wondered just how fine everything really was going to be.

Confession: I have become the other woman.

I made it all the way to Monday night without giving in to the urge to call Derrick, which was pretty good considering that Jade was MIA since Saturday and unavailable to talk me out of it. I was worried about what might have happened to her, until I called *Threads* on Monday and learned that she had, in fact, reported in at 10:00 a.m. that morning, before she went out on a shoot. I might have called Alyssa again, but I couldn't bear the thought of knowing Richard might be in the background and in danger of overhearing me blast her. Since she was in court all day today, I would have to wait before I had a chance to tell her just how unspeakably cruel I thought she was for doing what she was doing to Richard.

But by the time Monday night rolled along, I felt entitled to call Derrick. After all, it was now over a week since we had last spoken. And so what if he hadn't called again, aching to talk to me, after that initial realization of how much he missed me? He *had* given me his number right? Maybe he was waiting for *me* to call *him.* And because I was the type who would never let anyone suffer too greatly on my account, I waited until just after midnight, passing the time jotting down lame ideas for that damn proposal on the older bride for Patricia, then carefully dialed his phone number, which, I'll admit, I had already memorized from staring at it so often.

After one ring, I knew I had done the right thing.

At two rings, anticipation filled me.

At the third ring, I started to plot my next move. Leave a message if he's not home? That would put the ball in his court. Not a good idea in my current state of mind.

At the fourth ring I wondered if he had even gotten a machine yet. If he hadn't, he would have no idea I was calling him. Hell, I could ring him all night, unless of course he had caller ID. Unfortunately I had no way of knowing that.

Suddenly a breathless and—God help me—*female* voice came over the line. "Hello?"

"Uh. I, um...I think I have the wrong number?"

"Who are you looking for?"

"Derrick Holt?"

"Nope, you've got the right number," she chirped perkily. "He's not in right now, can I take a message?"

So thrown off was I by this woman—whoever she was—I didn't think about my next best move. I answered dumbly, "Just tell him Emma called."

"Emma? Does he have your number?"

Yeah, sweetheart. Emblazoned on his brain. "Yes, he has it."

"Okay, I'll give him the message."

"Thanks," I replied weakly, my head spinning.

"Have a good night," she said pleasantly, and hung up.

Who was she, dammit? My mind immediately sorted through the possibilities until I settled on the one that hurt the least. The roommate. Relief washed through me. She had to be the roommate. There was no way Derrick could have gotten cozy enough with a new girlfriend this fast, right? Not enough so that she'd get key privileges. Hell, I didn't get a set of Derrick's keys until we were dating a solid six months. And even then I had to demand them.

The roommate. Okay. I could live with that.

Then a new dread filled me. Richard and Alyssa had practically been roommates once.

I called Jade, knowing she was the only one who could talk me out of the terrible turn my thoughts had taken. At the sound of her message, I started to panic. "Where the hell *are* you?" I all but shouted at the sound of the beep.

"Emma?" came Jade's groggy voice as she picked up.

"Oh God, I'm sorry, Jade," I said, feeling immediately guilty. "Are you sleeping?" I glanced at the clock. It was midnight, after all, though I knew Jade stayed up pretty late most of the time.

"It's all right," she said.

"Is everything okay with you?"

"Yeah, fine. Just tired." Then she laughed, the sound rich and satisfied. "I've been on a marathon of sex ever since Saturday night."

"Saturday night?"

"Yeah, after you got out of the cab, I decided there was no reason I had to be alone. I headed straight over to Enrico's. I didn't get home until a few hours ago."

"You've been with him the whole time?"

"Well, except for a brief intermission today when I went on a shoot. Otherwise, I've pretty much been in the horizontal." She laughed throatily. "And the vertical. Did I mention my little Enrico used to be an athlete back in Italy? *Mmmmm,*" she purred.

Apparently Jade had managed to exorcise thoughts of Michael the only way she knew how. With lots of mind-blowing sex. "You must be beat. I'll let you go."

"Is everything all right?"

"Derrick has a roommate," I blurted, the memory of the woman's happy little voice filling me with newfound angst.

"So what? You knew that, didn't you?"

"A *female* roommate."

"Oh."

"Now all I can think about is him coming home to her every night. Them sharing dinners. Videos. Next thing you know, she's more girlfriend than roommate!"

"Emma—"

"I know what you're going to say, Jade. I should forget about him. After all, he's not my boyfriend anymore. He's not in my life. He has the perfect right to move on."

"He hasn't moved on, Emma. He just got a roommate."

"Yeah, well, it's easy enough to fall in love with your roommate.

Look at Richard. He fell in love with Alyssa when she was spending so much time at his apartment.''

"You have to take your mind off this. You are not going to get anywhere with—"

"I *can't* take my mind off it. In fact, it's all I've been able to think about ever since I hung up the damn phone. All I can see is Derrick talking with his roommate, laughing with his roommate, telling his roommate all about his day. His next screenplay idea. His hopes and dreams." I sighed. "And I'll just be that girl he used to know on the East Coast. I can't bear the thought of… of…becoming an anecdote. A part of his past." My voice broke. "I still love him, Jade."

She sighed, and it was one of the saddest sounds I've known to come out of Jade. "I know, honey." She was silent then, and I knew that space of quiet was filled with understanding. She knew what I was going through. Hell, she suffered from the same ailment.

"You need another guy," she said finally, her voice full of determination, "someone to take your mind off Derrick. What happened with that guy you met Saturday?"

"Not a peep out of him yet." A pit formed in my stomach. Maybe I was just not the kind of woman men pined for, chased after, romanced. Apparently I was the kind that drove men away. As in, clear across the country.

"Well, it's too soon anyway," Jade said. "He didn't look like some desperate geek to me. In the meantime, let me see if Enrico has any friends."

"No, I don't want to—"

"Emma, sex is the single girl's Prozac. Trust me on this."

"Forget it, Jade. I'll manage," I said, then realized that my cupboards were currently bare of anything resembling binge food.

Dear God, how was I going to survive this?

Suddenly my eye fell on a dusty bottle of Baileys Irish Cream, a gift I had gotten last Christmas and had yet to open.

Oh God.

"Do you think I'm an alcoholic?" I asked, eyeing the bottle with dread.

"Whoa. Where did that come from?" Jade said.

"I did drink an awful lot on Saturday. Three or four drinks in as many hours. And then there were those shots Manny bought for us. That's not normal. I could have a problem."

"Three or four drinks and a few shots of Tequila on a Saturday night only qualifies you for a hangover."

"But it was almost like I *had* to get drunk in order to…to function."

"Gimme a break, Emma. You are *not* an alcoholic. I know you think just because your father had a problem—"

"*Has.* My father *has* a problem, Jade," I cut in. Then, with an exasperated sigh, I confessed all. "He fell off the roof of his house last week. He didn't say so, but I suspect he'd been drinking again."

"Oh, shit. Is he all right?"

"Beyond a broken shoulder and arm, he's fine. As fine as he'll ever be, anyway. All ready to sue and blame it all on someone else."

She was quiet again, and during this silence I imagined she was putting it all together—my need for alcohol to carry on a conversation at a party, my father's need for alcohol before he climbed up on top of a house.

"Look, Emma, I'm sorry about what happened to your dad. I really am. But all you're doing is using this incident with your dad to take your mind off Derrick, when I have a much better solution."

"Sex? Sex is a better solution?"

"It's a healthier one. Good cardiovascular. And not bad for your self-image, either."

I sighed as I realized I had no desire to have sex again. The whole idea seemed suddenly exhausting. I couldn't even imagine being naked with anyone but Derrick. Then I realized that there was a very strong chance Derrick would soon be getting naked with someone else. "At this rate, I don't think I'll ever have sex again. And least of all with some oversexed twentysomething immigrant boy you might round up for me."

"Okay, but you don't know what you're missing…."

Oh, I did, I thought. It just had nothing to do with sex. And everything to do with a certain screenwriter who was on the sure path to happily-ever-after. With someone else.

Confession: I don't even like me anymore.

The next day at work, I struggled to concentrate on the nightmare project I had gotten stuck with all because of my glib comments in the editorial meeting last week. What the hell did I know about the first-time older bride? Heck, I'd be lucky if I even made it to that category, at the rate I was going. Maybe I should be working on a Senior Brides issue. That was more my speed. With a sigh, I tried to picture Patricia, who had married well into her thirties, looking demure while her future husband got down on one knee. But all my mind conjured up was a vision of two people seated at opposite ends of a negotiating table, each armed with lawyers as they carefully negotiated the terms of what they would and wouldn't give to the person they intended to share their life with. Who could blame me? After all, it was common knowledge around the office that Patricia herself had devised a pretty hefty prenup. And the word was her groom-to-be had presented her with a contract just as massive. The romance of it all was almost too much to bear.

I sighed and looked at the clock. It was already two o'clock, and I had wasted half a day on this proposal, letting all my other responsibilities pile up and my life become even more miserably busy. Patricia wanted to see something on this in less than a week, and I had barely put together two sentences on the beauty and wonder of being a first-time bride pushing forty. Where was the magic? I wondered.

Shoving aside my scribbled notes, I picked up the phone and dialed, not even questioning what I was doing. He was probably home, after all, with the irregular hours he kept now that he was living my dream life as a writer. Probably home and just ignoring the fact that I had called him more than twelve hours ago and left a message.

"Hello?"

"Derrick," I said, my nerves singing with relief at the sound of that voice I knew better than my own.

"Hey, Emma, what's up?" he replied, a smile in his voice.

He was glad to hear from me! But then suspicion filled me. "I tried you last night. Left a message, in fact. With a…a woman who answered?"

"Oh, Carrie didn't tell me you called."

Bitch. "Carrie?"

"My roommate. She's a little…ditzy sometimes."

I smiled inside. She was definitely not Derrick's type. Of one thing I could be sure—he *never* went for ditzy. "Oh, yeah? Well, I guess what can you expect in a *roommate,* after all. It's not like they really *care* whether or not you get your phone messages. Or even what kind of day you've had."

"Nah, Carrie's great. In fact, she's an excellent cook. And since she weighs about ninety pounds and cooks like she's going to feed an army, I reap the benefits. She has so many leftovers, I may never have to cook for myself again."

Oh God, he was a goner. "So…how did you find this, uh, room-mate? Carrie?" I asked around my tight throat.

"Actually, someone at the studio sent her my way, knowing I was looking for an apartment and she was looking for a roommate. She's an actor. You might even have seen her on TV. She does a lot of commercial work. In fact, she's in a toothpaste ad right now. Close-Up, I think. You know the one where the girl runs into the guy in the elevator?"

"Uh, no. Don't think I've seen it. So you two must be pretty close by now."

"Close? Well, we're getting to know—" He stopped suddenly. "Emma, what's going on?"

"Going on?"

"You're jealous, aren't you?" Then he laughed. Actually laughed.

"I am not!"

"Okay, you're not." He chuckled again and changed the subject. "So what's up with you? Get that promotion yet?"

I looked down at the sprawl of magazines on my desk, pulled

from every magazine rack within a five-hundred-yard radius of the office, and all purchased with the idea that they would inspire me to belt out a promotion-winning proposal. Eventually. "Uh, I'm working on it," I replied, while my mind frantically scrambled for a way to steer the conversation back to the hateful subject of his thin, and probably beautiful, actor roommate. "So, I bet it must be nice living with a woman this time around."

"Yeah, it's fine. Hey, did I tell you I got the thumbs-up on the first script I doctored? Some crazy horror film, but I had fun with it."

"That's great, Derrick."

"Yeah, well, it's not the same as hearing my own script is going into production, but, hey, I'll take it. I mean, at least until I get some word on what's happening with the screenplay I sold. But I was happy to get some good feedback."

"You must have celebrated your success, huh?" I said.

"Yeah, well. I had a couple of beers with Carrie when I got home."

My heart sank, and suddenly I wondered why I had fought so hard to get back to a subject that could yield me no comfort. "That's, uh, nice."

"Yeah. In fact, I hate to cut you short, but I'm on a serious deadline. Can I call you back some other time?"

"Uh, yeah," I replied, even more miserable. "If you want to."

"Of course I want to, Em. Hey, is everything all right?"

"All right?"

"I mean you seem a little...down or something."

"Me? No, I'm fine. Just fine," I replied. Nothing that a few tubs of Ben & Jerry's wouldn't cure. Or worse, a few drinks. Maybe even some meaningless sex.

"Good, good. Listen, we'll talk soon. I want to get done before Carrie gets home. She's always so distracting, I can't get anything done. What are you gonna do, right? Roommates."

"Right." I laughed weakly, and after a few more parting words and empty promises that we'd "talk soon," I hung up, my chest feeling like it had all but caved in at the spot where my heart once was.

And just in case I wasn't miserable enough, moments later Rebecca turned up in my cubicle. One look at my face and her bright smile faded. "What's wrong?" she asked, sitting down in my guest chair, her face sympathetic.

"Oh, nothing," I said, "Just talking to Derrick." Then, remembering she didn't know the state of my life, I amended, "Uh, you know. He was being your typical guy. So busy with work he doesn't even have time...to...to have dinner with me tonight. No big deal."

"Yeah, well, I know how *that* is," she said, rolling her eyes. "Last week I had to remind Nash that my birthday was coming up. I mean, I think he would have forgotten *entirely* last year if I hadn't dragged him to Bloomingdale's to show him what I wanted." With another roll of the eyes, she continued, "If I hadn't tipped him off, I might *never* have gotten my Bulova." She held up her arm to show me the diamond-encrusted watch she knew I coveted.

Suddenly I found myself admiring Rebecca. Here was a woman who clearly knew how to get what she wanted. I could learn something from her.

"I don't think Nash forgot my birthday this year, though," she continued. "In fact, when I brought it up last week, he told me on the phone just now he was going to try to get us a reservation at Le Colonial."

"Wow, pretty snazzy. When are you going?"

"Saturday—my birthday, of course," she said with surprise, as if she had expected me to remember the day.

I cringed at her next words.

"I think it's going to happen this time."

"Happen?"

"Well, Nash is going to propose, of course! I mean, why else would he be taking me to one of the best restaurants in town? I mean it *is* my birthday, but it's not like it's my thirtieth or anything."

Noting painfully that she said "thirtieth" as if it were a dirty word—Rebecca was still a youthful about-to-turn-twenty-nine—I said, "Well, I suppose anything's possible."

She seemed disappointed in my lack of enthusiasm for her prospects. And then, as if she hoped to take her revenge, she asked, "So how's the proposal coming along?" I saw her eye roam over the stacks of magazines, the doodles I had made on my notepad, the half-eaten Twinkie on my desk.

"Oh, great. Just had a great, uh, brainstorming session," I lied. "How's yours going?"

"Mine?" she replied with eyebrows raised. "Oh, mine is done. I just want to proofread it before I hand it in," she said, patting the side pocket of her suit, where, I noticed, she had placed a packet of carefully folded pages.

Inwardly I wanted to scream. Would I ever win at anything? I wondered with sudden sorrow.

"Well, guess I'd better run off. I have a meeting with Patricia this afternoon. She said she had something important she wanted to talk to me about."

Apparently I wouldn't, I realized as I watched Rebecca all but skip away with my hopes and dreams neatly tucked into the side pocket of her designer suit.

Confession: I discover monogamy means never having to say you're sorry.

When Alyssa finally returned my call late that afternoon, she cut off the lengthy speech I had prepared on Richard's virtues with the words, "Meet me at the gym at seven-thirty." When I had tried to protest, she simply replied, "Look, you need to work out. And I really need to talk."

Now, as she stood above me on the bench where I lay, spotting me as I pushed two weights above my chest in an exercise that promised to keep my breasts pointing north for a few more years, she blurted out, "I'm going to sleep with Jason."

My arms released and I dropped both weights to the sides.

"What?"

"You're not going to talk me out of this, Em," she said quickly as I swung my legs around and sat upright to face her.

"I am *so* going to talk you out of this. Alyssa, do you realize what you're doing? You could potentially jeopardize the most important relationship in your life all because of...of...raging lust.''

She folded her arms defensively. ''It's not raging lust. It's...it's more than that. You should have seen Jason when I met him for coffee the other day. I mean, the fact that he agreed to meet me when his office was closed because he didn't want me to spend the rest of the weekend worrying about Lulu just shows you what kind of man he is.''

''A martyr?''

''No, compassionate. And sensitive. I can't remember the last time Richard gave a thought to what I might want or need.''

''Alyssa, I happen to know that Richard cares a great deal for you. You should have heard the worry in his voice when I talked to him on the phone the other day. He loves you.''

She looked away, her eyes momentarily glassy before she blinked away her tears, along with any doubts she might have had. ''I can't think of him now. I need to think of me. Everything is coming down on me right now. Lulu...'' Her voice cracked. ''Lulu needs surgery.''

''Oh, no. What's wrong?''

''Well, one of the scans showed a cyst on her bladder. Jason says it could be benign, but it's what's causing her so much discomfort. He doesn't think the surgery will be major—the cyst is small. But Lulu is fifteen and—'' she shut her eyes, squeezed back tears ''—anything could happen.''

I stood and put my arms around her in a hug, which she accepted gratefully until my next words. ''I think you should let Richard be there for you during—''

She pulled out of my arms. ''Stop it, Emma. Please. And don't you dare think you have the right to judge me if I want to take a little...a little comfort from someone I feel a strong connection to.''

Though I didn't think ''comfort'' quite described what Alyssa might get out of sex with a guy as hot as Dr. Jason Carruthers, I swallowed my biting retort and said, ''All I'm saying is that you should just think about what you stand to lose. Richard and you have a lot of years together. And you could very well have a *life* together.''

Alyssa folded her arms across her chest defensively. "Would it be fair for me to enter into a lifetime commitment with him if I had doubts?"

She had a point there. Suddenly I wondered what I would do if I were in this predicament with Derrick, whom I was having serious doubts about ever since our last conversation. Could you ever really know the person you loved until you broke up with him? I mean, I never saw Derrick as actually befriending, much less falling in love with, some bimbo actress.

Still, I wasn't ready to let go of my belief that some people, at least, were absolutely meant to be together. "We *all* have doubts, Alyssa. But we choose to forgo them if we want to have a life with someone…with someone we love. How *else* are we supposed to get married, have children? Commit ourselves to a life with another person?"

She sat down on the bench with a sigh. Pressed her towel into her chin. "I'm beginning to think commitment is overrated. You know, human beings are one of the few species that mate for life."

"Oh, brother. Is this the kind of line a veterinarian-on-the-make feeds to his prey?"

She looked up, as if shocked I would think of *her* beloved veterinarian in such a manner. "Jason is not on the make. God, I wish he were." Her brow furrowed. "No, in fact, maybe I like him precisely because he *isn't* on the make." She sighed. "The funny thing is, I don't think I would like him as much if he were the type to put the moves on a woman who was practically engaged to someone else. That's why I haven't told him about Richard."

"Oh, terrific. Let's protect the good doctor's innocence—at least until you find yourself beneath him on a bed at some Motel 6."

"There is no Motel 6 in NYC."

"Alyssa, you are *not* considering cheating on Richard on his own turf! At least, go through the Lincoln tunnel and get yourself safely in New Jersey."

"You're crazy. What does it matter *where* I sleep with him—"

"Look," I said, picking up the weights and thrusting them into her hands. "You are talking to someone who doesn't want you sleeping with him at all."

"That's not an option," she said, taking the weights from me and lying on her back along the bench, her resolve showing in the jut of her chin.

"Could you at least promise me one thing?" I said, standing above her as she positioned herself to begin the exercise.

She looked at me, waiting for whatever outrageous request she imagined I might come up with.

"Could you at least wait until after Lulu's surgery?"

She smiled. I think she was almost relieved I hadn't asked something else. Like that she refrain from penetration or something. "That's seems manageable. Lulu is scheduled for surgery next week. I think I can last that long."

I looked at her determined face as she pushed the weights upward, and firmed my own resolve.

One week. I had one week to convince Alyssa that she was about to make the biggest mistake of her life.

Confession: I discover a fat-free substitute for despair.

I am always amazed at how many little tasks I can get through while procrastinating on something infinitely more important—like the proposal I had yet to hand in to Patricia. I started my day composing a clever list of "Top Ten Reasons Why Sex is Better With The Man You've Lived With for Five Years," which I promptly e-mailed to Alyssa. Then I felt a sudden inspiration to do my filing, which I had kept piling up in a carefully hidden place between my desk and the cubicle wall. Rebecca dropped by that afternoon to inform me that Patricia absolutely adored her proposal for the second-marriage issue and had even asked her to start assigning articles. Then she had the nerve to ask *me* if I wanted to do a piece on my mother's third marriage. I, of course, promptly declined. After all, I told her, I would probably be preoccupied with putting together my issue on Older Brides. I didn't tell her that I had yet to even draw up the proposal.

Once she left, I realized I needed to get cracking if I truly wanted to compete with Rebecca. But a glance at my watch told me it was close to four and way too late to get started on such a huge project.

So I dialed Jade's office, hoping to get her take on the whole Derrick/roommate situation, now that I knew Derrick's roommate was not only female, but thin and beautiful enough to do ads for Close-Up, which was clearly one of the sexier brands of toothpaste on the shelves, at least from a marketing perspective. I had already filled Alyssa in on the situation as we showered at the gym the night before, but she had been unable to offer any consolation other than that I should consider therapy. "Not on any sort of permanent basis," she had said when she saw the alarm in my face. "Just to help you get through this. Get over him."

I, of course, quickly discarded this advice by informing her that she was the last person who should be recommending therapy. Let's just say there was an abrupt change of subject after that.

"Hey," came Jade's cheerful voice on the other end. Clearly sex on a regular basis was doing wonders for her state of mind, I thought, feeling a bit guilty for heaping more Derrick angst on her. But after we exchanged greetings, I couldn't help filling her in on how Derrick was cozying up to his new roommate. I knew it was wrong, but I needed something to make my life seem a little less miserable than it was. Even if that meant tearing into good old Carrie, who seemed like the kind of woman Jade and I normally took great delight in attacking. Thin. Distracted. Blond—this last part was my assumption. After all, she did live in California.

"Oh, and get this," I said, warming up, "she's an actor. Derrick claims she's starring in a Close-Up ad, of all things."

"I think I saw that ad," Jade replied mirthlessly. "Girl runs into an elevator. Bumps right into this tall, handsome guy."

"Oh God. What a cliché. And I'll bet she's a cliché, too. What did she look like? I'll just bet she was your basic blond anorexic." I said, waiting hopefully for Jade to confirm my assumptions.

"She had nice…teeth," was Jade's only comment.

Feeling vaguely nauseous, I rushed her off the phone, claiming I had to do some urgent errands on my way home. What I really wanted was to take refuge in my apartment and bury myself somehow. Find some way to relieve myself of the burden of painful truth: Derrick was moving on. While I…I was doing a breath-stealing jog…in place.

As I reached my corner, I couldn't bear the thought of going home to my claustrophobically tiny apartment. Especially as I had just realized it was Wednesday and the last possible day I could reasonably accept a date with Max Van Gelder for the weekend without looking desperate, at least according to Jade's Guide to Guy Hunting. He had yet to call, and judging from the way my day was going so far, I sincerely doubted he would.

I almost headed to the Korean deli, visions of snack cakes dancing in my head. Almost. Then the feel of my still-aching abdominal muscles reminded me how far I had come, how the blood, sweat and tears I'd expended in the gym last night would be all for naught if I allowed myself even this pathetic little pity party. So I turned left instead, suddenly remembering I had other options.

I headed for Healthy Dee-lites, a little health-food store I used to go to when I was trying to prove to Derrick how health-conscious I was. It was during a period in our relationship when we had experienced the first lull in our sex life, and I had become painfully afraid that I had bloated up too much to be attractive. Later, when my sexual powers had been restored, I used to go simply because I had developed an addiction to Healthy Dee-lites' flagship product, Skinny Scoop, a frosty ice-cream-like substance that I had managed to convince myself was low enough in fat and calories to eat whole tubfuls of without gaining an ounce.

Once I hit University Place and the cheerful red awning came into view, I remembered the sweet old couple who ran the place and wondered why I had ever stopped shopping there. As I walked into the pretty little shop and eyed the rows of organic vegetables and shelves of snack food designed to comfort the mind without destroying the waistline, I knew I had found my mecca again.

"Well, hello there," chirped the kind-faced, sixtyish woman who ran the place with her equally adorable husband. He stood ready at the register, a broad smile on his face.

"Hi, how are you?" I replied, feeling slightly embarrassed for having abandoned them for so long. I hadn't thought they would actually remember me.

"We're great. Haven't seen you in a while," the woman said,

beaming up at me as if I were one of her prodigal children come home.

"Yeah, well. Busy and all," I replied, not wanting her to think I'd been forgoing her and her husband's happy little shop for the new vegetarian superstore across the street.

"Double Mocha Chip, right?" she said, naming the Skinny Scoop flavor I used to faithfully come to purchase during that long, vague period of my Derrick Days. I was mortified to be so... obvious. It was as if she could see my gaping wounds beneath my slenderizing skirt outfit.

"You guessed it," I said.

Then she paused. "You know what? I think we might have just sold our last pint. Gosh, Ed—do you think we might have any more in the freezer downstairs?" she said, turning to her husband, who seemed to think deeply about this.

Struck by an idea, he brightened and said, "I know, why don't you call down to Griff and see if he can check for us?"

The woman smiled at her husband, as if what he'd just suggested was pure genius. "Good idea." Then she turned to a phone on the wall and, after a moment or two, spoke into the receiver to some faceless person on the other end who apparently waited there to do her bidding. "Do me a favor, Griffin, and check the freezer down there to see if we have any more of that delicious Double Mocha Chip Skinny Scoop." She winked at me. "And bring it up if we do."

She hung up the receiver. "We just had this intercom installed, and it works like a charm." She smiled. "Our son recommended we get it. He's always thinking, that one. He's very smart. In fact, he runs his own design firm." She turned her beaming face on her husband for a moment, then refocused it on me.

I returned her smile, wondering what was so pathetically wrong with her son that she felt a need to sell him to me, her disloyal female customer. She continued to beam, then turned her attention back to some sales flyers she had been folding into envelopes. Her husband, seeing her struggle a bit with the seal on a fresh box of envelopes, immediately came over to assist. It was then I remembered the other thing I had loved about coming to this store: seeing these two together. My heart ached inside, wistful. I realized that I, too, could make a life for myself wearing a goofy apron and standing behind a peach-colored counter if I could find a man who cared for me the way this man obviously cared for his wife.

As I watched them work together in companionable silence, the door to the back sprang open, and out stepped the most beautiful man I had ever seen. Before I could even prepare myself, he stood before me, wearing a pair of ancient blue jeans and a dirty T-shirt that looked like it had been smeared with every flavor of Skinny Scoop Heavenly Dee-lites had to offer. But none of that took away from the fact that he was broad-shouldered and lean-hipped, with gorgeous brown eyes surrounded by thick sooty lashes. Even his short brown hair managed to look silky, despite the dusting of powder that seemed to have settled over it from whatever work he was doing down in the basement. And there, in his large tanned hands, was the biggest vat of Double Mocha Chip I had ever seen.

"You the customer who wanted the Double Mocha?" he asked.

"Uh, yeah," I said, helplessly.

"We only had the gallon size," he said, holding the container out to me. "That okay?"

Mesmerized by the way his chocolately brown eyes focused in on me as he spoke, I replied dumbly, "That's perfect." Then, realizing what I must look like, standing there alone and agreeing to an ungodly quantity of ice cream that might not be quite as low calorie as its name implied, I added, "Me and my roommates are absolutely *addicted* to this stuff."

He smiled, grabbed a plastic bag from under the counter, dropped the gallon in and handed it to me. "It's all yours. Enjoy," he said. Then turning to the old couple, who seemed suddenly caught up in contemplation of the glue on one of the envelopes, he said, "Let me know if you need anything else," and disappeared down the steps as they smiled after him gratefully.

After I paid the old man for my consolation prize, I headed home, my head full of illicit fantasies of going back to Heavenly Dee-lites at closing time and seducing the sexy new Skinny Scoop man. I wondered what his function was there. Was he just doing some repairs, or was he a regular employee? With a frown, I realized it would be much better if he were some kind of mechanic. I mean, I couldn't allow myself a fling with a man who made just above minimum wage, could I? A girl had to have some standards, after all. The old couple seemed to be on pretty familiar terms with him, though. Maybe he was the creator of Skinny Scoop who they kept in the basement, churning out vat after creamy, lucious vat of the kind of frozen dessert designed to make women feel indulgent and satisfied, yet safely free from elastic waist pants. God, if that were true, he would be the perfect man. My soulmate. Maybe I had been looking in all the wrong places.

I snapped out of my reverie as I approached my building. Who was I kidding with my ridiculous delusions of happily-ever-after with the Skinny Scoop man? Clearly I was losing it. The reality was not that I was some midnight seductress haunting a health-food shop. I was a slightly overplump, recently dumped ex-girlfriend, who was heading home alone, and in serious danger of eating an entire gallon of Skinny Scoop once I discovered my answering machine contained no messages from Max—or Derrick, either, for that matter.

Opening the front door with a heavy sigh, I came face-to-face with Beatrice, who had apparently just arrived home herself, her arms loaded with groceries as she attempted to get in the door to her apartment.

"Hello, there, my friend," she sang out at the sight of me.

"Hi, Beatrice, how are you?" I replied by rote.

"Oh, I'm all right, aside from the fact that my arthritis is acting up. Of all days, when I had to do my grocery shopping!" Then, her eyes lit up as an idea struck her. "Do you think you could help me in with these packages?"

Though I was reluctant to get any more involved with Beatrice than I had to, I went over and relieved her of a few of her bags, then followed her into her matchbox apartment.

At first glance, one might say her apartment resembled mine to a tee. But then I took in the walls, which were covered with brightly painted watercolors, many of them signed by Beatrice herself. Some of them were even quite remarkable, although others looked like the work of a child.

"Did you paint all of these, Beatrice?" I asked.

"Why, yes, when I was a much younger woman," she said, placing the bags on the table and turning to study the walls with me. "Now, I can barely see them," she said, squinting at them through her thick glasses.

"Well, they're quite beautiful," I said, looking at her with new interest and wondering if perhaps there was more to Beatrice than I had originally thought. Maybe she wasn't just some lonely old woman doomed to a life of despair. Maybe she was an artist, or at least a former artist. Suddenly I allowed myself to imagine her current solitude as the result of a conscious decision to devote herself to the ascetic life of an artist, rather than some tragic flicker of fate. As I looked at her now, I tried desperately to see beyond her brown teeth, her bad hair, her short, stout figure and discover the woman beneath. The artist in charge of her own destiny.

"Why, thank you, Emma," Beatrice said effusively. "Everyone at the rehabilitation center thought I had a good eye for color."

All my visions disappeared in the blink of an eye and Beatrice became...Beatrice again. A lonely old woman with very little social grace and a dubious sexual orientation.

And just as I was about to march off and leave Beatrice to her miserable little existence for my somewhat elevated one of the fourth floor, I saw her pull a large plastic tub out of one of the bags with a label that looked menacingly familiar:

Double Mocha Chip, I realized with sudden deep dismay. The low-calorie confection of the lonely. And the lovelorn.

Nine

"Never let him see you sweat—at least not until you've got
him in your bed."
—Jade Moreau, Über Single Girl

Confession: I have become the ex-girlfriend from hell.

Maybe it was my newfound and extremely uncomfortable asso-
ciation with Beatrice that made me do it. Maybe it was the message
from my father I came home to Thursday night, asking me if I had
found a lawyer—or, better yet, an attorney-husband—who might
represent him in his latest lawsuit and perhaps give him a few
grandkids. Maybe I was just so damn tired of waiting for Derrick
to call and apologize for moving in with a woman who could make
him happier than I ever could. Whatever it was, I did the unthinkable, at least according to Jade's Guide to Guy Hunting. I agreed
to meet with Max Van Gelder on a Friday night, despite the fact
that he waited until Thursday at 10:00 p.m. to ask.

Though I knew it made me seem desperate, dateless and otherwise dull to be so available, I wasn't thinking this when I came
home on Thursday from another unproductive day at the office. I'll
admit I was somewhat bloated after spending the previous evening
with a tub of Skinny Scoop and feeling as if there wasn't a male
in the universe who might even find me remotely attractive. Even
the construction workers who had been rebuilding the Union Square
Station for the past decade failed to acknowledge me with the usual
wink or smile as I passed by them on my way home.

Needless to say, when the phone rang at 10:00 p.m., I was desperately glad. And when I discovered Max Van Gelder on the other

end, I was so supremely happy, I would have agreed to meet him right then and there.

But of course I didn't tell him this as I sat across from him the following evening at a cozy little table at a pub called the Chelsea Square, my first in a very long line of tequila and ginger ale drinks in front of me. Instead I was thinking how incredibly handsome he looked in his baby-blue button-down shirt and jeans, and how glad I was that I had opted for jeans—topped with a clingy tank—and looked sufficiently casual and, I hoped, effortlessly sexy.

I will admit that even then, a small part of me still wondered how I had become so fortunate as to be sitting before a man who was articulate, well-read and utterly intimidating.

"Makes me think of Dickens," he was saying now, in response to my rather bland, silence-filling comment that I had never been to the Chelsea Square before.

I smiled weakly at this and took a good slug out of my tequila. After all, I was one of the few English majors who had managed to get through a B.A. *and* a masters degree without ever having opened Dickens, who bored me to tears when I was force-fed *Hard Times* in high school. I considered my successful avoidance a point of pride, but I wasn't going to mention that now that I was busy being Max's captive audience.

When he was through discussing the finer points of the pub's crowded, gloomy interior, I promptly changed the subject. "So did you finish that piece for *The New Yorker?*" I asked.

"Oh, yes. In fact that was one of the reasons I wasn't able to call sooner," he replied, matter-of-factly. "Deadlines, you know."

"Oh, I know," I said, with a roll of my eyes, another sip of my drink. He was drinking a Bombay martini, which I found quite impressive though I barely batted an eyelash as he ordered it.

"Yes, you mentioned you were a writer, but I don't think you had a chance to tell me what it was you were writing."

The moment of truth had arrived. And before I could even mentally prepare my self-deprecating speech about my job at *Bridal Best,* my mouth went off in another direction. "Actually, I'm working on a novel."

"Ah, kindred spirits," he said, his perfectly cute eyebrows raised.

This bit of encouragement gave me all the fuel I needed. Well, this and another healthy sip from my drink. "Yes, I've been working on it for some time now." All true, I rationalized. I had started a novel just after graduate school. Though since Derrick, the only thing I'd done was angst over the work I *hadn't* done on it.

Another sip of my drink brought a semitruth. "Actually, I've been kinda stuck on it for a while. Maybe it's writer's block." *Or maybe I've given up.* I smiled weakly. "Or maybe it's my space. You know, I've been thinking a new desk might just be the thing. I have a computer, but I really don't have a good place to sit comfortably and write."

He smiled. "Yes, well, when the need arises, I find I can write just about anywhere. I think one just has to find one's subject."

Feeling as if he had seen right through my thinly veiled excuses, I polished off my drink. Rallying myself, I realized I needed to turn attention back to him—and fast. "So what is your subject, if you don't mind my asking?"

"Well, it's a kind of coming-of-age novel. A young boy loses his father and has to find his way in the world."

This explanation irked me. Why was it men were always writing about young boys on the brink of manhood? As if anyone were really interested in the philosophical ponderings of the prepubescent. Still, I nodded in recognition of the genre. "Ah, a *bildüngsroman.* Fascinating."

His response was a wide smile that melted me all the way through to the lacy black bra I'd worn, just in case. "Well, first it looks like we need to get you another drink," he said, gesturing to my empty glass and then signaling the waiter.

As I glanced at his nearly full martini, I was embarrassed. "Gosh, I guess I was thirstier than I thought. You've barely made a dent—"

"A Bombay martini must be sipped if one expects to find one's way home. Don't worry about me, enjoy yourself."

And I did, finally relaxing over my second drink and listening as he spoke about the inspiration for his book, the death of his own father. By my third drink (his second), I was sufficiently lubed to admit to my day job, and began regaling him with tales of days spent penning what amounted to marriage manifestos. I even took potshots at Patricia. "Everyone in the office suspects the groom in her wedding photos is a cardboard cutout," I said to his amusement. I went on to describe the mania to get to the altar our editorial content seemed to fuel, and to make myself seem even more above it all, I described, to great hilarity, Rebecca's manic attempt to beat a wedding proposal out of her perfect boyfriend.

Max was not only amused, he was practically in tears of laughter when I was through. I would have said it was the martinis, but he'd ordered a beer on his second round.

"God, Emma," he said, finally getting control of himself again, "I'll bet you're a damn good writer. This is terrific material." Then, seeing my glass was once again empty, he signaled the waiter.

My head was swimming. "No, no, I don't think I can drink another."

"Are you sure?" he asked, then, "I'm going to have another beer."

It was all the encouragement I needed. After all, I hadn't felt this good in a long time. Max liked me. He thought I was funny. He imagined I was a damn good writer.

Pour me another one, I say.

So we had another, while I continued to be equally charming and, I hoped, utterly desirable. I batted my eyelashes. I swatted his forearm playfully. I made eye contact. And when we were done, he walked me home, his arm linked in mine. Maybe because he felt as warmly about me as I did about him. Or maybe because I started to weave the moment we hit the concrete.

When we finally reached my front door, that alcohol-induced warmth had already flowed into the pit of my stomach, making me liquid inside and aching with unquenched desire for this man who seemed to find me so captivating. I realized then that I was perfectly capable of sleeping with Max Van Gelder, and on the first date no less. Jade's warning voice all but drowned out by the flow of tequila in my veins, I looked up at him as we came to a stop, my eyes slumberous and, I hoped, suggestive.

He kissed me then. And not just a good-night peck, but an open-mouthed plunder. I would have characterized it as the action of a man with only one thing on his mind, had it not been for that hesitancy I felt in him, as if he were merely testing the waters.

Pulling back, he looked up at my building, as if seeking out my window, then gazed at me once more with a small smile. "I think it might be safest if we say good-night here."

Max. Precious Max, I thought in my hazy mind. Such a gentleman. The kind even Grandma Zizi would admire, I thought, realizing his height and good looks also met her other qualifications. Hell, he might even be rich. I smiled up at him, feeling something like love welling up inside me. Except we don't call it love, not this soon. Not until we are renting videos on Friday night and sharing a toothbrush on Saturday morning.

He smiled back. Then, removing my arms from around his neck gently, he clasped my two hands in his and held me away from him, his eyes studying me in a way that made me giddy, and slightly nervous.

Then he laughed, breaking the tension. And he spoke, breaking my bubble. "I still can't believe you drank four tequila drinks in—" he dropped my hands to look at his watch "—as many hours." He chuckled again, eyebrows raised.

Suddenly those four drinks lurched in my stomach, in serious danger of making a comeback, all over his soft leather loafers. I laughed uneasily as he stepped back and with the most gentle, most innocuous wave, said, "I'll call you."

I was certain, in that moment, that he never would.

As I stumbled up the steps to my apartment, my head fuzzy and my eyes burning with something that felt frighteningly like tears, I realized there was only one thing to do. And that thing was guided by a faint ache in my soul that alcohol only heightened, and the sight of my empty apartment made absolutely imperative.

I called Derrick. Don't ask me what I expected. I wasn't even sure myself. All I knew was that in the face of Max Van Gelder's apparent rejection, I felt an almost painful yearning to hear the voice of the man who once told me he loved me more than life itself.

As the phone rang in my ear, I consulted my watch: 12:20 a.m. New York time meant 9:20 p.m. California time. He could be home. He could be out. He could be having sex with his roommate. I quickly blotted out that last thought. That's one of the great gifts alcohol brings: denial.

"Hello?"

"Derrick!" I said, relief evident in my voice.

"Hey, Em, how are you?" he replied. I was certain that was warmth and happiness I heard in his voice. He was glad to hear from me. Maybe even jubilant.

"I'm good, good. How's everything with you?"

"Excellent, in fact. I'm just getting ready to go to a screening party for one of the studio's new films." He chuckled. "And this time I have an invitation, being an employee of the studio. My days of party-crashing are over."

"That sounds great," I said wistfully.

"So what are you up to? You must be just getting home from somewhere?"

"Um. Chelsea Square?"

"Oh, I used to love that place."

Must be a guy thing. "Yeah, it was okay."

"That's the one thing I really miss about being in New York. L.A. just doesn't have the same kind of cool old bars that you find everywhere in New York."

I bristled, then joked, "Oh, so that's the *one* thing you miss about NYC?" Fear filled me as I waited for his reply.

"And you, of course, Em," he said to my relief. "That goes without saying."

My heart trilled inside. *He loves me, he loves me, he loves me.*

"So who did you go out with?"

"Jade," I replied quickly, then realizing I could inflict my own torture, I added, "and a few of her model friends. Just some *guys* she did a shoot with."

"That's cool," he replied, clearly unfazed by the fact that I allegedly spent the evening surrounded by the most beautiful men NYC had to offer. "How is Jade doing?"

"She's fine. Alyssa's fine, too. Though Lulu isn't too good. Poor little thing needs surgery."

"Oh, no, really? God, I hope Lulu's all right. I loved that dog."

You did? Then why, oh why, did you leave Lulu? Why did you leave *me?* Swallowing my angst, I said, "I hope she'll be all right. Alyssa's pretty broken up about it."

"Well, give her a hug from me."

"I will." I felt so light suddenly. He cared about me. Even my friends. Hell, he cared about my friend's *dog.*

Then he went and ruined it all. "Listen, Em, I gotta run. Carrie should be home any minute. I'm supposed to be ready to go when she gets here, and I haven't even showered yet."

"Carrie? I thought you said *you* got the invite to this party."

"I did. But I asked Carrie to come with me," he replied innocently.

"But she's your *roommate,"* I insisted.

He laughed. "Yeah, and? Is there some kind of secret party law that says you can't take your *roommate* to a film-opening bash? I figured it would be a good opportunity for her to make contacts. She is an actress and—"

"Tell me the truth, Derrick."

"Truth?"

"You're sleeping with her, right?"

"What?"

"Okay, maybe you're not sleeping with her. Yet. But it's only a matter of time. A few dinners at home, a few parties. Next thing you know, you guys come home one night, tumble into bed. *Next* thing you know, you're downsizing to a one bedroom."

"Emma—"

"This is just like you, Derrick. Always doing whatever the fuck you want, no matter who you hurt. Well, I'm tired of it. I'm tired of everything."

He was silent on the other end, which only encouraged me to go on.

"How dare you walk away from me after two years and call me

up as if everything is fine between us?'' I said, a well of anger
rising in me that I had not known existed until now. ''Then you
have the nerve—the nerve!—to start fucking your roommate and
think this isn't going to bother me? Well, it does bother me, dammit. I know maybe *you* can tell someone you love them, and then
move three thousand miles away. But I can't. I said I loved you
and I still love you. You can't just change the rules on me. You
can't.''

As I paused to catch my breath, I realized he still hadn't said a
word. And it was starting to make me nervous.

''Aren't you going to say anything?''

He sighed. ''Maybe we shouldn't talk anymore.''

That made me really furious. ''Oh, here we go. Typical male
solution. Let's just not talk anymore. Why talk about anything?
Why even try to have a relationship?''

''We aren't *having* a relationship, Emma.''

I stopped dead in my tracks. He had me there. And the truth
coming out of his mouth stabbed painfully, right in the center of
my heart. ''I thought we were friends,'' I said weakly.

''Maybe we can't be friends. I don't know why I ever thought
we could. Hell, it amazes me we even lasted so long as a couple.
You're so damn...difficult, Emma. You can never just let things
be what they are.''

I was difficult? *I* couldn't let things be? ''Is that right?'' I asked
now, my anger bubbling again. ''If you're such a genius at relationships, why don't you fill me in on what exactly I'm supposed
to *let be?*''

''Us, Emma,'' he said in a lethal whisper. ''Let *us* be. We're
over, dammit. Over!'' he yelled in my ear.

I was stunned into silence by his words. And suddenly, achingly,
sober.

''Look, Emma,'' he said, his voice softer. ''The last thing I want
to do is hurt you. Maybe it was wrong of me to think we could be
friends right away. Maybe we need a time-out. To...to cool off.''

My throat clogged as I realized what he was suggesting. I
couldn't imagine not talking to Derrick. Not hearing his voice. ''I
don't think that's a good—''

"Stop thinking so much, Emma. That's your problem. You think too damn much. About everything."

"Sorry, I hadn't realized I was such a *problem*," I replied, taking comfort in anger once more.

He sighed again. "We are going to get nowhere with this. Listen, let's just take a break, okay? Let's just agree we won't talk for, say, a month."

A month? My insides quaked, but I rallied behind my anger. "A *month?*"

"It's not such a long time."

I was furious now. Furious and sad that he was so over me he could go an entire month without even hearing my voice. Without knowing whether I was dead or alive. Still, my temper caused me to drive in the final stake, knowing, even as I did, it would ultimately destroy me. "I don't think a month is long enough!"

And with that, I slammed down the phone and finally, *finally,* allowed myself to cry.

Confession: The truth has set me free: I am truly dumped now.

Something broke inside of me. I wasn't sure if I needed whatever it was, but I certainly felt freed from a burden I had not even realized I carried. I woke up Saturday morning, and my first thought was that I was alone. Completely, utterly alone. My second thought was that I didn't have time to dwell on it. I had things to do.

I spent the day in front of my computer. I didn't just sit there, I wrote. I shut off the ringer on my phone and just wrote. And within a few hours, I had composed what I believed to be the strongest and best and most innovative proposal for *Bridal Best* that I had done in my whole career there. I waxed poetic on the choices facing older single women, I belted out ideas for articles. I was brilliant.

When I went to work on Monday, dressed appropriately in my black blazer and matching trousers, which suddenly felt like a power suit, I confidently handed my freshly printed pages to Patricia's admin, Nancy, who eyed me with surprise. Then I marched over to Rebecca's cubicle to gloat, only to discover a note proclaiming her out sick.

Poor baby, I thought sarcastically. She was probably home polishing up her new engagement ring, hoping to blind us all with its
glare when she came in tomorrow. Well, she wouldn't find me
hovering over her, exclaiming with the rest of the staff about its
large size and glowing brilliance. I couldn't care less.

And as I worked out at the gym that night with Alyssa, I even
acted blasé about her upcoming and long-anticipated fling with Dr.
Jason Carruthers. Suddenly I was a strong advocate of her taking
what she needed and not worrying about the consequences. I mean,
really, what was she waiting for? The big wedding? Who wanted
to be tied down anyway? I asked as I heaved weights into the air
with more fervor than usual.

When she eyed me suspiciously, I finally confessed that I'd had
an eye-opening exchange with Derrick the night before. I could tell
Alyssa felt vindicated. "See, I told you you were angry," she said.
But she still looked at me worriedly when I suggested she call in
advance to book the hotel room for her and Jason's rendezvous.

On Tuesday I had drinks with Jade at Bar Six, served to us
compliments of Enrico, who was working that night, probably
harder than he ever had, in order to keep our glasses no less than
half full and us completely happy. Jade, of course, was quite
pleased with my new attitude, and we spent the evening taking great
delight in ogling any unsuspecting male who sidled too close to us
whenever Enrico disappeared to handle another table. We laughed.
We smoked—yes, I even allowed myself one mind-tingling, breath-
stealing cigarette—and we sat back in our chairs, our bare legs
crossed lazily and alluringly in front of us, feeling like two women
too wise in the ways of the world to be taken for granted by some
man.

By Thursday, things started to fall apart.

First, Caroline called me into her office as soon as I got in to
work, and in her usual pleasant manner, informed me Patricia had
read my proposal and had passed it on to her for review. "As your
manager, she thought I should have a look at it," she said with a
somewhat uneasy smile.

Then, in a more careful tone, she asked, "Is everything okay,
Emma?"

"Everything's fine," I replied confidently.

"In your personal life?" she coaxed.

I frowned. "My life is…great. Why wouldn't it be?"

"Good," she said, sitting back in her chair and looking somewhat relieved, yet still uneasy. "Well, I have to say after reading your proposal for the new issue, I was a bit concerned."

"About?"

"Well, Emma. I don't know how to say this, but—" She paused, biting her bottom lip. "You've written what amounts to…to an antimarriage manifesto."

My eyes widened and I opened my mouth to defend myself, but for some reason, nothing came out.

"Look, I understand if this project got away from you for…for whatever reason. But this proposal is just…unacceptable. There is no way *Bridal Best* could do an issue with articles like—" and she began flipping through the proposal, scanning the pages "—'Understanding Your Man: When I Do is Not the Right Answer.' Or—" she flipped another page "—'Life Beyond the Altar—You Don't Have to Marry to Have it All.'"

Though fear had begun to invade my senses, I rallied. "Well, I had thought since *Bridal Best* is devoted to the *whole* woman, we might explore a woman's options outside of marriage. I mean, the more I thought about this, the more I realized that if a woman waits long enough to marry, she might come to realize that marriage isn't the only—or even the best—answer." There, now I had her.

But Caroline's face only creased further with her concern. "Emma, I understand what you are saying, and you may, in fact, have an excellent point." She paused. "But *Bridal Best* is a *wedding planning* magazine." She smiled, as if trying to get me to see the humor of it all. "I mean, really, Emma, where would we be—where would our advertisers be, for that matter—if we started preaching that women shouldn't get married? I don't imagine we'd sell a lot of wedding cake, now would we?"

She had a point. An extremely major point that somehow, in my surge of creative expression and newfound single-girl freedom, I had completely forgotten. I was mortified. What the *hell* had I been thinking?

"I...I guess I *was* a little...distracted when I...I put the proposal together."

Then Caroline, in her warm and forgiving way, smiled. "Don't worry about it, Emma." She handed me back my proposal. "Why don't you give it another shot now that you've gained some... perspective. Let's see what you can come up with."

I nodded weakly, taking the proposal from her in one boneless hand and rising to leave. "Thanks, Caroline. I...I'll see what I can do."

Back at my desk, as I sat pondering how I had managed to make such an utter fool out of myself to everyone who was anyone at *Bridal Best,* Rebecca showed up at my cubicle. She was the last person I expected to see, as she had been out sick for the past three days, and I was fairly shocked when I saw her face, which was red and blotchy and masked in what looked like Calamine lotion. "Are you all right?" I asked, stunned by how unattractive she looked.

"I need to talk to you. Drinks tonight?"

"Sure," I muttered, curious. Then, with a glance down at Rebecca's ringless left hand, I knew this little outing wasn't going to be pretty.

We went to Rio Grande, sitting outside so Rebecca could keep her sunglasses on and cover most of the puffy madness of her face. She told me on the way over it was poison ivy, though she refrained from any further explanation until we were seated across from one another, margaritas in front of us.

"So tell me how the hell you managed to get poison ivy in the middle of New York City," I said.

"I didn't get this in New York City," she said, looking at me as if I were some kind of dimwit. "Nash and I drove upstate on Saturday morning. Turns out he couldn't get a reservation at Le Colonial for my birthday, and he had a little surprise planned for me up there instead." She took a healthy sip of her margarita. "Boy, did he ever."

I cringed inwardly when I realized I hadn't even wished her a happy birthday, then figured that judging by the look on her face, she wasn't in the mood for any sort of merriment.

"So I'm imagining a cozy cabin. Moonlit strolls. Plenty of opportunities for him to pop the question,'' Rebecca continued, her face a mask that hid whatever emotions she was feeling. ''I mean, I had certainly dropped enough hints that I wanted to be engaged by my twenty-ninth birthday!''

I nodded my head encouragingly, and neglected to point out that, at thirty-one, I was far from engaged.

''So we are driving through this wooded area in the Berkshires. Absolutely beautiful. I'm looking everywhere for that cozy cabin, when Nash turns onto a dirt road with a sign that says ''Lakeview Campgrounds.''

''Oh, I went there as a kid!'' I exclaimed.

This information did not impress her. ''Apparently so did Nash. With his dad. Seems he was trying to relive some boyhood memories. Don't ask me why he thought this would be the perfect thing to do on *my* birthday.''

''You know guys. They always seem to think that we're going to adore their fantasies. I think it's a defect of the male brain.'' Then I laughed. ''Did I ever tell you that Derrick brought me to a *batting range* for our one-year anniversary?''

''Yeah, well, I was trying to be a good sport. Tried not to shudder when he pulled out the tent and gleefully asked me to help him set it up. After all, in my mind, I was getting engaged.'' She shrugged. ''I figured it would make a good story to tell our children someday.''

I nodded, trying to imagine Rebecca, with her manicured hands and careful bob, as a mother. Somehow the Calamine dotting her face was helping me conjure something up, but it was an image far from maternal.

''So we get the tent up, and while he's merrily puttering around the campsite, I decide to walk down by the lake and take a shower.''

''Oh, didn't you love those outdoor showers—with the view of the mountains—'' I stopped at the sight of her raised eyebrows. Apparently not.

''When I come back about an hour or so later, Nash suggests we take a walk. And he's got this silly little grin on his face that tells me he's up to something, right?'' She shook her head and took a fortifying sip of her drink. "Oh, he was up to something all right. But not what I was expecting."

I leaned in close, completely drawn in.

"He takes me on this little nature walk through the woods. And we're walking along for about twenty minutes when suddenly before us is this perfectly wrapped gift, sitting on a stump."

I raised my eyebrows. "Was it...?"

She shook her head. "No, it wasn't. In fact, one of the first things I noticed was that it was way too big to be an engagement ring." She held up her hands about twelve inches apart. "It was about the size of a kitchen appliance. Which is *exactly* what it was." She shuddered. "A Cuisinart. He bought me a fucking Cuisinart."

"I don't get it. The whole walk through the woods, what was he trying to do?"

"Apparently it was something his dad used to do for Nash's birthday when they went camping together. He'd run off into the woods in secret and plant a gift for Nash. Then he'd act all surprised when they came across it, as if he had no idea how it had gotten there, but he was certain it belonged to Nash." She rolled her eyes. "It was some sort of game with them." She sighed. "I suppose I can't blame him. His dad died a year ago, and this is really Nash's first summer without him. I guess he wanted to somehow bring back the memory. But a *Cuisinart!*" All sympathy that had flickered briefly on her face dissolved into anger and disbelief.

"A kitchen appliance is a significant gift," I said. "It shows he thinks of you in a domestic way. A...a wifely way."

"Yeah, well, I would have been more confident of that if there had been a ring on that tree stump, and I told him so, right then and there."

"You *did?*" I replied, aghast. Rebecca wasn't one to mince words, I was discovering, especially on the marriage issue.

"I did," she said, then downed the rest of her drink. "I was so damn mad, I even took that damn Cuisinart and fired it into the bushes!" She laughed mirthlessly. "All that got me was this horrible poison ivy." She sighed, then explained, "He looked so hurt after I sent that Cuisinart sailing, I felt bad, so I waded through the brush to find it and walked right into this...this plague! Now I wonder why I even bothered. How dare *he* act all hurt! As if *I* had somehow missed the point of the whole weekend. I mean, we've been together two years, for chrissakes!''

I smiled sadly. Two years. It really didn't mean anything in the whole scheme of things. After all, Derrick and I had been together two years. And maybe I had a few more two-year relationships in my future. The thought depressed me.

"I'm not getting any younger," Rebecca said. "Now that I'm starting to meet some of my career goals..." She paused, as if realizing how this might sound to me, then blundered on. "I want to get started on some of my other goals. Like marriage. A family."

The little life plan she laid out made me painfully aware of how behind I was on all of my own goals. I sighed and almost—*almost*—confessed to the recent demise of my relationship with Derrick. But then I felt a ball of emotion gathering in my throat and stopped myself. I was too vulnerable after that last damning phone call. I would probably start bawling. And the last thing I wanted to do was cry in front of Rebecca. Especially when I heard her next words.

"Well, now that Nash finally has a clue about what *should* be happening with us," Rebecca continued, "I expect he'll start shopping for a ring." Then she frowned. "Maybe I should leave more of those photos of engagement rings I borrowed from the magazine around again. I mean, he clearly didn't notice them the first time. After all, I wouldn't want him getting me a ring I didn't like—like one of those horrible heart-shaped diamonds. I mean, there are some things I just won't wear. Not even for love."

"I suppose," I said, but I could no longer focus on the conversation. My mind had moved on to contemplate Derrick and all he hadn't done for me. Not even for love.

Confession: My self-image has become painfully dependent on the sight of the blinking red light on my answering machine.

The weekend came without one message from anyone of the male persuasion, not even my father, whom I couldn't bring myself to call back. Of course, Derrick wouldn't call. He could always be counted on to stick to his promises, and if he said he wasn't going to call, I was pretty damn sure he wouldn't. As predicted, Max didn't call, either. Though I told myself I expected him to blow me off, his rejection still stung. What was so wrong with me? I wondered as I shored myself against another Saturday night at home. I had already called Alyssa, mostly to check in on Lulu, who'd had a successful surgery last Thursday was already recovering at home, but also because I felt the pinch of loneliness. After reporting that Lulu was fine, only a bit sore and uncomfortable, Alyssa declared that she and Richard were staying in to tend to her that night. "You can come over if you want," she added as an afterthought, but I was too depressed even to contemplate spending an evening with Alyssa and Richard. Besides, Lulu didn't need my negativity while she was trying to recover.

I called Jade, too, only to discover she and Enrico were going out dancing. Of course, I was invited to come along, but the thought of shaking myself nonsensically on a dance floor, especially after I had just stuffed myself full of the last of the Skinny Scoop, did not appeal to me at all.

So here I was, alone again on Saturday night. I tried to turn it into a positive. With the thought that I might get some work done, I opened up my computer. And as I sat there trying to figure out how to make my disastrous proposal for the Older Bride Issue more wedding-friendly, I resorted to an old procrastination technique of mine that I used whenever I wanted to avoid writing. I started scanning through some of my old files, starting with one I had simply titled Notes. I discovered, with surprise, that it was actually a very tentative beginning to that novel I once thought I'd write. As the title of the file indicated, it was mostly scraps of information on characters the book might contain, scenes I imagined would work. As I skimmed through, I came to a section where I had actually started to flesh out a scene. It was only a few paragraphs about a woman who was sitting before her mirror, making up her face before she went out. But as I read it, I was drawn in. And when I got to the end of the final paragraph, the strangest thing happened. I began to type, filling in the rest of the scene. What she wore, where she was going. Before I knew it, I had written three pages.

Feeling inordinately pleased with myself, I shut my computer and took a soothing bath. By the time I closed my eyes to go to sleep that night, I felt a satisfaction I hadn't known since graduate school, when I finished the collection of short stories for my master's thesis. I was writing again. Really writing. It was as if I was starting over as the person I most wanted to be.

Confession: Okay, okay—I wasn't totally content. Not until the phone rang...

Like a sign from God that I was finally on the way to my new life, the phone rang Sunday night, breaking the silence I had spent a good portion of the weekend in. I had done some more writing and, I will admit, quite a bit more cleaning. Since I was in the midst of carefully going over the five pages I had eked out, I decided not to answer, letting the machine pick up.

At the sound of Max Van Gelder's voice, I froze.

"Emma? It's Max. Remember me?" Chuckle. "Sorry I haven't been in touch. Got this last-minute assignment I couldn't turn down. *Rolling Stone Magazine.*" Another chuckle, this one sounding a bit smug.

Well, la-dee-da, I thought, though my insides were racing with excitement.

"Anyway, I wondered if you wanted to get together this week. Give me a call. My number is 555-7684. Hope to hear from you. Take care."

Shell-shocked, I immediately got up from my computer and began a little jig. He called! Max Van Gelder called!

Unwilling to celebrate this victory alone—and wanting to keep myself from immediately dialing his number—I called Jade.

"Hello?" she answered in a throaty voice.

"Are you sleeping?" I asked in disbelief. It was only eight-thirty.

"No, no. Just resting. Enrico left about an hour ago and I'm exhausted,'' she replied, the satisfaction of a well-pleasured woman in her voice.

"He called," I burst out.

"Who called?"

"Max. Max Van Gelder. The writer I met at the *Bone* party we went to?"

"Took him long enough. What did he say?"

"He's been on deadline—got a last-minute assignment from *Rolling Stone.*"

"Hmm," she said, her tone indicating that she was vaguely impressed. "So what did he want?"

"He wants to get together!" I replied, refusing to let her dampen my spirits.

"Huh. So he calls on a Sunday night? He's gonna need some training. You didn't make plans yet, did you?"

"Plans? No, no. He left a message. I have his *number.*"

"Don't call him back—"

"Jade!"

"I don't mean *ever,* I just mean don't call him back right away. Make him wait. He made *you* wait."

Waiting, I knew, was going to be a lot harder on me. "How long?"

"At least until Wednesday. Then you can make plans for the weekend."

"He said this week. He wants to get together this week—"

"Emma, listen to me, honey. We're not talking about what *he* wants. You start giving in to that from date two and you're finished. Make him jump through a few hoops."

She was right, I realized. I needed to get a grip. It was just that I had been so sure I would never hear from him again, the sound of his voice had thrown me into a state of temporary insanity. Now that I had regained some measure of control, I said, "You know what the strangest part of this is? He called right while I was in the middle of...of...writing. It's like it was a sign or something. I mean, he's a writer. I want to be a writer."

"You *are* a writer, Emma."

"Yeah, well, to be honest I haven't been doing a whole lot of writing lately. Outside of *Bridal Best* anyway."

"Doesn't mean anything. Just because a musician isn't in a band doesn't mean he can't play the guitar."

"When did you turn into the philosopher?"

"Good sex will do that to a woman. You'll see."

"It's not like I haven't had good sex, Jade. Derrick and I—"

"Oh, no, *no*. Let's not go there. Derrick and you are *over*."

"Okay, okay."

"Don't yes me. Now, do you have any good underwear? If not, you need to hit Victoria's Secret this week."

"It's not like I'm going to sleep with him on the second date—"

"You never know. Besides, I'm thinking it might do you a world of good. Remember, sex is—"

"—the single girl's Prozac. I know. I know." But the thought of sleeping with Max—of sleeping with anyone other than Derrick—was utterly frightening all of sudden. And absolutely thrilling. "I better hit the gym this week."

"That's fine, but do it for *you*. You don't *need* it. You look great."

"When was the last time you saw me naked?" I replied, running my hand over my abdomen.

"I don't need to see you naked to know you're in good shape. I'm a clothes stylist, remember?"

I smiled. Maybe I *was* beautiful. I certainly felt it at the moment, with Max's message still blinking on my machine and the thought of returning his call churning my stomach with anticipation. "Thanks for the vote of confidence, Jade."

"Yeah, well. What are friends for?"

Confession: I am suddenly boy crazy. And I barely have a boy in my life.

Monday afternoon at work, after I had banged out version two of my proposal and proofed it three times, I handed it in to Patricia. I wasn't totally sure it was now what my editor-in-chief was looking for, but I felt a sudden strange indifference. It wasn't my novel after all. My novel. The one I had worked on over the weekend. The one I would casually drop into my next conversation with Max, whenever I decided to call him back. After all, he was a writer. He would understand.

I called Alyssa when I got home, to check on Lulu's progress and to keep myself from calling Max back too soon. Plus, since Lulu had made it safely through her surgery, I had to keep a careful eye on Alyssa. Now that I had regained my sanity, I wanted to take back all the encouragement I had given her on sleeping with Jason. And I had reason to worry on that count. When I had tried her at the office earlier today, I'd learned she'd taken the day off—allegedly to run Lulu into the vet. I tried to contain my panic, so as not to alarm her secretary, but I was worried. Even more so since I hadn't heard back from Lys all day.

Her voice was exuberant as she breathed a cheery hello into my ear.

"What's going on?" I asked, hoping she wasn't in some kind of pheromone high after spending the afternoon with Dr. Jason Carruthers.

"I'm in love," she declared.

Oh God. It was worse than I thought.

"And I have you to thank, Emma. I am so glad I waited until after Lulu's surgery before I—I…you know…"

"Alyssa," I began to protest, "obviously, you're feeling vulnerable after the surgery. You *can't* be in love with Jason—"

She laughed. "Emma, it's not Jason I'm in love with, it's Richard!"

My heart leaped with hope. "Okay, back up. Start from the beginning."

"Well, you know Lulu came home Saturday to recover."

"Yeah, how is she doing?"

"Oh, she's fine. Better than ever."

"Good," I said, then waited for her to go on with whatever revelation had occurred that had knocked the sense back into her.

"She was really uncomfortable all day Saturday, so Richard and decided to give her some of the painkillers Jason prescribed to her sleep that night."

"Uh-huh."

"We crashed about eleven on Saturday night. We were both exhausted after caring for Lulu all day, and she seemed to be resting comfortably, so we figured it was okay for us to go to bed."

"Right," I said, still wondering where the in-love part came in.

"About one-thirty in the morning, Richard jumps out of bed. Turns out, he heard a strange noise coming from the kitchen, where we had set up Lulu's bed."

"Was she all right?"

"No, she was vomiting uncontrollably. And every time Richard and I tried to help her or comfort her, she just whined and threw up again. I was never so scared in my life."

"So what did you do?"

"What else could I do? I called Jason."

"And?" Suddenly I was envisioning Jason in Alyssa and Richard's living room at 2:00 a.m., poised to save Lulu's life and carry off Alyssa.

"He wasn't around. I got his answering service."

Aha. So Mr. Wonderful had finally shown his true colors. "Is that right?"

"He called back within the hour, but by then Lulu had stopped vomiting, though she was very weak."

"Did he come by?"

"No. Turns out he had gone out to Fire Island for the weekend and there was no way he could get back to the city until Sunday, what with the ferry schedule and all. He just advised us to keep fluids in Lulu, to keep her from dehydrating. So that's what Richard and I did. We sat up with Lulu all night, taking turns feeding her water from an eyedropper, which is the only method we could find to get water into her. And we comforted her. And each other. Emma, I never realized how much Richard really cared about Lulu. About me. We just held each other through the night and talked. Really talked. It was…beautiful."

My eyes misted over and a lump thickened in my throat. "That's wonderful, Alyssa."

"And get this," she continued. "I took Lulu in to see Jason

today. Apparently she had had an allergic reaction to the painkillers
he prescribed!''

"The bastard."

"It's not Jason's fault. How could he have known she was allergic? She had no history."

"Still, he might have done some tests...."

"Emma, I'm very grateful to Jason. Especially since he also gave
me the news today that the biopsy on Lulu's cyst showed it's benign."

"That's wonderful!"

"I know. I was so happy, I gave Jason a big hug. And the best
part is, I didn't feel a smidgen of attraction for him anymore. Can
you believe it?"

"Yes, I can," I said, disavowing all images that suddenly came
to mind of Dr. Jason Carruthers and his blatant sensuality. I was
so damn happy Alyssa and Richard had found each other again.

"You know, I'm even considering going homeopathic next
time," she continued. "Natural remedies might be easier on Lulu's
system. There's a vet in the East Village who specializes in holistic
treatment. I've been doing some reading, and I'm starting to realize
that Jason might not be as up-to-date as I thought he was."

I smiled. One thing was certain: No matter what happened with
Lulu, I knew Alyssa and Richard had passed a test that showed
they would withstand anything together. Forever.

"I've got to go," she said now. "Richard is cooking *me* dinner
tonight, and from the sound of clanging pots in the kitchen, he
might need some help."

We hung up a few minutes later, and I was filled with hope once
more. I had known Alyssa and Richard were Meant-To-Be. I had
felt it in my bones, and I had been right. And now, as my thoughts
turned to Max, I felt an odd tingling inside that filled me with
anticipation, and with hope. Maybe my intuition was telling me he
just might be The One for me.

Ten

"Love is a sweet hell only the truly courageous can escape."
—Bart Freely, director, *The Lone Lover*

Confession: My body has been taken over by a brave new woman: the Über Single Girl.

With all these good vibes in the air, I couldn't hold out much longer on Max. By Tuesday night, there was no stopping the inevitable. I called him. I couldn't help myself. And at the sound of his happy voice on the other end of the line, I knew I had done the right thing.

"Emma! Good to hear from you. How's everything?"

"Wonderful. Yourself?"

"Great, great. Sorry I took so long to get back to you. I—"

"Long? I hadn't noticed. Been so busy and all," I fibbed. "Working on a proposal for a special issue of the magazine. Writing a novel. You know how it is."

"Oh, I do," he said with a chuckle. "So, you up for a little entertainment?"

"Depends on what you have in mind," I replied, though I knew in my heart even if he suggested watching football with a roomful of his beer-swilling fraternity brothers, I'd go.

"Well, the new Bart Freely movie is opening this weekend—*The Lone Lover?* Freely's one of my favorite directors."

A shiver went through me. Bart Freely was Derrick's favorite director, too. But this thought was erased by Max's next words.

"It's playing at the Beekman Theater, right by my apartment. Thought you might want to try the Upper East Side for a change.

Besides, the Beekman is a great old theater and it's been renovated recently.''

He was inviting me into his 'hood. My antennae were raised. *He wants to show me his world. Maybe even...his apartment.* Gulp. "That sounds like fun," I replied, as if the sexual implications of his suggestion didn't even faze me.

"I could pick you up at your apartment, if you want..." he started.

Amazed and flattered that he would suggest something so insanely chivalrous as coming all the way downtown to pick me up for a movie all the way uptown, I quickly replied, "Oh, that's not necessary. How about I meet you at the theater?"

"Great. Great," he replied, relief evident in his voice. "There's a nine-fifteen show. Maybe we can meet there about eight-thirty? You know how crazy it is getting seats on a Friday night."

"Oh, yeah," I said, remembering how anal Derrick had been about getting to the movies early to insure himself a center-screen, midtheater view that hopefully wouldn't be impeded by some pituitary case. Since I had already lived with this particular neurosis for two years, I knew I could handle it. "That's fine."

"Then it's settled. See you at eight-thirty on Friday."

"See you then," I replied.

Then he added, "I'm really looking forward to it, Emma."

"Me, too." I replied. And I was. If I didn't have an anxiety attack due to sheer nervous anticipation.

Confession: I finally understand why sex is a four-letter word.

"You don't *have* to sleep with him, Emma, just because you're in his neighborhood," Jade said when I called her later that night to tell her about my big date plans.

"I know *that,*" I replied, though I had already mentally picked out my whole outfit, right down to my black lacy underwear.

"In fact, I changed my mind. I don't think you should sleep with him just yet," she said.

"Look's who's advocating celibacy!"

"Yeah, well, I don't like how he's maneuvering things. You

need to keep him reminded of who is in charge. If you don't sleep with him, he'll realize he can't run things his way. Believe me, they will always *try* to run things their way. Even Enrico, dewy youth that he is, likes to think he's the one running the show. I humor him sometimes, only to keep the peace. But I'm really the one calling the shots."

"So I gather you and Enrico are going strong?"

"Going strong?" she said defensively. "We're not *going* anywhere. We are having sex."

"Okay, okay. No need to get so touchy."

"Who's touchy? I'm just tired of reminding everyone, including him, that we are *not* having a relationship. We are having sex. Amazing sex, I might add. In fact, the other night, I'm getting ready to go out and he's waiting for me in the living room. Or so I thought. Next thing you know, he's in the bathroom with me as I'm putting on my lipstick, yanking my skirt up and shoving me against the mirror." She sighed at the memory. "He took me right there on the bathroom sink. All my hair products and cosmetics flying everywhere with one swipe of his beefy forearm. Totally fucking amazing."

I tried to picture Max and me having a wild moment of passion in my bathroom. Then I realized the sink was a little too close to the toilet in that tiny space to make it anything but a rather awkward affair. I tried to picture Max naked, and it wasn't a bad image. It was so good, in fact, I had to force myself to refocus once more on the conversation at hand. "Good sex is important to a relationship—not that you're having a relationship," I added quickly before driving my real point home. "It's too bad Enrico isn't a little older. And more your type. You guys might have something."

Jade sighed. "That's the problem with you, Emma. You're always thinking a man and a woman together has to equal happily-ever-after."

"I do not!" I said, suddenly defensive. "I was just thinking how nice it could be. Me and Max. You and Enrico. Alyssa and Richard."

"You're assuming way too much there, Emma. I mean, even Alyssa and Richard aren't sure where they're going...."

"Oh, yes they are," I replied happily, then proceeded to fill her in on all the heartwarming details of Alyssa and Richard's reunion.

By the end, I could tell she was pleased for them. How could she not be? I knew Jade saw Alyssa and Richard as soulmates, just as I always did. Of course, she couldn't help but turn the tide of the conversation from warm and fuzzy coupledom back to sexually adventurous femaledom before we hung up.

"Does this mean that Dr. Doggie is free?" she asked.

"You are insufferable," I replied.

"That's why you love me," she said.

"It's true. What would I have done after Derrick without you to remind me of all the other fish in the sea?"

"You mean vermin in the basement, don't you?" she replied. "This is New York City, after all."

"Jade!" Her sexually adventurous side I could accept. It was her cynicism I worried about.

Confession: Cynicism might be my only protection right now.

Friday night came way too fast for my taste. I only had time for one gym session, and even that was somewhat halfhearted, as Alyssa and I spent most of it dawdling in the steam room and talking about her and Richard's relationship revival. A surprise bouquet of roses sent to her office on Monday. A full body massage when she got home on Tuesday. He'd even shut off the Yankees game last night so they could spend some quality time together. All this plus Lulu was back to her perky self again. I was amazed at how far a little personal trauma could take a relationship.

I had also barely had time to recover from two jarring bits of news I received during the week. On Wednesday I learned my proposal for the Older Bride issue had ultimately been nixed by Patricia. Though Caroline did suggest, in her usual soothing tone, that I could do an *article* on the older bride for Rebecca's special issue on second marriages, I didn't respond warmly to the idea. Especially since Rebecca, Marcy Keller and anyone I happened to strike up a conversation with at the office these days couldn't help but inform me how beautifully Rebecca's special issue was coming along.

The second bit of news, which I received via voice mail on Thursday, was considerably more disturbing. My father's wife, Deirdre, had called me at the office, and finding me away from my desk, left three menacing words after the beep for me to return to: "He's drinking again." Then, in a voice somewhat more resigned, "Call me when you get a chance."

I will confess up-front that I did not call back right away. I couldn't go there, couldn't descend into my family's particular brand of madness while I was trying so hard to make my life resemble something normal, if not fairytalelike. It wasn't as if I could do anything anyway. I'd had such messages before over the course of the past few years. I knew the drill. Three or four days of drinking, lack of appetite and sleeplessness. Two days where he attempted to sober up. One day of helplessness and self-pity. Then, if things got really bad, rehab.

I just wasn't ready to deal with it.

So I avoided it for the time being. Even managed to mercifully blot it out of my mind completely as I blew out my hair on Friday night and slid on my best pair of jeans. After throwing on my slides and a sleeveless, funky orange T-shirt that Jade had discovered at a sample sale and given to me after having worn it only once, I was ready to face my date with Max Van Gelder. As ready as I would ever be, anyway.

Max was waiting in front of the theater when I arrived, much to my satisfaction. Jade had advised lateness, and though it was a struggle for me, I managed to make myself a full five minutes behind our scheduled meeting time. "Hey," I said, as I approached.

"Hey, yourself," he said, his eyes roaming over me. Then he kissed me, hard and fast, on the lips.

Well, I thought. Things were certainly getting off to an... *interesting* start. That kiss felt awfully like the kind of casually intimate kiss one received from a...a boyfriend.

Then he grinned at me. "You look great."

More points for Max. "Thanks. You're not so bad yourself," I replied.

Another smile, while his eyes studied mine for a few moments, almost as if he were measuring something. It made me vaguely nervous, but in a shivery, exciting way.

"Want to go in and find seats? I already got us tickets," he said, taking my hand.

He led me into the theater, and I thrilled at the way we must look together, he in dark denim with a groovy camouflage T-shirt, me in matching denim and funky orange. We looked more the part of the hip New York couple than Derrick and I ever had, I realized with satisfaction. After all, Derrick was from *New Jersey.* And there was no hiding that fact, no matter how many black turtlenecks you owned.

But then my brand-spanking new beau did a perfectly Derrick thing: He started obsessing over the seating arrangements.

First, he buzzed me past the snack bar, muttering something about finding seats first before the crowds got there. Then, once he opened the door to the theater, I saw him survey the room. "Okay, looks like some strong possibilities in the center aisles still, though some of them may be too close to the screen. Wait—" With a firm hand to my back, he escorted me to an aisle that was completely filled, except for two seats which still remained empty midrow. "Can you excuse us?" he said to the burly guy on the end, who looked down the row first, almost in disbelief that there were still any seats left. After we plowed through the left half of the row and took our coveted position, Max sat down carefully, inspecting his view from every angle, even slumping down a little bit to see if the somewhat short person in front of us might obstruct his view at any angle other than the straight back position. Once through with his routine, he turned to smile at me. "Perfect," he whispered. "How are you? Comfortable?"

"I'm fine," I said, smiling dumbly at him, amazed at how similar he suddenly seemed to Derrick. It was almost as if I were experiencing déjà vu. Were all men like this? Maybe it was just a New York thing. Overcrowded theaters and all.

"Want anything from the snack bar?" he said.

"Uh..." I gazed at the row of people to our right, hoping he would choose to disturb *them* this time, rather than push past Burly

Guy and his group of disgruntled friends once more. "Okay. A Diet Coke?"

"Sure. And I'll get us some popcorn." With that, he made his way down the right half of the row, thank God, leaving me to openly gaze upon his beautiful posterior. I sighed. Suddenly the night felt full of promise once more.

Max came back about fifteen minutes later, gallantly juggling two sodas and a giant vat of popcorn. Once settled in beside me, he handed over a soda and gave me another one of his toe-curling smiles. "I've been waiting all week to see this movie," he said, then positioned the popcorn strategically between us as the lights dimmed and the first preview lit up the screen. After a few barbs passed back and forth concerning the ridiculous quality of the three movies previewed, we settled into silence as the opening credits rolled. Judging from what I remembered about Derrick's movie fanaticism, I knew a word uttered during the feature film could be damning when on a date with a true film buff, so I kept my mouth shut.

During the course of the movie, which followed the life of a young urbanite torn between his love for his impossible neighbor and the woman he has lived with for seven years, I became painfully aware of two things. First, that Bart Freely, director extraordiniare according to Derrick and Max, seemed to structure all his films around the utter impossibility of two people ever finding each other on any sort of emotional level. And second, that there seemed to be a somewhat jarring amount of physical space between Max and me for the entire duration of the movie. His eyes were forward, knees a careful yet relaxed distance from mine, his arm embracing the popcorn like a lover. Plus, he took over my armrest, as did the other male movie-goer to my right, leaving me with no other option but to keep my hands folded on my lap. We weren't even touching shoulders. It was as if I were at the movies by myself, so cut off from him was I.

By the time we got to the final scene in the movie, which closed on a shot of our young hipster hero reading Nietzsche in a dimly lit restaurant mere weeks after having been thrown out by his live-in and abandoned by his lover, and looking incredibly content in his solitude, a strange, ominous feeling began to pervade my system. I risked a glance at Max, who was completely engrossed in the movie, his handsome features highlighted by the flickering screen. It was as if he had completely forgotten I was there.

This felt suspiciously like a bad sign, though I couldn't—or wouldn't—put my finger on why. Instead I closed the distance between us by grabbing his hand as the credits rolled up.

And when he flashed me that killer smile, all my fears faded away.

"What did you think?" I asked, gazing up at him.

"Ecstasy. Sheer filmmaking ecstasy. Freely never disappoints. I mean, how he manages to convey the beautiful, yet painfully nihilistic quality of human relationships, it's just…pure genius!"

Shoving that warning voice deep into the basement of my brain, I tried to look suitably pensive and responded with the ever-ambiguous "hmm."

Fortunately I was saved from expressing my true feelings, as Max seemed to have fallen in love with the sound of his own voice, and went on and on about the "genius" of Bart Freely as we strolled away from the theater together. He waxed poetic on everything from the loneliness of the human condition to the sad state of Hollywood, which had no place for such a diverse (yeah, right) and unique (to whom, men?) filmmaker as Bart Freely.

Finally we arrived at what I discovered was to be our next destination for the evening. A bar on East Seventy-First Street which seemed to be called simply Bar, either because the owner couldn't afford to fix the half-torn-down sign, or he was attempting to be clever.

"You up for something to eat? Maybe a few drinks?" Max asked hopefully.

Apparently Bar also had food. "Sure," I replied, somewhat relieved he hadn't made any presumptions and led me straight to his apartment.

Once we were seated, shades of our first date came back to me. As I looked at Max seated across from me once more, I remembered why I was attracted to him in the first place: a) he was hot b) he was intellectual and most of all c) he was a writer—a successful writer. And he looked it, I thought, studying him as he scanned the menu thoughtfully.

"Why don't we start off with a couple of drinks?" he suggested, "Then, if we want, we can have a couple appetizers. Unless, you're hungry for dinner...?" he continued, eyeing me speculatively over the top of his menu.

Like I would really admit I was hungry enough for a four-course meal with him looking at me like that—as if food was so beside the point for us intellectual types. Suddenly I wondered why I never seemed to get dinner when I was out on a date. "That's sounds good," I replied.

"Well, I know what I'm having," he said, shutting the menu with a smile. "My beloved Bombay martini." Then he half squinted, as if trying to pull out a memory. "And what was that you were drinking last time? Some kind of tequila drink?"

Suddenly his parting words on our first date came back to me, and an image of my father, four drinks lined up in front of him and a grin on his weary face, flashed before me.

"You know, I think I'll go with a glass of Merlot tonight." After all, I didn't want him to think I had some sort of...problem.

He seemed somewhat disappointed in this selection, though he cheerfully ordered for both of us once the waiter showed up.

"So how's the book coming?" he asked once we were alone again.

"Fine, fine," I replied, but inwardly cringed when I realized I had barely looked at it since Max's call on Sunday night. It was as if I suddenly redirected my efforts from the moment I had heard his voice on my machine. "And you? Have you finished the article for *Rolling Stone?*"

"Oh, yeah. It was just a book review. Nothing I couldn't handle," he replied with a shrug.

I ignored the fact that this simple task had previously been the excuse for why he had been too busy to call me for over a week. "That's cool. Good book?"

"Nothing special. I was rather glad to get back to my own writing," he said, a gleam in his eye.

As our drinks arrived and we talked more about writing, I realized I was performing a dance I had performed once before, two years earlier. It was as if I weren't talking to Max, but to Derrick. The nuances were the same—two writers struggling to show each other what their true passions were and maybe not hearing each other at all, judging by what had happened between Derrick and me. But I didn't want to feel that gap, didn't want to see it. And so I pushed it away, focusing on the moment instead, on the way Max got animated every time he felt the conversation was feeding whatever point he was making. And he always had some brilliant point or other. I was becoming enamored in spite of my doubts. How I could I help it, with the Merlot warming up my veins and taking a heavier toll on my senses than I expected, probably because we never did order any food and it had been a long time since I'd ingested anything solid enough to absorb alcohol. I wasn't drunk, not by a long shot. I'd barely even touched the second glass Max insisted I order, probably out of some vague desire to keep myself a safe distance from the ominous memory of Deirdre's phone message. I can only assume it was my vulnerable, post-Derrick haze that had me positively glowing with a wealth of warm feelings toward Max as he called for the check and ushered me out the door a few hours later.

Whatever strange emotions I was feeling, not even the cool night air that blasted me in the face once we hit the streets could drive it away. In fact, I found myself nodding eagerly in response to his suggestion that we go back to his place. Just for a quick look, he said. Apparently Max had a killer one-bedroom with a wood-burning fireplace, all for $1,500 a month. It simply had to be seen to be believed.

Yeah, right.

We walked there arm in arm, my head resting on his shoulder as if we'd been together for two years rather than two nights. I couldn't help but relax into the warmth of him. He felt so solid. So male. And I suddenly realized how much I missed a good, solid male.

Then I saw the apartment.

With one flick of the switch, the room glowed with warmth and color. And I found myself standing in the kind of expansive living space a downtown dweller like myself could only dream of.

"It's wonderful," I breathed, turning to look at Max.

His smile was smug, as if he himself had laid every brick in the fireplace that sat cozily on the far wall. "Let me give you a tour."

He proceeded to lead me through a kitchen. Not a line of appliances against a wall or stuffed into a alcove that had once been a closet. But a full-blown, actual eat-in kitchen, complete with table and chairs and—even rarer—a window. I swallowed hard, speechless as he took my hand and pulled me toward the pièce de résistance.

The bedroom.

Vaulted ceilings, a wall of windows and a bed so beautifully made up in blues in grays, I might have suspected he was a bit light in the loafers—except for the purely predatory look I saw in his eyes when I turned to look at him once more, my mouth agape.

I wanted to sleep with him. With all of it—the wood-burning fireplace, the eat-in kitchen, the twenty-foot ceilings. I was in a state of pure, unadulterated lust.

"Can I get you something to drink?" he asked, breaking the tension and allowing me to get a grip on my senses. "I think I might even have a bottle of Merlot, since that seems to be your poison of choice this evening."

"Great," I said, meekly following him back through the kitchen in an effort to keep myself from crawling into the cozy little bed and begging Max to make love to me until my name was added to the lease.

"Have a seat in the living room," he said. "There are some CDs in the rack by the fireplace. Pick something out."

I did as he asked, enjoying the fact that he put me in charge of the music selection. I needed something to grab on to, to help me gain control. But as I began to browse through Max's CDs, I found myself spiraling further into the unknown. I didn't recognize anything in his collection. All he seemed to own were obscure British imports of bands I never heard of, and classical recordings, which I knew virtually nothing about.

Finally I spied a Billie Holiday CD and grabbed it. Why not? It

was romantic in some ways. So what if it was the blues? It somehow seemed…appropriate, I realized as the first strains of "Lady
Sings the Blues," wafted silkily from the speakers. Yes, I thought
as I seated myself carefully on the sofa, I was ready for whatever
Max had on his mind. And I was pretty sure I knew what that was.

Confession: Reader, I slept with him.

When Max returned with two glasses in hand, I had managed to
transform myself into the kind of cool and courageous chick who
felt perfectly at ease in a hot guy's apartment. I had even kicked
off my slides and slid down deep into his sofa, though my insides
quivered a bit at the sight of him standing before me, his look
speculative once more.

"Billie Holiday. Nice choice," he said, handing me a glass and
seating himself right beside me.

I had barely taken a sip before Max took the glass from my hand
and pulled me into his arms for a kiss so sexy yet so tender it was
oddly…heartbreaking.

I did the only thing I could. I brought things up a notch. I
couldn't help myself. The tenderness was too much to bear, and
the only way I could fight it was by ravishing his mouth, nipping
savagely at his lips. His eyes widened in surprise, then he responded in kind, and soon enough, my bra was on the floor next
to my T-shirt and Max was easing me into a reclining position.

"I need to feel you," I said, yanking his T-shirt up and pressing
myself against him. I was blind in that moment, though I noted
vaguely once he was bare-chested that he was a little on the skinny
side, but toned, athletic. Solid. It was all I needed.

Apparently Max needed more. "Let's go into the bedroom," he
breathed in my ear, and I answered by coaxing his tongue into my
mouth and sucking hard. He groaned and got up, pulling me with
him, past that beautiful brick-covered wall, through the spacious
kitchen and into that plush, inviting bed.

I suddenly couldn't remember the last time I had smelled a man's
scent against cool, crisp sheets. All I knew was that it felt incredibly
good to lie in Max's bed. With a quick kiss, he left me there tem-

porarily while he shucked his jeans. I felt a momentary panic at the sight of his narrow hips and his—oh God—Fruit Of The Looms. He suddenly looked so foreign to me, unfamiliar. This body, hairless, gaunt and suddenly strange to my eyes, was one I did not know. It was as if my muddled brain were expecting someone else, someone familiar...someone like...Derrick.

I closed my eyes against the thought, waiting for the weight of Max, the feel of his tongue in my mouth once more, his hands roaming over me. It did feel good, after all. I will not lie. I was attracted to Max Van Gelder in a way that went beyond his surprisingly narrow body and somewhat clumsy hands. Allowing him to slide both my jeans and panties down my legs, I decided to let things run their course.

And when things had reached some sort of fevered pitch for Max—I was aroused myself, though something had been muted inside me—I watched stoically while he slid off those Fruit Of The Looms and fumbled in the nightstand for a condom. I had all those giggly little thoughts about the ridiculous look of a man's cock covered in latex—not that it was a bad cock, somewhere above my lifetime average and maybe even slightly larger than Derrick's— take that, you bastard!—and waited patiently while he poked and prodded at me, attempting to find the place nature had put in the same spot on every woman yet most men couldn't find on the first try.

Suddenly he was inside me, staring at someplace on the pillow beneath my head, a look of relief on his features. He began to move, slowly at first, as if the action caused him more pain than pleasure. Initially I felt a little strange myself, staring up at this man I barely knew as he pounded away at me in some heightened state of plea- sure I was not yet privy to. And my feelings must have shown on my face, for he suddenly closed his eyes.

I watched him for a few moments, studying his features and wondering how they had suddenly turned so vulnerable-looking they made me want to cry. But I didn't cry. Hell, I was having sex. So I did what every single girl must when she found herself pleas- antly engaged with a man she found attractive and willing, if not perfectly suited. I shut my eyes. And enjoyed myself.

For the friction had started to warm me, the feel of him between my thighs began to excite me. I will admit, I did for a moment imagine it was Derrick above me, sweating and grunting and acting like his efforts would somehow save the world. And though the memory thrilled me, it was only a momentary thrill, followed by a seething anger that I could banish only by focusing on the friction once more. *C'mon,* my brain screamed. "Harder," I heard myself cry, just like one of those women in the porno flick Derrick brought over once, hoping to spice things up between us.

And with one ear-shattering groan from Max, it was over. Oh, not for me. No, no, no, don't go thinking I got so lucky. The only reason *I* knew it was over was that foreign and now very sweaty body was limp on top of mine, which was still tingling hopefully, unaware that there was nothing to hope for anymore.

Suddenly he lifted his head, a goofy grin on his face as he looked down at me. "Wow. That was amazing."

I smiled back, deciding to swallow my disappointment and face the moment bravely. Besides, when I looked up into those satiated features, I saw the old Max again. The one I found so attractive, in that intellectual New York guy kind of way. I even liked him again. More than seemed warranted, judging by the outcome of this particular sexual encounter.

Then came the fatal question. "Did you, uh…?"

"Oh, yes," I said instantly, batting away the voices that immediately began protesting in my head. I don't know why I lied. Maybe I wanted to believe it was true, that I had found some kind of satisfaction with this man who was so perfectly right for me, yet suddenly so impossible to…to love.

He smiled, his relief evident. "I was a little worried there. I didn't, uh, last very long…." Then he chuckled. "Guess it's been a while."

I smiled at that, supremely glad to learn that Max Van Gelder wasn't some Upper East Side stud.

He kissed my lips, then touched the back of his hand to my face, his eyes glancing down at our bodies still entwined as he said, "Don't worry. It will get better. Once I get to know your body, I mean." That hand moved from my cheek and slid down my breast, coming to rest at my waist. "Every woman is different. And I don't know where you're...uh, sensitive."

By the time his gaze came back to mine, I realized he had already found my most sensitive spot—my heart. He was making me promises. Promises of next time that I suddenly wanted desperately to believe in. I looked up at his face, the face that had lured me here, and I tried hard to imagine it as part of my life. Images of us flashed through my mind, walking hand in hand through Central Park, sharing coffee and intimate conversation at the Peacock, dancing at my mother's wedding while Grandma Zizi looked on with pride and joy. Suddenly it all seemed possible. That Max could be The One. That I could fall in love again.

Still, I decided not to spend the night. It didn't feel like the right thing to do. Besides, I hoped, by making an early escape and leaving him longing for more, to preserve some of the magic that might have been dispelled by my having given it up on date two.

When I announced my plans to leave a short while later, Max didn't make any argument, and something pinged ominously inside me. I tried to disregard the feeling as I crawled out of his bed and began gathering the clothes strewn around his apartment, all the while gazing at his cozy kitchen, the charming fireplace and other accoutrements as I passed them, as if committing it all to memory. *Stop that!* my mind screamed. *You'll be back.* Though I grew more and more uncertain of this as I slid into my clothes and reentered the bedroom, where Max was already engrossed in a book that I had seen lying on his bedstand earlier.

Because he seemed bent on doing the right thing, he threw on his clothes and walked me downstairs, stood with me in the chill of the early-morning hour and hailed me a cab. We didn't say much, and I assumed it was because neither of us wanted to spoil the sudden intimacy that had sprung up between us. I tried not to think that it might be because we had already said everything we needed to say to each other for tonight. Or any other night, for that matter.

"I'll call you," he said as a cab pulled up, and the words chilled me for some reason. Maybe because I had thought it was under-

stood and thus unnecessary to say. And maybe because I realized
I was wrong.

After a quick, hard kiss that seemed more like an awkward
bumping of noses, I slid into the cab and headed home, feeling
more alone. I was feeling more alone than ever.

Confession: Things could definitely get worse.

"You *slept* with him?" Jade said with disbelief as we sat across
from one another at breakfast. Since the weather was beautiful, we
went to French Roast and took a table outside. I had made my
confession mere moments after we had placed our order with the
waitress, hoping Jade might find some positive angle to this whole
thing. But I realized my mistake once I saw her reaction. And now,
with the bright morning sunlight flooding our table, there was nowhere to hide my dismay.

"What? As if *you've* never slept with a guy on the second
date...."

"Not if I was really interested in the guy," Jade said, putting
down her coffee cup and sliding a cigarette out of the pack on the
table.

"Who says I'm interested in Max?" I replied defensively.

She paused in the middle of lighting her cigarette, eyebrows
raised.

"All right, so I fucked up. Okay?" Suddenly I felt ill. "He's
not going to call again, is he?"

"I don't know, Emma. He might. But it probably won't be because of your sparkling conversation. It's really hard to go back
and do the whole getting-to-know-you thing once you sleep with a
guy."

"I don't think Max is like that. Besides, he did say something
about how great the sex would be when he got to know my body
better. Which implies at least a few more dates. Or sexual encounters. Whatever you want to call them."

Jade puffed on her cigarette. "Did he say this before his orgasm
or after?"

"After," I said smugly.

"Well, then, maybe he was being honest. Or feeling like he had to make some sort of promise. Did you come?"

"Uh...no."

"Oh." Jade glanced away, as if suddenly interested in the people passing by on the sidewalk.

"What?" I asked, desperate for some sort of reassurance that I was not about to be blown off by Max Van Gelder. But Jade wasn't about to give me any false hopes.

"Well, he might have said that as a...consolation."

"Oh, please, Jade. He didn't know I didn't come. I...I told him I did."

Her eyes bulged, then she rolled them. "You've got a lot to learn, Emma."

Our food arrived then, and while I watched Jade stub out her cigarette and dig into her French toast, I suddenly felt no appetite at all for the pretty little plate of eggs Benedict before me. Max wasn't going to call. I felt it in my bones. But I had felt that once before and he *had* called, I reminded myself. Maybe if I believed he wouldn't, then Murphy's Law would take effect and he would.

Then another thought struck me: Did I *want* him to call?

I immediately dismissed this one, as well as any other disparaging thought I might have had about Max Van Gelder during the course of our very brief relationship. After all, whether or not he was a great guy was almost beside the point. I needed him to call, even if I decided I never wanted to see him again. My ego demanded it.

So when I came home from breakfast and discovered a big fat "O" on the message light of my machine, I felt the walls of my apartment closing in on me. Shouldn't I have at least gotten a courtesy call after the milestone of last night? A "had-a-great-time-can't-wait-to-see-you-again" acknowledgment? We'd had sex for crissakes. And I didn't even attain orgasm. Hell, I deserved a dozen roses!

I thought about calling Alyssa, then realized she was probably still busy falling in love with Richard all over again. Not that I wasn't thrilled for her—I just couldn't deal with someone else's happiness at the moment.

I decided to call my father instead. After all, I had to face the music some time, and it *had* been three days since Deirdre's voice mail informing me that my father had fallen off the wagon once again.

She picked up on the second ring. "Hello?"

"Hey, Dee, it's Emma."

"Hello," she replied. I couldn't detect any emotion in her voice: no anger, no disappointment. I was on safe ground so far.

"How's everything going?"

"Fine. Your father's in a rehab."

I sighed, then swallowed whatever bubble of feeling threatened. I had learned long ago that it was a waste of emotion to feel anything in the face of my father's transgressions.

"Drove him over to Rolling Pines this morning to start the detox program," she continued, her voice stoical. "Thank God they had a bed for him."

My heart sank. This wasn't the first time my father had willingly entered a rehabilitation center. In fact, his visits there had become yearly events, and I realized with dismay that this was actually his fourth stay at the Rolling Pines Recovery Center. I sighed. Since a midweek visit was not an option, I asked, "What time are visiting hours on Saturday?"

"Ten to four. Though today is out because they don't allow visitors the first couple of days—"

"I know, I know," I replied. I was way too familiar with the detox program at Rolling Pines. Three days of detox before they even allowed friends or family to visit.

"Should I pick you up at the station next Saturday, then? Around noon?" she asked.

After we had settled on a time, I listened while she let loose on my father, how she couldn't keep the alcohol away from him, no matter how she tried. How their lives had fallen into some awful pattern not worth continuing. I couldn't blame her for being angry. I wouldn't even have blamed her if she told me she was leaving him. I hadn't blamed my mother, either. Who could live with a man who cared so little for himself?

With a promise to check in during the week and confirm train arrival times, I hung up with that same hollow feeling I always felt after one of my father's episodes. Then I did what I always did in this situation: sealed it up inside until I felt nothing. Absolutely nothing.

Moments later, the phone rang again. "I heard about your father," my mother stated sadly on the other end. "Shaun called me."

I sighed, not wanting to get into things but knowing it was inevitable.

"Are you okay, sweetheart?" she said.

"I'm fine. Why wouldn't I be? It's not as if I'm *surprised.*"

My mother was quiet after that remark, and I could tell she was tabulating the amount of psychological damage my father's most recent episode had caused. "Well, maybe he'll get some help this time."

"Oh, he's already checked into rehab. Deirdre drove him over this morning." Not that it mattered, I thought to myself.

"That poor woman," my mother said, "I don't know how she takes it." Then: "So are you coming in next Saturday to see him?" She knew the drill, too, after all.

"Yeah," I admitted, knowing that a visit with my mother would be unavoidable if I set foot on Long Island this weekend. "Deirdre's picking me up at noon. I'll have her drop me off at your house afterward."

"Good, sweetie. I'll make us a nice dinner and we can take some time to talk. You really shouldn't keep your emotions so bottled up."

"Don't worry, Mom. I was planning on having a few stiff drinks and a good cry later."

"Emma!"

"Just kidding. Look, I have to go. See you Saturday afternoon, around four?"

"We'll talk about this then," she warned, and I knew I wouldn't be able to sneak back to the city that night without having my emotions picked apart by my mother.

If, between Max and my father—not to mention residual Derrick Damage—there was anything left for the picking.

Confession: It seems that I am destined to spend Saturday night alone. Probably until the end of time.

Once I had finalized my depressing plans for next Saturday, this Saturday night loomed before me, cold and empty. Since Alyssa was spending a romantic evening at home with Richard and I knew Jade had plans to go out with Enrico, I knew I was fated to spend it alone. No longer did I wait for a call from Max. I didn't even torment myself with thoughts of Derrick. Instead thoughts of my father's illness infested my mind, making me question every hope I'd ever had for my own future. Every dream I'd been unable to achieve.

I shuddered, forcing back tears. Then I did the only thing I could to keep myself sane. I cleaned.

I started with the living area, pulling all the books off the shelves and dusting each one individually. Then I moved on to the desk, filing papers, polishing the surface. Next the floor was mopped, then the kitchen scrubbed. The bathroom was sprayed down and wiped until it sparkled.

I showered, then fell onto the bed exhausted. My gaze fell on the clock—4:00 p.m. Too early for bed. I did another stare down with the phone, which remained silent and menacing. I imagined Max Van Gelder walking up the stairs to his apartment, just about to insert the key in the door when he is attacked by a band of thieves who beat him and leave him battered and bruised in the hallway, before they proceed to ransack his entire apartment, stealing everything except the Billie Holiday CD. When he comes to consciousness again, the only thing he hears is the soulful sound of "What a Little Moonlight Can Do," and the only person he thinks of is me.

I sighed and glanced at the phone once more. It remained silent.

I could go to the gym. But that would mean rounding up Alyssa before she settled in with Richard for the night, as I could gain access to the gym only by the grace of her seemingly unlimited supply of guest passes. And since I couldn't deal with her helpful words of wisdom right now, I could just forget about going to the gym. What I really needed was to get a membership of my own....

As I lay there contemplating my nonoptions, a quietness finally fell over me, and I drifted off into a brief and somewhat blissful sleep, during which I dreamed I was in Max's bed. Except when I rolled over to wake him, I discovered Derrick instead. "Hey," he said, blinking sleep out of his eyes. "I hoped you would drop by." And then he pulled me into his arms and made love to me, really made love to me, simultaneous orgasm and all.

I woke up to darkness, achingly aware that I was completely alone.

I slid out of bed, then went to the bathroom to splash water on my face and run a brush through my rumpled hair, which had kinked and curled from falling asleep on it while wet. After slipping on my slides and, as an afterthought, dabbing on lipstick, I headed down the stairs in search of dinner fare.

Once I hit the cool night air, I knew what I had to do. I headed for the bodega on the corner. And Smiling Man. To hell with good eating habits.

But by the time I got there and responded to his cheerful, "Hello!" my resolve broke. I couldn't bring myself to destroy everything I had worked for up until now, no matter how bad I felt. I slinked past the Hostess snack cakes, past the freezer full of Ben & Jerry's and grabbed a container of skim milk, a can of tuna and a granola bar, just to save face.

"Is that it?" he taunted as I placed the items reluctantly on the counter.

"*Yes,*" I replied, practically hissing the word at him. He didn't seem to notice my ire as he perkily poked at his register, then held out his hand to receive my money.

"Have a good night!" he insisted cheerfully as I took my bag and walked dejectedly out the door.

I couldn't go home like this, I realized as I turned toward my building once more. I needed *something* to lift my spirits.

As if on autopilot, I headed for Heavenly Dee-lites, and was filled with dismay when I saw the Closed sign hanging in the door. Then alarm bells went off in my head when I saw *him* standing just inside, turning the key in the lock. I tried to back away, but it was too late—he saw me. The Skinny Scoop man of my recent seduction fantasies. Except that he looked even more irresistible, in a clean T-shirt and a pair of faded jeans.

Spotting me, he opened the door. "Hi," he said. "I was just locking up, but if you need anything—"

Suddenly I remembered my rumpled hair, my makeup-free face. Thank God I had at least opted for lipstick.

"Uh…no, I'm—"

"Hey," he said suddenly, his beautiful face filled with recognition, that sexy mouth turning up into a smile. "Double Mocha Chip, right?"

I was mortified. He remembered me. He remembered my flavor. Which probably meant that he remembered I had purchased a whole *gallon* of the stuff mere weeks ago. "Uh, yeah." I replied, numbly. There was no way to get out of this gracefully now. Smiling weakly, I admitted, "You guessed it."

"I have a feeling you're in need of a refill," he said, opening the door invitingly. "Come on in. It'll only take a minute."

I nodded and stepped over the threshold, my senses on full alert. After all, by inviting me in at closing time, the Skinny Scoop man was coming dangerously close to fulfilling my recent seduction fantasy. I felt heat rising to my face as a sudden image of us going at it against the freezer case filled my mind. "Just a pint," I said weakly once he faced me again from a safe distance behind the counter.

"You got it," he said, reaching into the glass freezer between us.

Nice forearms, I thought as I watched him dig through the containers in search of the Double Mocha. I thought of Jade and her love of this particular part of the male anatomy. That's right—he's more Jade's type anyway. Whom was I kidding? Clearly I would have nothing in common with this guy anyway. After all, he was a…a…stock boy. Or something. Not that Jade would have anything in common with him, either, but that didn't matter to *her.*

The beautifully tanned hand attached to the beefy forearm finally found the Double Mocha Chip, plucked it out of the case and plopped it in a bag. "There you go," he said, handing it over. "That will be two-seventy-five."

I dug around in my pocket, pulled out a five and handed it to him, my fingers grazing his. That's when I felt it. That tiny electric zing that I had read about but never actually encountered in real life.

Maybe I didn't need to have anything in common with the Skinny Scoop man. Maybe I just needed—

I banished the thought as he handed me back my change, and I noticed the nonchalance with which he performed the function. No way would a guy like this even be interested in me. He was pure sex, while I...

I didn't know what I was anymore. "Thanks," I replied, pocketing the change and giving him a meager smile.

"Hey, no problem," he replied, flashing me one of those amazing smiles once again.

God, I wanted to have sex with him. But, instead, I turned myself around and marched out the door. What had I become, some kind of sex-crazed maniac? Suddenly Jade's whole M.O. was thrown into relief. Maybe this was what happened to you when the love of your life brutally dumped you, destroying all your belief in soulmates and true love. Maybe you just roamed the city streets, in search of drink and debauchery....

"See you soon," he called out as I made my way through the door.

I swallowed. Hard. Maybe I *would* see him soon. And not just for Skinny Scoop.

By the time I got home and was safely under the covers, the pint of Skinny Scoop in my hands and my spoon poised as I contemplated the Saturday night pickings, the thought of a life of promiscuity and restlessness filled me with sorrow. I dug into the pint, spooned in my first mouthful and swallowed, the sweetness less than the anticipated balm to my wounded, threadbare soul. I stared numbly at the TV screen, settling on a channel that had some mindless sitcom on, as I realized that all the good TV was reserved for nights when people were expected to be home. Like any other night but Saturday. And just when I thought I had finally managed to achieve the numbness of couch potatodom, the sitcom I had tuned into broke for a commercial, and I watched, horrified, as the most beautiful blond woman I had ever seen stepped into an elevator with an incredibly handsome man, their mouths coming dangerously close as a tube of brightly packaged toothpaste flashed up on the screen.

Close-Up.

Oh God. It was even worse than I'd thought, I realized as I took in Carrie's winning smile, her generous breasts and narrow waist.

Derrick had found someone else. And she was perfect.

Eleven

"Men: You can't live with them and you can't
permanently institutionalize them."
—Deirdre Carter, still married to Emma's father
(believe it or not).

Confession: I begin to question my own sanity.

By the time my phone did ring, it was Sunday morning and I was
in a deep and mercifully dreamless sleep.

It was Jade. "You're sleeping?"

"No, no, I'm up," I lied, glad to hear a familiar voice after an
evening filled with my own torturous thoughts.

"Meet me at Joe Jr.'s?" she said, naming our favorite diner,
conveniently located down the street from me. "Half an hour?"

"Okay," I said, then hung up and glanced at the clock: 10:00
a.m. There had to be something wrong. There was no way Jade
could be up so early on a Sunday morning otherwise.

As was my habit, I arrived at Joe's a few minutes before Jade,
and was greeted by the cheerful staff. Joe Jr.'s was a family-owned
diner, and if you went there often enough, you became a member
of the family. Right now I was ready to trade in my own family
for this one.

Jade arrived shortly afterward. Once we had slid into a booth
and ordered coffee, I asked, "What's going on?"

"It's over," she said, smiling gratefully at the young waiter as
he filled our coffee cups.

"Over?"

"Enrico and me."

My heart pinged oddly. "What happened?" I demanded.

"Fucking guy shows up at my apartment last night with this bulging knapsack," she began as she tore open sugar packets and dumped them into her coffee. "At first, I'm not thinking anything. I mean, I told him he could stay over, so I figured he had a change of clothes in there. Well, I'm putting my lipstick on and getting ready to walk out the door, when he pulls out a…a…bathrobe!"

I was confused. "I don't get it."

"Neither does he, apparently. He tells me he figured he could keep his robe here, so he'd have it whenever he stays over. Then he proceeds to go hang it on the back of my bathroom door!"

Uh-oh. Enrico was getting territorial. "God, he might as well have peed all over the place. What did you do?"

"What else could I do? I told him to stuff that terry-cloth nightmare right back in his bag."

"Ouch. Poor Enrico."

"Poor Enrico nothing. Poor *me!* I mean, everything was going great, we were having amazing sex, good times. And then he has to go getting all boyfriendy on me."

"So you broke up with him?"

"What else could I do?"

"I don't know, Jade. Maybe you could have just told him to take his little bathrobe home and carry on as you were before."

"Oh, I tried. Believe me. But he was so furious that I didn't want his robe hanging around my place, he started accusing me of sleeping with other guys."

"Uh-oh."

"Yeah, the whole night was a mess. Not even his bathrobe survived." She smiled somewhat guiltily. "After I yanked it off the hook and tried to hand it back to him, we got into a tug-of-war and…well, the sleeve kinda came off." She cringed. "I feel a little bad about that. Maybe I'll have my contact at Ralph Lauren send him a replacement."

Now I was sure her tryst with Enrico truly was over, as it was Jade's habit to load up her man with gifts just before she gave him the heave-ho. It was as if she felt a hidden guilt at ending things. Even Michael, asshole that he was, had gotten six new CDs. And

Carl, who lasted no more than a month, got a weight-training belt. "So what now?"

"Nothing. Like I said, it's over."

At that moment, Alex, our usual waiter, came over. "Hello, ladies. What can I get for you today?"

Without hesitation, Jade rattled off a version of an omelet with extras that had enough fat and carbohydrates to make her blood stop moving in her veins. When the waiter turned to me, I nodded numbly. "I'll have the same."

Once he was gone, I asked Jade, "Do you think something is wrong with us?"

She narrowed her eyes at me. "What?"

"I mean, neither one of us seems to be able to maintain a relationship."

"For your information, Emma, I am not looking for a relationship. And the demise of *your* relationship had nothing to do with *you*."

I studied her for a minute, wondering how much truth there was behind her statement that she didn't want a relationship. After the Ted episode, I was convinced it was only a matter of her meeting the right guy. But this was a subject I couldn't broach with Jade without getting my head bit off. So instead I said, "Max never called me."

"The writer guy?"

"Yeah." I studied her face, waiting for her to show some sign that she thought there was something wrong with me, too.

"That's New York men for you. The good ones aren't really available. And the others are so needy, all they really want is someone to replace their mothers."

"Maybe *I'm* the needy one. Maybe Max saw that. I didn't tell you this, but I drank four drinks on our first date. In about as many hours."

"And?" she replied, as if this statement meant nothing.

"That's not normal. I mean, he even commented on it."

"He did?"

"Yeah," I said, embarrassed. "And then he seemed really disappointed when I acted more sedate and drank Merlot on date number two. Not that that stopped me from acting like some drunken girl and sleeping with him.''

''Maybe you just wanted to get laid.''

''Maybe I'm just a mess,'' I replied. Then, with a resigned sigh, I blurted out, ''My father's in a rehab.''

''Oh, Emma. Not again,'' she said, her face full of sympathy.

''I'm beginning to wonder if maybe my whole family is fucked up—including me. I mean, I did drink a lot that first date, and Max—''

''Uh-uh. Don't go there, Emma.'' Jade shook her head. ''If I know you, you were nervous as hell when you went out with Max. I mean, he looked pretty intimidating to me, the way he looked down his nose at everyone and everything. A lot of people drink too much when they're nervous. Besides, it doesn't sound to me like you drank all that much on the second date. Sounds more like Max was just being your typical guy looking to get laid and hoping to grease your wheels by plying you with drinks.''

''Yeah, well, I wouldn't worry so much if my father didn't have such a...a problem with it. These things are hereditary, you know.''

Jade sighed, then leaned back in her seat. ''You're determined to find some reason why no man in the world will want you. I'm telling you, Emma, there's nothing wrong with you. You're intelligent and beautiful, and the only reason Derrick left was because he got a job offer. There's no explanation for the Max thing. There never is. Look at Ted. We had a great time together, and he's disappeared off the face of the earth.''

As our order arrived and as Jade and I dug into the fatty concoction of eggs, cheese and ham, I wondered if she was kidding herself about men being the real problem and not us. After all, *she* had just thrown a man out of her life for bringing a bathrobe over, for chrissakes. Could it be we were just the innocent victims of the New York City dating scene? Or were we part of the problem?

Confession: It is now public knowledge: I am a complete and utter failure.

By Monday morning I was a mess, especially since Sunday night—the very night Max had called me last week—passed without a word from him. The phone remained silent, except for one poor fool who had haplessly dialed my number in error and had his head bitten off by me for not being anyone I desperately needed to hear from. Like Max. Or Derrick, for that matter. Not that I expected to hear from *him* again. And that thought hurt even more than Max's indifference ever could.

Now I plodded numbly along the subway platform, hating the crowds that surged and swarmed around me and suddenly understanding why Sartre had said, "Hell is other people." After boarding the train, I stood among the sweaty throngs, gazing blindly up at a hemorrhoid ad while I analyzed my date with Max for the sixteenth time.

Somehow this gloomy Monday morning, all the minute details that led to this moment of desolation seemed glaringly apparent. The way he'd maneuvered me up to his neighborhood, probably with the sole aim of getting me into his apartment at some appropriate moment. That damn Bart Freely movie, after which he'd waxed poetic on the virtues of solitude. The way he plied me with drinks I didn't want, probably in the hope that I would be drunk enough for him to work his seductive magic.

Turns out he didn't even need to do that. I hadn't been drunk, I'd been lonely. And desperately missing Derrick, though I was loath to admit that, even to myself.

By the time I got to the office, I was too depressed to register the significance of the hum of excited chatter going on behind the cubicle walls. Too numb to see Marcy Keller hovering, hoping to get my attention as I walked into my own cubicle and clicked on my computer. When I turned around and caught her looming in the doorway, I simply brushed past her, muttering something about coffee. I didn't want to deal with whatever gossip she had to share. And, frankly, I didn't care, even if the rumor turned out to be that *Bridal Best* was about to fold and that all our jobs were on the line. I took a dejected kind of satisfaction in picturing myself cleaning out my office drawers and, later, after I'd worked through what little savings I had, being tossed out of my tiny rent-stabilized nightmare. The thought gave me a momentary sense of freedom.

Until I realized that unemployment and eviction would only mean one thing: moving home—at the age of thirty-one—to my mother.

Once I returned to my cube, coffee in hand, I discovered an e-mail from Caroline in my in-box, beckoning me to her office, "at your earliest convenience."

Since anything was better than dealing with the mounds of paper that sat waiting for immediate attention in my in-box, I set my coffee down on the desk and headed down the hall to Caroline's office.

"Emma! Thanks for coming by," she said when I knocked softly on her open door. "Come in," she encouraged. "And close the door behind you."

Uh-oh. Something was up. And judging by her expression, which seemed poised to send condolences to yours truly, it wasn't good. Still, I did as I was told, then sat in the seat before her, waiting for the ax to fall.

Caroline smoothed her hands, somewhat anxiously I thought, over her rounded abdomen. "First, I want you to know that at *Bridal Best* we truly value your contribution as a writer and as an editor." Then she smiled. "You've written some of the strongest articles this magazine has published in the past few years."

Pretty heavy-duty compliment, I thought, and couldn't help but feel proud. Then suspicious. God, *was* I getting fired?

"Second, I want to emphasize how very *competitive* the choices were for the new senior features editor."

A sense of foreboding filled me. I knew what was coming now.

"Unfortunately, however, we could only choose one candidate," she continued, a pained expression filling her features, "and that candidate was Rebecca Sanders."

It amazed me how hollow I felt, how without feeling I was when she said the words I both expected and feared. And aside from the rush of heat and emotion that filled my head and clogged my ears, I think I was quite poised as I heard myself thank her for the opportunity to apply for the position and express my belief (I did believe it, right?) that Rebecca would do a fine job.

Caroline went on to explain that though we both were strong candidates, Rebecca had had management experience at her last job.

"I think that's what gave her the edge, Emma. After all, the senior features editor is largely a *management* position," she said, looking at me carefully as she emphasized the word. Then she smiled as I gazed at her, trying to make out whatever secret message she was trying to send me and coming up empty.

Caroline was still beaming me that sad little smile as I nodded at her, then stood and turned to walk on somewhat stilted legs to her door. She stopped me once I had my hand on the knob, calling out my name in a soft, sympathetic voice that might have induced tears if I hadn't managed to squash anything resembling emotion down into the pit of my stomach.

"Emma," she began. "I know that right now this might seem like a terrible blow, but you might consider what other options are available to you. You're a very strong writer. Not everyone has that gift. Not even the senior features editors."

I looked at her uncomprehendingly. Was she trying to encourage me to look for another job? Maybe she didn't even want me on her staff anymore, much less as a peer. Oh God.

She smiled again, this time encouragingly. "Look, you can come and talk to me anytime. About anything. Your writing. Future plans. I'm here for you."

"Thanks," I said in a half whisper, then opened the door and stumbled blindly out into the hall.

Reality hit like the blast of cool air I felt once I stood out in the corridor, my wounds bared for all the world at *Bridal Best* to see. I noted Lucretia peering out over her cube and Nancy making somewhat slow progress to the photocopier, her gaze on me. And of course there was Marcy Keller, hovering by the water cooler, just waiting for me to walk by and break down, telling her everything. I decided right then and there I would not show Marcy—nor anyone else—that I cared. And with this decision, I suddenly wasn't sure if I *did* care. After all, did I really want to be senior features editor at a magazine that wouldn't even acknowledge the existence of women like me—hopelessly single and with no future prospects of registering for more china and cookware than was humanly necessary? Fuck them. They weren't getting a piece of me.

I brushed by Nancy, nodded curtly at Lucretia as she ducked

away once more and smiled bravely at Marcy as I passed her without a word. I even managed to sit looking strong and unruffled less than an hour later at the editorial meeting, when Patricia proudly announced her choice for the new senior features editor. And as Rebecca stood beaming before us, I smiled and applauded just as wildly as the rest of my colleagues. But I didn't dare lower my gaze to look anyone directly in the eye. I didn't dare let anyone know what I really felt.

Like I was dying inside.

Confession: There is no cure for the common heartache—at least not without a prescription.

That night I sat on a stool in Alyssa's kitchen. She had already slid her vegetable lasagna into the oven and sat before me, her expression alternating between outrage and sympathy as I told her all the gory details of my day, then glided into the ugly facts of my date with Max and his ultimate rejection, just to make myself feel especially crummy. A glass of wine sat untouched before me. I was afraid to drink it, for fear I would somehow burst into angry flames or, worse, cry.

"What is so wrong with me?" I asked, my sorrow now sharpened into an anxious pain in my gut.

"There is *nothing* wrong with you," Alyssa insisted, grabbing one of my hands as if she were going to use it to knock some sense into me.

"Yeah. There's nothing wrong with me. That's why men are moving across the country to escape me. And even the ones that still live in this fine city seem to be avoiding me as if I had some sort of...of plague." I sighed and felt no relief from it. "Let's face it, Alyssa. Clearly I'm a mess that no one wants to be a part of. Not even *Bridal Best*—a fucking magazine that doesn't even acknowledge life beyond the wedding day—sees me as not qualified to join the glorious ranks of their management team!"

"Emma..."

"There's nothing you can say or do, Alyssa. I'm just...tired. Tired of being put down, left behind. Tired of...of everything."

Silence reigned for a few moments. Until Alyssa squeezed my hand in comfort, and I finally 'fessed up to the other thing that had been clawing at my gut. "My father's in rehab again."

"Oh, Em." Alyssa's eyes filled with fresh sympathy. "When did he go in?"

"Saturday. Deirdre drove him over. He started drinking last week, I guess. I don't know for sure, because by the time I called back, he'd already sunk to the next level. Not that there was anything I could have done...."

"No, there was nothing you could have done," Alyssa said firmly.

"I'm going to see him this weekend."

"Do you want me to come with you?" Lys asked.

I smiled then. Good ol' Alyssa. If nothing else, I could count on her to be there for me. The thought gave me some comfort. "I'll be fine. Besides, my mother's already on the case. I'm going to her house afterward for a solid dose of psychobabble and comfort food. She's cooking me dinner."

Alyssa sat looking at me for a few moments. Then: "I know you don't necessarily believe in all that self-help stuff, and frankly I'm wary of a lot of it myself. But maybe, just this once, you should consider counseling. Just to sort things out."

I sighed. "Alyssa—"

"Look, I went myself. After my mother died."

This bit of information floored me. Alyssa had seen a shrink? She seemed too...too normal for that.

"I know what you're thinking, Emma," she said with a small smile. "But everyone needs help at some point in their lives. Some things are not so easy to deal with yourself. And with your father in rehab, well...." She sighed. "You need to absolve yourself from the blame you're assigning to yourself. You need to break the chain."

I smiled at her, wishing I could see the events of my life as merely a problem that could be fixed rather than an ultimate disaster in the process of unfolding. It was suddenly very clear to me why some people—my mother included—resorted to prescription drugs.

And I wondered if maybe I wasn't one of those people. After all, I was my parents' daughter, wasn't I?

Confession: I realize now that some women are meant to be alone and miserable, while others are effortlessly happy.

I was inconsolable that week. Especially after I told my mother I had lost the promotion and she was strangely silent on the subject. In my paranoia, I imagined she had suddenly realized her daughter was a complete and utter failure at both life and love. I confided this theory to Jade.

"She does not!" Jade insisted as she dragged me through Bloomingdale's on Wednesday night in a vain attempt to help me through my despair with a shopping spree. I couldn't bring myself to buy a single thing and instead followed Jade around as she searched for the perfect bikini to take to Fire Island with her for the July Fourth weekend, which, I realized with sudden horror, was the weekend after next.

I sighed as I watched Jade arm herself with hangers that dangled scraps of material, and followed her numbly as she headed for the dressing room. Apparently a photographer friend of hers was throwing some big bash at his beach house and had promised Jade not only a bed to sleep in, but a bevy of beautiful men to help her get over her recent loss of a sexual partner. "Maybe he has room for one more," she said enticingly. I immediately refused. Though I certainly didn't see any spectacular plans of my own looming on the horizon, I didn't think donning a suit and spending a weekend with supermodels and the people who dress them, photograph them and adore them would do anything good for my mental state. Besides that, I had decided to withdraw from the manhunt for a while. I just couldn't bear any more rejection.

There was one thing good about going to Long Island this weekend—I had the perfect excuse not to attend the little outing the girls in the office had planned on Saturday night, in honor of Rebecca's promotion. I even managed to look disappointed that I would be forced to miss the festivities, until Rebecca dropped by and gleefully informed me that she suspected Nash had finally gone shopping for a ring and a proposal would be forthcoming. Suddenly I felt drawn once more into that strange karmic loop that said I was to get nothing and Rebecca, everything.

I tried not to be bitter. Tried to hold my chin high as I muddled through the week. By the time I got off the train at Huntington on Saturday afternoon, I had hardened myself against any sort of feeling at all. And when I looked at Deirdre's somber face as I got into her car, I realized she had, too. As we drove over together, I noticed for the first time how much she looked like my mother. Deirdre had the same oval-shaped face and, except for her blue eyes, similar coloring. It was almost as if she were an older, more exhausted version of my mother—my mother, had she stayed with my father. Even Dee's hair, which fell in rumpled, faded waves to her shoulders, looked tired.

"How is he?" I asked finally, as we neared Rolling Pines.

"Same as always," she said. "He's already handpicked a selection of drug addicts and alcoholics he's decided are definitely worse off than he is. So he's feeling pretty good about himself."

"Have Shaun and Tiffany been by to see him?"

"Shaun came last night. And Thursday. Tiffany's in the middle of the kitchen renovation and couldn't get free."

Nothing like a little drywall and spackle to keep one from witnessing the dirty underbelly of family life. I sighed. I wished I'd had some suitable excuse to avoid this visit, but being the only daughter left me with few outs.

Moments later we pulled into the parking lot, got out and began to cross the carefully tended lawn of Rolling Pines. As we neared the facility, I saw that a number of the residents were seated outside at picnic tables or propped up in lawn chairs, for their official dose of fresh air. I spotted my father right away, seated alone at a table that seemed cut off from the rest, as if it had been tossed beyond the tree line without thought or care to its placement.

"What are you doing sitting way out here?" Deirdre called out to him as we approached.

Dad looked up, as if startled to see us there. "Shade. It's damn hot out here, and they won't let us go inside yet." He glanced at me almost as if he were embarrassed to acknowledge my presence.

"Hi, Emma," he said finally, half standing to kiss my cheek before he plopped himself back down again.

He looked terrible, with his arm bound in a sling and his face pale. I noticed a cut above his brow and wondered if that came from his tumble off the roof or if he'd suffered some other accident. His face was ashen, and his hair seemed dusted with even more gray than before. He looked old. And fragile.

I couldn't help commenting, "You look awful, Dad."

"Thanks. You're not so bad yourself," he said. Then, turning to Deirdre, "Did you bring me cigarettes?"

She handed over the bag she had under her arm and he took it, sliding the carton of unfiltered Camels into his one free hand. "No lighter?" he complained. "I told you to bring me a lighter." He sighed. "Someone stole my damn lighter in this godforsaken place. Bunch of thieves around here..."

She fished around in her pocketbook, then dropped three books of matches on the table before him.

"Matches are no good. How am I supposed to light my damn cigarettes with my damn arm like this—"

"I'm going to get a cup of coffee," Deirdre said, ignoring him. "You want anything, Emma?"

"No, thanks," I replied.

"I'll take a cup," my father said hopefully.

Without a word, Deirdre marched off across the grass, toward the gray building that housed—along with a few hundred substance abusers and the people who tended them—a cafeteria. I turned to my father, who had placed a cigarette between his lips and was struggling to light a match single-handedly.

"Can you give me a hand with this?" he asked when he saw I was staring at him. I took a book of matches off the table, struck one and reached across to light his cigarette.

"Thanks," he said, inhaling deeply and blowing out smoke as he stared off into the distant trees.

I didn't say a word, only watched him. What *could* I say? No lecture would make my father, Burt Carter, sober up for good. No warm, loving speeches would turn him into a *Brady Bunch Dad,* or *My Three Sons* kind of dad. He was my flesh and blood. My father, for better or for worse. And there wasn't a damn thing I could do about him.

Finally he spoke, surprising me. "Ah, Emma, I'm getting too old for this kind of thing."

"Me, too," I replied, ducking my head to avoid the stream of smoke that came out of his mouth as he turned to look at me.

"You?" he replied, his eyebrows raised. "You've got your whole life ahead of you. You have yet to make your first million!" Then he laughed, enjoying his familiar joke with me. "So how's it going with the job and all? Get that promotion yet?"

"No," I replied, resignation filling me. "They gave it to someone else."

He turned to look at me for a moment. Then with a last tug on his cigarette, he dropped it into the dirt below the table and stepped on it. "Ah, well. That happens sometimes. Too bad, though. The money would have been nice, huh?"

And the self-respect, I thought, but I didn't say anything, only nodded.

"But you'll be okay," he continued. "You don't need them, right? Once you write that Great American Novel, you'll show them who's boss."

I looked up at him now, trying to see if he actually believed what he said. Believed that his daughter would succeed at the one thing she'd dreamed of ever since she was a young girl. But I only saw a pair of faded, bloodshot eyes that quickly glanced off into the distance the moment I caught his gaze.

Turning my head in the same direction as his, I saw Deirdre heading toward us once more, a cup of coffee in each hand, her head raised as if she was trying to avoid looking at the men and women lazing around on the chairs surrounding the building, their faces pale and their bodies broken and tired.

"How's your mother?" my father asked, still watching Deirdre's approach. "Your brother tells me she's getting married again." He shook his head with a smile. Apparently he found the thought of my mother's third attempt at marriage humorous. I guess he figured if she didn't succeed this time, he could continue to blame her for the demise of their marriage.

"Yes, she is. And I think she found a good guy this time," I said, surprising myself with my sudden defense of my mother and Clark.

"I hope so," he said, glancing at me and popping another cigarette into his mouth as if making up for lost time. "The main thing is, you gotta find someone who will stand by you no matter what."

As if on cue, Deirdre placed two coffee cups on the table, glancing between my father and me. "How is everything? All right?"

"Just fine, darling," he said. Then, pulling the unlit cigarette from his mouth, he reached up and planted a kiss on her cheek. "Isn't she great?" he said.

"Too good for you," Deirdre replied, rolling her eyes at me, though I could see she was pleased.

"Help me out, will you, hon?" he said now, handing her the matches and settling the cigarette between his lips.

As I watched her strike the match and hold it to his cigarette, I was filled with a strange mixture of sorrow and, oddly enough, relief. I had finally realized that this burden was mine only if I chose it.

And I didn't want it. For once, I was sure of something.

Confession: I am forced to accept a higher power—my mother.

By the time Deirdre dropped me off in front of my mom's house, I was actually looking forward to seeing her. After a day spent in the gloom that perpetually surrounded my father, the prospect of my mother's relentless cheer was a welcome contrast. But when I entered the kitchen and saw my mother's friend, Dorothea, sitting there, I immediately went on red alert.

"Emma, you remember Dorothea, don't you?"

Of course I did. Dorothea was my mother's tennis partner turned best friend after mom had divorced my dad. Dorothea was also a trained psychologist, whom my mother shamelessly preyed upon for advice whenever she or one of her children seemed in danger of succumbing to any kind of feelings other than the most cheerful and optimistic ones. "How are you, Dorothea?" I asked, plastering my best phony smile on my face.

"Good, good. How are *you?*" she said now, her eyebrows arching above her dark, carefully made-up eyes. Clearly I was the target of my mother's most recent concern. And this thought was confirmed when, mere moments after I had seated myself at the table, my mother jumped up and exclaimed, "Look at the time! I'll have to hurry if I hope to pick Clark up at the college before they lock him in for the weekend!"

"What happened to Clark's car?" I asked suspiciously.

"Oh, your brother is using it today—he needed an SUV to pick up Tiffany's new kitchen sink at Home Depot. I won't be long," she said airily, grabbing her keys from the hook where she kept them and heading for the door. "Why don't you two have a little chat while I'm gone?" she added encouragingly. And with a wink at Dorothea, who actually had the grace to seem embarrassed, she disappeared.

I smiled wanly at Dorothea as she smoothed a carefully manicured and much-beringed hand over her shiny black bob. "Sorry about this, Emma," she began, waving a hand helplessly in the air. "Your mother seems to think you might need someone to talk to…you know, because of all that's happened recently. With Derrick. Your father," she continued, her eyes widening at me as if trying to say I *could* talk to her, if I wanted to, but she wasn't going to push it.

"My mother seems to think I can't manage my life without her butting into it periodically," I replied.

"She cares about you, Emma. She wants you to be happy."

"I am happy," I protested. *I think.* Why was it that I always seemed happiest in opposition to my mother's attempts to *make* me happy?

Dorothea smiled as if *she* was satisfied with my answer. "I'm sure you are." Then, "Are you still living in the city? West Village, wasn't it?"

"Yes…yes, I am," I said.

"I love the West Village. I used to live there myself years ago. When I did my master's in Social Work at the New School."

Now that the subject had safely turned to New York neighbor-hoods, we fell into a comfortable rapport, as Dorothea regaled me with tales of her days as a young single woman in New York, before she met her first husband—she had since divorced and re-married happily—and moved to suburbia. "Those were the days," she said now, and looked at me with something close to envy. "And you can never go back to them," she added philosophically. "I know you've probably heard this a million times Emma, but these really are the best years of your life. Take it from one who knows. Don't be in such a hurry to run to the next step. You're living in the greatest city in the world. Enjoy it while you can!"

Attempting to dispel some of the embarrassing exuberance her words cast over the room—bonding with my mother's friends al-ways made me uneasy—I started in with my usual round of self-denigrating apartment jokes. "Well, I might enjoy it more if I were occupying the greatest *apartment* in the greatest city in the world. You know, living in the hippest neighborhood does have its price. My apartment is so small, the wall-to-wall carpeting says Welcome on it."

This earned me a laugh. Then: "What are you in, a studio?"

"You could call it that," I replied. "Most people living fifty miles or more outside of NYC might classify it as a walk-in closet."

"Rent stabilized?"

"Yep." Then I laughed. "Ah, the chains that bind us."

"Don't I know it," Dorothea said, waving a hand in the air. "In fact, the apartment where I used to live on Thompson Street is a rent-stabilized one bedroom, and to this day, I still haven't managed to let go of it. A friend of mine is living in it right now—and it turned out to be the perfect spot for her after her divorce." Then, as a new thought struck her, her eyes lit up and she looked at me with renewed enthusiasm. "You know, last time we spoke, she was pretty serious about the guy she was seeing. They had been talking marriage, with a move back to suburbia and everything. Maybe I'll give her a call. If she gives up the place, you're welcome to it. It's a nice space. And not too far from where you live now."

My heart started pumping madly, as it always did when anyone dangled a larger but still rent-stabilized possibility in front of me. "I'd love to take a look at it. I mean, if your friend *is* moving."

"Well, even if she isn't, it's only a matter of time," Dorothea said. "Stacy hasn't known what to do with herself since she lost the status of Suburban Wife. She'll be married and back on Long Island soon enough."

Her words filled me with glee, and by the time my mother returned with Clark in tow, I was brimming with barely contained excitement.

"Well," my mother said, eyeing us speculatively, a smile lingering on her lips, "I can see you two have had quite a nice little chat while I was gone."

Dorothea winked at me, and I couldn't help but smile back. "It was quite a nice little chat indeed," I replied, feeling something strumming inside me that I had not felt for what seemed a long, long time.

Hope.

Twelve

"Even the mentally insane need love."
—Beatrice Simms, mascot, Building of the Incurables

Confession: I have discovered the price of happiness, and it is below market value.

It amazed me how much the hope of space in New York could be a balm to my soul. I practically skipped to the subway on Monday morning as a vision danced in my head of me lounging on a sofa that did not double as a bed in some spacious future living room.

It was enough to make me think I needed nothing and, more specifically, no one. To hell with Max and his twenty-foot ceilings and slightly larger than average apparatus. If I got this apartment, I could do anything—even brave the Pink Pussycat Boutique. I was ready for sex toys, service for one and—you guessed it—that miniature schnauzer, who yelped joyfully at me as I passed the pet store on my way home from work that night. My life felt new again, and anything was possible.

My father came home from rehab on Tuesday—whether for good behavior or because his insurance had run out, I didn't know and was afraid to ask. But when I spoke to him he sounded unexpectedly cheerful. Turned out he'd hooked up with a new lawyer in rehab. Apparently Stan Farber had an occasional problem with barbiturates, but other than that, he was a pretty damn good attorney. And though I was afraid that my father's happiness would last only as long as his lawyer's patience, I was ready to relinquish him to his new god.

The work week flew by, with me suddenly productive now that no one expected anything more than my usual contributions. The flutter over Rebecca's promotion had suddenly died down, due to new rumors—sparked mostly by Marcy Keller—that Patricia's marriage was on the rocks. Though I didn't think Patricia had enough of a marriage to warrant much excitement over her divorce, I was relieved to relinquish the role of object of everyone's speculation. In fact, everyone pretty much went back to ignoring my existence, much less the fact that I had been so recently and embarrassingly passed over for a promotion.

By the time the weekend came, I was feeling increasingly optimistic. In fact, I even caved in to Jade's insistence that I go to Fire Island with her for the July Fourth weekend. Especially since, after donning my bathing suit, I saw how much firmer I looked all around. Firm enough to allow myself to get on a scale—and discover I had lost seven pounds! And though my beach weekend did not result in any new romance—every man there was much too pretty for my taste—it served to solidify my relationship with Jade on a new level. For we were two women bonded by something even stronger than our growing-up years—we were both single women on the make who needed nothing and no one except each other and the latest shade of lipstick from Bobbie Brown—available, of course, in Jade's up-to-the-moment makeup stash. We ruthlessly prowled the bars on Fire Island in provocative clothing, flirting with the kind of men I once would have been frightened to share elevator space with. And then we blithely left those same men standing alone in the bar at the sight of even the slightest flaw—an open fly, a hair out of place, a blatant display of machismo. I had never felt so powerful. Or so sexy, despite the fact that I hadn't had so much as a good-night kiss since my ill-fated fling with Max Van Gelder.

But within two days of returning to the city, the bottom fell out—for me, that is. "You're never going to believe this," Jade said when we met for drinks at Revolution after work on Tuesday night, hoping to somehow recapture the holiday weekend revelry despite our reluctant return to the nine-to-five life. "I'd believe anything at this point," I replied, sipping a Tequila Linda as I studied her enigmatic expression.

"Ted is back."

Tequila practically came out of my nose. "You're kidding?"

"Nope. And it gets even better," she continued, her eyes filled with a mixture of disbelief and, I have to admit, excitement.

I waited, wondering what any man could have possibly done to arouse Jade to such a heightened state of emotion.

"Apparently you were right about him," she said.

"That he was an asshole? A brainless musclehead?" I said, combing my memory for any epitaphs I might have devised for Ted in those early dismal days when Jade thought she would never hear from him again.

"No, no," she replied, shaking her head. "Remember the first explanation you gave for why he didn't call me?"

I thought about this for a minute, then finally came up with it. "That he was hit by a bus?"

Her raised eyebrows and ridiculously large smile said it all.

"You have *got* to be kidding me!"

"Nope. I came home last night and there he was, waiting on my front stoop and looking just as scrumptious as ever, though he had this incredibly sexy scar on his chin."

Leave it to Jade to find inflamed tissue appealing. "What the hell did he say?"

"That he'd been in and out of the hospital for the past couple of months. Apparently he got up the next day after our date, hopped on his bike for a trip down the West Side Highway and met a bus head-on. He was in ICU for the first two weeks, and—get this— when he finally got out, the first person he thought of was me. How much he wanted to call me, let me know how much he enjoyed being with me."

I was filled with disbelief at the sight of Jade's dreamy-eyed expression. "So why *didn't* he call?" I asked suspiciously. After all, one of us had to remain rational here, and clearly it wasn't going to be Jade.

"Well, it wasn't so easy for him once he got out of the hospital. He was forced to face a new reality. His body was broken, his face scarred. His modeling career was essentially...over," she finished, her face long with sympathy.

"So what? Did you tell him you only dated models or something?"

Jade eyeballed me as if I were some sort of dimwit. "No, no. It was nothing like that. It was that he no longer had a *job*. His confidence dropped, and he fell into a kind of funk. He figured no woman, especially one as successful as myself, would want anything to do with a jobless loser."

"Hmm…" I said. Though I didn't want to forgive Ted, I was starting to understand. While women suffered from body issues, men suffered from provider instinct. If they couldn't bring home the bacon, they didn't feel very appetizing themselves. Still, I resisted. "I don't know, Jade."

But judging by the look on her face, she wasn't listening. "You know, he even thought I wouldn't find him attractive anymore. I mean, not only is his face scarred, but his back is, too. The funny thing is, I thought he looked kind of…of rugged with all those scars. And it was so sweet the way he looked at me—like he wanted me but was afraid I…I wouldn't want him."

"If he wanted you so bad, then why didn't he *call?*" I insisted. "I mean, being injured is one thing. And the job thing, well, that's understandable. But to make you wonder all these months, not just pick up the phone and—"

I came to an abrupt halt when I realized Jade was staring at me. "What has gotten into you, Emma? I thought you'd be happy for me. I thought—"

"I'm sorry," I began, "You'll have to excuse me if I'm a little distrustful of anything a man has to say these days. Especially when it borders on the absurd!"

She relented a little. "Look, I was mentally right where you are when I came home last night and saw him sitting there. I was ready to make a few cutting remarks and walk on by. But then he started talking. And maybe it was the sight of those forearms, but I started listening." She smiled at the memory. "He explained that when he first came out of the hospital, scarred and out of work, he didn't even dream of calling me. He pretty much put me out of his head. And after a month or so of physical therapy, and lots of soul-searching, he realized he needed to move on with his life. So he got a job with a friend's construction company. Once he started working with his hands for a while, he felt a satisfaction, a confidence, he hadn't known before. He said he thought of me all the time at that point. Wished he'd called me earlier and thought now it was probably too late." She looked me straight in the eye then. "He said he'd felt this…bond, this *connection* with me from that first night. Can you believe that? I guess I *didn't* imagine it…" she said, her expression growing dreamy once more before she continued. "He knew I'd slam down the phone if he even tried to call, so he came to my apartment last night and just waited until I got home, trying to figure out how he was going to get me to at least listen to him, never mind go out with him again." She leaned back in her chair. "And believe me, when I saw him there, I was shocked. And angry. Until I saw that look…" She sighed.

"That look?" I inquired.

"There was something in his eyes, something that told me that this wasn't bullshit. Something…real."

Suddenly realization crashed down on me. Dear God, was it possible? I studied Jade's eyes, and when I saw the emotion glowing in them, I knew. Jade, my best friend, soul sister and newfound partner in Single Girldom, was on the verge of falling hopelessly, maddeningly, in love.

Confession: Ted isn't the only one with scars…

Okay, so I wasn't exactly happy to be left alone on the brink of my newfound Single Girldom. And, yes, I'll admit that it took me some time to be happy for Jade. In fact, it wasn't until I saw her and Ted together the following Friday—we had all met for dinner, that is Alyssa and Richard, Jade and Ted and me, playing fifth wheel—that I started to come around. I needed to see for myself the evidence of Ted's recent bodily injury. Yes, it was real. And when I witnessed the goofy glaze of happiness that came into his eyes whenever he looked at Jade, which was often, I knew that Jade had found it. True love. The kind that could wipe away any lingering doubts that the men who had come before might have placed in her heart. The kind that could heal.

So there I was, spending Saturday night alone again, but this time it felt different. *I* felt different. For one thing, I had heard from Dorothea and learned that her friend Stacy had, in fact, gotten engaged and was happily making plans to move back to the burbs in about three months' time. By mid-fall, I would be living in an adult-size apartment, complete with wood-burning fireplace, which I discovered with great delight when I dropped by after work to view the apartment. After being greeted by a glowing Stacy, who couldn't help showing me her 1.5 carat marquis as she escorted me through the rooms(!), I thrilled to the sight of the high ceilings, picture-frame moldings and even a claw-foot tub. This was a place I could truly make a home. And maybe, I thought as I eyed the spacious bedroom and ample storage, share with someone someday.

But as I headed down the steps of my own dilapidated building that Saturday night, hoping to escape my four walls temporarily while I sought out something that might resemble dinner, the dream of a new man seemed impossible. The best vision I could conjure up was an image of me in my new apartment, curled up in front of a blazing fire, a book in my hand and a schnauzer at my feet.

As I descended the final flight of stairs, I was stopped dead at the bottom by the sight of Beatrice barreling—somewhat merrily, I noted—out her front door. And in a dress, no less. True, it was neon floral and could probably provide temporary shelter for a small family stranded on a desert plain, but she did look somewhat more…feminine.

"Hello, neighbor!" she bellowed when she turned and caught sight of me sneaking past her to exit.

"Hello, Beatrice, how are you?" I replied, resigned to have a bit of chat with the lonely old gal.

But Beatrice breezed by me, apparently in a hurry herself. "Wonderful, wonderful. Except I'm very late." As she pulled open the outer door, she turned to me and whispered confidingly, "I'm meeting my *man friend* at the park. We're going to have turkey sandwiches and pound cake together!" she exclaimed, holding up the shopping bag she clutched in one hand, a girlish grin on her gruesome features. And with that, she was gone, leaving me holding the door, dumbfounded.

Even Beatrice, it seemed, was no longer without a man. While I...

Suddenly I knew what I had to do. I turned toward Heavenly Dee-lites, realizing that if a woman really wanted something in this city, she had to go for it, no-holds-barred. And I was determined to have the one man who had stubbornly taken up residence in my fantasy life, ever since that fateful day I first laid eyes on him over a gallon of Double Mocha Chip. The Skinny Scoop man. Who cared that he probably earned slightly more than minimum wage? He was gorgeous and he was male and I had come to believe that if I asked for much more from a man, it was asking too much. I felt powerful all of sudden, as I marched confidently toward Heavenly Dee-lites, checking my reflection in a storefront as I went by. I looked powerful. I was Jade before Ted. And that wasn't so bad, was it? Better that than the mopey, pathetic ex-girlfriend of Derrick I'd been for so many weeks.

When I finally reached my destination, I combed my fingers through my hair one more time for courage, pulled open the door, which jingled madly in anticipation, and stepped inside.

Only to be greeted by the sweet old familiar face of the woman who owned the place.

"Well, hello there!" she called out to me pleasantly as I moved helplessly toward the counter.

"Hi, how are you?" I replied, noting how very tanned and relaxed she looked.

"Wonderful! My husband and I just got back from a cruise to Barcelona!" Then she smiled. "A little gift from our son."

Swallowing my disappointment that they weren't still away cruising while I seduced their stock boy, I replied, "That sounds wonderful. Your son is very generous."

She beamed. "He is such a *good boy*. He almost never thinks of himself, and yet he works so hard. I swear the only time I see him relax is when he comes over to play cards with us on Friday nights. My husband and I have a bridge group," she added.

I smiled, trying to imagine this perfect son, shuffling cards and dealing them out to the old folks on a Friday night. And I thought *I* didn't have a life.

"You know, I think he just needs to meet the right girl," she said, looking at me with new interest.

Oh, dear. Now I was being eyeballed as the prospective date of their son, Nerd of the Western World. So much for my grand seduction plan. "That's, uh, sweet of you to say so, but I, uh, well you know, I already have a boyfriend."

"Oh?" she said, looking puzzled. As if my presence alone in her store on a Saturday night for the umpteenth time somehow didn't coincide with the picture I was attempting to create of my alleged coupledom. She shook her head then, as if remembering herself. "I'm sorry, dear. I'm rambling on. What can I get you? A pint of Double Mocha Chip?"

As my gaze fell upon the freezer full of Skinny Scoop, a fresh wave of sadness swept over me. Suddenly I wasn't ready to relinquish hope of seeing the succulent stock boy tonight. A plan began to form in my mind, as my eye fell on the Double Mocha Chip, fully stocked and ready to purchase. If I could come up with a flavor that might not be so readily available, that might require a call down to the basement....

"Do you have Banana Nut Crunch?" I said, naming the flavor that Derrick had always loved and I had despised. It had been a point of contention between us during our relationship, as I never really could relate to a man who didn't like chocolate. Now, I realized with growing glee, there wasn't a pint of Banana Nut Crunch to be found in the freezer case, and that simple fact might just bring me closer to—

"You know, I don't see it here," the woman said after a thorough search of the freezer. "Let me just call downstairs," she continued, and headed for the intercom on the wall.

I started to panic as I heard her ordering a search of Banana Nut Crunch. What would I do when he arrived, Skinny Scoop in hand? How could I subtly let him know my intentions, without alarming this nice old woman who thought me good enough for her sweet, doofy son?

As the door to the basement opened, my heart thundered madly in my chest. Perhaps I could somehow slip him my number, or make some allusion to a bar in the neighborhood where we could meet—

My mind came suddenly to a halt at the sight of a man—specifically, the kind old husband of the aforementioned kind old lady—standing at the top of the steps, a pint of Banana Nut Crunch in hand.

"This the one you wanted, Gloria?" he said, smiling gently at her as he held out the container.

"Yes, that's it," she said, walking toward him and taking the container in her right hand. Then she reached up with her free hand and touched him gently on his softly wrinkled cheek. "Thank you, sweetheart."

They stared at each other for a few moments, their gazes filled with so much love I felt a lump thickening in my throat at the sight, followed by a flood of shame as I remembered the lustful designs I'd had on their stock boy. Once the old man retreated through the door again and the woman had bagged my purchase, I quickly paid her and made my exit, heading home to my too-lonely apartment with a container of my least favorite flavor of Skinny Scoop and a heart full of sorrow.

As I crammed the container of Skinny Scoop into my freezer, untouched, I wondered how I had failed so miserably at being the bold Single Woman I imagined myself to be. After all, Jade would never find herself stuck with Banana Nut Crunch when she craved Double Mocha Chip.

But then, Jade had never been desperate enough to do anything she could, at the cost of her own well-being, to please a man.

Suddenly my life fell into relief. How I had tried so hard to be what Derrick wanted me to be that I didn't pay attention to who I really was, what I really wanted. All that time I was trying not to care that he didn't want to move on to the next step in our relationship, trying to pretend I was just as much a solitary artist as he was, I forgot who I really was.

After that revelation, everything else sort of fell into place. I didn't blame Max for not calling me. Who would call a woman who thought so little of herself that she practically threw herself at him from date one? Heck, the fact that we had a second date at all probably only meant he was hoping to at least relieve some sexual tension with the first willing girl he found himself remotely attracted to. After all, I knew what New York City was like, how hard it was to get close to anyone still breathing, much less sexually active. And there I was, sitting by the phone, like an operator standing by to fulfill his every sexual desire. Wondering when he was going to pick up the phone and give my life meaning again.

What an idiot I had been!

It was all going to come to a stop, I decided. The waiting. The hope that someone else could somehow make my life go from barely tolerable to remotely happy. Emma Carter waited for no one anymore.

Confession: I fall prey to the shopping gods—and exorcise a few demons.

When I went into the office the following week, more revelations followed. Especially when I caught myself hovering by the copy editor's cubicle while she read my latest piece on headgear, waiting for whatever compliments on my clever turns of phrase she might toss my way. Suddenly I realized I was doing exactly what I had said I wouldn't do: waiting for someone else to tell me I was spending my life in some worthwhile way. On the way back to my own cube, I saw Rebecca holding court in Patricia's office, the two women obviously engaged in the kind of tête-à-tête that would more than likely land Rebecca the office next to Patricia's someday.

But instead of feeling dejected, instead of blaming all those misguided souls at *Bridal Best* for not recognizing my genius, not begging for my leadership, I let go of the strange hold their opinions had over me. Who was Patricia, after all, to decide what kind of work I was or wasn't suited for? She didn't know me, her anonymous employee. Hell, I doubt she even knew her own husband. I was the master of my destiny, not her. And not Rebecca. Not even Derrick, dammit. It was up to me to decide what life had in store for Emma Carter. And after the initial high these revelations induced in me, I headed home at week's end determined to discover just what that life was.

And realized I didn't have a clue.

Which is probably why I fell prey to my mother's machinations first thing Saturday morning.

"Emma, I'm glad I caught you," she began, when I picked up the phone in the half haze of sleep.

I opened my eyes and did a half turn to glare at the clock on my bedstand. "Where else would I be at eight-thirty on Saturday morning?"

Ignoring my irritation, she continued, "What do you have planned for today?"

"Nothing," I muttered, then realized I spoke without thinking, leaving myself open to whatever scenario my mother had in mind.

"Wonderful! I thought I'd come into the city and do a little shoe shopping. Macy's is having a sale and the one on Thirty-Fourth Street has five shoe departments—so much better than the one at the *mall*." She said mall with a distaste that surprised me, coming from a woman who pilgrimaged there at least twice-weekly. "The wedding is two months away, and I still need shoes! I thought I could pick up some new sandals for the honeymoon. Maybe some strappy heels for evening…"

If there was one thing my mother and I had in common, it was a weakness for footwear. The only difference was, she had more buying power. And maybe it was this compelling fact that per-suaded me to spend all day Saturday shopping with her until my shoulders ached and my soul cried out for something more sub-stantial than the contemplation of the virtues of open-toe versus enclosed shoe. Or maybe it was just that I hoped to avoid any more time spent alone after a Friday night spent obsessing over where my life was going and wondering whether I did, in fact, *have* a life.

Now, as I sat exhausted in a chair next to my mother's while she tried on her fifth pair of open-toe, low-heeled, neutral-colored sandals—a pair she claimed she would need in case her outfit called for something other than the open-toe, low-heeled black sandals, strappy silver high heels, black slides or red mules she'd already purchased in addition to the off-white pump she would wear to marry Clark—I wondered how I had gotten into this mess. Then I eyeballed the bags surrounding my feet, two of which were mine and contained the sexiest, strappiest red heels and the most adorable pair of sneakers I had ever seen, and remembered that it had been my own greed that had been my undoing.

Finally my mother looked up from where she'd been trying without success to adjust the strap on her current shoe selection so that it didn't leave so much of her big toe exposed. "You know what?" she said, sudden reason dawning in her eyes. "I don't really need these anyway. What do you say we put this to rest and go get some lunch?"

Since eating was always my favorite option, I readily agreed. Once we had negotiated the crowds and made our way out of Macy's, we opted to get away from the maddening midtown scene and hopped a cab downtown. We decided to eat at Zen Palate, as my mother had just finished reading a book on the virtues of soy and was eager to jump into her next phase: vegetarianism.

An hour later, halfway through a plate of curried udon noodles with tofu and vegetables, my mother put down her fork. "You know, this is good," she said, picking up her napkin and patting her lips, "but I don't know if I can go the whole nine yards with this vegetarian stuff." She smiled. "I grew up on meat. It seems unnatural *not* to eat it!"

I smiled back at her, feeling in good spirits again now that we were safely away from any beckoning sales and my tummy was full of sautéed eggplant and fried bean curd. "Yeah, well, I haven't officially crossed over myself, though Alyssa swears soy is the answer to everything."

"How is Alyssa doing?"

"Alyssa's great. She and Richard are doing great," I replied, remembering how happy they had looked together last time I'd seen them. "I bet they'll be engaged any day now."

"Oh, that *is* good news," my mother replied, her smile shining in her eyes. "And Jade? Is she dating anyone?"

"As it turns out," I replied, "Jade is in love."

"In love!" my mother exclaimed, her joy evident. "With who?"

"This guy Ted she met at the gym. Real sweet. Nothing like Michael."

"Thank God," my mother replied. She had met Michael once
or twice and even on such short acquaintance could tell what a self-
absorbed jerk he was. I guess that's one of the benefits of dating
into your fifties—you gain a sixth sense when it comes to men and
can spot a creep at five hundred yards. "It was about time Jade
met someone good," Mom continued.

An awkward silence fell between us, during which I was positive
my mother's thoughts had turned to me, her daughter, who I'm
sure she deemed well overdue for Mr. Perfect.

"What?" I said, trying to wipe the look of anticipation off her
face. Did she think I had actually met someone who had any sort
of potential and then deliberately kept the news from her?

"Nothing!" she replied. "I was just wondering what was going
on with you."

I immediately became defensive, spoiling the pleasant mood between us. And though I regretted it later, some demon inside me
drove me to it and I couldn't help myself. "Do you want to know
what's going on with *me,* or do you want to know what's going
on in my *love life?* Because if it's the latter, I have nothing to say
on the subject. But if it's the former—"

"Emma! What's with this attack? I thought we were having a
nice time. I thought—"

"Maybe that's the problem with you," I said, an anger surging
over me that I hadn't even realized had been simmering. "You
always want to think we're having a *nice time.* Well, maybe if
you'd just lay off the meds for a few days, you'd realize life isn't
so rosy most of the time. That maybe we aren't always having a
nice time. That maybe life just plain *sucks* most of the time."

My mother's face crumbled with a mixture of hurt and concern,
causing the first wave of regret to crash over me. What had I done?
And *why* had I done it?

I sighed, my anger morphing into self-hatred. "I'm sorry. I didn't
mean—"

She held up a hand, cutting me off. "First, in defense of myself
I want to say that I haven't so much as touched antidepressants
since…since a few months after I met Clark. I know I depended
on them a lot to get me through the rough patches over the years,

but those days are over for me. Ever since I met Clark, everything is different. *I'm* different.''

Needless to say, I was shocked, and a little suspicious. ''Don't you worry that your happiness is too dependent on Clark? I mean, didn't you just trade one drug for another? Antidepressants for love?''

She shook her head emphatically. ''No. Because when I met Clark, I was in a different place emotionally. I had been through counseling. I was down to only five hundred milligrams a day. I felt like...like I understood myself better. Like I knew what I wanted out of life. So when Clark came into the picture, I was sure it was him.''

Now I was truly shell-shocked. It seemed my mother, while blundering through her marriages and seemingly making a mess of her life, had managed to find happiness. I ached with a mixture of shimmering hope and utter despair.

Because I realized I could be happy one day, too, but it wouldn't be something I could easily find in Macy's shoe department, or even at the bottom of a Skinny Scoop container. In fact, I suspected I had a lot more hell to go through before I even got close. But for the first time, I realized with tremulous hope as I studied my mother's satisfied expression, I *would* get there. *If* I gave it a chance.

Confession: I am forced to shed my role as office pariah—and ex-girlfriend.

The following week I felt as if a great load had suddenly been lifted off my shoulders. I even summoned up the courage to call my dad to check up on him. The good news was that he appeared to be laying off the alcohol, and had even started to attend some Alcoholics Anonymous meetings, which was a good sign, considering that he usually wrote them off, saying that the only people who went to those meetings were people who ''really had problems.'' For years, my father seemed to think he fell into another category. I suppose this had a lot to do with the fact that he had managed to stay functional even during his hardest drinking days.

He held down a job, renovated his first home and, when he remarried, completely overhauled his second home, though he was a bit older and a lot less fit for the job. All with the assistance of good old Johnnie Walker. But now that he was retired and found himself falling off of rooftops, I guess he figured it was time to face a few facts.

I began to feel cautiously optimistic about him. And I might have been more hopeful if Deirdre hadn't mentioned that he was still vigorously seeking a new lawyer for his lawsuit against the harness company. I guess he still couldn't let go of the need for a scapegoat yet.

And I should know. I had a few scapegoats of my own, I discovered. Namely, Rebecca, who, I realized, I had turned into the one reason why I would never succeed in life.

It seemed that in the weeks following Rebecca's rise to power I had become the unsung heroine of the weary and disgruntled among the ranks of *Bridal Best.* People like Lucretia Henry with her dead-end job and Marcy Keller, who lacked an inner emotional life, took every opportunity to let me know how strongly they felt that the promotion should have been mine, how I had been a victim of the kind of mismanagement that would one day bring the magazine to its knees. I will admit that my survival at *Bridal Best* in the weeks after Rebecca moved into her freshly painted office, complete with a door and a window with an East River view, was dependent on this kind of bitter commentary. How else could I go on if I didn't convince myself that Rebecca, with her power suits and freshly trimmed bob, hadn't blindsided Patricia and everyone else into thinking she was better than she actually was?

For a while there, I was doing just fine as the disgruntled, passed over contributing editor. In fact, a strange calm had settled over me. A calm that allowed me to compose articles and develop captions and savvy headlines in a more timely and efficient manner than I ever had before. It was as if I had become indifferent to the impact my work would have on others, and this attitude, oddly enough, made my job easier to do. It was like sleepwalking during a hike up Mount Everest. Though I would probably never make it to the top, I would somehow manage to get by, as long as I didn't open my eyes and see the jagged cliffs below.

Then Caroline went and stirred things up. I was sitting cross-legged in my cubicle, meticulously renaming all my file folders as part of my newfound desire to see myself as one of the holy organized few, when I felt Caroline's now very pregnant presence in my doorway. As I greeted her cheerfully, I saw a look of concern in her expression that I wondered at, until she asked me to meet me in her office for "a chat" when I had "a free moment."

Naturally I was worried. Had someone overheard me mimicking Patricia's soft-spoken speeches about the magic of *Bridal Best?* Did Marcy let out that I was the one responsible for the decapitated bride layout that was hung anonymously on the lunchroom wall?

I dropped everything I was doing and hurried after Caroline. Though I was not really ready to face my fate, I was clearly unable to live with the unknown.

By the time I reached her doorway, Caroline had already seated herself among the mounds of paper that filled her office. Despite the fact that she was on the verge of leaving for three months on maternity leave, she seemed just as unfazed as ever by the endless deadline pressure and general insanity of life at *Bridal Best.* She even looked serene as she bent her head over the layout before her. I almost ran away, suddenly not wanting to disturb her, when she looked up, blinking at me in surprise. "Oh, Emma. You're here already. Well, come in," she said, gesturing to the seat across from her. "I'll just be a minute."

I obeyed, sitting anxiously while she finished reviewing the spread before her. When she finally looked up at me, I saw the same concern I'd seen earlier still creasing her brow.

"How's everything going, Emma?" she asked.

So determined was I to wipe that worry from her brow that I immediately launched into a relentlessly cheerful speech about how wonderful everything was, how focused I was lately, how organized I was becoming. How my desk was so clean and well maintained that I could perform surgery there, if necessary—this last said with my usual token laugh.

Caroline was not amused. "That's all well and good, Emma. But I want to know how *you're* doing."

Suddenly I knew what was coming. Caroline was that kind of touchy-feely boss who likes to make sure on a regular basis that the employees in her care are feeling happy and loved. And since I had so recently exhibited signs of despair, I felt sure she wanted to get to the bottom of things with me.

I stifled a sigh. "I'm great. Life is great."

"How's the writing going?"

"Good, good," I replied. After all, I had handed in my last two articles on time and after little toil. Suddenly I worried that maybe my lack of toil was resulting in lackluster writing. If that was the case, then I needed to know. "Uh...has there been...I mean, have you had some negative feedback on me, uh, recently?"

"No, no. Not at all," Caroline said, shaking her head in denial. "I was just concerned, that's all. I thought you might have been...distracted by recent events in this office."

I knew the "events" she referred to. Rebecca's promotion. My downfall. Since the subject could no longer be avoided, I launched into it. "Well, to be honest, Caroline, things have gotten...easier for me since the decision to promote Rebecca was made. I'm concentrating better on my writing. And everything is just going... easier."

She smiled. "I'm glad to hear that."

I smiled back, relieved to have reestablished my position as a contented employee with Caroline.

"The truth is," Caroline continued, "I was surprised you ever wanted the senior features editor position at all."

This took me aback. What did she think I was doing here, anyway? Did she expect me to be some sort of corporate slave forever, endlessly belting out copy on the magic of happily-ever-after and all the nightmarish preparation that went into planning for it?

As if she read my mind, Caroline continued, "I don't want you to take this the wrong way. It's just that I've always seen your writing as your strength. It's one of the reasons I wanted you on my team as a contributing editor. Truthfully there's very little writing involved in the senior features position. Mostly management stuff.'' She rolled her eyes. ''I should know.'' Then she smiled. ''I don't know if I ever told you this, but I used to fancy myself a writer. Right after college I wrote a lifestyles column for a newspaper back home in Ohio. Of course, that was before I met my husband and his job brought us to the East Coast and me to *Bridal Best.* When I first got here, I was the reigning writer on the staff, until I got offered a spot in management and spent more time assigning articles than actually writing them.'' She smiled. ''You know, when you came on board, I saw a little of myself in you.''

Now I was really shocked. Caroline, Miss Perfect Wife, Mother and Manager, saw herself in *me?*

''Of course, I could have kept up the writing on the side, but a lot of other things got in the way of my pursuing that dream,'' she said. ''All good things, of course. Miles and I bought the house, and it needed so much work to make it a home. Then Sarah came along, surprise, surprise.'' She chuckled.

Surprise, surprise, indeed, I thought. Up until now, I had always believed Caroline had carefully orchestrated every moment of her life, from puberty on. First boyfriend, first husband, first cozy Connecticut farmhouse and then three perfectly behaved and beautiful children.

''By the time my second child was born,'' she continued, ''I was up for a management position. How could I turn down that money when my family needed so much? When my husband and I wanted so much for our kids?'' Her face suddenly took on a wistful expression, and my heart leaped out to her. I had always seen Caroline's life as a dream-come-true—not as something that might have stifled a dream.

As if she read my mind again, she said, ''Don't get me wrong. I don't regret the choices I made. My life with my family is good, and it gave me great satisfaction to build it with my husband. The writing—that will come someday, in its own time.'' Then her gaze focused on me. ''But for some of us, that time could come sooner, if we don't let ourselves get sidetracked by...misplaced ambitions.''

I swallowed, hard, ever ready to deny that I had any ambitions other than to be one of the best at *Bridal Best.* But I knew Caroline wasn't looking for my pledge of allegiance to the company. She was looking for something more. Like my hopes and dreams. Things that, for reasons I didn't want to look at, were a lot harder to pledge my allegiance to.

By the time I eased myself out of her guest chair, Caroline and I had moved on to other, safer subjects, like my thoughts on the layout she was currently reviewing. But before I left her office, she had jotted down the name of an editor friend of hers at the magazine *Today's Woman,* encouraging me to contact her if I ever had an idea for an article that might not fit within the scope of *Bridal Best.* I knew by the smile behind her words that she was referring to my passionate though misguided proposal on women who said no to marriage. But I didn't take it the wrong way. Suddenly I felt as if Caroline was on my side. Rooting for me, even.

It was a good feeling, for the most part. Especially when I sent off a query letter two days later to Caroline's editor friend, proposing an article on, of all things, breaking up with the love of your life. Clearly I had struck a chord with the senior editor, because a week later she called to offer me a thousand-dollar advance to write the piece for the Relationships section in their fall issue. I was both thrilled and shocked, and called Jade and Alyssa immediately to tell them my good news.

Jade couldn't help giving me an "I-told-you-so" attitude.

Alyssa proposed a minicelebration the following Saturday night. Dinner and drinks. Just us girls. "Besides," she said, "it's been so long since the three of us got together."

By the time Saturday night arrived, our minicelebration had turned into a megacelebration. For Alyssa showed up at Miracle Grill on Bleeker, our chosen restaurant, with the most beautiful engagement ring I had ever seen and the sparkle of pure love in her eyes. She insisted she didn't want to upstage me, and ordered a round of drinks to toast my success as a writer, but as we waited for our food to arrive of course, Jade and I demanded all the details of the proposal scene.

It seemed Richard had gone for true romance. First he asked Alyssa to meet him at Central Park after work on Friday night for a free concert on the Great Lawn. As Alyssa stood waiting to meet

him at the Seventy-second Street entrance, suddenly out of nowhere
Lulu came running toward her. Alyssa admitted she was confused
at first, until she saw Richard in tow, a picnic basket in hand.
Though he calmly explained that Lulu "seemed lonely at home,"
Alyssa was naturally suspicious. Even more so when he led them
away from the Great Lawn and toward an alcove of trees further
in, which Alyssa immediately recognized as the place where they
had carved their initials into a tree in the weeks after they had
moved to New York together to share their first apartment. Richard
claimed he thought they would have a private little dinner before
the concert, but by then, Alyssa's heart was thrumming with anticipation. And once the blanket was laid with Lulu perched on the
edge as if she knew exactly what was going on, Richard got down
on one knee and told Alyssa just how much he loved her, how
much he hoped to make her his wife.

Even Jade had tears in her eyes by the time Alyssa was through.
"More drinks!" she immediately announced, gesturing to the
darkly handsome waiter at whom she barely batted an eyelash as
she ordered us another round.

"How's Ted?" I asked, after we had sufficiently toasted Alyssa's
engagement and settled in to contemplate just how good life was.

"Ted is perfect," Jade said. Then: "But he's trying to get me
to quit smoking."

"Good for him!" Alyssa said.

"Yeah," I chimed in, "you really do have to quit, Jade. Smoking
is just so passé."

"Listen to you," Jade said, "the hip new writer for *Today's
Woman* magazine."

"Yes, I can't wait to read your article!" Alyssa said, "What's
it about, anyway?"

I smiled as I lifted my glass, "Getting over your ex-boyfriend."

Jade and Alyssa lifted their glasses. "I'll drink to that," Jade
said.

And we banged glasses yet again. But the merriment surrounding
us at the moment didn't stop Alyssa from doing a little check on
my emotional state.

"So how are you doing, anyway? I mean, I haven't asked because I didn't want to bring up the *D* word, especially since things have been going so well for you,'' Alyssa said.

"I'm fine," I replied, my token response. "Though I have to say, when I got the offer from *Today's Woman,* I wanted to call him up and tell him."

"Have you heard from him?" Jade asked.

"No, not since I bit his head off for having a good life without me."

They were both silent for a moment, which made me suddenly feel bad. As if I should be feeling worse about the fact that Derrick hadn't called. To be honest, I did feel sadness, but the kind of sadness that comes when you've shared your everything with someone for two years and now didn't even dare speak to him rather than the sadness of someone who knows she's lost the great love of her life.

"I guess I'm doomed to be that angry girl he left behind in New York," I said, trying to muster up some humor about the situation. "The Eternal Ex-girlfriend."

Jade put down her glass with a thud. "Emma Carter, you are no longer an ex-girlfriend."

I looked up at her, both confused and hopeful that she had found some better definition for me.

Then she smiled. "You are officially a Single Woman. And believe me, that's not such a bad thing."

And with another bang of our glasses, we drank to my new incarnation.

Thirteen

"Being blond isn't everything. But it helps!"
—Sebastian Yeager, lapsed Beauty Queen

Confession: I am an ex-girlfriend's best friend.

Now that I had moved on to the next phase of my life, I was able to let go of a few things. Like my anger. I even relented on my noncompliance with Rebecca's stance and managed to belt out a pretty damn good article on my mother's upcoming marriage to husband number three for Rebecca's special issue. Of course, our newest senior features editor was thrilled to receive it, and I was proud of my efforts. Still, I couldn't help feeling, with a certain amount of resignation as I watched her slip my article into her shiny leather satchel, that there were just some women who got everything in life. The great job. The great man. And others, like me, who didn't. And even as she promised me a quick read that evening as she headed out the door, all I could think about was Rebecca curled up in front of a fireplace reading my article while Nash looked on adoringly, just waiting for her to finish up so he could carry her off to bed for a full-body massage followed by a thorough review of the kind of engagement ring she wanted. For I knew that would come in a matter of time. Just last week Rebecca told me that Nash had been at Tiffany.com. Not that she was snooping, she said, she just happened to notice that address line on his home computer while she had been surfing, signifying he had recently visited the site.

The next day, anxious to get her take on my article, which I'd fretted over for some reason the night before, I hovered by her new office, wondering desperately where she was. Rebecca was *always* on time, and it was nearly nine-thirty already. I had even managed to convince myself that she'd called in sick in order to avoid telling me how bad my piece was, when I saw her storming down the hallway toward me, gripping her leather satchel in front of her, her eyes downcast. I stumbled toward the water fountain near her door, not wanting to seem too anxious, and proceeded to fill one of the paper cups there. When she saw me, sipping nonchalantly, she lifted her gaze to mine and I was struck by the well of sorrow I saw in her blue eyes. "Can I talk to you?" she practically begged, her mouth curling dangerously, as if she might even cry.

"Sure," I said, crumbling my now-empty cup and tossing it in the wastebasket nearby. I followed her into her new office, and she immediately exercised her prerogatives as a senior features editor by shutting her brand-new door soundly behind us.

Then she dropped her leather satchel on the floor and sat down, gesturing to the guest chair across from her desk so that I would join her. She sighed, then—looking me straight in the eye—declared, "He fucking dumped me."

So thrown off was I by the sound of an obscenity coming out of Rebecca's pretty little blueblood mouth, I asked dumbly, "Who?"

"Nash!" she all but shouted at me, her eyes bulging. "Who else?" And then, as if saying his name caused her great pain, her lower lip began to tremble.

"Ah, Bec, I'm sorry." And I was. I couldn't bear to see anyone—not even Rebecca—suffer over a man. Especially after my own recent experience, which still stabbed at me painfully whenever I allowed myself the liberty to torture myself over it. "What happened?"

Her watery gaze sharpened suddenly, bolstered by a new, more satisfying emotion. Anger. "Well, last night he took me to Lutèce, which he knew I'd been dying to go to," she began, swiping a hand under her eye to dash away the tear that threatened to fall. "He had the reservation since last week, and I'm thinking, this is it, he's going to ask me to marry him." She smiled tremulously. "I was even going to tell you about it, but I was afraid of jinxing myself, you know? But I was so sure. I mean, he'd just been to

Tiffany.com, confirming his order—or so I thought. Apparently he'd only gone to check out a pen to buy for his boss's retirement gift!'' Swallowing back the surge of anger that admission had so obviously caused, she continued, "What else was I to think? I mean, I had practically wallpapered his apartment in ads featuring their Lucida-cut diamond, which is Tiffany's newest style. You know the one I'm talking about, right? Square-cut?''

I did have a vague memory of some stunning, square-shaped diamond in a Tiffany ad I'd seen in a recent layout we'd done, so I nodded my head once more.

"Pretty amazing stone, huh?'' she said, eyebrows raised.

"Beautiful," I agreed, recognizing in her the kind of engage-ment-ring lust that drove women to marry lesser—albeit wealth-ier—men.

"Anyway," she continued, harnessing her anger once more, "he takes me to Lutèce, and we're sitting across from each other at the most beautiful little table." Her eyes welled up at this point, and though I was curious as to the kind of emotions the memory of silverware and expertly folded napkins could conjure up, I grabbed a Kleenex from the box on her desk and handed it to her.

"Thanks," she said, taking it and giving her delicate little nose a rather indelicate honk.

"So we're sitting there, freshly poured glasses of Bordeaux be-fore us, and I'm looking at him and he's looking at me and I'm thinking this is it, he's going to ask me. I mean, he even looked *nervous,* and idiot that I am, I'm thinking, isn't that cute? He's nervous. Maybe he's afraid I might say no!" She tossed her crum-pled tissue onto the desk before her with leashed fury. "So I reach across the table encouragingly and say, 'Darling, you look so ner-vous, relax.' So he smiles and says, 'Oh, there are just so many things I need to say to you tonight.' Now my heart is beating so fast, I'm thinking I'm going to have a heart attack before he pulls out that ring, so I say, 'Oh, darling, you know you can talk to me about anything. Ask me anything. We *love* each other, after all.'" This last came out on a squeak as Rebecca's tears sprang free and she practically howled with a mixture of sadness and bitterness. There was nothing I could do but reach over and grab her hand in heartfelt sympathy.

"And then," she continued, once she'd contained her sobs again, "the bastard breaks up with me. Can you believe it?" she asked, looking up at me in confusion and sorrow.

In truth, even as I stared at this red-eyed, puffy-faced version of Rebecca, I couldn't believe any man would willingly leave such a paragon of good breeding and wifely suitability by the wayside. "Why?" I asked, in disbelief. "Did he give any reasons?"

"Oh, he had reasons. Lots of them. But all of them having to do with the fact that he's just an immature beast who wouldn't know a good thing if it bit him in the ass." She reached over and tugged another Kleenex out of the box. "He's got things he wants to do, he says. He's not ready, he says. His mother—his *mother!*— still relies on him to take care of her." She let out a snort. "As if Frederic Fekkai didn't already have *her* needs covered."

I stared at her for a few moments, taking it all in. And then I did the unthinkable. I laughed. I couldn't help myself. It just burst out of me. It wasn't as if Rebecca's breakup didn't bother me, it did. I felt terribly sorry for her. And it wasn't even the image of Nash and his well-coiffed mother that did it. There was just something about the whole thing that seemed incredibly absurd all of a sudden. As if suddenly all the angst we spent over men—boys, I should really say—was completely ridiculous.

Vainly attempting to stifle my mirth, I watched anxiously as Rebecca turned to look me straight in the face. I worried that I seemed hopelessly callous in the face of her recent distress. Then I saw a smile crease her tearstained face. And suddenly she was laughing, too. The kind of guffaw I hadn't seen from her since the days when we traded barbs aimed at Patricia and her army of ladies-in-waiting.

When we had all but busted a gut and were wiping away fresh tears together—tears of the merrier variety—Rebecca sat back in her chair and sighed, fresh sadness carving lines in her face and making her look older. "This is not going to be easy," she admitted. "In fact, this is probably the worst thing that will ever happen to me."

Not by a long shot, I thought to myself, remembering ever more painful things that I had to deal with in my own Post-Derrick period. But I knew what she meant. Knew all too well the intense feeling that immediately followed when the man you loved suddenly decided to call the whole thing off. It was as if your entire life had just shattered into a million impossibly painful pieces.

"It feels like the worst thing right now," I said carefully, "but it won't always."

When she looked up at me hopefully, I continued, "You're going to feel abandoned. You're going to feel bereft. Hell, you're going to feel like shit. But it gets better, believe me. Suddenly you'll remember that person you were before," I said, as if realizing this fact myself for the first time. "You'll remember what it is that you want out of life." Then I smiled. "And you'll go for it."

She nodded her head thoughtfully, then turned to me. "And just how did you get so smart, Emma? I mean, is that what happened to you before you met Derrick?"

"Noooo," I said, with a small smile, "that's what's happening to me now."

And then I did it. I confessed all. Told her everything, from the pitiful way Derrick announced his imminent departure from my life, to his new life with the Goddess of Good Dental Hygiene, to our last painful phone call.

When I was through, Rebecca sat looking at me in shock. "God, Emma, I can't believe you went through all that. And you didn't even tell me! How did you survive?"

I smiled, despite the fact that there was still a part of me that wondered the very same thing. "That remains to be seen."

Confession: There are some things only good hair can cure.

And so it was that Rebecca and I became friends again. I even took her to Alyssa's gym, having joined myself now that I had used up all of Alyssa's *and* Jade's guest passes. Of course, Rebecca had her own gym—how else had she managed to maintain that perfect power-suit shape? But it was a good bonding experience for us, especially when I showed her how many demons a good Stair-Master session could exorcise in the post-breakup stage. We even went out for drinks one night, and I got her tipsy enough to trade jabs with me once more about the psychotic world of wedding planning that is *Bridal Best.* Of course, Rebecca was a bit more subdued about it. After all, she was management now.

So it went. I was now officially single, complete with gym membership. And officially thinner, as my membership included a session with Tom, a buff and beautiful personal trainer whom I even contemplated asking out, until he asked me to step onto the scale. Despite the fact that I trembled initially, moments later I was practically shrieking with joy. I had now lost a total of ten pounds! Ten! I was positively…trim! For me, at least.

I was also, officially, a writer of sorts. Once my article for *Today's Woman* was complete, I actually bought a *Writer's Market* with the idea that I would pursue other opportunities.

Sure, I was happier. I will not lie and try to play the disgruntled ex-girlfriend anymore. But still something was missing. Something that made me ache to call Derrick. Made me fret over the mistakes I'd made with Max. Made me resist taking up with Tom, the buff and beautiful personal trainer. And I might have fallen into some sort of malaise, had I not been momentarily saved by none other than St. Sebastian himself.

"Emma!" came his surprised and delighted voice when he caught me at home on a Friday night.

Well, if wasn't my prodigal hairdresser, I thought. "Sebastian, how are you?"

"Magnificent. How are you?"

"Good, good."

"Are you in love?"

"Uh—"

"*I'm* in love," he continued, not waiting for whatever lame answer I might come up with. "In love with life."

Whew. I was worried for a moment that yet another of my friends had jumped the Singles ship.

"Oh, Emma, I have learned so much from my guru. You really should come to a session with me. I'm meditating every day now, and I can't tell you how much it's deepened my awareness of all things. In fact, they're starting a new session next week. You really ought to come."

Uh-oh. I began to fear Sebastian was going to start peddling spirituality to me. Your Unconscious Life Wiped Clean, in three easy sessions. "I, um—"

"So tell me, tell me, tell me—what have you been up to? How's your hair?"

Aha. Now I had uncovered the true purpose of Sebastian's call. "Still not blond."

"Hmm. Maybe we can remedy that. What are you doing tomorrow afternoon?"

I smiled. Good old Sebastian. He always came through with some highlights whenever he was running low on cash. I guess his inner peace just wasn't paying the bills. Not wanting to miss out on this opportunity, I quickly agreed to meet him at his place on the Upper East Side, where I would surreptitiously dump a wad of cash on his dresser and in return receive the glossy golden lights I craved.

As it turned out, Sebastian was just what I needed. The next day, as I sat in a chair in a kitchen decorated in the kind of bold yet soothing color combinations that could make Martha Stewart swoon with delight, I was filled with that old satisfaction a woman only knows when she feels truly cared for. With my head half full of aluminum-foil-wrapped color and Sebastian humming a soft, soothing rhythm while he applied the finishing touches, I knew I had found something resembling happiness.

Once he was done with the foils, Sebastian set a timer and busied himself making us tea. As I watched him gently sift the tea leaves into a cast-iron container then pour hot water over the top of them, I studied his economy of movement, his grace. Wrapped in his relaxing presence, I realized that no matter what small task he did, he did it with the greatest pleasure.

Clearly something had happened to Sebastian. Or some*one*. After he had set the tea in front of me and took a seat across the table, bowing his head briefly to pray, I asked the question I'd been wondering about since I'd first arrived today and witnessed his glowing presence. "So, are you dating anyone?"

He shook his head and sipped his tea, heaving a great sigh of pleasure.

I sipped *my* tea, and when I discovered the thin, dank taste, I wondered if I were drinking a different brew. "I'm not dating anyone, either," I offered, though he hadn't asked. "And it's starting to get on my nerves."

He smiled and waved a hand at me. "Oh, Emma. You just need to get laid."

My eyes widened. I certainly didn't see that one coming, not with Sebastian sitting there in his oriental robe, looking so serene and content. I was expecting something more along the lines of say, a quick chant to calm the mind.

"What?" he said, looking mildly offended at what I imagined was the surprised expression on my face. "Did you think I had become a monk, Emma?" He rolled his eyes. "Please!"

Then he raked his fingers through his curly blond locks, a look of mischief coming over his cherub face. "I have learned the key to all relationships is no relationship." He shrugged. "I am just better when I am by myself. More at peace. Probably because I don't have to deal with another person's *mishegoss.*" He rolled his eyes again. "After John, I've had enough to last me two lifetimes." Then he shrugged. "I don't really need anything from anyone else. Except sex. And that can be had easily enough."

Ah, to be a gay man in New York City, I thought to myself. Was it that effortless to get laid without getting…screwed? "So is that your secret?" I asked.

"Secret?"

"To happiness," I explained. "You just seem so calm. So happy."

He smiled beatifically. "I have learned happiness from my guru, Emma. No man can teach you that," he said, gesturing to the framed photo on his bookshelf of that wise Indian woman he'd shown me the last time we'd gotten together. As I studied her smooth, clean features, her carefully placed bindi, I wasn't convinced. Though she had that same beatific smile on her face, her eyes seemed somewhat…sad.

"Do you think some people were meant to be alone?" I asked now, fearing the answer.

"Only if they want to be," he said. "It is a choice. Everything in life is a choice, though most people don't see it that way."

With that, the timer went off and Sebastian jumped into action, checking a few foils, then beginning the careful process of unwrapping my hair. Once the foils were out, he guided me to the sink and gently washed out the color formula I hoped would change my life for the better. As was his practice, he kept me away from all mirrors until he had completed the blow-dry—he liked the drama of watching my expression once I witnessed the complete transformation.

I didn't disappoint him. Once my hair had been blown into smooth, shiny waves about my face and I stepped before the mirror and saw all that glossy gold color lighting up my features, I couldn't help but smile with pure joy. "I'm beautiful!" I exclaimed, then turned to hug him.

"Oh, Emma," he said, pulling me into his embrace. "You were *always* beautiful." Then he leaned away from me, studying his handiwork. "Now you're simply...*more* beautiful!"

And as I turned to see my reflection once more, I realized, with a flow of happy warmth through my veins, that he was right.

Confession: I am blond. Hear me roar!

That evening I headed home with my tummy pleasantly full from the soba noodles and vegetables Sebastian had fed me once he finished my hair, and the number for my local yoga institute tucked away in my wallet. Though I wouldn't accept the guru, Sebastian had managed to convince me of the value of meditation. I didn't know that I would try it, but I took the card anyway. As I came to my corner, I stopped then turned toward Heavenly Dee-lites, thinking I might indulge in a little Double Mocha Chip. Not because I was feeling blue and hoping to drown my sorrows, just because it had been a good day and now I wanted to finish it off with a sweet, low-calorie treat. Besides, I hadn't been there in a while and I didn't want the sweet old couple who ran the place to think something had happened to such a loyal customer.

The moment I stepped through the front door and saw *him* inside, I panicked. I thought he had quit, or been seduced by some other desperate customer and promptly fired. But there he stood, broad-shouldered and beautiful in a T-shirt that stretched across that amazing chest, and a pair of perfectly faded jeans hugging those slender hips. I was immediately tongue-tied.

"Hey," he said with a smile that zipped through me, "if it isn't Ms. Double Mocha Chip. Where've you been?"

I immediately became defensive, which caused my tongue to untie and unleash the kind of comment a woman should never make to a man she fantasizes about sleeping with. "Yeah, well, sorry to disappoint you, but I do have a life. And the name is Emma Carter—"

"Whoa, whoa," he said, "slow down, Emma. It was just that I...I was kinda wondering what happened to you."

All the anger drained out of me. He was?

"And my name's Griffin Rivers. But you can call me Griffin. If we're going to continue to see each other, I think we should at least be on a first-name basis." He smiled. "Now, what'll it be? The usual?"

I sighed, embarrassed. "Yes, the...usual."

I shivered as I watched him sift through the freezer between us, pull out that familiar container, then pause before he dropped it into a bag. "I'm sorry, did you want the gallon-size or this pint-size?"

"The pint, of course," I answered quickly.

"None for the roommates?"

I frowned. "Roommates? I don't have any—" I stopped, suddenly remembering the fib I had told to cover my gluttony. I smiled. "Turns out they've all...moved out."

"Ah..." he said, a smile lingering on that beautiful mouth as he bagged the pint, then proceeded to the register to ring me up.

When he handed me back my change, his hand brushing mine, I felt it. That zing. That powerful connection I'd only read about a zillion times—and experienced only twice, both times with him. Griffin. The Skinny Scoop man. Suddenly Sebastian's earlier suggestion that I needed to get laid rang through me. No woman in her right mind would leave this store without securing a date with such a promising bed partner, minimum-wage worker or not. He was just too...hot. But how? How did I go about getting this man in my bed? I was way out of my league. He was a god. Jade's kind of god. Not the kind of bespectacled geek I usually warmed up to.

Drawing on all my courage—somewhat heightened when I remembered how absolutely fabulous I had looked upon leaving Sebastian's this afternoon—I started in. "Thanks." I smiled. *Now what?* In a last grab at straws, I held up my purchase. "So now that I'm without roommates, looks like I won't be coming by so...often."

"I don't know," he said. "That stuff's pretty addictive."

No kidding. "Well, just in case I don't make it here next Saturday night, maybe we should meet up anyway. You know, go for drinks or something. Maybe somewhere—" I looked around the small store, lined with organic fruits and vegetables "—somewhere less healthy. Like a bar."

"Or a restaurant," he offered. "Why don't I come pick you up at your place after closing? Say nine or so. You must live nearby...."

"You know what, why don't I meet you here?" I replied, a sudden image of us pleasantly entwined in the nondairy section filling my mind. Besides, I didn't him want him to catch a glimpse of my hovel too soon. Or, worse, run into Beatrice and get the lowdown on her digestive problems. I liked to save that stuff for later, once I had hooked a man with my charm.

"See you here at nine on Saturday then," he said.

"Sure. See you then," I said coolly, as I turned and walked out the door, my insides trembling so hard I thought I would shatter into a million pieces.

Oh God. I had a date. With the most beautiful man I had ever seen. The most beautiful man I had ever hoped to seduce.

Catching a glimpse of my gorgeous new reflection in a storefront on my way home, I realized I was a changed woman. A woman who knew what she wanted and wasn't afraid to go for it. Maybe it was the hair.

Or maybe it was just...about time.

Confession: I discover something even more satisfying than sex.

I spent the next week preparing for my big seduction scene.
"Are you sure you want to just *sleep* with him?"

This from Jade, who, oddly enough, immediately shot down my proposed plan when I called her to apprise her of my cute boy coup. "What else am I going to do with him? The guy peddles ice-cream substitute, for crissakes."

"You are *such* a snob," she countered.

"To quote you, before you began spending your Saturday nights baking pies for Ted—"

"I baked one pie! As an experiment," she protested. "Ted likes pie and…and I wanted to see if my oven still worked—"

"As I was saying, I'm simply using the justification you used when you turned poor Enrico into a sex toy. Griffin is *not* my type. Yes, he's hot. Yes, he has a day job—of sorts. But what could we possibly have in common?"

"He could be an artist of some sort and he's just doing this to pay the bills," Jade argued.

"Even Derrick wouldn't sink so low as to be a counter boy in a veggie store. It just doesn't pay enough to support any sort of dream, artistic or otherwise. Griffin is probably one of those granola types who does it just because he feels he's serving some kind of purpose for Mother Earth."

"What's wrong with a guy like that?"

"Jade—"

"Okay, okay," she said. "Just be careful, all right? Remember how you felt after you slept with Max and didn't hear from him."

Though the reminder caused a plunging feeling in my stomach, I persevered. "This is different. When I went out with Max, I was looking for a relationship. Now all I want is sex. And I intend to get it."

"My, my, Emma, I never thought I'd hear *you* say those words," Jade said, a smile in her voice.

"Yeah, well, it's the new me."

"That's fine," Jade said. "Just remind the 'new you' to bring some condoms."

"Yeah, yeah," I replied, as if I were an old hand at this.

But in truth, as I purchased condoms from the smirking sales-clerk at Duane Reade—a traumatic situation in itself—and later slid them into my purse as I readied myself to leave the house on Saturday night, I'd never felt so nervous. Exhilarated, too, but that only seemed to make my quivering stomach more prone to pole-vaulting.

I glanced into the mirror for courage. I had to admit, I looked pretty damn good. I had opted for a black skirt and deep khaki green camisole ensemble, as a concession to the August heat but also because I wasn't taking any chances. I wanted Griffin to want me. And with my soft, sun-streaked hair and Midnight Plunder-tinted lips, I felt ready to do battle. The silky red bra and panties I wore beneath my outfit bolstered me further as I slid on my mules, picked up my bag and headed to Heavenly Dee-lites for something I hoped would be even more gratifying than a whole freezer case full of Double Mocha Chip.

He was waiting outside for me, freshly showered and dressed in a dark brushed cotton T-shirt and what looked like a pair of those high-tech fabric trousers Jade claimed were all the rage and I knew to be very expensive. And if this didn't make me wonder, the magazine he read, as he sat comfortably on the little bench out front of the store, did. *Advertising Age* wasn't usually the preferred reading of the vegan set, or the type of thing a man who spent his Saturday nights fetching and selling Skinny Scoop might enjoy.

I didn't have time to ponder these contradictions, though, because the moment Griffen looked up and saw me there, a pleased expression settling over his incredible features, all thoughts flew out of my head.

"Hey, Emma," he greeted me, and next thing I knew he was before me, holding my two hands in his and looking at me as if he would eat me alive. Only he didn't. Not even a kiss, though I could see he wanted to—as if it were the most natural thing in the world for two complete strangers to do. But suddenly we didn't feel like strangers. And for a brief moment I looked into his thickly lashed eyes and saw something—someone—I felt I knew down to my very soul. I swallowed. Hard. Then a completely unexpected thought blew through my mind: Our child would have those eyes.

Oh God. I needed to get a grip. I glanced away and carefully disengaged my hands from Griffin's, laughing shakily. When I looked up again, he was already picking up his magazine from the bench. As if nothing at all had just passed between us. Clearly I was out of my mind.

"Let me just put this inside and lock up," he said, unchaining the bench from the storefront and effortlessly carrying it into the darkened store, along with the magazine I still wondered about.

When he came out front once more and locked the door behind him, I became curious about him again. How had he spiffed himself up so well, especially after a day of churning and serving Skinny Scoop?

"So I guess the store is, uh, equipped with a shower?" I inquired with a short laugh. "I mean, you seem to have no evidence of a hard day's work on your, uh, clothes," I continued, eyeing his effortlessly casual yet clearly expensive outfit once more.

"My parents have an apartment not far from the store. I showered at their place," he said matter-of-factly, then took my hand and started leading me down the street.

I tried to hold on to my senses though the strength in that big hand as it folded around mine certainly muddled things. "Um, your parents. They live here? In the city?" *Please God don't let him live with his parents,* I prayed silently, though it sure would explain a lot. His designer threads on a minimum-wage salary for one thing.

"All their lives. I was born here. They thought to retire to Florida a few years back, but they weren't ready to give up the store."

"The store?" I asked, dumbfounded.

"Heavenly Dee-lites," he said, turning to look at me as we strode farther downtown on University Place. "I'm sorry, I thought you knew that. The couple who run the store—they're my parents."

"Ohhhhh," I said, realization dawning. The sweet old couple were his parents. Then that meant—

"I'm lucky I got out of there tonight." Then he laughed, the sound deep and rich. "They almost suckered me into a bridge game with their friends. Not that I mind spending time with them—I mean, it's only been about six months since I've moved back to New York. I was out in Chicago for a while. And they are getting older. Truthfully, I think they should give up the store and just relax. I've been coming in on Saturdays to help out, but it's not easy. I mean, I've got my own business to run...."

Oh my, oh my, oh my. This was not some minimum-wage worker and potential boy toy I was out on a date with. This was a *man.* An incredibly good-looking man who not only had the most beautiful forearms I had ever seen, but was kind and gentle enough to spend some of *his* Saturday nights with his sweet old parents, for crissakes. Playing *bridge.*

And that wasn't all I discovered about Griffin that night. During dinner at Nobu, where I ate some of the most decadently delicious food I'd had in a long time, I learned that he was a graphic designer with his own firm. Apparently he worked with a lot of advertising firms, hence his choice of reading materials earlier in the evening. He had grown up in New York, helping his parents with the store during high school. After college at Princeton, he had gone on to Chicago to do design work for a big firm there, before returning to New York to start his own firm. Spending Saturday nights at Heavenly Dee-lites was certainly not his idea of a good time. But he wanted to help out his parents, who, he worried, were working too hard and couldn't be convinced to take off time unless they knew the store was in good hands.

And what good hands *he* had. I shook inside every time he reached across the table to grab mine.

To top it off, he had an apartment in the hottest new neighborhood in New York City. And not some above-market rental. Not my Griffin. He *owned* his place. He'd just showed up in his hometown of New York City six months ago and set down roots, starting with a loft space with floor-to-ceiling windows and original prewar details.

Not that I saw this illustrious space after our date. Oh, no. Reader, I did not sleep with him that night. It somehow didn't seem...appropriate. In my heart of hearts, I felt like I shouldn't even be sharing the same room with this man, much less the same bed. I was way out of my league.

Which is why I was filled with fear when he put me in a cab after dinner, with no more than one utterly delicious and entirely too brief kiss. "I'll call you," he said.

In my dreams, I thought, although I had taken it as a hopeful sign when he'd asked for my phone number as soon as we'd given our orders at the restaurant.

By the time the cab pulled up to my dilapidated building, I was filled with resignation. And maybe a little bit of relief. I wasn't ready for someone as magnificent as Griffin. But I knew one thing for sure. If he never called, I would be just fine. Better than fine. After all, I had myself, didn't I? And that was good enough for me.

Confession: I never even saw it coming.

When the phone rang at eleven the next morning, I had no expectations. That's why I was completely unprepared for the sound of Griffin's smooth, rich voice wishing me good morning, telling me what a great time he'd had the night before and how much he looked forward to getting together again. He wasn't even worried about looking like some overeager geek by barely waiting a day before calling. And in truth, I wasn't even worried that he was some overeager geek. He liked me. Really liked me. Just as much as I liked him.

So we did go out the following week. And the following weekend. We even spent the long Labor Day weekend together, which even Jade agreed was significant, considering how new our relationship was. Soon, spending our weekends together was a natural thing. As if we found being apart more bizarre than being together. And we became, without my even noticing it, a couple.

"You've got it bad," Jade said, as she and I sat over cappuccinos at French Roast with Alyssa, whom we had just helped pick out the most amazing wedding gown at Vera Wang. I had just regaled them with a detailed description of how absolutely gorgeous Griffin looked while asleep when Jade pronounced me "in deep." Who could blame me? Last night, Griffin and I had made love for the first time. And it was the most beautiful, intimate experience I have ever had.

"Well, I'm happy for you, Emma," Alyssa said, looking at me

with that dreamy-eyed expression she got whenever she contemplated what she deemed the beginnings of true love.

"What's not to be happy about?" Jade said, lifting her mug of cappuccino to her lips. "She looks just like me the day after Ted and I first spent the night together." She sighed. "God, I think the sex between us has gotten even better, if that's possible."

"I think it always gets better over time," Alyssa said sagely. And when Jade gave her that raised-eyebrow look, she added, "I mean, there *are* lull periods. But when things are good..." She sighed, and her expression said that things between Richard and her were good. Very good.

"Here's to good things," I said, raising my mug of cappuccino in toast. And smiling like the satisfied cats that we were, we banged mugs and drank deep, savoring the sweetness of it all.

Confession: Okay, I still have my moments....

I won't lie to you. As Griffin and I skated toward coupledom, things were a little scary. First, there was my mother's wedding. Since it came in the early weeks of my relationship with Griffin, it didn't seem right to subject him to a weekend on a cruise ship with my family, whom he hadn't met yet, of course. I was a little worried over his meeting them someday, so I hoped to save "someday" until things between us were a little more secure. I think I feared Griffin might find my family somewhat...unusual, to say the least. My mother, for one, had married me off to him from the first phone call in which I dared speak his name. My father still thought I should have stuck with the lawyer. Grandma Zizi, who when I called to wish a happy ninety-second birthday, only wanted to know if he was tall. "Six-one, Grandma." I replied. I thought she might go into immediate cardiac arrest, she was so happy.

And there were other fears to contend with, I discovered. As I was about to leave for the wedding weekend, I had my first fight with Griffin. Mostly because I was having an anxiety attack over the fact that while I was sailing off to watch my mother say those sacred vows she knew so well to the sound of waves crashing in the distance, Griffin was going to Fire Island for the weekend with a bunch of old college friends for one last beach hurray. I wouldn't have minded so much, had he not accidentally mentioned that his "sort-of" ex-girlfriend was going to be there.

"I know how easy it is to...to...fall prey to old partners," I argued. "One minute you're having a few drinks, laughing over old times, next minute you're *reliving* them in each other's arms!"

"You're crazy," he said, looking at me in that way that always assured me he wasn't the type to be troubled by such fits of anxiety. He was so different from me that way. Which was probably why we got along so well.

And so it was I watched my mother walk down the aisle for the third time, a mariachi band playing in the distance. I even managed not to burst into tears—or have a complete anxiety attack—when I felt the wooden platform I stood on to do my reading of John Donne's "The Ecstasy" begin to shift and creak beneath my feet in the high winds. Somehow during all the craziness of renting a gazebo to put on the beach for the ceremony, picking out a restaurant and tying up bags of birdseed to toss at the happy couple, none of us had seemed to remember that September was hurricane season in the Caribbean. But we made it through the ceremony, which culminated in a flurry of trained doves, which swooped down upon the happy couple, seemingly from nowhere, just as the groom kissed the bride. A last-minute touch my mother had not even told me about and I am sure would never have been condoned by the wedding nazis at *Bridal Best,* considering the fuss that was created when the trainer of said birds tried to corral them back into their bamboo cage. Let's just say we had about a fistful of birdseed left to throw at my mother and Clark once the ceremony ended. But it was enough. More than enough. For I realized, as I watched my mother and Clark together that weekend, that they didn't really need luck to make this marriage work. It was clear enough to me that they had something more. Like love.

I will say that despite the relative sanity of my mother's nuptials, they did produce a strange effect on me. Though I realized it was completely unreasonable to contemplate marriage to Griffin—after all, we'd been together a little more than a month—I came home with visions of my own happy day dancing in my head. I hated myself for being so predictable, and yet I couldn't help but wonder if that day would ever come. "Relax!" Jade said, but I couldn't. "Take it day by day," Alyssa advised, but I was already mentally two years down the line, envisioning Griffin walking out of my life, leaving me thirty-three, single and utterly without hope. And though I managed to keep my growing anxiety from Griffin, who continued to be his sweet, loving self, I lived each day as if an ax were hanging over my head.

Then, like a sign from God—or maybe just a well-timed maneuver on Sebastian's part—I got a beautiful printed card in the mail, announcing that Sebastian was now officially a healer, and that for $99.95 a session, I might purge myself of whatever it was that was eating away at my soul.

Well, I wasn't ready for the full program, and frankly, I wasn't sure I would ever trust anything that promised mental prosperity while destroying my financial future. But I did dig that card out for the yoga institute that Sebastian had given me all those weeks ago, and after obtaining a list of schedules, I started attending classes.

Now, I can't say that I made any inroads on the meditation front. In truth, I realized by class number three that I was more prone to either fall asleep midway through, or have an anxiety attack at the thought of life free of anxiety. But during my fifth session something happened. And while the spiritual character of this event was suspect, I did gain a greater understanding of myself.

While in the midst of doing the salutation to the sun which started off the class—a set of maneuvers that at first felt awkward and now was somewhat soothing—I caught sight, out of the corner of my eye, of a face I had not seen since my days in the M.F.A. program at NYU. It was Professor Diana Young, the first creative-writing teacher I really respected at NYU and the advisor I eventually chose to guide me through the short-story collection I put together for my M.A. thesis. By the time we got into second position, I knew she had seen me, too.

The effect of her presence on me was odd. I was completely thrown and incapable of concentrating on anything. By the time we lay on our backs to meditate for the final portion of the class, I was a mess. Instead of focusing on the soothing voice of the in-

structor, who gently coaxed us into some deeper state of consciousness, I was plotting ways to make my escape without sharing more
than a wave and a brief greeting with the woman whom I had
struggled before for a whole semester, showing up in her office
with story fragments and, more often, excuses why I had missed
another one of the deadlines she had set for me. By semester's end,
I had managed to get six stories on paper and qualify for my degree,
but I was unable to believe a word of the praise she gave my work,
though I had taken careful note of whatever criticisms she had
made, gentle as they might have been.

Now, as the yoga instructor led those who had managed to let
go of it all—myself not included—back to reality, I quickly stood,
picking up my towel and working my way nonchalantly toward the
door. Maybe Professor Young hadn't seen me. Maybe she didn't
realize I'd seen her—

"Emma! Emma Carter, is that you?" she said now, approaching
me.

"Professor Young, how are you?" I replied before I had even
turned around to confront her soft, gently wrinkled features and
lively gray eyes that always seemed to see right through me. Her
hair, which she wore long despite the fact that it was mostly gray
and might benefit from a good cut, was pulled back in a messy
ponytail, and her wand-slim figure was in a leotard the most hid-
eous shade of green I had ever seen. But that was Professor Young.
Completely oblivious to the dictates of fashion or even taste, for
that matter. Still, she was an amazing writer—a real genius with
words—and I had always worshiped her. And feared her.

"Good, dear. How are *you?*" she said, those all-knowing gray
eyes searching mine.

"I'm good. Really good," I said. I was, wasn't I? Or at least I
had been, until I saw her.

"Are you still writing?" she asked now, and I realized the source
of my discomfort because I replied in what sounded to my own
ears like a defensive tone.

"Of course. In fact, I have an article in the issue of *Today's
Woman* coming out next month."

"Well, that's just wonderful," she said, her eyes gleaming with genuine happiness for me. "What's it about?"

Suddenly I felt ridiculous. How was I going to explain to her that it was one of those angsty piece on breaking up aimed toward the recently dumped? "Uh, it's on relationships. That type of thing."

"Interesting," she said, studying me. "So, did you ever finish that novel you started just after graduation?"

The question did me in. My insides crumbled and my happy little facade of peace and prosperity fell apart. I doubt she even noticed, judging by the way she still smiled at me. Despite my freelance magazine writing career and my amazing new boyfriend, I suddenly felt like a failure. "Actually, um…no."

At her perplexed expression, I started babbling about how I had gotten this great job writing for a magazine—I didn't mention names—my immediate and surprising success there, my subsequent promotion—I didn't mention titles—and how one thing led to another and here I was, writing for magazines.

By the time I was through, she seemed satisfied. Still, before we parted ways, she looked at me one last time, studying my eyes in that way she had, then said, "Well, I always saw you in fiction, Emma. But I guess you never can tell, right?" Then she hugged me, congratulated me on my success and even invited me to come up and see her at her office at NYU.

I plodded home feeling like the bottom had fallen out. And later that evening, as Griffin lay beside me in bed, caressing my cheek and wondering at my silence, he asked the question that unplugged the dam. "What's wrong, Emma?"

And so I told him. About meeting Professor Young. About my life after NYU. Up until then, the only impression Griffin had of me was of the successful magazine journalist, penning articles on whatever diverse and interesting subjects I could dream up. He had no idea that I had a folder on my laptop that housed notes toward a novel and all my real dreams. Now that he knew, I worried that he would see me as weak. After all, here was a man unafraid to pursue *his* dreams. Hell, he'd left behind a six-figure job in Chicago to start up his own design firm in NYC, with little more than a few investors and a lot of hope.

But when I looked into those thickly lashed and incredibly beautiful eyes—eyes, I realized in that moment, I had fallen deeply in love with—I did not see judgment, nor even fear. I saw hope. And—dare I say it—love. From his lips came the three simple words I most needed to hear in that moment.

"Just try, Emma."

Then he smiled that smile that never failed to warm me inside, and I knew he was right.

Fourteen

"Ex-boyfriends are like wrinkles.
A few good ones give you character."
—Emma Carter, Ex-Girlfriend Extraordinaire

Confession: I have become the "It" girl of my own little world.

Five months later, I was sitting at home on a Saturday night. Alone. And infinitely satisfied.

Okay, things could have been better. Griffin could have been there and we could have been cuddled under the covers together on this snowy winter night. But he was away on business and it couldn't be helped.

So there I sat on the sofa, an old movie in the VCR and a pint of Ben & Jerry's New York Superchunk Fudge in hand—a secret indulgence I had recently switched to and didn't have the heart to tell Griff about—having a little quality time with myself. I would have made it a girls' night, except Jade was off on a skiing vacation with Ted and Alyssa was with Richard, probably listening to yet another rendition of "Always and Forever" by some overaged yet ever-hopeful musicians in cheap tuxedos who were auditioning to play at their wedding. I couldn't call Sebastian, either, as he was off in India, where he'd gone to finally meet his guru. I was happy for him, but I sincerely hoped he came back. Not only did I miss his soothing presence in my life, but my highlights were in need of a touch-up.

I barely saw Rebecca anymore, now that I had freed myself from the world of *Bridal Best* and gone full-time freelance. From what I heard, she was now burning the midnight oil and playing Patricia's best pal. According to Marcy Keller, whom I bumped into at

D'Agostino's one day, Patricia needed friends now. My former fearless editor-in-chief was in the midst of a divorce from her phantom husband and on the verge of something that looked frighteningly like a nervous breakdown. I'm sure Rebecca was earning big brownie points by attempting to hold Patricia's hand through it all. Or maybe Rebecca felt a bond with Patricia. After all, her own breakup with Nash was still a not-so-distant memory.

I didn't mind spending the evening alone. My four walls didn't get to me anymore, now that they had expanded to twelve walls— sixteen, if you counted the bathroom. My rent-stabilized one bedroom had finally come through, once Stacy had gone off to life in suburbia with her new husband. According to Dorothea, they were already expecting their first child. Me, I was expecting a new oriental rug, to go with my freshly painted walls and magnificent marble fireplace. It was due to be delivered next week.

I had just dug my spoon into a particularly fudge-laden hunk of ice cream when the phone rang.

"Oh, good, you're home," my mother said when I picked up.

"Hi, Mom."

"I was worried. It's snowing terribly outside. You can't be too careful in this—"

"I know, Mom," I said. "I'm thirty-one years old. I've seen enough snow to know how to negotiate those drifts."

"Where's Griffin?"

"California."

"What?" my mother said, her alarm apparent.

"On *business,*" I said. "He's coming home Tuesday," I continued, with a glance out the window at the snow that still came down. "Weather permitting."

"Oh, business. Of course," she said, her relief apparent. I think my mother sometimes believed this magnificent man who had dropped into my life—for my mother had declared him husband material from the moment she first met him this past Thanksgiving—would somehow disappear in a puff a smoke the minute she stopped keeping tabs. I guess I couldn't blame her. I had to pinch myself every time I walked down the street beside him and saw women give him the once-over—and me a killing glance. But there we were. A couple. His parents were as bad as my mother when it came to having obvious wedding fantasies—they never tired of reminding us that they'd in a way introduced us—but God knew what the future held. Griffin and I just took each day as it came, good and bad. And it was all I needed now.

"Well, since he's not around, we can really talk about what's going on with you," my mother said.

Uh-oh. Here is comes. "Mom—"

"I just need to know where you're at. It's been six months!"

"Mom, these things take time. Rome wasn't built in a day."

"Just give me an update. Please. I've already bragged to all my girlfriends about you. Dorothea has been bugging me for news ever since!"

I smiled. "Okay, okay. Page 175. But it's only the first draft—"

My words were drowned out by the sound of my mother's shriek of joy. I couldn't help but muffle a squeal of delight myself. From the moment she had learned I had started a novel, my mother had been my biggest fan, though she had yet to read a word of the manuscript. I had kept it from almost everyone so far, except Diana Young, who had given the first one hundred pages a read and declared them "quite promising."

"Oh, Emma, I never dreamed…" my mother all but breathed into the phone.

Frankly, neither had I. Not really. Not until now.

"You know Clark has that editor friend at Random House who said he would take a look—"

"You told me, Mom." And I smiled. It was only about the fiftieth time she'd mentioned it.

"Clark and I can't wait to see it. You know he's so proud of you, too."

Then I simply listened as she moved on to the subject of Clark, what a kind man, what a good man he was. It was as if she couldn't help saying it, even six months after the wedding.

By the time we hung up, I was over my Ben & Jerry's craving. I got up and placed the container back in the freezer, realizing that if I didn't eat it before Tuesday, I would have to confess my lack of allegiance to Skinny Scoop to Griffin.

He could take it, I thought. Like most anything else I dished out, it seemed.

Even my father liked Griffin, and he really hadn't been partial to any of my boyfriends. But he was in better spirits himself these days, having enrolled, believe it or not, in law school. I will admit I was dubious at first about this late career move. Deirdre had told me last fall that he'd applied. As she explained it, though, it was apparently some long-held dream he'd never realized—and, she thought, something he had probably sublimated into all those loony-tune lawsuits. Besides, she explained, it couldn't hurt him to have the law background now that he'd started his own small financial consulting business in his retirement. There weren't many accountants in New York who held dual degrees, and it could more than triple his already exorbitant fee. The promise of money always seemed to fill my father's heart with joy.

I couldn't help but feel hopeful for him. He hadn't had a drink since last summer, not that this was any long-standing record for him. Still, he seemed to have a better attitude about things. He'd even dropped his lawsuit against the harness company. Though watch out if you get caught on the phone with him these days. Once he gets started on tax law reform, he can talk the leg off a donkey. My mother claimed he would lose his one-track mind once Shaun and Tiffany got pregnant, which judging by the fact that the kitchen renovation is now complete, and there are no new home improvements on the horizon, will probably be any day now. Then again, my mother might just be doing some wishful thinking again.

The morning after the near binge on Ben & Jerry's, when I woke up and sat down to write, a pot of coffee brewing and filling my cozy apartment with that richly satisfying smell, the thought of Derrick flickered briefly through my mind. Maybe it was because he had called me not two months ago, "just to talk" he said, though it was clear he was lonely. The most miraculous thing about our conversation was that I felt no need to toss my new boyfriend in his face, though I couldn't help but mention my progress on the novel. He was happy for me and even sounded wistful as he congratulated me. When I probed further, I learned that his screenplay, though it had earned him a handsome option fee and brought him to L.A., had ultimately been shelved. Worse, he seemed to be spending more time these days doctoring other people's scripts than writing his own, especially now that his "perfect" roommate had gotten a boyfriend who seemed have taken up residence in Carrie's bedroom. Apparently said boyfriend had a penchant for performing loud sexual antics on a nightly basis.

Okay, maybe that part made me feel a little...gleeful. But once I got over the sick feeling of gratification at the thought of Carrie and some oversexed mongrel wreaking havoc on my ex-boyfriend's life, Derrick and I did something we hadn't done in a long time. Probably since the first few months of our relationship.

We talked. I mean *really* talked. About writing. About life. I found that I had much wisdom to offer him on both counts. I could tell he was more than a little impressed. And maybe even feeling a little bit of regret about the girl he left behind. Not that I cared. Okay, I cared. But only in that thrilling little way a woman feels when she knows she's a force to be reckoned with.

Now, as I clicked on my computer, doing all those little exercises in procrastination I still resorted to occasionally—like rubbing the cuticle cream I kept handy on my desk into my nailbeds and sorting through some junk mail I found lying there as well—I realized I was really happy. Don't get me wrong: my life is far from perfect. After all, freelancers live from check to check and my book isn't even finished, much less sold. Too, Griffin and I have yet to talk about the future. In fact, we're both so engrossed in our careers it hasn't really come up, except as a fearsome worry in my overactive imagination. I'm sure I'm the only one worrying, of course. After all, worrying over the future is a particularly female malady, I think.

Still, as I sat comfortably at my computer, I knew I had a lot. Good friends. Days spent in the way I most wanted to spend them. Regular sex—a thing not to be taken lightly in this city of one-night stands. But most of all, I had found the person I had never thought to look for in those frantic weeks after Derrick walked out of my life.

Myself.

And that's all any woman really needs. Ex-girlfriend or...otherwise.